But Not For Love

Also by Edwin Shrake

Fiction

Blood Reckoning
Blessed McGill
Strange Peaches
Peter Arbiter
Limo *(with Dan Jenkins)*
Night Never Falls
The Borderland

Nonfiction

Willie *(with Willie Nelson)*
Bootlegger's Boy *(with Barry Switzer)*
Harvey Penick's Little Red Book *(with Harvey Penick)*
If You Play Golf, You're My Friend *(with Penick)*
For All Who Love the Game *(with Penick)*
The Game for a Lifetime *(with Penick)*
The Wisdom of Harvey Penick *(with Penick)*

But Not For Love

Edwin Shrake

Foreword by Dan Jenkins

Afterword by James Ward Lee

TCU Press

Fort Worth

The Texas Tradition Series Number Twenty-nine
James Ward Lee, *Series Editor*

First published 1964 by Doubleday & Company, Inc.

Shrake, Edwin
But not for love : a novel / by Edwin Shrake ; foreword by Dan Jenkins
afterword by James Ward Lee.
p.com.—(Texas tradition series ; no. 29)
ISBN 0-87565-233-6 (pbk : alk paper)
1. Nineteen sixties—Fiction. 2. Young adults--Fiction. 3. Middle
clas—Fiction. 4. Texas—Fiction. I. Title. II. Series

PS3569.H735 B88 2000
813'.54--dc21 00-036428

This reprint edition of Edwin Shrake's *But Not For Love*
is part of RetroFest 2000, Fort Worth's community-wide festival
focused on the decade of the 1960s.

for Creagan *and for* Ben

And why dost thou not pardon my transgression,
and take away mine iniquity?
For now shall I sleep in the dust;
and thou shalt seek me in the morning,
but I shall not be.
—*Job 7:21*

Men have died from time to time,
And worms have eaten them,
But not for Love.
—*William Shakespeare*

Foreword

It behooves me to confess—and I haven't been behooved in over a week, by the way—that my wife and I took a certain amount of pride in the fact that we hosted the affair. I speak of the somewhat notorious cocktail party in what was our home at the time on Sunset Terrace in Fort Worth, the social event that inspired a particularly hilarious scene in this novel by Bud Shrake, one of the city's very own, and as fine a writer for my money as ever fondled the English language.

A novel, mind you. A book in hardcover. Not a page out of the old *Fort Worth Press,* where the two of us labored side by side, covering desperately important sports events in the region, and sometimes even in Houston. That was back when we were working under the guidance of the legendary Blackie Sherrod, who was either our Mother Teresa or Don Corleone, depending on his view of the story you'd written that day.

Yeah, a novel. Something men who wore beards and women who wore glasses usually wrote when they weren't sitting around sidewalk cafes in Paris, discussing pathos and humor in Russian literature. A thing to put up on a shelf and blow smoke rings at, or take down to gaze at the jacket photo and wish it had been taken when you were staring out wistfully over the Bosphorous.

When *But Not For Love* came out and actually turned up in bookstores, Bud's pals, all of us, couldn't have been more excited if the title had been *Moby Paschal* or *Farewell to the TCU Drug.*

For one thing, Doubleday, a big-time book company, published the novel, and this confirmed what we'd always hoped might be the case: that you didn't have to sit around sidewalk cafes in Paris to become a novelist. You could sit around Herb Massey's on 8th Avenue.

Herb's was our Algonquin Round Table in those days, but better. Dorothy Parker and George S. Kaufman and the others didn't have any truck drivers, railroad workers, and liquor salesman to converse with, or chicken-fried steak and cream gravy to dine on—or a puck bowling machine, for that matter.

Not that Bud wrote the book then. The all-night table at Herb's, the all-day booth at the TCU Drug, and all those hours in the quaint city room at the *Press* were merely where his talents had been honed. Incidentally, the quaint city room at the *Press* was where almost any writer would have found inspiration from the soot that rained down on his shirt from what was supposed to be the cooling units in the windows or the editor who ate cold green peas out of a can.

The fact is, Bud didn't write *But Not For Love* until he'd moved on to the *Dallas Morning News,* and he practically wrote it with one hand. With the other, he was covering the fun-loving Dallas Cowboys of the early '60s and various other sports events. Meanwhile, of course, he didn't miss out on any social functions or tavern closings, which you might could say made the effort all the more heroic.

There's a saying that the two greatest motivations for a writer are poverty and deadlines.

Bud knew back then, as did I, that there was an infinite truth behind the humor in that. We had wives and kids and car payments, and the two of us had yet to be called to toil for *Sports Illustrated* amid the steel and glass towers of Big Town Gotham the Apple. Thus, we learned to type faster, and one day *But Not For Love* simply crawled out of his old Smith-Corona portable.

A quick way to describe the novel is to say it's about the charm and zaniness of Fort Worth vs. the cold-blooded money-grubbing of Dallas. Critics of the era liked it as much as all of us did, as well they should have. To quote the blurbs, "Multimillionaires . . . ruthless, amoral, sexy . . . their palatial homes, yachts, and decorative wives . . . it's vivid . . . violent . . . excellent."

The house where the big birthday party occurs in the novel was the one my wife and I had discovered and bought and remodeled. It was near the heart of downtown, hidden on a leafy, block-long street that ran along a bluff and offered a view toward all of West Texas. Painters and poets who gathered at the rustic Brooks Morris apartments and "art colony" across the street knew about Sunset Terrace, but most people in Fort Worth weren't even aware it was there.

The party that evening was one of those things we did quite often, in honor of the fact that it was Friday night. Good friends from Paschal and TCU and Texas A&M and Texas, those who lived in Fort Worth and Dallas, would gather for food, beverages, weighty discussions, wicked criticisms of current lifestyles, occasional divorces, Sinatra on the hi-fi, and replays of all the parties that had come before. And smoking. Everybody smoked incessantly, which brings to mind the immortal line of writer Fran Liebowitz: "Smoking is the entire point of being an adult."

Some people say it was the blackbottom punch, which contained every known form of alcohol, that caused the game of "nekkid bridge" and encouraged so many of our women friends to participate.

There is still debate as to whether the game was invented by Bud, Gary Cartwright, or Jerre R. Todd—"Jap" Cartwright and "Rounder" Todd having been cohorts in those giddy days at the *Press.* They all detested the serious game of bridge, which my wife and I played with other friends two or three times a week.

In any case, it was a party game in which numerous gentlemen and wives and girlfriends stood around the dining room table in front of a large picture window and were dealt hands from a deck of cards and were commanded to ditch an article of clothing each time the hand didn't contain enough face cards.

That game of "nekkid bridge" was much more tame than the one in *But Not For Love,* although several guys got down to their boxer shorts and two attractive ladies, one giggly wife and one numb girlfriend, were rather fetchingly reduced to their panties and bras before an alarmed June Jenkins, my wife, rushed out of the kitchen to call a halt to it all.

I should mention that my mother and grandmother had recently moved into the two-story house next door, and while they should have been reading or watching TV, it had been easy enough for them to see what was going on through the big dining room window.

We didn't know until a few days later when my ladylike grandmother smiled and nicely said to Bud and me, "Who was that basketball team you all were entertaining the other night?"

I think I said it was a combination of Paschal and Arlington Heights.

Looking back on it now and enjoying *But Not For Love* again, it's easy enough to understand how almost everything that went on back then was all about something that would be in a novel someday.

Bud knew it first.

Dan Jenkins
Fort Worth, Texas

Part One

KISSES ARREORO

All morning Jacob Iles, who had a purple eye and a black ear, sat in the lemon sunlight on the afterdeck of the yacht *Silver Spoon* and wound line onto fishing reels. It was a job he would have left for the mate, but on this particular morning Jacob Iles felt the need of doing simple and boring work as a penance. His head ached, there was a pain in his chest that made him reluctant to breathe, and his vision blurred as he looked through dark glasses. When he finished each reel, Jacob Iles would check to see that it was seated on its rod, and then he would lay the equipment on the deck and put his feet up onto the rail and look between his white tennis sneakers at the tanker unloading crude oil at the refinery across the channel. The tanker rode low with the water flapping at its black hull. As oil flowed through the long pipe the tanker's red underbelly would begin to rise from the water and then the pipe would withdraw and the tanker would slide down the channel into the Gulf of Mexico. Many of the men Iles could see on the tanker's deck would never come back to Port Agness, and in a way that morning he envied them. Iles reached up beneath the rim of his dark glasses and touched the bruises around his left eye. He frowned and lifted another reel out of the tackle box beside his chair.

After three weeks of wind and rough water the day had broken clear and calm and the channel was flat as a mirror. The white and silver tanks of the refinery shone like pearls against the blue steel of the sky. Two small shrimp boats dragged nets through the gray water. Around the shrimpers swarmed clouds of gulls waiting for the winches to turn and the nets to rise and the trash fish to be thrown over the sides. It was a reassuring sight for Jacob Iles. No matter how unclean he felt when he awoke in the morning, he began to purify himself when he reached the water. Boats and fish and the Gulf were like ventilating fans that blew sweet air through his soul; these things, he felt, were basic; they took him back to the very beginning, to a time of innocence, to a God.

The sounds of the dock cradled him. He shut his eyes and listened to ropes creaking, to water sloshing at the pilings, to the jungle bird screeching of the gulls, to spraying and cursing as captains along the dock hosed down their boats. Fifty feet away was the noise of an electric drill punching holes for screws that would fasten a new windshield into a flying bridge. Iles could smell the salt breath of the water, the paint, and gasoline, and grease, and the smoke of exhausts. Because of the long period of bad weather no charters had gone out that morning, but perhaps by noon the fishermen would come and nearly every boat along the dock would be pounding down the channel toward Corpus Christi Bay or into the open Gulf. That was where Iles wanted to be, seventy miles into the blueblack water, trolling for billfish.

Jacob Iles opened his eyes as a shrimp boat sidled up against the dock beside the *Silver Spoon.* A hundred gulls swooped around the shrimper. The birds, white with black heads and black wings, perched on the winch boom or dived at the fish trapped in the nets or floated marvelously still above the boat with wings extended and eyes wild and hungry. The noise of the gulls made Iles take his feet down from the rail, drop the reel and spool of one-hundred-thirty-pound test line into his lap, and light a cigarette. He drank from the can of beer that he kept in a wire holder on the rail and looked at the loafers sitting on a bench outside the store. They were three old men who crossed their legs like women and showed the ill white of their ankles. They wore clothes that were dark with sweat and fish blood, and they squinted out at the bright channel water as if each man was deciding for himself how soon the wind would return. Iles knew they had been talking about him. Everybody along the dock had discussed him that morning. He frowned again and then shrugged and began watching the man in the shrimp boat.

The shrimp boat was twenty-eight feet long and thumped easily against the rubber tire bumpers as it came against the dock. The captain, who worked alone, roped his boat fore and aft to the pilings. Iles watched him dip a small net into one of three wooden bins behind the cabin and bring up a squirming, bulging capture of sea life. The captain dumped the contents of the small net onto a table in front of the bins and began quickly to sort his catch. The shrimps he threw into the first bin. He tossed the little squids and some of the crabs into a bucket. The trash fish fell onto the deck to be washed overboard by the streaming hose or to be grabbed by the gulls which glided around the boat. Iles saw a crab swept off the table onto the deck, where it lifted its claws and began to scramble sideways. The crab snapped a tiny silver fish in one of its pincers and waved the fish like a club at the threatening gulls. Caught in the water from the hose, the crab skidded into the drain where it wedged against a hardhead which was stuck there with its gills heaving and its tail slapping the deck. The gulls screamed down at the crab but pulled up short of its claws. Finally the captain noticed that the drain was blocked. With the handle of the dip net, he poked the hardhead through the opening. The crab slid through behind and plopped into the water. Iles watched the crab sink beside a piling, the silver fish still bent in its grasp, claws raised as if the gulls might yet strike at it beneath the surface.

"You eat them squids?" Iles said.

The shrimp boat captain looked up from the bins.

"Them squids you're throwing in the bucket. You eat them things?" said Iles.

"Yeah. I fry 'em like oysters," the shrimper said.

"Turns my stomach," said Iles.

The shrimper didn't look directly at Iles but talked as if he were addressing the roof of Ernie's Wharf store. Iles had put down the reel and stood with a foot on the rail and the can of beer in one hand.

"Makes me sick to think about squids inside a human stomach," Iles said. "You got a human stomach, ain't you? It's big enough and fat enough to be human, anyhow."

"I guess," the shrimper said.

"Get much today?" asked Iles.

"Fifty pounds since five o'clock."

"Don't feel like talking?"

"I'm working, Jacob," the shrimper said, wiping his hands on his khaki shirt. "I got to fill up them bait bins. Somebody liable to want to catch a fish here again some day or other."

"Don't get sassy with me, you goddamn channel hauler."

The captain didn't answer.

"You trying to get sassy with me?"

"Look, Jacob, I don't want no trouble with you," said the

shrimper. "We got no argument with each other. I just mind my own work. I never want no trouble with nobody."

"Why don't you paint your boat?" Iles said. "That green paint is peeling off like dead skin. It looks like leprosy. You ratty shrimpers make this whole dock look bad." The sound of the electric drill had stopped, and Iles spoke louder to be certain they all heard him. "It's a disgrace to have you ratty shrimpers alongside the *Silver Spoon.* A lot of you cruddy charters, too. Some of you guys ain't got enough sense or self-respect to handle a rowboat in a stock tank. If they're gonna call this a fishing dock, they ought to get some real fishing boats and some real fishing captains and scuttle most of these wrecks."

"That go for Burney, too, Jake?" somebody yelled.

"Who the hell said that?" said Iles.

Except for the gulls it was quiet along the dock. The three loafers had quit talking on their bench in front of the store. Iles looked at each of the dozen boats moored at the dock and saw that nobody was working now; they stood silently, listening.

"Whose voice was that?" Iles said. "You got the guts to speak up again?"

A big tanker moved down the channel three hundred yards out, its screw turning noiselessly. The gulls screeched and hovered around the shrimper. Iles saw that his mate had come up on deck and was holding a wrench behind his back. Finishing the beer, Iles crushed the can with the pressure of his thumbs and lobbed the can into the water.

"Oh crap," said Iles.

Iles sat down again. A stitch of pain crawled around his left eye behind the dark glasses, and his left ear had begun to throb. He glanced up at his mate, a tall man with slick black hair and skin turned the color of peanuts by the sun. The mate grinned at him and put down the wrench. The sounds began again: the electric drill, the hoses, the splashings of the dip net, the cursing of the captains, the muttering of the three loafers.

"You trying to start a war, Jake?" asked the mate.

"Oh crap, Billy," Iles said. "Some hangovers just no good at all. I feel like I swallered a rabbit."

The mate looked down the dock.

"No action out of 'em," the mate said. "I guess that ought to handle it."

"Till I catch up to Burney, anyhow."

"Why don't you let it drop?"

"You know how it is," Iles said. "This is a hell of a life. If you're not cock of the walk, you're nobody. If you let these guys tromp on you, they'll tromp on you."

"They know you ain't scared."

"They know Burney like to of tore me apart over at the Sporting Life last night. Some of 'em got the idea if Burney can do it, they can do it too. Be a lot simpler for me to find Burney and kick his face in. Might save me half a dozen fights."

"Only thing is, can you do it?"

"Now, Billy, ain't you got faith in me?"

"I'm trying to look at it straight, Jake. You didn't do it last night very good."

"I've thought it all out," Iles said, "and I don't believe he can whip me again. I had him down last night, Billy, and I had him by the heel and I could of killed him. He knew it and I knew it. He couldn't move. All I had to do was boot him a little. He give up and waited. Remember that guy in Campeche? It was the same thing. Only I let Burney go home. He'd done almost pulled my ear off and knocked my eye out, and I let him go home."

"You and Burney used to get along."

"We still get along all right. We'd been drinking it up and I started telling everybody how to catch billfish and Burney said I was wrong and I laid him twenty to one that I could kick the crap out of him. He picked up the money. Damn, I'd forgot about the money. If Marge knew about the twenty dollars, she'd run me clean off."

"How does Marge feel about you fighting again?"

"How do you think? But I'll tell you one thing, it's only her feelings that are hurt. I'm a lot worse off than she is. How about bringing me some more aspirins? I'm sore today."

The mate went into the cabin and came back with the aspirin and two cans of beer. Billy gave one can of beer to Iles and then sat in the other fighting chair and looked up at the thin aluminum outriggers locked against the cabin of the *Silver Spoon.* Iles took three aspirin with a drink of beer. He rubbed a finger across the cold wet can and touched the damp finger to his bruised ear. His white tee-shirt stuck to his chest with sweat, and moisture glittered in the curly bleached hair on his forearms. Iles usually worked with his shirt off, but there were six red-purple welts on his ribs, and four red streaks dug into his back by Burney's fingernails, and teeth marks on his shoulder. Iles's skin felt greasy, and he knew that if he let himself go for a moment he would vomit. His eye, his ear, his ribs, his back, and the smaller cuts and bruises on his face were each separate agonies, although none hurt as much as the pain inside.

"What time you got to go to the airport?" asked the mate.

"Guthrie said he'd be here about noon. That means about two, but I'd better be there by noon in case there's some kind of screwup in Dallas and he gets here when he's supposed to."

"You look a sight. Want me to go instead?"

"Naw. I got to let 'em see me sooner or later. I'll take the station wagon. One of the niggers from the house can take the pickup for the bags. You finish cleaning the boat and getting the tackle ready and make sure the bar is stocked and the bunks are made and we got plenty of groceries on board. I imagine we'll pull out about five A.M. I'll tell 'em three, they'll think that means four, and they'll get to the boat at five."

"No chance they'll want to fish today?"

"They'll all be drunk except Guthrie. He won't make me take 'em out when they're drunk."

"In the two years I been on the *Spoon* I seen Mr. Guthrie on maybe fifteen trips," the mate said. "He's always got a drink in his hand. I don't care whether it's dawn or midnight. He's got Bloody Marys in the morning and beer at noon and scotch all afternoon and night, and he's always more sober than I am."

"You see him when he's partying with a bunch of drunks," said Iles. "It used to be I'd take him out alone. That was way back before we had the *Spoon*, when we just had that forty-five-foot Chris-Craft. Just Sam and me would go out to fish. There wasn't no drinking. Only a few beers when it was real hot and after we'd worked hard on a fish. We'd have a nigger to cut bait and help with the tail roping and gaffing and stuff, but we sure didn't have no bartender. Now Sam's always got a lot of people with him. Politicians and big company owners and guys like that. While they're drinking and playing, he's drinking and thinking."

"He's pretty sharp."

Iles looked at his watch and stood up.

"Guthrie's a funny guy, Billy," he said. "Sam got out of the Air

Force same time I got out of the Infantry, in 1946. He had a stake of five thousand dollars. I had eight thousand. He was three years younger than me. So he run his five thousand into I don't know how many million, and I did a little magic and turned my eight thousand into about eight hundred hangovers and a wife and three kids. Three and a half."

"Some sonabitches got the touch," said the mate.

"Yeah, don't we?" Iles said.

His wife was hanging wash outside their trailer when Iles drove up in the Ford station wagon.

"Jacob, you blow dust all over the clothes when you drive so fast," she said.

She wore a loose housecoat draped over her swollen belly. She had wrapped a scarf around her hair, but the shiny tips of curlers stuck through. Iles noticed that the flesh sagged from her arms as she raised them to the line. The sight bothered him, gave him a sense of loss, an impression of fading time: How long, he wondered, since her arms had been slender and brown? He stood and looked around the trailer camp. Seven trailers parked in a row with sand paths between them. Five of the trailers, including Iles's, were propped on concrete blocks. He had planted grass in a rectangle the size of a burial plot in front of his trailer and had enclosed it in a fence of small white pickets. Red bougainvillea grew along the side of the trailer. It was nice in the hot evenings to sit on the porch and look at the flowers and at the lights in the windows of the other trailers, and to hear the radios and televisions and the kids laughing, and to smell the wet wind from the Gulf. If he couldn't be on his boat out in the moonglistening water, then the trailer porch was a good place to be when the sky was grape-colored.

"How you feel, baby?" his wife said, picking up the dishpan she had used to carry the clothes.

"Not bad. Okay."

"You're lying. You feel like hell. Don't you think I can tell?"

"I don't feel no worse than I ought to. Not as bad as I deserve."

"Come on inside and drink a beer."

"I like you, Marge. You understand a man."

"No, I don't understand you at all," she said.

Inside the trailer, Iles sat at the kitchen table while his wife scuffed to the refrigerator in her slippers and brought him a beer. Her eyes were tired, and her skin was blotchy. She was getting heavy. This pregnancy seemed to have asked too much.

Looking at her now, as she was, with her flabby forearms and narrow eyes and cracked lips and blue networks showing in the calves of her legs, Iles tried to remember how she had been the day he met her fifteen years before. She was a tall, slender girl then, alive, with red hair and blue eyes, and she could laugh. She was a waitress at a cafe three blocks in from the beach at Fort Lauderdale, and Iles went to the cafe to drink beer and to look at her. He was working as captain of a party fishing boat that loaded up twice a day with tourists and took them offshore to let them tangle their lines and get sunburned and throw up and take photographs and yell at each other and invent deep-sea fishing stories. It was a job that Iles hated. He had got it through a corporal who had been an assistant squad leader in the platoon that Iles, a sergeant, was in charge of when the lieutenant was absent, which was often. The only part of the job that Iles liked was being united with the sea again. He preferred the Gulf of Mexico because he had been born on its shore, in Port Aransas, but he had listened to the offer from the corporal and had moved after the war to the east coast of Florida. The party boat did not suit him, and the tourists did not suit him. But the Atlantic did, thundering out green and blue and turquoise and gray from Fort Lauderdale and Pompano Beach and Hollywood, where he guided the broiled, retching tourists. Occasionally Iles would take his days off and catch a charter out of Miami or would go across to the Bahamas to fish or would plug for tarpon in the rivers. Mostly, though, he drove the tourists or went into the cafe in the evenings to drink beer and to look at the tall, red-haired waitress.

By the time he got her pregnant, they had decided to be married anyhow. Iles owned a piece of the party boat, as the only tangible asset he had acquired with any of his eight thousand dollars, and he and his bride rented a house in Fort Lauderdale. The house was on an inland canal and had a green lawn and palm trees. They lived in it for three years before Iles went to work a midweek charter out of Miami and met Sam Guthrie. During the fishing trip Guthrie hooked and fought and landed a three-hundred-pound mako shark, and meanwhile baited and captured what Iles, listening casually, took to be a rather large contract for the electrical work in a series of Florida shopping centers. Pleased with his fish and his contract, Guthrie invited Iles to a drink after they docked at Miami. The drink lasted two days. They discovered they had been raised as neighbors—Iles in Port Aransas and Guthrie in Port Agness—and had entered the armed forces in the same month and had been discharged only two months apart and had both been stationed for a while outside London and both loved the sea. They went back to Fort Lauderdale together. The next day, Guthrie returned to Dallas. Iles began packing. He and Marge left their house with the green lawn and the palms and moved to Port Agness to await delivery of Guthrie's Chris-Craft, which Iles was to operate as a charter when Guthrie wasn't using it. In the next few years they shifted the boat around from Port Agness to Rockport, Houston, Mobile, New Orleans, Tampa, Key West, Miami, and again to Port Agness. Marge and the children followed Iles in a trailer. She never had another house. Looking at her as she was now he remembered that, and he was sorry.

"Honey," Marge said, raising her eyes with an effort from a stack of towels she was folding, "are you gonna talk to Mr. Guthrie today?"

"If I get a chance. He's got a party with him. You know how that is. Lot of drinking and carrying on up in the big house. Lot of crazy business. We don't get much chance to talk.

"We got to know soon."

"Don't bad mouth me about it. I'll talk to him when I can."

"It ain't just me, Jacob. You act like it was just me."

"Okay."

"I mean you act like it wasn't the kids involved too," she said. "They're your kids the same as they are mine. I'd think you'd want what's best for them."

"I said okay."

"You're gonna ask for more money? Not for that other thing?"

"What other thing?"

"You know."

"If I knew would I ask?"

"A job," she said. "A job back at one of his plants."

"Marge, I told you a thousand times I can't do that."

"You don't want to."

"Why would he hire me? I don't know about nothing but boats."

"You could learn. You're only forty-one years old. You do the electrical repairs on the *Spoon* yourself, don't you? It ain't like you're stupid about it and couldn't handle a job."

"I don't know."

"You and Mr. Guthrie been together a long time," she said. "You're friends. He owes you."

"He don't owe me nothing except what I earn," said Iles. "We're friends, all right, because I know about boats and I do him good work and see that he catches fish and see that nobody drowns in one of his parties. But if you take that away, then we ain't friends. You don't know how these rich guys think. They're your friend as long as you make your own way and got something they can use and don't ask a lot of favors. When that's gone, you're gone."

"I can't believe that," she said. "As many times as you and Mr. Guthrie sat out there on that porch and drank beer? You mean you ain't friends? He brings presents for the kids, he eats dinner with us sometimes. That don't make you friends?"

Iles leaned his elbows on the table and lit a cigarette. Marge had put down the towels and was looking hard at him with an expression he knew was close to tears.

"It's always been him coming to us," said Iles. "If it was me going to him, it'd be different. Anyways, he ain't eat dinner with us in a while. The kids been getting their birthday presents by mail. He ain't had any of us up to the house in a long time, has he?"

"At least you can ask for more money."

"He paid two hundred and twenty-five thousand dollars for the *Spoon*. It costs him about thirty thousand dollars a year to run it. I'm supposed to tell him it's gonna cost more?"

"You're small-minded," she said. "What would a thousand more make? He's got millions."

"I guess so."

"You know so."

"Look, if he got it in his mind to come and say Jake I'd like to give you ten thousand dollars to see that your kids can go to college when the time comes, why that'd be fine and he wouldn't think none the less of me if I took it. But I've seen the look he gets on his face when guys ask him for favors. Out on a fishing party they'd be pals, drinking and telling jokes, and then some guy would get too much to drink and feel pretty friendly and he'd go too far. He'd say something out of line. It'd get awful quiet. And that poor bastard that went too far, he'd know what he done. He'd know they wasn't really pals at all. He'd want to kill hisself. I'd never see him on the boat again."

"This ain't any ten thousand dollars and it ain't a favor," his wife said. "It's a raise in pay we're talking about. It's due you."

"I'm just trying to live simple," said Iles. "Can't nothing be simple any more? All I want to do is get out on the Gulf and fish and then come home, and everthing keeps getting all screwed-up. How come it's so hard to be simple?"

"You got responsibilities."

"Yeah. I got one right now. I got to go shake up that nigger. If I don't, he'll be late and then we won't have no job at all to worry about."

"You'll ask Mr. Guthrie?"

"Sure. I'll ask him."

She followed him to the door. She was very heavy this time and she walked as if the weight and the aching of her womb would pull her to the floor if she didn't concentrate on holding herself up. Toys and clothes and magazines cluttered the living quarters of the trailer. Iles could see from the slump of her shoulders that she despaired of picking them up.

"Jacob, I'd like to have a house," she said.

"I know it, honey."

"Let's stop moving so much. Let's get away from the water. I hate it. Any more, I just hate it."

"I'll see what I can do," said Iles.

"I'm sorry to be talking about this today, Jacob. I know how much you hurt."

"I ought to be used to hurting."

"Give me a kiss?"

Iles was faintly surprised, but he bent forward and kissed her dry lips. She smelled like cold cream and tasted like fried potatoes. Her belly nudged against him. Lifting his head he saw the oily shine of her nose, and he turned and went out and let the screen door slam. At the car, Iles stopped and waved. She waved back from behind the screen, standing limply as if abandoned of hope. Iles got into the station wagon and started the engine and roared away through the sand. In the mirror, past the white dust thrown by the wheels, he saw her disappear from the screen. He knew she would go to the bed now and lie down on it and cry.

Port Agness is an island, a link in the necklace of islands which sits off the South Texas coast like a great barrier reef extending down into the waters of Mexico. It is an island of sand dunes piled in some places high as a house. Hardly anyone lives in Port Agness. The winds blow most of the year, shifting the dunes and raining the island with sand and salt spray. There is a channel much like a river between the islands and the mainland, and a series of bays cut up into the coast. Other channels slice between the islands as openings to the Gulf, and the nature of the land is such that the autumn hurricanes occasionally close some channels and tear out different ones so that the charts must be made over and the captains must be mindful of the changing passages. Driving the Ford station wagon down through the dunes from the big house Iles passed an area that had been a channel when he was a boy but that now was a range of dunes. He went by the timbers of what had begun ambitiously as a bridge to the mainland before a hurricane caught it much less than midway. His car spinning through the dunes like a mad beetle, Iles came across a patch of earth flat as a tennis court where once there had been a small hotel. Each of these things registered automatically in his mind, as a man accustomed to observing landfalls and noting mutations, and he drove onto the ferry with absolute timing. Across the wide channel, he pushed the Ford to eighty miles an hour along the highway to County Airport. He arrived just at noon, saw with relief that Guthrie's airplane was not there, and parked the station wagon beside a tin shed. At 12:30 the Negro drove up in the pickup truck, looked at Iles in angry remembrance of their conversation at the big house, and immediately went to sleep.

Iles waited for more than an hour beside the station wagon. With the patience of a man who had spent most of his life on fishing boats and the rest of it in the Infantry, Iles sat on the shady side of the car and leaned against the fender. He scraped up handfuls of gravel and tossed the pebbles against the tires of the pickup. Both doors of the truck were open in search of whatever slight breeze might happen along. Iles could see the Negro's feet sticking out. The Negro had gone to sleep in the front seat. Whenever Iles found a larger pebble, he would throw it against the fender of the pickup and the plunk would make the Negro's feet jerk. Iles grinned at the feet. Then, finally, he mashed out his cigarette, dropped the gravel, wiped his hands on his pants, and stood up. He had put on a white shirt, but he had unbuttoned it to the navel. Now he began to button his shirt again. He had seen the speck against the sky.

"Hey, nigger," Iles said.

The feet didn't move.

"Hey, nigger," said Iles. "Sit up and look like you're human. I think that's the plane."

The feet twitched, stopped, twitched again, pulled inside the cab, and the Negro's head appeared in the window. The Negro scratched his scalp. His walnut face shone with sweat. His wide yellow eyes looked at Iles; they were sullen eyes, dull with dislike and sleep.

"You got no call to talk to me that way," the Negro said.

"What're you hot about?"

"I don't like what you called me. You cussed me at the house and called me that, and you called me that again. I don't like it."

"You mean nigger?" said Iles. "You don't like me to call you a nigger? What are you, a Indian?"

"I'm a man," the Negro said. He climbed out of the truck and put on his white dinner jacket. He searched his pockets for his bow tie, and snapped it on. The collar was dark and wrinkled. His black trousers were crumpled, and the jacket was immediately stained with sweat.

"You can be a man and a nigger at the same time," said Iles. "Don't make it no worse than it is. I live like a nigger myself. Some of 'em when they call me Cap, they say it the same way they do when they call you waiter. The big advantage I got over you is I can go into the Sporting Life Bar and get my ass knocked off, whereas you can't."

"Don't try to be friends with me," the Negro said.

"You one of them damned Muslims?"

"I'm not your friend."

"Screw you then," said Iles. "You'll be lucky if Mr. Guthrie don't take one look at how you sweated up your suit and tie a rock to your tail and use you for an anchor."

"I didn't make the sun to shine," the Negro said.

"Screw you is what I said."

The plane was coming in over the tops of the mesquite and scrub oaks at the far end of the runway. It was a twin-engine transport, painted white with a red streak from nose to tail and with a red G and lightning bolt on the rudder. The wheels touched, the plane bounced once, then settled smoothly onto the asphalt runway. Iles smelled burning rubber. There was a roar as the pilot reversed his engines. The plane began to taxi toward where the cars were parked, in front of the maintenance shed. Iles walked out to meet the plane. The wind from the props whipped his pants and blew dust in his eyes, and he had to hold his cap. Then the noise quit. The door opened. The co-pilot stuck his head out and began to lower the ramp.

"Hi, Iles," said the co-pilot.

"What say," Iles said.

"Not much. Any fishing?"

Iles turned his thumb down and shook his head. The co-pilot stepped back inside. A woman appeared in the doorway. Iles looked up at her through his dark glasses. She was still very pretty, small and fine boned, with nice hips and with ankles that were a bit too thick. Her hair was black with brushings of gray. She wore her hair short, which Iles liked. Dark glasses hid her eyes, but she smiled when she saw Iles. He reached up to take her hand and help her down the steps and she squeezed his fingers. Behind him he heard the motor of the pickup turn over and the truck start slowly toward the plane.

"Hello, Jacob," the woman said.

"Miz Guthrie," he said. "Good to have you back again."

"My God, Jacob, your face!" she said.

"We had some weather," said Iles. "I fell off the bridge."

She glanced down at his legs and quickly looked up his body until her eyes were on his face again.

"No broken bones?" she said.

"No, ma'am. Busted up my pride though."

"You have vanity to spare, Jacob. You haven't lost anything."

"No, ma'am. Nothing I can't get back."

The others were coming down now. Mrs. Guthrie released Iles's hand, and he stepped around her to be at the bottom of the ramp. Each of the descending people looked at Iles, and he looked at them. He recognized the first one: a tall, frail, dry-looking man named Senator somebody. The Senator had been at the island a couple of times before. The Senator was all right, except that if he ever hung into a good fish he got tired and needed help. But most old men were that way, especially if they'd never done any hard work and their muscles were soft, and the Senator was never too apologetic about it. Iles didn't know the next two: a man with clipped red brush hair and horn-rimmed glasses, and a tall blonde woman. Iles nodded to them, but neither of them returned the nod. The man was small and thin and seemed graceful despite the fact that his face had little grace to it. He went past Iles with a quick look that warned Iles he did not want, would resent, to be touched or helped. Iles reached up to take the hand of the tall blonde woman, and she allowed it, coldly. She looked at the bruises on his face as if they were markings on the hide of a strange and mildly curious beast. Iles decided he didn't like either of them, but then there had been plenty of Guthrie's visitors Iles didn't like. His job was merely to entertain them and to take them to where fish were, not to try for their friendship.

"Hey, Jake!" a voice said. "Goddamn, it's good to see you, skipper!"

"Hey, Sam," said Iles, smiling.

Guthrie ran down the steps in three bounds, shook Iles's hand, and put an arm around Iles's shoulder. Guthrie was four inches taller than Iles and forty pounds heavier, and he steered Iles away from the others as easily as if he were guiding a child. Iles winced as Guthrie's hand touched the scratches and bruises on his back, and the hand immediately lifted as if Guthrie understood from the purple eye and the black ear what was also the matter beneath the shirt.

"How's Marge?" Guthrie said.

"Okay. Pregnant as usual."

"Kid's due in July, isn't it?"

"Early July. How the hell did you remember that?"

"I never forget anything, Jake, that's of any importance to me. Four kids. Isn't that something? If I was you, I'd take to locking myself in the bathroom for a little while ever night just before bedtime. That'll sure get rid of your tensions, and at the same time it'll cut down on your future grocery bills."

"Don't sound like much fun to me."

"That's the trouble of it. Obviously I don't take my own advice." Guthrie looked around the airport, which had been bulldozed out of a stumpy wood of mesquite and scrub oak, and he lifted his arms and laughed. "I've missed this place. How long since I was here? Four months?"

"Five, almost. Last time was December."

"I've been busy, Jake. Been working like hell."

"Big deals?"

"Pretty big for an old South Texas boy like me."

"If they're big for you, they're big," said Iles.

"I hope they're not too big, Jake. These things can get all out of whack, can wrap you up like a crab in a net, can flip you upside down and give you a boarding before you know it. Anything that keeps me from going fishing for five months might be too big."

"Sam, can't we hurry?" Mrs. Guthrie said. "It's hot."

"Do let's get cool," said the blonde woman.

"That ain't heat," Guthrie said. "That's the warm, loving breath of God. It'll do you good to let that soaked up air-conditioning evaporate for a while."

"It might help my eternal spirit, but it's going to bother the crap out of my sinuses," said the man in horn-rims.

"Okay, we'll move," Guthrie said. He saw the Negro. "Look at him! A dinner jacket and tux pants! He president of the local chapter of the NAACP?"

"It was Roger's idea," said Iles. "He got them new outfits for all the boys at the house, and he bought new uniforms for the women. Roger's proud of 'em. He lined 'em up this morning and marched down the line inspecting 'em like a general."

"Showy," Guthrie said. "Awful showy. But I wouldn't want to hurt Roger's feelings. He likes it, I guess it ought to be all right with me."

Iles looked at Guthrie as they walked toward the car. Guthrie looked as vigorous as he always had, although his waist was fleshier where his golf shirt tucked into his beltless slacks. Guthrie was a big man. Iles looked up at his large straight nose, and at the cleft in his heavy rounded chin. There was a mole on Guthrie's left cheek where the whiskers grew thicker and blacker, and Guthrie had not shaved that morning. Guthrie's skin was dark, as if from some Mediterranean ancestry, and his hair was heavy and black. He walked like a man who was aware of his body, lightly, bobbing on the balls of his feet, slightly swaggering, shoulders held back, turning quickly and tightly, hands held free for sudden movement. He frequently rubbed his stomach as he was talking, as if to reassure himself that it was still reasonably flat. His eyes were large and misty brown, soft as warm chocolate, but Iles had seen all expression leave them during times of anger or concentration. At those times the eyes went blank and hard as agates. Guthrie's smile was wide and white with perfect, capped teeth. He walked past Iles and opened the rear door of the station wagon.

"I'll crawl back here on the little seat so you girls don't have to wrinkle up your dresses and Waddy's sinuses don't drain," Guthrie said. "Waddy, you and Beth and the Senator take the next seat. Jane, you sit up front with Jake, our favorite fisherman." Guthrie swung himself easily through the narrow opening and dropped onto the folded-down seat. "Lord, it's good to be away from that city. I'm starting to feel like a man again. I'm starting to get something in my lungs besides smoke and perfume and the smell of brief cases. Oh, Lord, it's good. One blue marlin, Jake, early in the morning, and everthing I got is yours. I'll swap with you clean."

"What'll you give me to boot?" said Iles.

Through a window of the Convair, Sam Guthrie could see the gray water of the Gulf glittering between pieces of cloud. Guthrie leaned sideways and looked down at the shadow of the airplane as it glided across the flat green and brown geometry of the earth where the clouds had left it bare. Off to the right were clouds like cotton mountains, and below the clouds drifted in thinner trailing wisps. But ahead Guthrie could see that it was clear over the Gulf. They were flying, he guessed, at about four thousand feet, and they would be on the ground in less than fifteen minutes. Guthrie looked at the waiter and made a circle in the air with his finger. The waiter, at the bar in the galley, nodded and began pulling bottles out of wooden racks that were padded with foam rubber. Guthrie sat back. He crossed his legs with difficulty under the card table and realized Waddy Morris was looking at him.

"I'm surprised you don't remember that game, Sam," said Waddy Morris.

"What game is that?" Guthrie said.

"The game I was talking about. It was the damnedest run I ever saw. This TCU back, McKown I think his name was, or some sort of name like that, was the slowest guy on the field. He couldn't outrun my wife in a sheath dress. But he ran fifty or sixty yards right through the middle of the Aggies for a touchdown and the whole Aggie team tried to tackle him and couldn't and tried to chase him and couldn't catch him."

"Oh, Waddy, make it eighty yards and have people come down from the *stands,* for God's sake, to try and catch him," said Beth Morris. "Make it an outstanding story if you're going to tell it."

"Fifty or sixty yards is far enough," Waddy said. "You study your cards. You play poorly enough without interrupting other people's conversations. Sam, I saw that All-American, Swink, make some great runs for TCU a few years later. I saw Doak Walker in every game he ever played for SMU after he got out of the Army. But Swink and Walker could run, and McKown couldn't. McKown didn't have their ability. He got his touchdown and won the game because he wanted to so damned bad. That's why I say it's the greatest run I ever saw."

"When was that?" said Guthrie.

"McKown? Ten or twelve years ago."

"Ten or twelve years ago I didn't have time to see many football games," said Guthrie. "I was buying season tickets to the SMU games for business reasons, but I never went unless there was somebody to be romanced."

"He didn't even have time to see me, and I was right in his pocket," said Jane Guthrie.

"I would think you're somebody to be romanced," Waddy said.

"Oh, Waddy, for God's sake," said Beth Morris.

"Study your cards," Waddy said.

Guthrie smiled at his wife, who sat beside Waddy Morris across the card table from Guthrie and Beth Morris. The plane took a sudden swoop downward, and the waiter steadied himself at the bar. Beth Morris's shoulder and knee touched Guthrie as she leaned around him to look out the window. Senator Rose, who sat on one of the two couches in the middle of the plane, looked up from his magazine and smiled.

"It'll be rough for a few minutes," Guthrie said.

"You were a flier during the second war, weren't you, Sam?" asked Beth Morris, straightening up. "I'm knocking for two. Play the ace of spades, darling."

"Three points," Guthrie said, throwing down his cards. "I flew bombers in Europe."

"That must have been thrilling," said Beth Morris.

"Sure. It was lots of fun," Guthrie said.

"Were you a general or something?" she said.

"He was a major, damn it," said Waddy. "Why this fascination with wars?"

"I thought oil men loved wars, for God's sake," Beth Morris said.

"If you say 'for God's sake' once more, I'll divorce you, for God's sake," Waddy said.

"Well, nobody wants to talk about football," said Beth Morris.

"How many do we need to go out in the third game?" Waddy asked.

"Thirty-seven, darling. They need six. We're down three boxes and a hundred and eighty dollars. That's nearly a whole afternoon's telephone bill for you, darling."

Waddy Morris peered at his cards. He bit his upper lip and squinted through his glasses. His red hair, the thin color of tabasco sauce much watered, lay about in bunches like the bristles of a brush that had been stepped on. His small mouth puckered, as if drawing on an imaginary cigarette. With one finger he touched a red blemish on his chin, and then carefully and with an attitude of sly, private amusement, he discarded and smiled at Jane Guthrie.

"I feel that I've just been raped," she said.

"Not quite," said Waddy. "But I'm following you down a lonely alley."

"I love the way you've done your plane, Sam," Beth Morris said. "It looks a lot like our Convair."

"A little bit," Waddy said. "It looks more like the DC-3 we just had redecorated. This Convair looks a lot better than our Convair. Our Convair is starting to get worn-out-looking places in the carpet. Not that it matters. The way the tax laws are getting, our Convair is going to stay parked until the tires go flat or I buy my own Congress."

"If Sam can fly his, we can fly ours," said Beth Morris.

"But, darling, Sam is *rich,*" Waddy said.

They all laughed.

"I tried to make the plane comfortable," Guthrie said.

Guthrie grinned to himself. A decorator had laid the floor in heavy beige carpeting and had hung matching drapes the length of either side of the sitting area. They had removed the old seats and replaced them with overstuffed armchairs and two long couches. Guthrie had sent electricians from Guthrie Electronics, Inc., to install a stereo sound system for records and radio, to put altimeters and speedometers and compasses and rate of climb indicators into a folding panel for the guests. They had put a new bar up front, and a smaller bar in the rear, and had built in three more cold boxes for ice and beer. The cabinetmakers had put in cabinets that looked like mahogany but were of a light synthetic for cigarettes and glasses and bottles and playing cards and magazines, and there was a bookshelf filled with *Reader's Digest* condensations. Four card tables swung out from the walls, and each had four armchairs arranged at it. A new galley had been installed near the pilots' compartment, a new coffee urn, containers for the tomato juice they used for Bloody Marys and the apple juice they mixed with vodka and the water with which they took their aspirin and vitamins. There was one small cabinet which held a sterilized syringe and packet of needles and bottle of vitamin B-12 compound for urgent recovery of the more debilitated. Both toilet compartments were built to the specifications of those in the big jet airliners and were carpeted and mirrored. When he'd bought the Convair, a year earlier, it was purely for business: the interior bare except for seats along one wall, three desks along the other, and two bunks in the rear. Now the plane would carry nineteen passengers as elegantly as if they were in a hotel suite. It no longer looked like a flying office, Guthrie thought. But it was comfortable, all right. The wonder was that it would get off the ground.

The waiter brought the last round of drinks as the red warning lights went on. Waddy Morris put down his cards and said, "Gin."

"Drink 'em up," said Guthrie.

"Damn, I went around the world to throw you that three of hearts," Jane Guthrie said. "Would the six have helped?"

"Not at all," said Waddy. "The three hit me right in the middle. It was the only card that would have ginned me." He swished the ice cubes in the scotch and water. "I'm starting to believe, seriously, that I'm a marvelous player. I concentrated on that card until you were helpless to keep from throwing it. The powers of the mind. The compelling of the will."

Waddy leaned back in the chair. He had a vaguely puzzled grin, as if he were interested in what he saw before him but not ready to be fully involved in it. With himself, he seemed pleased. With everything else, he seemed dubious, holding back, testing. Guthrie glanced at Beth Morris. She was blonde and handsome, a former high fashion model, with large clear artful eyes and a wide mouth and a regular profile that did not have the flaw that would make it especially appealing. She was handsome in the way that a perfectly bred and groomed animal is handsome. Guthrie had seen her at the various society charity balls and opera parties, tall and sleek, shining with diamonds and apparently like a diamond herself. He hadn't known her in her gaunt, dieting, strapped-down period as a fashion model. But evidently as Waddy's wife she had uncorseted and allowed her body the freedom to expand, and Guthrie admired the result. Guthrie looked at Waddy Morris. Waddy with his big glasses, short pugnacious chin, pale wet blue eyes, pinched mouth, freckles, uncertain complexion. Without the freak of birth, Guthrie thought, Waddy would probably be a physics instructor with a fat wife, a house full of children, and a yearning to buy his own bowling ball someday. But Waddy had certainly taken advantage of what accident had provided him.

Guthrie's wife nudged him.

"You're very pensive," she said.

"Huh?" said Guthrie.

"Dear, the light's on. Fasten your seat belt."

"Sorry."

"Sam needs this weekend," Jane Guthrie said. "He's been working so hard on this proxy fight that he's almost turned himself inside out. He never sleeps any more. I don't think he can even remember the children's names."

"That vote counting is next week, isn't it?" asked Waddy.

"Yeah," Guthrie said.

"Got it won?"

"I think so. I damn sure better. According to my proxy fighters, I'm gonna win, but that's what they'd be expected to tell me I guess. For the money I'm paying them, they're not supposed to disillusion me."

"You need nearly all the rest of the uncommitted proxies, don't you?" asked Waddy.

"Nearly. Except I've pulled a couple of tricks the other side doesn't know about yet."

"It's been a tough one," Waddy said quietly, cutting the two women out of the conversation. "I've followed it since you started buying that Ramco stock under a street name. I had some of the stock, you know. Friend of yours in Denver bought it from me. I'd have held it if I'd been absolutely sure it was you. But you'd bounced the price around. My dad had some that he sold on the street. You were causing a pretty good bunch of rumors before you took it to the SEC. Then that kid lawyer started hitting you with those injunctions. That bother you much?"

"It annoyed the hell out of me. But I don't think all that crap he put out in the newspapers has affected the stockholders to any great extent. He knew he couldn't get anywhere with his injunctions. He just wanted to spread propaganda against me."

"I understand A. C. Johnson is the biggest stockholder in Ramco," said Waddy. "He's a good friend of mine. We went to Texas Country Day together, and then to the same prep school, and then for some damn reason he went to Yale. I went out to Stanford. For some damn reason."

"I wish A. C. Johnson was a good friend of mine," Guthrie said. "Which way's he going?"

"The old board is sure he's going with them. But my proxy guys are rushing him like he was the sweetheart of the student body. Who the hell knows? Nobody can find out for sure until next week. He hasn't registered his proxies for either side."

"I'm simply dying to see your house down here," Beth Morris said.

"I'm sure it's nowhere as grand as the one you have on your island, but we enjoy it," said Jane Guthrie. "The children spend the summers down here, and Sam always gets a kick out of coming back. He was born here."

"I didn't know that," Beth said.

Waddy nodded. "I'd heard it," he said.

The plane had dropped through the covering clouds and had come into hard sunlight. Beyond was the landing strip at County Airport, where the corrugated iron buildings seemed on fire from the sun, and beyond that lay the shining water of the Gulf of Mexico.

"The ground is so flat here," said Beth, leaning against Guthrie again to look out the window. "I wish the Texas coast had cliffs and mountains, for God's sake, like California or Oregon or Washington. It's so damned *boring* to look down at all that flatness for miles and miles and miles."

"This used to be the floor of the ocean," Waddy said. "The mountains were up around Austin, but they eroded. They wore down like teeth without enough calcium and left those hills that the students drive their cars off of. Down here the water pulled back and left all sorts of things."

"Like what?" said Beth.

"Sea shells," Waddy said. "And oil."

"Why doesn't somebody develop this land the way they did Florida?" said Beth. "Really, this is no more awful looking I suppose than Florida. We don't have all those nasty swamps. They could build a lot of big hotels and night clubs and plant palm trees. It could be fun."

"Somebody will," Waddy said.

"I hope not," said Guthrie. "I like it the way it is. I can start from near my house at Port Agness and drive forty or fifty miles down the island and never see a soul. Only the cranes and the herons and the gulls and a few cows. That's a good feeling after being in the city too long. It gives you perspective. I don't want to have to drive along past a hundred hotels with traffic lights and fat people waddling over to the beach."

"Do your parents still live here?" Beth asked.

"My father drowned when I was ten years old. My mother died of pneumonia when I was nineteen," said Guthrie.

"Oh, I'm sorry," Beth said.

"So was I," said Guthrie.

The others looked at him.

"I didn't mean that to be funny," said Guthrie. "I mean it as the truth. I hated it like hell for both of them. My old man tried to make it as a fisherman, but he never had much luck. Maybe he wasn't the type. I remember him as a gray-haired old guy who always needed a shave, but he was only thirty-four when he drowned. Strange how kids remember things, isn't it? He went overboard off a shrimper during a storm in the Gulf. Poor bastard. He never had any luck at all. His own boat disappeared in a hurricane. It wasn't much of a boat, but it was his. He lost at everything. Cards, women, fights, drinking, he always lost. I remember the look he used to have in his eyes. Like he really wanted so much more. Yearning, I guess would be the word. He never had too much to do with me. Acted like he was embarrassed to have me around, to have me looking at him. Like he didn't want me to see him the way he was. I hated it when he drowned. I really hated it."

"Sam, dear, don't light that cigarette," his wife said. "We're on the way down."

"That rule's for the airlines, not for me," said Guthrie.

The Convair floated onto the runway, bounced once, rolled to a stop as the engines hammered into reverse, and then began to taxi. Looking out the window, Guthrie saw Jacob Iles waiting near the station wagon. The sun hit the windshield of the car and flashed off the chrome. He watched Iles come toward the plane shielding his eyes and holding his cap against the blowing dust.

"There's Jake," Guthrie said. "There's a good man."

"Who is he?" asked Beth.

"Skipper of my boat. Hell of a guy. You'll see in the morning, Waddy. If the fish are there, he'll take us to 'em."

"He looks primitive," Beth said.

"All fishing captains look primitive," said Waddy.

"I think Jake would take that as a compliment," Guthrie said, smiling.

They heard the doors slam open and the ramp go down. Guthrie raised the card table and locked it against the wall. Senator Rose was already up. He stretched, snapped his portfolio case shut, and tossed his magazine onto the couch. The Senator was a tall old man with a red face and white hair, and he wore a rumpled seersucker suit, a soft button-down collar, and a black knit tie in a tiny knot. He had drunk a great many Bloody Marys during the flight, and now he kept opening his mouth and squeezing his lower lip with thumb and forefinger as if he had been anesthetized.

"I'm strongly in favor of a nap, Sam," said the Senator. "I hope you don't intend to fish this afternoon. I wouldn't want to miss it. But I'm afraid age demands its tribute from me."

"No fishing today, Senator," Guthrie said. "We'll take it easy today. We'll be downright slothful. Hey, smell that? I'm not even outside yet and I can smell the sun and hot wind and salt water. It makes you come alive again."

"You really *like* this place, don't you?" said Beth Morris, looking at Guthrie as he took her elbow and guided her down the aisle. In heels she was nearly as tall as Guthrie; her legs, it struck him, were longer than his. She had white, transparent skin, faintly blue under the surface, and wore purple eye shadow. Her arm felt brittle under his fingers, as if he could snap it by twisting his wrist.

"Sometimes I think I never should have left here," Guthrie said. "Sometimes I think I can't ever really be happy anywhere else. When you grow up on the Gulf like I did and then you leave it and go after other things, it's like you strayed or something. It's like you've been thrown out of paradise. Like you've left what's solid to chase after something you can never quite get your hands on. I don't know. Something like that."

Beth Morris smiled at him, and Guthrie could tell she had no idea what he meant.

"Waddy doesn't feel that way about anything," he said. "Waddy doesn't need it. He's beyond it. He's enough with himself. He makes his own rules and sort of handles everything that's put in front of him. But I wake up at night sometimes smelling the Gulf and I have a hell of a time forgetting it and going back to sleep."

"If that's what you think about Waddy, you don't know very much about Waddy," said Beth.

"I know a considerable amount about Waddy," Guthrie said. Then he laughed. "Anyhow, watch out for this sun. It's treacherous. It'll broil you."

"I'm not the outdoor type," she said. "I take my pleasures where it's air-conditioned and there are soft things to lie on. I'm afraid I'd rather have music and perfume and silk pillows than a sunburned nose and messed-up hair."

"You shouldn't leave without getting a tan. I'd consider it an insult to my ability as a host. You could get a little brown in a couple of days."

"I don't like the white places," she said. "Could you arrange for me to get a tan without the white places?"

"For God's sake, come on," Waddy said from the doorway. "I haven't had a drink in two and a half minutes."

Jacob Iles met them at the bottom of the ramp. Guthrie grinned when he saw the bruises on Iles's face; he knew immediately what had caused them. Iles was not at all a large man, about five-ten and one hundred seventy pounds, but Guthrie had seen him in saloon brawls several times. Iles was a vicious fighter, who fought as if the object were to hurt his opponent as badly and as quickly as possible. Iles took off the white yachting cap, the clean one he usually wore when meeting the plane or for the first hour when there were strangers on the boat. After clawing one hand through his sunscorched hair, he put his cap back on and adjusted his dark glasses. Sweat bubbled on his face and in the pockets below his cheekbones. Iles's face was a rough, upside-down triangle with the point at the chin. His ears stuck out. The left ear was a bruised blueblack with a red spot the size of a quarter at the lobe where it joined his head. Guthrie wondered whether the ear had been yanked, struck, chewed on, or possibly all three. Iles's left eye was a purple mound that made his glasses sit crookedly. With the back of his hand, the captain rubbed sweat off his forehead. He has a bad one this time, Guthrie thought, and then he went to Iles, shook his hand, and put his arm around the captain's shoulder. Through the damp shirt, Guthrie felt the ridges of Iles's wounds and lifted his hand.

They drove away from the airport in the station wagon. The grass along the highway had been burned dead yellow by the sun. As they went past the carbon plant they saw the grass, the trees, the sand, colored by the smoke. The grassy hillocks of the dunes were black as heaps of coal. The sun was white, intense, painful. Senator Rose, squinting, fumbled in his coat pocket for his dark glasses. All the others except Guthrie already wore them.

"Looks like hell, doesn't it?" Guthrie said. "You ought to see it in the middle of the summer when it's hot. You might think this is hot, but this is only late spring. In the summer it's not real. People are paralyzed. Nothing moves. I swear you could sit here and watch a ladybug crawl across the road and not see another living thing all afternoon. Oh, maybe a few grasshoppers."

"But it's not like this at Agua Verda," the Senator said. "Sam has built himself a palace there."

"Agua Verda?" said Beth Morris. "I thought we were in Port Agness or some damn place."

"Agua Verda is the house," the Senator said. "I believe the architect named it that. It means blue water."

"Green water," said Jane Guthrie. "Actually the color of the water changes all the time, and the house is hardly a palace."

"My dear, you're being modest," Senator Rose said.

They passed beside two small towns which sat to their left on a bay. In one they could see the masts of shrimp boats tied up at the docks, and the houses were painted pastels, and in the yard of a red stone school children bounced a basketball in the dirt under the shade of an oak tree. Then Iles swung the station wagon farther to the left up a shallow rise through a cluster of oaks. They went along a street of stores and shops from whose windows eyes looked out at the speeding car. From the crest of the rise, the station wagon dropped down onto the bridge across the flats. To either side lay the brilliant water. Below the bridge people walked slowly in the sand or fished off a rock jetty with surf foaming at their ankles. Inside the station wagon the passengers were quiet. Waddy Morris stared out the window, frowning, as if he had begun to regret the trip. Beth Morris had shut her eyes. The air-conditioner hummed. In his cramped rear seat Guthrie mashed out a cigarette on the floor and twisted to watch the ferry landing approach.

There were two tankers at the refinery when Iles drove the station wagon onto the ferry, tires rumbling. The passengers got out. The bar came down behind them. The ferry captain sounded his whistle and they started across. A porpoise splashed and wallowed beside the ferry, black back running water as the porpoise dived. Spray filmed the dark glasses of the passengers. Guthrie stood at the bow with his hands around the iron rails that were hot from the sun and watched the island come nearer. It was like a great sandbar upon which people had absurdly built houses and tried to live. To the right the island stretched as far as he could see and the surf was white in the sun. To the left he could see the jetty which marked a Gulf passage and split the island from the neighboring island to the northeast. Straight ahead was Port Agness, a scattering of buildings like a child's toys left in the sand. Guthrie never returned without a jolt to his emotions. He wondered how the island had been the first time his father saw it: a pale, bare arm of land erupted with sand mountains and ponds of rain water. Now there were new houses going up, a new marine laboratory, motels, taverns. Downtown Port Agness was a sandy square of wooden buildings beside the channel docks. In the summers the few roads were crowded with tourists who didn't come again unless they were fishermen. There was not much else to offer a tourist except dangerous sun and blowing wind. When Guthrie was a boy the island had two hundred permanent residents. Now there were eight hundred, and they paid taxes, and police had shut down their dice games and roulette wheels and had made them hide their drinks across the bars. The chemical plants were creeping closer from either side of the island under clouds of orange smoke and suffocating odors along the coast, the huge chemical plants with their maze of smoke stacks that made them look like an insane designer's idea of a battleship, frightening and forbidden places with wire fences. The refinery had been built where there had once been a fishing village, on the mainland. They were laying waste to the country, Guthrie thought, inviting destruction. They were pouring salt on the earth.

"Someday," Guthrie said, "this will all be flattened. All these oil tanks, and those factories on the coast, and these frame shacks and cheap stores will be blown away. Someday this island will be purged. It might put the whole island under water. The Gulf won't put up with all this crap for very long at a time, but people keep forgetting it."

"What are you talking about?" said Waddy, who had taken off his coat and come to the rail. "I'm dying of thirst."

"Hurricanes," Guthrie said. "We haven't had a big blow here for fifteen years. The last one wiped it clean. That's the town, over there where you see the Coast Guard tower. Well, the last blow was like the hand of God swept across the island. It raked most of that stuff into the bay. Blew away the docks, crushed the stores and cafes, drowned the business area, destroyed every house or building that wasn't anchored. Everything that didn't have a good moral foundation to it was squashed."

"Moral foundation?" said Waddy. "That's an odd way to put it."

"You know what I mean. The things that had been built honestly and with patience and good materials, some of them stood."

"A lot of people couldn't afford to build that way," Jane Guthrie said.

"They were lazy," said Guthrie. "It's hard to believe you're going to be destroyed, so they were lazy about it. Anyhow, it's nothing to me. The hell with it."

"Oh, God, would I like to have a drink," Beth Morris said.

At the ferry landing they got back into the car. The chocks were yanked from the wheels, and Iles drove onto the island. Iles paid the toll, drove past a battered wharf that mothered two rusty shrimp boats, and pulled up at a stop sign.

"You can see the *Silver Spoon* over there," said Guthrie. "There by that gray building. To the left. The building is Ernie's Wharf. That's where we'll leave from in the morning."

"It's a pretty boat," Beth Morris said.

"You make it sound like an outboard," said Waddy.

"The *Spoon* is molded Fiberglas," Guthrie said. "Jake and I got together with the builder in Miami and told him exactly what we wanted. Jake stayed with them night and day while they put it together. You won't see many like it. Sixty-eight feet long. Has VT-12 600 horsepower turbocharged diesel engines. Carries two thousand gallons of fuel and six hundred gallons of fresh water. Range of eight hundred nautical miles. The *Spoon* has everything in it you could ask for."

"It has a bar, I suppose," said Waddy.

"We've never run dry," Guthrie said.

"Neither has Waddy," said Beth Morris.

"You talk like I'm a drunk," Waddy said. "I'm not a drunk. I'm thirsty. I'm very simply and plainly thirsty."

"Oh, all right," said Beth. "For God's sake."

"You're the one who was saying how much you wanted a drink," Waddy said.

"*Don't* let's quibble, Waddy," said Beth. "We can *both* have a drink."

Iles turned the station wagon into a road that curved through a gathering of stucco tourist cabins with patches of St. Augustine grass and then past a trailer camp where red bougainvillea grew. There were a few palms along the road. The car climbed into the dunes toward Guthrie's house on the Gulf side of the island. Other houses stood among the dunes on stilts, most of them small unpainted houses that appeared to be riding precariously above upreaching sand. As they came closer to the Gulf, they could hear the surf smashing against the beach. The dunes masked the water. Iles swung onto a bouncing sandy road between dunes higher than the car, and he honked the horn as he came to hidden turns with the sand floating around them and flying back from the tires. At the top of the road they came to Agua Verda, which was yet above them.

Without pilings, as the other houses had, Agua Verda squatted heavily into the sand hills at the highest point of the island. From the rear of the house the passengers could see only that it was stone and concrete and glass with no acute angles. It was like a stone grinding dish turned upside down and pressed into the sand by a monstrous hand so that sand partly buried it around the edges. A long flight of steps led down from a glass door on the rear side away from the Gulf wind. By the time the station wagon stopped, a Negro in a white jacket had suddenly arrived. It was not clear whether he had come down the steps or had emerged like a spider from a secret door in a deep cellar or had popped out of a dune. But he was smiling and bowing as he opened the station wagon doors, bow tie bobbing on his fat neck with each movement of his mouth. Guthrie slapped him on the back in greeting, and Waddy shook his head as if that were a habit Guthrie would have to get rid of. The Negro houseman bowed them toward the steps, and they followed Guthrie up.

At the head of the steps and behind the glass door they entered an enclosed courtyard. The courtyard was roofed with transparent plastic that had been tinted green to soften the sun. Cactus and flowers grew from gardens with low rock walls around the court. In the center of the court was a fountain with a piece of abstract black metal sculpture from which water poured as if from the head of a bent, distended phallus. Guthrie pointed toward the sculpture.

"That's a crazy thing," he said. "The architect stuck that in, last thing he did to the house. Looks like the tail of a sick cat to me. I'd rather have had a naked woman there or old Neptune with his pitchfork, or, hell, even a naked man. But Jane likes it. Jane and the architect bought it from some nut who lives in Austin and makes these things in his shop."

"Boone? How interesting," said Beth Morris.

"You know about art?" Guthrie said.

"Waddy and I are collectors in our modest way," she said.

"Modest way!" said Waddy. "For God's sake, I wouldn't call the prices you pay for that crap modest."

"Darling, it's our civic duty to further the cause of Dallas culture," Beth said.

"I've heard that speech," said Waddy.

"I got another statue that I like," Guthrie said. "I picked it up at an exhibit Jane drug me to. Come on."

They followed Guthrie down a hall that opened off the courtyard and entered a room fifty feet long with a wall of glass facing the water. The carpet was bottomlessly soft, and despite the glare of the afternoon the room was dark and cool, almost cavelike in its feeling of security. The walls were egg white and were hung with abstract paintings in bright colors. The glass wall that looked upon the Gulf was divided into panels twelve feet high. Each panel had a golden indention on its frame for a handle so that the panels could slide.

"We got some big shutters we can bolt over that glass from the outside, but we still cut the wall into sections," Guthrie said. "I'd hate to be replacing that solid sheet of glass every time we had a little breeze. I don't believe the insurance company would like it much, either."

On the opposite side of the room from the glass wall was a floor to ceiling glass window half as long as the one which opened to the Gulf. Through the smaller window they could see a swimming pool in another courtyard surrounded by the house. Aluminum deck furniture sat around the pool. There was a red and white candy-striped cabana beyond the diving board. Inside the shade of the cabana they could see two open doors which were dressing rooms with showers. A rim of concrete extended around the pool for four feet, and the rest of the courtyard was terrazzo except for the flowers planted beside the wall of the house.

"Seems kind of goofy to live on the Gulf and have a swimming pool," Guthrie said, grinning and rubbing his stomach. "But it's a long walk down through the dunes to the water, and most of the time the water's too rough and tricky for Jane and the kids, and the beach is just too damn dirty. Also, there's rattlesnakes out in the grass. Some people swear there isn't, but I've seen 'em. I could have the dunes scraped down and make a flat walk to the beach, but the wind would just pile 'em up again. I was going to put a roof over the pool. I don't know. That might be too phony for me. The water's heated, anyhow, in the winter. It can get pretty cold and wet down here."

The long living room curled at the far end from the hall by which they had entered. Around a flowing stone wall at the curve they found the dining alcove with a large, polished table and twelve chairs. In a niche in the stone wall was a face carved out of marble: a suffering, blinded face, mouth open as if trying to express an agonized knowledge that could never be grasped as thought or formalized into words.

"That's the one I like," Guthrie said. "That boy there, he's got the secret of something, whatever it is, and he'd like to tell us about it but he can't. That one gets me. I sit and look at it and try to figure out what that old boy knows that I don't know. I kind of *feel* what he's getting at sometimes, and then I don't feel it any more. Anyhow, it's a good statue. Frenchman did it. Marcel Mayer. Isn't that his name, honey?"

Jane Guthrie nodded. Guthrie pointed toward a roofed porch beyond a glass door beside the dining alcove. A covered walk extended back from the porch. The walk was like an arbor, with bougainvillea and honeysuckle writhing from a lattice.

"Bedrooms are down that tunnel there," Guthrie said. "Roger, the houseman, will get your bags up and unpack all the stuff for you. Let's go have a drink while we're waiting."

"I was just thinking about that," said Waddy.

"What a marvelous house," Beth Morris said. "Did you get your architect from New York or California? I've *got* to know who he is."

"Oh, God," said Waddy.

"We got some guys down here from Dallas to do it," Guthrie said. "Two young guys. I think one of 'em was a fag, but they were both pretty straight with me. They understood what I wanted in the way of a place that would stand up to the wind. They worked the fancier parts out with Jane. I like a more old-fashioned house like the one we got in Dallas, but I let Jane build the kind of house she likes down here. All I wanted was to be sure it wouldn't blow down."

They returned to the long room and sat on couches facing the water. The wind moved the grass on the dunes below. It was three hundred yards out to the beach. The dunes were irregular humps and forms, some like great hairy whales, some like sharks with high dorsal fins, some grassless white sand peaks freshly blown. The wall of glass was turning gray with salt. Far out the water was purple, then green coming in, then gray, and finally white and spewing as it tumbled against the beach. Gulls hung against the white sky.

"We're overdue for a big blow, a hundred and seventy mile an hour monster," Guthrie said, walking to the glass wall and looking out.

"I wish you wouldn't keep talking about it," said his wife.

"You're preoccupied with it," Waddy said.

"No, I just think ahead," said Guthrie. "But it wouldn't come this time of year. The big blows are in the fall or late summer. About the time the football teams start working out, Waddy. Even if one comes, we're safe. A division of artillery couldn't knock this place over. Besides, I know this country. Me and the Gulf are still good friends, I hope."

"You make it sound personal," Waddy said. "I'd never have thought of it as personal."

The Negro houseman brought in a tray of drinks. Bowing and smiling, he began to pass them around.

"We'll have a little vodka and orange juice to cool off, and then we'll turn on the power," said Guthrie. He sipped from his drink and slid back one of the panels of glass. The pages of a magazine fluttered on a table. Guthrie breathed deeply, like an asthmatic trying to clear his lungs at an inhalator. He shut the door. The door rolled quietly and clicked as the latch caught.

"I wanted to smell it," Guthrie said.

"Sam's a nut on this place," said Jane Guthrie. She sat on the couch beside Waddy with one leg folded beneath her and her short dark gray-touched hair down on her forehead in bangs. Guthrie looked at his wife. He had always thought she had an exceptional face, a pretty face with eyes intelligently wide apart, a face that showed emotions. She smiled at him and lifted her drink with her left hand, upon which she wore a plain gold wedding band and no other rings. Much of the time Guthrie tried to believe he loved her.

"How about a swim," Waddy said.

"I'd love to," said Jane Guthrie.

"You wear suits down here?" Waddy asked.

"Whatever you want," said Jane. "House rules are that each guest can do as he pleases."

"Waddy, for God's sake, don't go running around naked in the daylight," Beth Morris said.

"My wife won't let me have any fun," said Waddy.

"I have a few faults, but exhibitionism is not one of them," she said. "Neither is prudishness. But you've pulled enough crazy stunts for a while."

"Man's got to enjoy himself," said Waddy.

"What'd you do?" Guthrie asked.

"Really, I thought everyone knew," said Beth. She crossed her legs. "It was absolutely insane. You know Bob Francis, of course, you couldn't *help* but know Bob Francis."

"Yeah," Guthrie said.

"I saw Bob in Washington yesterday," said Senator Rose, who had seemed to be going to sleep until he was revived by the cold glass in his hand. "He was having lunch with Senator Growald, and several other very importantly placed senators."

"All of them bombed, I imagine," Waddy said.

"They were laughing a great deal," said Senator Rose.

"Bob's supposed to be working this week," Waddy said.

"On the housing contracts? He has been. He certainly has been," said Senator Rose, smiling and finishing his drink.

"Am I going to tell my story?" Beth Morris said.

"We're not stopping you," said Waddy. "We'll just talk above you."

"Waddy and Bob got drunk at Twenty One two weeks ago," Beth said.

"To be accurate, we got drunk at Sardi's East at lunch," said Waddy. "Then we went to Twenty One and got drunker. Or drunkest. Drunk, drunker, drunkest. Isn't that how it goes?"

"Waddy and Bob decided they *had* to ride around New York City in an *ambulance,* for God's sake," Beth said. "They came racing into Twenty One to tell me."

"What we came racing into Twenty One for was to have a drink," said Waddy. "Be accurate. Why the hell would we want to tell you anything?"

"I was so embarrassed," she said. "I pretended I didn't know them. They were in the bar, you know, with the airplanes on the ceiling? They were staggering around and coughing and saying they were sick. Bob was saying he had been run over by a New York Central commuters' train and had been castrated and he was going to sue Clint Murchison and Clint Murchison, Jr., and John Murchison and Allen Kirby and Bob Wagner and Mr. Rockefeller and the *New York Daily News* and who else?"

"The engineer," said Waddy. "Bob said the engineer was a man also named Bob Francis who had been Bob's wingman in the war and had always resented being the lesser Bob Francis."

"Bob kept putting in phone calls to Dr. Joyce Brothers to ask her how he could adjust psychologically to being a eunuch. Luckily, he never could find her. He tried to call Ava Gardner to tell her he loved her like a sister. He called the *Enquirer* to see if they wanted to buy his life story."

Beth laughed and paused to light a cigarette.

"I was in Twenty One once," Guthrie said. "I talked too loud and the waiter told me I'd have to shut up or get out."

"Waddy," said Beth, "was just as bad as Bob. He said he had been poisoned by Lamar Hunt. He said Lamar was jealous because Waddy was a better golfer and a better shot with a basketball and had got him with a piece of poisoned strawberry shortcake. Waddy was singing 'Oh Bury Me Not on the Lone Prairie' and saying he wanted to be cremated in a tub of cherries jubilee and served at a Salesmanship Club luncheon. It was awful, for God's sake. I got Pete Kriendler to hide me. They called an ambulance and had the men come right into the bar and carry them out on *stretchers.* They had another stretcher filled with bottles of scotch and pitchers of water and buckets of ice. It was a terrible scene. Bob got off his stretcher out in front and threw ice at a doorman. He said the doorman was the lesser Bob Francis who had come around to gloat.

"Then," Beth said, "they stopped at a florist on Fifth Avenue and bought these great big huge funeral wreaths to put on their chests. They had the whole damned ambulance filled with flowers. Waddy had the driver stop at a sporting goods store somewhere and bought two football helmets that they put on. They rode all over New York City in the back of that ambulance with flowers on their chests and wearing those *awful* football helmets, drinking scotch out of straws and sniffing oxygen, or whatever you do to oxygen, for God's sake, and looking out the windows. They had the sirens on and the lights were blinking. What would people have said? Can you imagine?"

"We went to see the mayor," said Waddy. "He was entertaining a bunch of ladies from the DAR when our bearers carried us in."

"What happened?" Guthrie said.

"I'm not sure," said Waddy. "I know Bob fell off his stretcher and went to sleep in the foyer with his football helmet for a pillow."

Waddy stood up, loosened his tie, and unbuttoned his collar. He looked at his wife.

"Anyhow, you are," he said.

"I am what?" said Beth.

"An exhibitionist. Every model is an exhibitionist at heart. If you're not an exhibitionist, how come you bought that bikini?"

"I wouldn't wear it at a public beach," she said.

"You wouldn't *go* to a public beach," said Waddy.

"Waddy does the wildest things," Beth said. "I think he does whatever pops into his head. He tried to buy a Navy blimp last year. You know what the Secretary of the Navy sent him when Waddy asked for a blimp? He sent Waddy a prophylactic."

"This is a very dreary conversation," Waddy said. His voice was hard and abrupt. He had suddenly quit smiling. "There must be something better for entertainment than to listen to my wife talk about rubbers."

Guthrie glanced at Beth Morris. She opened her mouth as if to continue her story, and then she stopped and looked down at the ceramic ash tray on the coffee table. Guthrie waited to see if there would be a challenge, but there was none. Beth smiled thinly and exhaled a stream of smoke and looked at it. Jacob Iles rapped on the doorframe at the entrance to the living room. Guthrie wondered how long he had been there. Iles still wore his white cap and dark glasses.

"What time you want the boat?" Iles said.

"What time you suggest?" said Guthrie.

"I was gonna say three. I'll say four at the latest. We'll have a ways to go, and I'd like to be there by sunup."

"That's the unpleasant part about fishing," Senator Rose said.

"The fish don't give a damn what time we have to get up," said Iles.

"Four, then," Guthrie said. "See you in the morning, Jake."

Iles looked at the people in the room, nodded to Guthrie, turned quickly and walked away down the hall.

"He doesn't care for us," said Beth Morris.

"That's not it," Guthrie said. "Jake gets uncomfortable around strangers, and he never has felt at ease up here in this house."

Guthrie held out his hand to his wife and helped her off the couch. She was more than a foot shorter than he was. He looked down at the gray in her hair, and he touched it almost tenderly, as if it were his own work. Then he turned toward the others.

"We'll show you where your rooms are," he said. "I guess we're all ready to swim."

They left Waddy and Beth Morris at the largest of the guest suites—bedroom, sitting room, dressing room, bath, and bar overlooking the dunes and the Gulf—took the Senator to a similar but smaller suite, and went to their own rooms. Guthrie walked to the glass door on the balcony and pulled back the drapes. The inside of the room became a harsh gray-white as sunlight flooded in through the salt-smeared glass.

"Leave it shut, Sam," his wife said. "It's so cool in here."

"I got to be able to see out there," said Guthrie.

The sliding doors to the closets were open, showing their clothes cleaned and neatly hanging. Guthrie and his wife kept wardrobes at the island house and brought very little luggage. Their toilet items were laid out on the dressing tables and in the two bathrooms. Leaving the drapes open, Guthrie walked into the bar. He took a bottle of scotch out of a cabinet and then put it back. He lit a cigarette, returned to the bedroom, and fell onto the bed. Guthrie looked at the ceiling and blew smoke, toward the light fixture, rubbing his stomach, squinting, his black brows pulled together. Jane had kicked off her high-heeled shoes and was unzippering her skirt.

"Aren't you going to swim?" she said.

"In a minute. I want to lie here."

"Did you notice Waddy?" she said. "He sure turned cold. I felt sorry for Beth. I didn't think I'd ever feel sorry for Beth Morris, but he put her down pretty hard."

"Waddy's that way," said Guthrie. "She ought to be practiced at surviving put downs. Waddy can be real polite, a nice guy, witty, obliging. I once saw him walk all the way across the club and bring back a Coke for the barber's little girl. But you never quite get through to him. Just when you think you've caught him really being human, he'll freeze up like he did a while ago."

"He's blunt, isn't he?"

"Sure. Blunt and arrogant as hell and aloof and he doesn't trust anybody. But you can't blame him," Guthrie said, rolling over to one side and propping himself on an elbow to watch Jane hang up her skirt. "He was born rich. He had to learn to protect himself. I think he might be pretty shy basically, but he'll turn around and act like a goddamn tyrant. I've heard him order executives around in a voice I wouldn't use on a bird dog. Men who make $50,000 a year or more."

"Why do they let him do it?"

"Because he can destroy them. That's his birthright. He was damn lucky he started with all that money. He's smart and shrewd, but he sure ain't got much charm or looks. If he wasn't one of the richest men in America he couldn't go out and con enough money to open an ice cream stand. But once it was opened for him, he could sell more ice cream than anybody in the world and never even show up at the stand."

"You know quite a bit about him," his wife said, opening a bureau drawer and taking out her bathing suit.

"I investigated him," said Guthrie, "and you can bet he investigated me. By now Waddy knows how often you and I make love and what I like for breakfast and how much I pay for my shirts and how many holes I got in my underwear. I'll tell you something. No matter what I do, how hard I work, how many people I murder, no matter what, I can never be as rich as Waddy Morris. It's too late to make that kind of money any more and get to keep it, and there's no depletion allowance in the electronics business. I think about that while I'm busting my ass to put over this merger. I can never be as rich as Waddy. I can be stronger, smarter, more of a man, but never as rich."

"Then why don't you quit trying?"

"I can't."

"Have you ever met his father?"

"No. I've never even seen him. He's been sick for a long time, but he still picks up the phone and tells kings what to do. That old man is something, I don't know, a giant. I ever tell you about him?"

"You haven't told me much at all lately," Jane said, hanging her blouse in the closet. She took off her garter belt and began to roll down her hose.

"He started off by winning some oil leases in a poker game. That's what got him interested. Then he started swapping leases around, buying and selling, scouting East Texas in a horse and buggy, talking to farmers. I've seen an old picture of him. He was a little guy with dusty clothes and an honest, country-looking face. He didn't know a damn thing about geology, but they say he could drive up in his buggy, look at a piece of ground, and smell oil. He could tell 'em what pine tree to drill under. He hit that big field at Caddo Creek, and the next year he hit down in the Big Thicket, and for a long time he was hitting everwhere. Now he's got railroads, publishing houses, trucking firms, pipeline companies, packing plants, tankers, so many different corporations it'll take a hundred years to untangle 'em when he dies. He's got fifteen million acres of oil property under lease in Africa, the Middle East, and Australia. When it comes to money, he's right up there with the Hunts and the Murchisons and Bob Smith and that mob. Guy told me the old man cried when his only daughter got married a couple of years ago back at that mansion in Dallas. They had the reception out in the front yard. It's only about seventy acres of cut grass in the front yard, but they didn't have many guests. Including us, I'll point out. They had lanterns hanging up, and an orchestra, and crepe paper draped all over the barns by the polo field, and the old man walked around crying. He had his first heart attack about a month later."

"Does Waddy *do* anything?" Jane asked.

"Sure. It ain't hardly proper to do nothing in Texas. Nobody takes much to playboys, and Waddy's not that sort anyhow. After the war Waddy went into drilling himself, and lost a half million dollars in a year. His old man said at that rate Waddy would be busted by the middle of the next century."

Guthrie grunted, swung his legs off the bed, and began to untie his shoelaces. One lace pulled into a knot. He bent over, yanked off the shoe, and threw it into the corner.

"Waddy's made a lot of money for himself since that bad year," he said, "and that oil keeps pumping all the state will let it and it keeps on bringing in three dollars a barrel, and the depletion allowance doesn't hurt him a bit. He's got a lot of leases around in other parts of the country too, where he can pump more than in Texas. But there's one thing I can't figure out."

"What's that?" asked Jane. She stood by the window in the sunlight holding up the bathing suit as if trying to decide whether to wear that one or get another one. The bathing suit was a dark gray-green, almost the exact color of her eyes.

"I can't figure out why Waddy wanted to come down here. He's the one who suggested the trip. He brought it up on the golf course. He just about invited himself. He started off by saying he wanted to run down to the border for Cinco de Mayo, and then he said he'd like to see our house at Port Agness. He knew I'd ask him as soon as he said that. Waddy and I play golf together and he took me fishing once over at Caddo, you remember, and we've been to, what, four parties at their house? But we're not in the same social set. We're not their bunch. Of course, the Morrises ain't like the old ranching or cotton or sugar families, either, but Waddy's Palm Beach and New York and Beverly Hills and all that crap, and he can take those old society families and make 'em play leapfrog if he wants to. But you and me are nothing but Texas new money. We give those big parties but, hell, everbody knows we're not in yet. I never would have asked Waddy down here. But when he brought it up, that made it okay."

"He likes you," Jane said.

"That's possible, I guess. Waddy *must* like a *few* people. But

I think he wants something. I've been wondering what I've got that he wants. He's never put a penny in electronics."

"Sam," Jane said, "have you got eyes for Beth Morris?"

Guthrie looked up from unbuttoning his shirt.

"Me? Hell, no."

"That wouldn't be very smart, would it?"

"Sure wouldn't."

"Please don't fool around with her."

"Why would I do that?" he said. "You're all I can handle. Come here."

"Not now," she said.

"Right now," said Guthrie.

She smiled and walked silently across the carpet in her bare feet and sat beside him on the bed. He looked at a mole on her neck; there were moments when it was distasteful to him. Her wide-set, sea-colored eyes were on him steadily, so close that he could see one lash that had got itself twisted slightly out of the regular order. Her face was still young despite a hardening at the corners of her eyes. He looked down at her flat stomach, down at her ankles, at the calluses on her heels. She could never have been a beautiful woman like Beth Morris because her legs were too short and heavy, but she was more human, more to be lived with, and in bed she was soft and compact and warm. Reaching behind her with both hands, Guthrie found the catch on her brassiere. He pulled the elastic band tight and began working on the catch with his fingers. It would simplify love, he thought, if someone would invent a brassiere that a man could take off easily with one hand. How many seductions had been prevented merely because the man had labored with the brassiere catch until he began to look clumsy and ridiculous, and the girl had laughed at him, and passion had vanished? Guthrie got the catch loose. He lifted the brassiere forward, and she raised her arms to let it slip free. As it fell he saw the dark sweat marks on the brassiere band. Her breasts sagged. Double stripes of pink circled her chest from the tightness of the band. Long ago, before there were three children, her breasts had been larger and had held up well without support. Guthrie remembered their honeymoon in a cheap tourist court outside Austin; the sickly green of the plaster walls in the bathroom, the weak yellow light from a fixture with two sixty-watt bulbs, one burned out, a fixture that they had quickly turned off and had opened the windows to the moon. He remembered how she had looked in the moonlight with her breasts high and her buttocks so peculiarly and charmingly thrusting, almost as if she were swaybacked, a posture that had somehow nearly disappeared through the years. He remembered the astonishingly clean smell of her, and the magic of being actually in bed with her, and the smell of her eagerness, and the touch of her knee, and how that night he had been desperately jealous at the thought that she might ever love anyone else, so taken with his jealousy that it had deeply affected the course of the night.

In their suite above the dunes he laid her against the pillow and straightened her body on the bed. His tongue touched her nipples, felt them become rubbery, and she began to squirm beneath him, burying herself under his body as if digging beneath a heavy blanket. He felt her hand on his stomach, groping down, unbuckling his belt, and he turned to allow her hand freedom, and then he felt himself exposed. Her hand was on him, massaging, fingers caressing, reaching down to cup him and creeping back up with fingernails lightly scraping. He heard the unsnapping, felt pressure release at his waist, then two more snaps, and the hand returned, stroking, rubbing, moistening.

"Not too much," he whispered. "Oh, be careful."

He stood up quickly and then he was naked. He leaned over her as she lay looking up at him, and he hooked his fingers into the elastic ribbon of her nylon panties and began to pull them down.

"I didn't get ready," she said.

"I can't wait for that," he said.

"I could do the other for you."

He dropped her panties onto the floor and lay beside her and kissed her, hurting, and she came against him as violently as if it were her first surrender.

"Both," he said.

And then later he said, "Janey, you've always been the number one."

And she said, "Sam, you're so precious to me, you're so good to me."

Afterward they showered together in the shower cabinet that had a ledge for sitting and was large enough for Guthrie to lie down in, and they dried each other and put on their bathing suits as if it were a new adventure. But then Guthrie seemed to have thought of something, and the pleasure ceased. He opened the cabinet doors in the bathroom, looked inside, and slammed them.

"Where're the big towels?" he said.

"Roger put all the beach towels in the cabana," said his wife. In the mirror she looked very small standing beside him. He rubbed his stomach and frowned. "What's the matter, Sam?"

"I can't get this proxy crap out of my head," he said. "I put more than five million dollars into that Ramco stock. Everthing we've got is in hock. I don't want to lose."

"You won't lose."

"Your confidence is appreciated," he said coolly, "but unfounded in fact."

"There won't be any more trouble in court, will there?"

"They gave up on that. I saw the guy this morning. That young lawyer? I believe I hate that son of a bitch. I try not to allow myself the pleasure of hating when business is involved. I try to be calm. But I think I hate that kid."

"He's only doing his job," Jane said.

"It's more than that to him," said Guthrie. "He got awful personal about it. He's gone after me like it was some kind of crusade. You know what he said to me this morning? The goddamn, floppy-eared, button-down snot. He said I was corrupt. Me, corrupt. I'm about the most uncorrupt man in Dallas. He said he didn't see how I could stand myself."

"He was angry. He didn't mean it."

"He meant it. He looked me right in the eye. If we hadn't been standing in the lobby of the First National Bank, I'd have knocked the hell out of him right then. He had no right to say that to me. His father is as corrupt as the mayor of Sodom. His whole goddamn family is rotten and full of corruption. And he walks over to me in the lobby and looks me in the eye and tells me I'm corrupt."

"Don't let it bother you so much."

"It doesn't bother me. It makes me mad as hell. If I win this proxy fight, Ramco is going to dump that young snot's law firm so fast he'll get the bends."

"He's done pretty well fighting you."

"He doesn't know how to fight. He fights standing up with a classical pose. That might look nice, but that ain't how you win. The kid is smart, all right. But he won't listen to reason. I know some of those guys on the Ramco board wanted to come in with me, and he talked them out of it. Damn it, I've had enough to worry about without him jabbing at me. I'm going to sink his goddamn boat."

Jane took two packages of cigarettes out of the drawer of the dresser, where there were several cartons.

"Let's don't forget these," she said, looking up at Guthrie. "I hate to get comfortable at the pool and find out I forgot the cigarettes."

Waddy, Beth, and the Senator were already at the pool when Guthrie and his wife eased back the sliding glass door and stepped into the sunlight. Guthrie stopped when he saw Beth. She stood beside the diving board with a rubber bathing cap that looked like a bouquet of yellow flowers in her hands. She wore a red and black checkerboard bikini that was like a narrow cloth belt around her breasts, and a diaper around her loins. The bikini bottom was cut so high that her sides were bare except for a thin elastic strap that held the front and back together, and the bikini was so tight behind that her buttocks swelled out on either side of the cloth like white melons. The top of the bikini covered the tips of her breasts but concealed nothing. Guthrie had seen strippers in Minneapolis and New Orleans finish their acts more properly dressed; Beth looked nakeder and more sensual than the nude show girls of London. In arched sandals she was nearly six feet tall. The vast revealed area of her flesh was without a blemish. The Senator lay on his back on a mat, his belly rising and falling as he breathed, sweat sparkling in the curly gray hairs on his chest, his legs hairless and grossly thin. Waddy sat in a deck chair, clutching a drink, his legs crossed. In a bathing suit Waddy was lean and surprisingly wide shouldered and looked athletic, like a welterweight. Waddy wore dark glasses, but Guthrie could tell Waddy was looking at Beth.

"Baby," Beth said, "smear some of that oil on me."

She walked around the edge of the pool, sandals clopping, long legs taking short steps, hips moving, breasts bobbing, her navel swinging, Guthrie thought, like a metronome. Waddy frowned and stood up. He began to rub oil onto her back and then into her buttocks and thighs like a man grooming a horse.

"I have looked into the abyss and seen a vision of wrath," Guthrie said softly to Jane. "I have seen the great cities of the plain laid to ruin. And now I will go and fall beside Senator Rose and shut my eyes and think pure thoughts. God help us all."

Jacob Iles awoke at two-forty-five, fifteen minutes before the alarm was to ring. He turned off the clock, sat on the edge of the bed with his face in his hands, slept another ten minutes in that position, then suddenly stood up. His wife lay on her back with her mouth open and her belly a mound under her cotton nightgown. She snored with a rasping sound, but her face had the gray, exhausted look of death. He saw that she needed to shave under her arms. A breeze stirred the curtains at the window beside the bed. From behind the partition that closed off the other bedroom, he heard one of the children talking in his sleep. The boy said, "No, no, you can't have it, it's mine."

Jacob Iles dropped off his jockey shorts, opened a bureau drawer, found that he had no clean shorts, looked at his wife, and put the dirty shorts back on. He went into the bathroom and snapped on the dim light. In the mirror he saw that the bruises were worse than the day before; his left eye was more swollen and bloodshot and the skin below the purple lump was turning a urinish yellow; his left ear, which had awakened him twice during the night when he had touched it against the pillow, was the color of raspberry jelly. Iles soaped a washcloth, gently dabbed at his face, splashed his face with water, and patted it dry with a damp towel. He gave up the idea of shaving. His beard was blond and light, and he didn't want to put a razor against his bruised flesh.

After examining the marks on his back and ribs, he pulled on a white polo shirt and a pair of khaki pants and laced his white sneakers. He brushed his teeth, combed his hair with his fingers, and went into the kitchen to cook his breakfast.

He put coffee into the percolator and turned on the fire under it. Iles laid three strips of bacon in the frying pan, dropped a chunk of butter on top, and let them fry until the bacon was turning brown and crisp. Then he flipped the bacon over, and cracked three eggs into the skillet. He remembered about the toast, buttered bread quickly and shoved it into the oven. Iles poured himself a glass of cold milk and looked out the window at the dark sky. He had put the plate of eggs and bacon on the table, and had got out the jam to put beside the toast, and was filling his coffee cup when his wife came in. She was yawning and scratching her head. She slumped heavily into the chair across from him and sighed. She was trying to shake herself awake. When she yawned her tongue looked as if she had been drinking sour cream. Her breath made him turn away.

"Damn if you're not lovely this morning," Iles said, sitting down.

"Why didn't you wake me up? I was gonna fix your breakfast."

"You looked like you was tired."

"Of course, I'm tired. I been carrying this baby."

"Want me to carry it a while?"

"What a comedian."

Iles picked up a piece of bacon with his fingers and ate it.

"Gimme a sip of your coffee," his wife said.

"I'll get you a cup."

"Never mind. I'll get it myself. You think I'm poison or something?"

"Well, there's no reason why you ought to drink my coffee when we got plenty of cups and there's a whole pot on the stove."

"Okay, I said I'd get a cup."

She poured her coffee and returned to the table, shuffling wearily past him as he tried to eat.

"Those eggs are brown around the edges," she said. "I thought you wouldn't eat eggs that was brown around the edges. Let me fix you some more."

"They're okay."

"Won't take me a second."

"They're *okay.*"

"You should of got me up. I like to see you off in the morning."

She lit a cigarette and coughed, holding her hand to her mouth and then looking at her hand and wiping it on her nightgown.

"My stomach's upset," she said.

Iles put down his fork.

"Goddamn it," he said. "I'm trying to eat my breakfast. I wonder if Miz Guthrie would come to her husband's breakfast table looking like hell and breathing all over him and talking about her stomach?"

"She would if she was married to you and lived in a trailer with three kids and was pregnant again and had to do all the work by herself and get up at three A.M. in the morning."

"Go back to bed."

"First place," said his wife, "Miz Guthrie goes to beauty parlors and buys nice clothes and has people to make her look good. She lays in bed all morning and has people to look after her kids and clean up her house and cook her meals. She don't have anything to do but set around all day and read magazines and powder her snatch so she'll smell good when Mr. Guthrie comes home."

"Maybe you ought to powder yours once in a while."

"It wouldn't make any difference the way you use it," his wife said. "On, off, and good night, leave me alone. That's really loving, ain't it? I'm nothing but a maid, a cook, and a whore. You want me to soak in bath salts and wear perfume and an evening dress when I come to breakfast? How am I gonna soak in bath salts in the damned little old shower in this damned trailer? I ain't had an evening dress since I was in high school. I ain't been to a beauty parlor to have my hair fixed in a year."

"That's not my fault," Iles said. "You can go get your hair fixed any time you want to."

"I can't remember when I wasn't washing diapers and putting iodine on you when you come home beat up and wondering where you was when you wasn't home and letting you push me down on the bed and mount me like a whore when a lot of times I was sick and didn't want to and you didn't even care whether I got my share of the fun out of it. You talk about how it would be to be married to Miz Guthrie! I wonder how it would be like to be married to Sam Guthrie. That's what I wonder, if he would treat his wife the way you do. You're killing me. Ever day you're killing me."

Iles pushed back his plate and looked down at the yellow of the eggs oozing into the bacon grease. His wife had started crying.

"It ain't worth it to keep on living just for all this crap I got," she said, looking at him with her eyes red and tears on her cheeks and the cigarette smoke drifting past her face. "You don't even love me, and I'm supposed to kill myself for you."

"Oh, Christ," he said.

"Now you're trying to insult me and pick a fight with me so you won't have to ask Mr. Guthrie for the one thing I want that I could get in this life. I'll tell you this. If you don't ask him, I'll leave. I'll get the hell out of here. I don't have to stay."

"Where would you go?"

"I don't know," she said. "But I'd find a place. Somebody would want me. I'm not all that bad that you say I am. I don't have to stay here another day."

"You couldn't find a place."

She was quiet for a moment. With her fingers she wiped her eyes. She drank a swallow of coffee and reached for another cigarette although her first one was still burning in an ash tray.

"I could kill myself," she said.

"Goddamn, this is a swell breakfast," said Iles.

"Would it make you sad if I killed myself?"

"Hell, yes. Do you think I'd go dancing?"

"You'd just get married again. You'd find some woman who was dumb enough. You wouldn't remember me ten minutes after they put me under the ground."

"There'd have to be somebody to take care of the kids," Iles said.

"I knew it," his wife said, and started crying again.

"Look, Marge. Look, honey, I was kidding. I didn't mean that."

"I wonder if I could kill myself."

"Quit talking crazy."

"I've got to do something. I can't stand it."

"It ain't exactly fun for me."

"Jake, don't say that. It hurts me."

"Maybe we'd both be better off if you did leave," he said. "If you went on the mainland somewhere and got a job. I could come see you and the kids. I could keep the oldest boy here with me and let him go to school and work on the *Spoon.*"

"Please, Jake, don't talk that way," she said, crying. "We all got to stay together. We're a family."

"You wouldn't leave, would you?" he said. "You wouldn't do a thing like that to me, would you?"

"No," she said.

"I swear, Marge, I'll try to make it better for you. I know you've had it rough." Iles glanced at his watch. "Damn, I got to get down to the *Spoon.*"

"You didn't eat your breakfast."

"I'll fix something in the galley."

"Let me doctor your face, baby," she said.

"There's nothing you could do for it."

"Jake," she said, "you're gonna ask him, then?"

"I'll try," said Iles.

When he went out, Iles couldn't get the gate open on his picket fence. Someone, probably the kids, had twisted the wire hoop that held it and the wire had dug into the wood. Cursing, Iles yanked at it and cut his thumb. He stepped back, placed one hand on top of a picket, and vaulted the fence. The shock of hitting the ground brought a sharp, then aching, pain from his eye and his ear. He got into the Ford station wagon and drove it to the docks and parked it in front of the gray wooden building where they bought supplies.

The wind sock on the roof hung out a bit from the pole, but the breeze wasn't enough to make the water rough. In the muddy darkness he could see several men standing on the dock. Lights were on in some of the boats, and he could hear voices. The cafe was open. The juke box was playing. A screen door slammed. The morning smelled like wet laundry. Somewhere off the dock a boat engine hacked twice and then began to run loud and unmuffled, like a car with a broken resonator. Jacob Iles walked across the sand of the parking lot and climbed the four plank steps onto the dock. The lights of the cafe reflected in the dark window of Ernie's Wharf store, and Iles saw himself, shadowy, going past. The boat engine throttled down and abruptly died. It was very quiet as Iles walked down the dock past the live bait bins and under the crossbars that had a sign saying Ernie's and a hook from which fish could be hung for photographing. Iles brushed past two channel shrimpers who mumbled to him. He went on without speaking, his sneakers quiet on the boardwalk. The water was dull gray near the dock, where lights swam in it, and then black out toward the channel. But it was calm. The water moved against the pilings with a sound as gentle as a child sloshing his hand in a bucket. Iles went on until he came to the long white bulk of the *Spoon.* He stepped on the mooring stump, then onto the fantail of the *Spoon,* and jumped lightly down onto the deck. The mate, Billy, appeared at the cabin door. The lights were on, and Iles could hear coffee perking.

"I slept on board," Billy said. "I think I got everthing ready. Want coffee?"

Iles nodded. Billy went to the electric coffee urn, a large silver one that made fifteen cups, held a cup under the spigot, and the coffee smoked as it came out. Billy was tall and brown and thin-chested with long black hair that curled on the back of his neck, and his shoulders were broad and bony. He wore only a pair of khaki shorts and rubber shower sandals.

"Listen, Billy," said Iles. "If you had any company on board last night you better go down to the crew quarters and make sure there ain't no lipstick on the pillow or nothing. Guthrie's liable to prowl all over the boat today, like he does when he ain't been here in a long time. You know Guthrie don't like us screwing around on the *Spoon.*"

"I didn't sleep in the crew quarters," Billy said, grinning. "I'm first mate, ain't I? You can't expect the first mate to entertain a guest way down there in them crew quarters."

"Where'd you sleep?" said Iles.

"In the big bed. Right there slap down in Mr. Guthrie's bed. My guest, she sure thought that was a big deal, too. She sure did show her appreciation, Jake."

Iles laughed.

"Don't worry about it," Billy said. "I put on clean sheets a few minutes ago and washed everthing and emptied the ash trays and polished the chest. I sprayed the whole damn place with under-arm deodorant."

"You get the ice out?"

"Yeah. I filled the ice buckets and put more water in the trays. We got fifty pounds of cubes, anyhow, in the refrigerator. I set out the vodka and the apple juice and the tomato juice and the Wooster sauce and the red hot sauce and got two cold cases of Tuborg beer on ice. I got another case of Tuborg, two cases of Heineken's, and two cases of Lowenbrau in the pantry. Oh, and a case of Pearl. If anybody wants Pearl when they could have Tuborg. Anyhow, it's done."

"Scotch and bourbon?"

"A case of each."

"Gin and vermouth?"

"Plenty. I bought enough groceries to feed the First Marines."

"Tackle?"

"Rigged. Bait's in the bait box. It's all done, I tell you."

"You sleep at all?"

"Enough," Billy said. "I didn't get drunk, anyhow, so I'll be all right. I took a couple of those diet pills Mr. Gutherie keeps in the cabinet. They make a man feel good."

"Where's the niggers?"

"The bait boy is asleep down in the engine room. The waiter ain't here yet."

"Let's have a Bloody Mary," Iles said. "I think we got time."

The Negro waiter arrived after Billy had made the drinks. He stumbled sleepily into the cabin. His dinner jacket was wrinkled, and his shirt collar was open with his clip-on bow tie dangling from one wing. They were the same clothes he had worn the day before and had not been pressed.

"You," said Iles. "Why'd they have to send you? What's your name?"

"No business of yours, cap," the Negro said.

"Nigger, I'd just as soon to punish you," said Iles.

"Name's George."

"George Washington Carver, I'll bet," Billy said.

"George Washington Simpson," said the Negro.

"Here," Iles said, pitching him the keys. "Take the station wagon back up to the house and wait for Mr. Guthrie and the others. While you're at it, put on a clean coat and a clean shirt. Did Roger get a look at you before you left?"

"Naw, I don't have to see Roger all the time."

"You better start," said Iles.

"What you want me to do with the pickup truck?" the Negro said. "I drove the pickup truck down here."

"Don't argue with everything I tell you," said Iles. "Just leave the pickup where it's at and get your ass up to that house."

The Negro scowled and went out the door. They heard him clambering onto the dock. Iles sprinkled two more drops of Louisiana Hot Sauce into his Bloody Mary, put in some more pepper, and stirred it. He looked at the red liquid sticking to the rim of the glass.

"Billy," he said, "this has started off to be a hell of a day."

Sam Guthrie awoke the instant the alarm rang and snapped it off. He sat up and stared at the clock, trying to read the luminous face, until his eyes could make out the position of the hands. It was three-thirty. Beside him, his wife slept. He looked down at her young girl's body veiled in a transparent red top and red panties, her breasts small and flat as she lay on her back. Through the glass door Guthrie could see the black humps of the dunes in the moonlight, and he listened for the surf but could hear only the hidden rumbling of the air-conditioning. Guthrie crawled out of bed, opened the glass door, and stepped onto the porch. Below, the cactus and the dunes and the splotches of flowers were weird patterns of shadows and creamy light. The Gulf and the sky melted together in a black continuum, as if there were no horizon. Standing on the porch in his white shorts, Guthrie breathed heavily and bent and touched his toes ten times. He was sweating when he finished and his skin felt soiled and greasy from the humidity and the salt spray. He saw a light go on in the guest bedroom at the Gulf end of the arbored walkway, and then he saw Waddy, in blue pajamas, stand up from the bed and put on his glasses and go into the bathroom. Guthrie walked to the railing of his porch. Through the rectangle of a lighted window he saw Beth Morris in bed, a twist of white sheets, one long bare leg, blonde hair against the pillow. He watched as she sat up and turned her head toward the bathroom. The sheet fell away. Guthrie whistled to himself. Waddy came out of the bathroom and switched off the lamp beside the bed and then returned to the bathroom, the light fading from the room as he closed the bathroom door. Guthrie turned away.

Down on the beach there was the noise of a car moving slowly along the sand; either lovers returning or surf fishermen going out. Guthrie heard a quick string of six popping noises, like exploding balloons, as the car ran over men-of-war that had washed onto the sand during the night. Guthrie wondered for a moment whether to stand and wait for Waddy to come out of the bathroom again, and then he shrugged and looked out at the black water. In the dark, with the sound of its deep churning, the Gulf was unknowable and frightening. Guthrie went back inside and slid the glass door closed. Jane had turned onto her left side and had pulled her knees up against her stomach. Guthrie went into his bathroom, flipped on the light, turned on the water at the basin, leaned over the toilet, and began to vomit.

After he had showered and shaved and dressed in Bermuda shorts, tennis sneakers, and a golf shirt, Guthrie smoked his first cigarette of the morning. He coughed. Jane opened her eyes and said, "I don't know how you can get up this early. I feel awful."

"It's a wicked, disastrous life," said Guthrie. "I'll never smoke or drink again."

"How about singing? You sang 'Dear Old Girl' with Senator Rose last night."

"I renounce it," Guthrie said. "Likewise I renounce having pushup contests with Waddy Morris."

"How many did he do?"

"Forty on his fingertips."

"He's cute," said Jane. She sat up and put her arms around her knees. "He's like a precocious little boy with big glasses and braces on his teeth and smarter than anybody else in the class. He's so unattractive and ungrateful that he's cute."

"From now on, I'm living pure and healthy," Guthrie said, coughing again. "I think I'll bug all the guest bedrooms with closed circuit television and put a bank of monitors in here."

"It'd be like having our own dirty movies."

"Yeah. I wonder what Senator Rose does when he's alone?"

"Don't get me excited, dear. I'm sleepy."

"Go to sleep, then."

"Thank you, sir."

Guthrie kissed her on the forehead.

"Catch a fish," she said.

The water was the color of old iron as it heaved against the *Silver Spoon* and then foamed away in a boiling wake that spread into wrinkles rushing out. The yacht sliced between the long rock jetties of Marino Passage. Cranes watched from the rocks, and the early wind was like a low chanting. The Gulf reached for the rocks of the jetties, washing them, pulling at them, depositing bottles and tin cans and pieces of dark wood. The water in the east, at the edge of the world, had begun to catch shots of light like millions of reflectors. The *Silver Spoon* throbbed, its engines tore the water into froth and flung it back. Inside the cabin Billy, the mate, was preparing breakfast for Guthrie and the guests. Billy had scrambled a dozen eggs and fried a pound of bacon and was taking two dozen biscuits out of the oven. The Negro waiter was setting the table which was covered with a cloth as white as a hospital sheet. Waddy Morris had mixed the second round of drinks, and Sam Guthrie sat at the table looking out at the water.

"Here go, Senator. Take this thing before I drop it," Waddy said, with three glasses squeezed together between his hands.

"I'm not quite through with my first one," said Senator Rose. The Senator sat on a couch, his thin legs crossed, his face purplish from tiny broken blood vessels under the hard light, his eyes tired. "But I suppose another might help me to digest Billy's cooking."

"This'll help you stay alive," Waddy said. "After all that hollering and yelling and loud talking you did last night, you must be worn out. How come you know how to do a cha cha and the twist, and I don't? You must be hell in Washington."

"Rugged constitution," said the Senator. "Comes from long years of activity. Try anything, Mr. Morris, that's what I say. One is never too old to learn a new dance step or admire a beautiful woman."

"Or be a fool," Waddy said.

Jacob Iles looked down from the step, where he stood at the wheel inside the cabin, and grinned.

"Here go, Sam," said Waddy.

Guthrie took the drink and glanced at Senator Rose, who had decided to smile. Waddy sat down at the table. He blinked through his thick glasses and scratched a red bump on his neck.

"Sore from the pushups?" Waddy said.

"I can feel 'em," said Guthrie.

"Wait till tomorrow," Waddy said. "If you don't do 'em regular, they'll make you sore as hell." Waddy sipped his drink, judged it, and nodded. "What're you looking at?"

"Outside. Watching the sun come up."

Waddy squinted through the window.

"First time I've seen that in quite a while," said Waddy. "But it hasn't changed much. It's still just a sunrise."

"A man never feels quite as good as when he's up early enough to see the magnificence of the sun rising to give the world warmth and a new day," Senator Rose said, yawning.

"That's a bag of crap," said Waddy. He looked at Guthrie. "Know something, Sam? You're making yourself a potful of enemies with this proxy fight. I could name a bunch of people who want to take a hunk out of you. Of course, they know you intend to merge Guthrie Electronics with Ramco, and they're wondering what will happen."

"They make a lot of noise, but they sound scared to me," Guthrie said.

"They're scared," said Waddy.

"The guys who are howling the loudest are the ones who're out," Guthrie said. "They know I'll bounce 'em. A merger would be a damn good thing for both companies. Ramco's earnings have been way down. The company's poorly managed. Anybody who's not smart enough to see that and want me to take over is not smart enough to work for me. By combining we can save a lot of money by cutting out duplication and not fighting each other. We can make the new company bigger, go after bigger contracts, bring more money into Dallas. It's good for the economy, good for the employees, good for me, good for everbody except a few executives who're going to get hurt and their friends who hate me for it."

"People aren't always reasonable," said Waddy. "Sometimes they don't even believe that I know what's best."

"If you get a whole lot of guys together in something, you get a situation where an ape could run it better," Guthrie said.

"I know all that howling from your opposition about anti-trust hasn't got anywhere yet," said Waddy. "But that's a dangerous word, Sam."

Guthrie turned toward Senator Rose.

"Senator, if I win this thing I don't want the Justice Department messing around in it," Guthrie said. "I'll handle the civil action, but I want you to watch those anti-trust boys. This isn't a violation of anti-trust. This is just smart business. The government's getting to where they try to tell me how to wipe."

"There's nothing I can do about the Justice Department," said Senator Rose.

"Just watch 'em."

"They take their orders from the Attorney General," said the Senator.

"I know where they take their orders from."

"But, Sam, I can't interfere with the Justice Department," Senator Rose said.

"We're talking as friends," said Guthrie, smiling. "All I'm asking is that you stay alert and help me if you get a chance. At least warn me. You know I can turn out high-class hardware. You know I can provide a lot of jobs."

"I'll do what I can," the Senator said.

"You're talking like you've already won," said Waddy.

"I've got to believe it. How about another drink, Senator? You finished that one in a hurry. George Washington, fix the Senator a drink."

Forty-eight miles out they came to a streak in the water where two currents met. Weeds and trash, bottles, beer cans, pieces of lumber, sea grass, were hung in the streak like refuse along a wire fence after a flood. The water on the near side was bluegreen, and on the far side it was like fine clear blueblack ink. Iles, who had gone to the wheel on the flying bridge, throttled back and cut a circling wake short of the streak while Billy and the Negro bait boy let down the aluminum outriggers and hooked Guthrie and Waddy Morris into two fighting chairs. The Senator came onto the deck but left the third chair, the middle one, vacant. Billy shoved the road butts into sockets on the chairs between the fishermen's legs. He adjusted the shoulder straps on the harnesses Guthrie and Waddy were wearing. The mate baited with four-pound skipjacks at the end of twenty-five foot wire leaders, clipped the one-hundred-thirty-pound test line onto the outrigger cables, and swiftly ran the line out on the pulleys. Iles looked down from the flying bridge. He had put on his old blue cap, which was jammed onto the back of his head, and his voice was high with excitement.

"We're going across the rip," Iles shouted. "Might hit something the first pass. Get ready."

"Be a sailfish this side or a marlin on the other side of the rip most likely," said Billy.

"Let's get after 'em," Guthrie said.

"Damn, this thing's heavy," Waddy said.

They trolled the streak for more than an hour, working toward the west. The sun began to heat the deck. Guthrie took his shirt off. The leather harness cut into him, and sweat rolled down his chest. Through polaroid glasses he watched the bait splashing far behind the boat; he kept his eyes a few feet beyond the bait, watching for the first foaming attack, watching for a dark fin coming like a blade through the water, and he listened for the hard ping when the line would be torn out of the clip on the outrigger. Waddy had removed his shoes and his shirt. He leaned back in his chair with his feet up on the railing and looked out at the water, at the sky going orange and thin blue.

"I'll have to take you to my island in the Caribbean," Waddy said. "The water's like lime Jell-O in my bay. I do a lot of skin-diving. It's great under there around those coral rocks. You never saw such beauty."

"You were a frog man in the Navy, weren't you?" asked Guthrie.

"Yeah. Underwater demolition and all that. Never blew up anything that didn't belong to our side, though. Good thing about it was I didn't have anywhere to fall like you did in that bomber. Ever do much skin-diving?"

"Not much. A little."

"You got a good build for it. A skin diver needs a deep chest. But some of us skinny fellows are better. I'm hollow. I can suck myself full of air."

"How about the fishing?" said Guthrie. "There must be great fishing at your place."

"Fishing bores me unless I really bang into something. I guess I started feeling too much like a fish, all the time I spent under there with them. I swim up to sharks and barracudas and take their pictures. I feel sort of brotherly to them."

"To sharks and barracudas?"

"They're misunderstood," Waddy said. "I'd like to have a beer."

"George Washington," said Guthrie, "snap us a couple of those Tuborgs."

Waddy stripped the tinfoil back from the neck of the green bottle.

"Sam," he said, "what do you think about the future of the oil business?"

"Hadn't thought much about it," said Guthrie.

"The oil business is finished," Waddy said. "In twenty years there won't be any oil business compared to what it is today."

"You mean we're running out?"

"Hell, no," said Waddy. "There's oil in the ground that they won't even let us sell and we don't bother to drill for. It'll be a long time before the oil is gone. I couldn't live long enough to pump out my known reserves. My daddy's got so much oil in so many different countries he can't remember them all."

"Tough luck," said Guthrie.

"We'll scratch by, somehow," said Waddy. He looked at Senator Rose. "Senator, would you mind going inside for a few minutes? I want to say something private to Mr. Guthrie."

"Not at all," Senator Rose said.

"Thought you'd oblige," said Waddy.

"I'm getting too much sun, anyway," the Senator said.

"Sam," said Waddy, after the Senator had ducked through the cabin door, "I don't like to stall around when I decide something. I'm going to talk to you straight. I've got a deal to offer. It's a good deal for both of us, and it's big, and it's far-reaching as all hell. You want to listen?"

"Sure," Guthrie said.

"All right. I'll get to the heart of it," said Waddy. "The big thing in your life is to take over Ramco and merge it with Guthrie Electronics. As it now stands, I doubt if you can do it. A. C. Johnson is sticking with the old board, regardless of what your proxy fighters tell you. As close as it is, Johnson can probably swing the voting. Surely you've studied it enough to know why Johnson won't go with you. Don't try to fool yourself about Johnson's position."

"Because of the Ramco president. Simmons is a friend of his," Guthrie said, feeling suddenly sick and weak, as if he had just received a death sentence.

"Johnson knows you'd throw out Simmons. You've stated publicly that you think Simmons is inept. That impressed some of the stockholders—but not Johnson. Johnson and Simmons are more than friends. They're tangled up in several ways. The earnings of Ramco may not be as high as they ought to be, but as far as Johnson is concerned Simmons stays as president. According to my estimate of it, you figure to lose the proxy fight. All that Ramco stock you bought makes you a big stockholder in Ramco, but it really makes you nothing but trouble."

Waddy took off his glasses and looked at the lenses.

"Damn salt water," he said, putting the glasses on again. "Don't look so stricken, Sam. You're not beaten yet. I've just started talking. I said I was going to get to the heart of it, and the heart of it is this: I want in. I want to buy into Guthrie Electronics now. I want a third of your shares in it. And then I want an option to buy stock in Guthrie-Ramco at the original issuing price. I want a year's option. Naturally, I think Guthrie-Ramco will boom. I think the stock will be worth twice as much in a year as it is the day it goes on sale."

"If I don't win the proxy fight, there won't be any Guthrie-Ramco stock," said Guthrie.

"Certainly. But you'll win if I buy in."

"Guthrie Electronics is mine," Guthrie said. "It's a privately owned corporation."

"You need money, Sam. You need to sell part of it to me. And you need to win that proxy fight. I can win it for you. All you have to do to win is promise me I can buy into Guthrie Electronics, promise me that stock option, and promise me you won't throw Simmons out right away. We can leave Simmons as president, but take all his authority away from him and ease him out later. We can do it so slickly that Simmons or Johnson, either one, won't realize it until it's done. Also, I want you to promise me that I name a couple of guys on the board of Guthrie-Ramco. I like to have my own men in there watching out for my interest."

"How can me letting you in guarantee I'll win the proxy fight?" asked Guthrie.

"I told you Johnson is my friend."

"He's a friend of Simmons, too."

"My name's not Simmons, Sam," Waddy said. "Would you rather have a friend named Simmons, or a friend named Waddy Morris?"

"There's not much choice, is there?"

"None, for an intelligent man. Look at some other advantages of having me in, Sam. Our new company would be in a position to use some of my contacts in Washington. Wouldn't you like to have Bob Francis and his friends working in behalf of Guthrie-Ramco? Of course you would. But there's even more to my offer than what I've told you so far, Sam."

Waddy tossed his beer bottle into the water.

"George Washington," said Guthrie.

Waddy accepted another beer without glancing at the waiter. Waddy held out his hand as if the beer was supposed to appear in it, and the beer appeared.

"The oil business is finished, Sam. There's going to be a new fuel. You understand? Something's going to take the place of the oil industry. Cars are going to run on batteries or something. Millions and millions and millions of cars, Sam. Maybe some kind of fuel that you drive into the service station and say let me have an eyedropper full. Maybe electronics. Maybe you drive in and say goose my battery for me, Sam, and check the transistors. Electronic highways where you put your car on a beam and let it cruise while you try to make out in the back seat. Airplanes flying around on this new fuel, boats going across the ocean, stuff up there in the sky with people in it, rockets going to the moon, crap like that. You can't pump a rocket full of ten million gallons of high test gasoline. The oil business is finished. Oil men are dinosaurs. But I'm not going to become extinct. I'm going to adapt myself. When the breakthrough comes, somebody is going to make billions. It's going to be me, Sam. And you."

Guthrie looked at Waddy, who took a deep gurgle of beer and sighed.

"Me?" said Guthrie.

"Why not?"

"Why do you want me?"

"First, you know this thing I'm talking about is going to happen."

"It'll happen."

"Damn right, you know it. You've been experimenting with solar power in one of your labs."

Guthrie grinned. "What we're doing in that lab is top secret."

"I know all about it. Anyhow, I think you're on the wrong track. But at least you're thinking."

"You still haven't said why you want me. Why do you even need me?"

"I don't really *need* you," Waddy said. "I could get it done without you. But I like to have good men. I like a guy who hustles and fights and thinks and has ambition. I like a guy who wants to keep getting richer. You've already got plants, labs, a lot of physicists. You've got the drive, the equipment, the ability, and you're pretty honest. What we'll do is split off some of your people and form us a little outfit and find out every damned thing the government has ever done in exotic fuels. Personally, I think electronics has the answer, but we need to know it all. We'll work at it, and experiment, and one of these days we'll tell everybody to come and look at what we've got."

"I don't have the right kind of people."

"You've got some geniuses in physics, Sam, maybe the ones we need. I know enough about your guidance systems and communications and that crap. I know enough physics to know the stuff you're building today was impossible a few years ago. The other guys we'll need, we'll go get them. We'll steal them from the Army or the Air Force or Russia or Germany or wherever the hell they are. I don't know exactly where we're heading, but the right people can find out for us. The question you ought to be asking is what you need *me* for?"

"Okay," Guthrie said. "What do I need you for?"

"Number one," said Waddy, lifting his forefinger as if testing the wind, "suppose you develop some super power source that would be perfect for the automobile industry. What would you do with it? Eat it? Detroit would bury you and throw your formula in the grave with you. But with me on your side, I believe we could swing it. I can make the deal. I'm a dealer. I've got influence. As a dealer, I make you look like a Cub Scout."

The fighting chair creaked as Waddy swiveled around to throw the second beer bottle into the water.

"Ought to oil that thing," Waddy said.

"What else? What's number two?"

"Number two is, I'm a better operator than you are. I'm smarter. I would never have got myself extended in this proxy fight without knowing I was going to win it. But you did. You got yourself ass deep in a tank of octopuses. I'm pulling you out. I think we'll be good partners, Sam. Deal?"

"Wait a minute," said Guthrie. "Let me think about it."

"We'll think about it later. We'll settle the price I'm paying to buy into Guthrie Electronics without any trouble, I assure you. I want to know right now: Deal or no deal? I need to get that proxy fight wound up this morning, one way or the other. I can do it with one telephone call."

"Good lord," Guthrie said.

"Deal?"

"Deal," said Guthrie.

"You make all those promises?"

"Yeah. I make all those promises."

"Looks like the seed is sowed," Waddy said. "Here go."

Waddy stuck out his hand, and Guthrie took it. The handshake was quick and brusque, as if Waddy were embarrassed to be touched.

"Well," said Waddy, "how does it feel to be the biggest electronics tycoon in the Southwest?"

"It doesn't feel real."

"It will. I'm investing in you as a man, Sam. Are you healthy? How's your sex life?"

"Strong as a goat."

"Great," Waddy said. "I think that's a sure indicator. Listen, I've got an idea for arranging us an exhibition in Mexico. I've worked it out like an architect. We'll need to buy a tape measure and find some ladies who are the proper lengths so they'll fit my geometric patterns."

"Anything you say, Waddy."

"I knew you'd go for this deal," said Waddy. "You judge everything by how good it'll be for you, don't you? Nothing wrong with that to my mind. This'll be very good for you. Next week we'll have us a nice meeting and talk business. It won't smear your reputation when word gets around that I'm in with you."

"I'm still stunned."

Waddy looked at his watch. "Johnson ought to be up by now," he said. "Got a ship to shore phone in the cabin? I'll go phone him. Having to count proxies is a terrible way to run a business. We want to get that all settled before the stockholders' meeting."

"Billy will show you the phone," said Guthrie.

Waddy unhooked his harness and looked down at the red prints on his flesh. "Son of a bitch," he said. He called Senator Rose to the chair, handed him the rod, and went toward the cabin massaging his shoulders.

"Hi up there, cap," Waddy said to Jacob Iles. "You as bored as we are?"

Senator Rose sat down in the fighting chair with the rod still sunk in the socket and let the harness lie in his lap. Guthrie lit a cigarette, thinking over what Waddy had said to him. The proposition was so immense that Guthrie couldn't take it in all at once. He knew he hadn't really considered it long enough. But the main thing, he thought, was that he had won the proxy fight. The rest of it, he would have to explore slowly. He was shocked and awed by the possibilities Waddy had presented him. Guthrie had grabbed at Waddy's offer as a prop to his destiny. That destiny, Guthrie thought, had been faltering, but suddenly it had gone up like a rocket rising from a pad, and Guthrie was dizzy with the rush of it.

"Sam," said the Senator, "when are we going to Mexico?"

"Tonight, maybe, or in the morning. Why?"

"I'm not feeling very well," the Senator said.

Senator Rose looked down at his canvas, crepe-soled shoes as if they were stuck to the deck.

"You've been hitting those Bloody Marys ever since we got aboard. When Waddy comes back, you ought to go inside and get some sleep," Guthrie said.

"I wouldn't want you to think I'm backing out on the party," said Senator Rose.

"I wouldn't think that."

"I wouldn't back out."

"Are you telling me you don't want to go to Mexico?" asked Guthrie.

"No, no. I've always been a goer, Sam. I've always been the last man home and the first man out of bed the next morning."

"I know you're a goer."

The Senator bobbed his head, and Guthrie saw that he was very drunk. With thin white fingers Senator Rose played with a buckle on the harness. He reached up to pinch his lower lip with the thumb and forefinger of his other hand.

"I wouldn't want you to think less of me," the Senator said.

"I don't, Senator. It's no disgrace to be tired."

"Yes, it is. It's a disgrace. I've been an active man, Sam. A dominant man. The last home and the first out of bed. I'm a goer. We all have our weak moments, though, don't we, Sam?"

"Everbody has weak moments."

"Everyone has moments of weakness. Everyone has times when it all gets too much for him. His resources are under hard attack and he gets flanked, and his resources fail. To fail is a disgrace. To be tired is a disgrace. Not to be a goer is a disgrace. To be weak is a disgrace."

"Senator, why don't you go take a nap?"

"I'm not weak or tired mentally, Sam. You don't think that, do you? You wouldn't have much patience with weakness, would you? You wouldn't grant me ease if I got flanked and my resources failed, would you? I'm not mentally weak."

"What's all this supposed to mean?" Guthrie said.

"I wouldn't want you to think less of me, Sam. I'm just physically tired is all. Feeling a little weary."

"Fin!" yelled Iles.

The line cracked off the outrigger and went taut as the water exploded astern and the bait vanished. Senator Rose grunted. The butt of the rod flew up from the socket and hit the Senator in the chest with a thump. The Senator caught the rod in his thin white hands and was jerked out of his chair and yanked toward the railing, one knee scraping the deck, the other leg flailing uselessly, clutching the rod butt as if only to defend himself from another blow, an expression of amazement and pain on his face.

"The drag!" Guthrie shouted, trying to free himself from his chair and scramble toward the Senator. Billy and the bait boy were running from the cabin. George Washington Simpson stood behind the Senator's chair with another Bloody Mary on a silver tray.

The Senator gasped. The rod bent crazily over the rail, lifting him until his head and shoulders were above the water, the rod wriggling and twisting in his hands. Just as Billy grabbed for him, the rod tore out of the Senator's hands. The rod jumped into the air, seemed to dangle for an instant, then plunged into the water and was gone. Senator Rose slumped beside the railing on his knees, his eyes mystified, hands on the railing as if he knelt at an altar. Billy gently pulled him around and unbuttoned his Italian silk sports shirt. The Senator rubbed the reddening blotch the size of a baseball on his chest.

"You all right?" Billy said. "Can you breathe? No broken ribs?"

"I'm sorry about the rod," said the Senator, looking at Guthrie and rubbing his chest.

"The hell with the rod," Guthrie said. "It's the fish I want."

"It was a marlin, Sam," Iles said from above. "Pretty good one for this time of year."

"I'll buy you another rod, of course," said Senator Rose.

"Screw the rod. You stupid old bastard. What did you tighten the drag for?" Guthrie said.

The Senator shook himself free of Billy and the bait boy, who had helped him up. Weaving, the Senator spread his feet and braced them against the deck. He lifted his fists, elbows against his stomach, knuckles turned in, and peered out from between his fists at Guthrie.

"Sir," Senator Rose said, "you can't talk to me like that. I'm a gentleman in my own right, as well as being a United States Senator. I demand that you stand up so that we can fight."

"Oh, God," said Guthrie.

"You have insulted me," Senator Rose said. "And furthermore, I didn't touch the drag. Please allow me the dignity of standing up so that I can knock you down."

"I'm not going to get up," Guthrie said.

Waddy came out of the cabin, walked in front of Senator Rose, started to sit down, stopped, and looked around.

"Where's my fishing pole?" said Waddy.

"Come on, Senator," Billy said, taking the Senator's right elbow. "Let's go inside and rest for a minute. That was a hell of a whop."

Senator Rose stared down at Guthrie. "Very well," he said, "if this man won't do me the honor of standing up to me." Then the Senator folded. He sagged against Billy. The mate and the bait boy helped him into the cabin. George Washington Simpson followed them, carrying the one Bloody Mary on a silver tray. Waddy watched them go.

"He sick?" asked Waddy.

"Drunk," Guthrie said.

"What happened to my pole? I left it right here."

"The Senator threw it overboard. What happened on the phone?"

"It's all set," said Waddy. "No problem."

"Look at that fin!" Iles yelled. "Knockdown!"

Guthrie's line leaped from the outrigger clip with a loud ping. A deep and tremendous power jolted him as the line whipped into the water and began running. The reel whined and the heavy rod warped. Guthrie lifted the rod in a short, quick, six-inch punch and looked up at the tip to watch the arc. If the arc lessened by an inch he would know the fish had slowed its run. But this fish was running. The line smoked off the reel. Streaming out, the line was dangerous as a power saw. Guthrie stretched his legs and pushed his sneakers against the rail, leaning back, holding the throbbing rod, watching the arc. He could feel the sun on his shoulders and arms and neck.

"A cap," Guthrie said. "Somebody get me a cap."

The bait boy ran into the cabin, returned with a baseball cap, and put it on Guthrie's head. The spool was getting thin, and still the fish ran. Don't sound right now, Guthrie thought, as the line whirred off the reel. Don't be a bulldog, be a lion. Up on the flying bridge Iles reversed the engines and began to back in the direction of the fish's charge. Guthrie saw the rod tip flicker and he wound rapidly, not pumping, to keep the curve in the rod. A long deep sound right at first took too much out of a fish, and this one had gone about four hundred yards already. But with the boat moving now faster than the fish, Guthrie was gaining line.

"You're sweating like a lawn sprinkler," Waddy said.

"Hey, Jake, what do you think it is? I didn't see the fin," yelled Guthrie.

"Blue, most likely. I think it's a big blue," Iles said.

"He's a sonabitch," said Guthrie.

"I saw a blackfish once bigger than this boat," Billy said. "Wouldn't it be hell to hook a big blackfish and get towed to Cuba?"

"He's coming, Jake! He's coming back!" shouted Guthrie.

Guthrie held the rod high and cranked the reel. Jacob Iles slammed the engines into slow forward as the fish moved toward the boat. Guthrie watched the rod tip, cranking to keep the line tight, to keep pressure on the fish. Abruptly, the fish changed direction. Guthrie, his lungs heaving, croaked a warning. The fish sounded again and then stopped. Guthrie began to pump the rod slowly and steadily, winding as he lowered the tip, gathering a few feet at a time, a slow, exhausting process.

"Feels like a piano down there," he said.

"I don't think it's fair for the captain to chase the fish around in the boat," said Waddy.

"Fair, my ass," Guthrie said. "I want that fish."

The rod whanged into a sudden bow and the outrushing line screamed against the drag. Far out, more than three hundred yards astern, a black glistening shape climbed into the sunlight. They saw the scythe of its tail, and its high dorsal fin, and the lance of its snout. It shuddered and fell back into the sea with a showering splash.

"An elephant!" yelled Guthrie. "A goddamned elephant!"

"Blue!" Iles shouted. "Four hundred pounds! Maybe more!"

Guthrie's biceps had begun to jump, and his left arm ached from the pull of the rod. His left shoulder socket was aflame. He wanted a cigarette and a glass of water, but in the thrill of seeing the fish for the first time he didn't ask. His tongue was swollen and his mouth was dry, and the sun was a white hot bath. Come on you beauty, he thought, you lovely beast. A big one like that shouldn't be in these waters, not so early; this was an autumn fish and it had come to him in May. In all the great deep water of the Gulf, this fish had found him. Oh God, my arms hurt, he thought. Oh Lord, my arms hurt.

The fish broke water again and Guthrie saw the wet lavender stripes on its sides.

I wish you'd swallowed that bait right into your heart, Guthrie thought as the fish fell with a whop as loud as a sack of concrete hitting a sidewalk. Oh don't shake the bait, don't tear the hook, Guthrie thought. He had to have this fish. Dimly he heard Waddy, the mate, and now Senator Rose talking behind him. Their voices angered him; they were standing back from the work. His arms were weak, numb, he could no longer turn the reel handle or feel the rod in his hands. But he kept turning, kept the pressure on, kept the rod bowed. He heard Waddy say, "Don't horse him too much." Guthrie scowled. He'd horse the sonofabitch right into the boat.

Waddy couldn't tell him how to fish. Back there long ago he had been the son of a fisherman. In this water, off this island, with his silent, embarrassed father, a gray-haired man in dirty dungarees with the stub of a cigarette between his lips and his face whiskery and a pained, hurt look in his eyes. They were so poor then that Guthrie wanted to cry out when he thought of it. The shack built out of driftwood and stolen lumber and tar paper and tin and cardboard. The old man would look at him as if to say that's how it is and it don't appear to be gonna get any better. His mother was quiet, always looking off, watching the sky as if waiting for something. Every Wednesday night, Sunday morning, and Sunday night she walked to the Baptist church in Port Agness, and most of the time Sam Guthrie went with her. Then, after the storm when his father didn't come back, people would look at Guthrie in a funny way, and he quit going to church. Guthrie went to work on a shrimper; they would go out in the morning with their nets and at night they would return to the bay to sleep. Out on the Gulf he would look into the dark mountains of water and wonder where his father rested, wonder how it had felt going down, cold, alone, embarrassed, unlucky, yearning, frightened, bewildered, wanting to smoke just one more cigarette one more evening and watch the sun go down behind the masts of the fishing boats, and to touch his wife one more time and maybe to see his son, and maybe to say something to them, something loving that now would never be said. Thinking of it tore at Guthrie's heart. He wanted Jacob Iles to come and take this rod out of his hands, to finish this elephant of a fish.

"That's five, Sam," said Waddy. "Five jumps."

Guthrie's glasses were streaked with sweat and salt spray. He mumbled and Billy took them and cleaned them while Guthrie squinted into the white light. The glasses were put over his eyes again blurred from having been wiped on the mate's shorts, worse than before. The rod bent. It was like pulling against a truck. The fish sounded, and the line ripped off the reel taking everything Guthrie had gained in the first hour. Billy poured water over the smoking reel. Guthrie leaned back in the chair, holding the rod tip high, the leather straps gnawing his shoulders, the reel whining, around him the noise of the water slapping the boat, the diesels thumping, the voices. Guthrie had begun to smell himself, some odor of bile and blood, as if he were being drawn out of his skin. Far below he knew the fish was swimming scared and hurt in the black water. Do you see him down there? Guthrie thought. Have you found his bones? When his father hadn't returned, Guthrie had left home, left the island, because he didn't want his mother to have to work for him. He always found a job. Gas stations, construction gangs, oil fields. In junior high school he worked in the cafeteria for his meals. He earned enough during the summers to get through high school with the help of extra work at nights. When he entered Texas A&M on a football scholarship he had one pair of shoes, two pairs of trousers, one coat, and two shirts. That was the year his mother died in the hospital at Corpus Christi and he wore his Aggie uniform to the funeral because it was the nicest thing he owned. Then in the Air Force he had more money than he'd ever known. He was stationed in San Antonio. He could eat in a restaurant without having to stop outside and count his money, without carefully studying the prices. That was when he had his first filet mignon, when he graduated from chicken fried steaks and hamburgers. On weekends when he could he would drive with some of his friends to Laredo, to Boy's Town. Beyond Boy's Town, on the Calle de Mina, there was a place named Lile's Club where he fell in love with a Mexican whore who had gold teeth. After he got his wings and began training as a bomber pilot, Guthrie would go down to Lile's Club as frequently as possible and sit in the bar with the whore, Arreoro. The bar had green lights. Guthrie would play the juke box and dance with Arreoro. They'd made an agreement that when she was approached by another customer she would go. She insisted on it. Otherwise, she said, she would stop seeing Guthrie. He would watch her go out with them, and wait, and torture himself with the thought of what she was doing. He would sulk when she came back, and she would laugh and hold his hand and push her soft breasts against him through her pink sweater. She was sixteen, and plump. She smelled like hair tonic, dried semen, and wool. She encouraged him to put his hands under her sweater and hold her breasts, and she would play with him beneath the table and laugh and bite his ear with her gold teeth. When Lile's Club closed at four A.M. Guthrie would walk with her across the courtyard to her room and they would sleep together in the soiled bed, above the head of which hung a crucifix. Guthrie wrote her five or six letters from London. His letters were full of himself, of his fear and loneliness. She wrote back letters like:

Hi sweethart, glad to hear from you we are all doing fine and busniss is good but i guess it make you unhappy to know that ha! There are a lots more of soldiers and Air Core boys all the time. I showed your letter to the other girls and they are glad you are fighting for our country too instead of in here chaseing away their date with your big angry face ha! ha! Maybe I love you too, yes, i don't know. But we can find out if you come Home with a lots of medals. Kisses Arreoro.

She finally quit answering his letters, and he discovered London. He flew thirty-three combat missions and came home on medical leave and found Jane at the North Texas State College for Women.

"Hey, nigger," yelled Iles. "Run fetch a damp towel and wipe off Mr. Guthrie with it. Don't stand around."

My hands, Guthrie thought, my hands will never open again, they're closed like pincers. The fish was sounding, stubbornly holding to its life. Above him the rod bent. Guthrie began the agonizing pumping again. Jane Saxton, he remembered. She didn't have a chance. The dance was in the big ballroom with the crepe paper on the ceiling and the chairs around the walls and the floor waxed and polished and the orchestra up in front. Guthrie was in his uniform, a twenty-three-year-old major with ribbons on his chest and an entirely unnecessary limp that made the college boys hate him and the girls stare at him. He had never felt exactly like that again, never exactly as proud and powerful as the night he found Jane Saxton and cut in on her and took her outside because he left the impression his leg was hurting too much to dance but he was too brave to admit it. Her date, a college boy, came out ten minutes later. Her date started crying and wanted to fight, but what kind of patriot would hit a wounded pilot? Guthrie laughed. Guthrie had taken off his coat, but the college boy, feeling guilty anyhow about not being in the war, had gone back inside crying. Later, Guthrie walked Jane Saxton to her dormitory and decided he was in love. He decided he wanted Jane Saxton to be part of him.

"Is that fun?" said Waddy. "It doesn't *look* like much fun."

Guthrie felt the cold wet towel on his forehead and then on his chest and shoulders, and the water wrung onto his back.

"Leave the towel," said Guthrie. "Put it over my head and get me some water to drink."

"Rub some sun cream on him," Iles said to the bait boy.

Guthrie was gaining on the fish again.

"Billy," said Iles, "better get the rifle and hand it up here to me."

"For sharks?" Waddy asked.

Billy nodded.

"Nine jumps," said Billy. "He ought to be wore."

"I am," Guthrie said.

"I meant the fish, Mr. Guthrie."

Jane in the white dress at the dance, Guthrie thought, with her hair cut short and a good tan and the white shoes. She was little, and it was great to touch her. It was six months before he noticed that she didn't have good ankles, but they were married by then and he was too busy even to think of wanting to look around. Out of the Air Force, he was no longer a hero. They moved into a garage apartment in a declining area of East Dallas, and they worked hard. Jane worked in an office all day and did the cooking, cleaning and washing at night and then listened to Guthrie tell her how tired he was. She never complained or asked for anything. Thinking about it, Guthrie felt that he owed her faith, love and gratitude, and if he couldn't always give her those he would at least buy her anything she wanted. But the children were bothering him. He would have to spend more time with them. He would have to make them understand how tough money was to get, and how tough it was to hang onto, and make them appreciate it. He didn't want them becoming snots. Maybe Jake could get the oldest boy a summer job on a shrimp boat. Good old Jake. Jake was dependable. Jake had brought him straight to this fish that was beating him to death.

Guthrie was going to stuff this great purple bastard of a fish and put it in his bedroom and use its bill for a tie rack. I apologize, fish, he thought, for saying that. The fish deserved better. That's what Waddy would do. Waddy would put the fish in an ambulance and ride him up and down Broadway and take him dancing at El Morocco. Old Waddy. Partner. Now wasn't that something? Wasn't that really something? Woodrow Morris, Jr., and Samuel Hooks Guthrie, partners. Own all the mysterious new fuel in the world and you got to get in line for it, boys. Beg a little. No, beg a lot. Richer and richer. Guthrie-Ramco Electronics Incorporated. Guthrie-Morris Mysterious New Power Supply Incorporated. Richer and richer. One day Guthrie would build a fishing boat that couldn't turn over and couldn't sink and nobody could fall out of it and down. No living soul would ever perish at sea out of Sam

Guthrie's boat. He was tired. He was beyond tired. Waddy Morris, partner. The thing to watch out for was any wrong step with Waddy's emptyheaded nogood tall blonde wife. Must never let anything show on his big angry face, or they could read it as Arreoro had read it. Not worth it anyway. Look into the abyss. Love is a fantasy, screwing is a game. Guthrie had to dominate all that. He had to be patient, ruthless and cunning. No hurricanes of the flesh, no bleeding hearts, no pity for snots like that lawyer Carpenter from the sick family. Carpenter's old man is the one who should have drowned. A hypocrite and a thief with a sugar-gutted, floppy-eared, Ivy League snot for a son. Somebody should have made that young Carpenter put all his savings into a guarantee on an electrical contract (*busniss is good ha!*) and work and build up something and then have some snot insult him for it.

"He's circling," Billy yelled.

"I see him," said Iles. "We'll outturn him."

"It's been a hour and forty-five minutes," Waddy said. "For God's sake, Sam, I've drunk four beers while you've been tugging on that fish."

The dorsal fin came up out of the water thirty yards away, and behind it the purple scythe of the tail. The fish lay inches below the surface, a long and strangely sluggish shape, distorted in color and size by the refraction of the water. As if at last depleted by its struggle and curious as to the nature of its enemy, the fish floated and waited, not yet in absolute surrender but allowing itself to be drawn slowly through the water, an impassive, gradually yielding mass, following rather than being pulled by the thin line that rose dripping sunlight.

"Oh," Iles said up on the flying bridge.

"What's the matter?" asked Billy.

"Maybe nothing," Iles said. "Get that tail rope ready. We ought to have the damned harpoon. Hey, George Washington, go get the harpoon."

George Washington Simpson, in his white jacket, looked up at Iles with yellow eyes, resentfully. "I don't know where it's at," he said.

"Crap. No, Billy, you stay on deck. You and the bait boy. Listen, George Washington, it's down forward by the crew quarters where we got all that equipment stored. Now you run get it and hurry," said Iles.

George Washington collided in the cabin doorway with Senator

Rose, who had given up and gone inside after watching Guthrie fight the fish for a while. The Senator was rubbing his eyes and drinking from a bottle of Lowenbrau. His shirt was open, showing his white belly and the bruise turning red-purple beneath the gray hairs on his chest.

"Is that still the same fish?" the Senator said.

"A little closer," Guthrie said aloud, looking out at the fish. Guthrie's cap had fallen off. The towel, dried by the sun and hard as crust, had congealed around his neck. Guthrie's biceps quivered; cords stood out in his forearms and neck. A piece of cigarette paper was stuck to his mouth. Sweat hung from the cleft of his chin. His voice was thick and dry; he licked at his lips but there seemed to be no moisture left in him. "Another twenty yards," he said. "*Espadón, aguja,* another twenty yards and you're mine."

"I didn't know a marlin had those purple stripes," said Senator Rose.

"He gets 'em when he's excited," Billy said.

"My wife breaks into a rash," said the Senator.

George Washington Simpson came out of the cabin and looked up at Iles, who had idled the engines and was leaning over the rail of the bridge studying the fish.

"Can't find no harpoon," the Negro waiter said.

"Look again," said Iles. "It's that long pole with a coil of rope tied to one end of it and a barbed spear at the other end. Hurry!"

George Washington walked into the cabin.

"Damn nigger probably doesn't know what a harpoon looks like," Iles said.

"What do they need with a harpoon?" said Waddy.

"Jake keeps it for big sharks," Billy said. "He's been trying to get one up by the boat and harpoon him."

"I don't see any sharks," said Waddy.

"No. We're lucky," Billy said. "I guess Jake thinks we might have to harpoon this marlin. He must see something from up there that we can't see."

"That's silly," said Waddy. "This isn't a whale."

"It's an awful big marlin for this stretch of water," Billy said.

The marlin was ten yards from the boat, a lavender torpedo with wide glass eyes. Guthrie braced his feet and reeled steadily, muscles twitching. Billy had put on a pair of heavy leather gloves that covered his wrists, and now he held the gaff between his legs and prepared the noose in the tail rope. The bait boy also put on a pair of gloves and picked up a gaff and placed a wooden club, a cut-off baseball bat, within quick reach. The marlin came in, twisting a bit in the curling water, turning its bill toward the boat, looking up at the white hull of the *Silver Spoon.*

"We're lucky," Billy said. "We're lucky."

The mate raised his left hand to reach for the wire leader to guide the fish in close. In his right hand, Billy gripped the gaff. The bait boy stood ready with the other gaff and the tail rope. The marlin slipped toward the boat. The leader began to appear from the water, nearly close enough for Billy to catch. With Billy's glove outstretched, Guthrie lifted the rod tip to bring in the leader.

The sound was like a diver cannonballing into the water beside the boat. A mushroom of water burst up and rained down on the deck. Guthrie fell backward. Waddy cursed and ducked his head. Senator Rose looked down at his Italian silk sports shirt, now thoroughly soaked. Billy turned around from the rail, water rolling from his face, his mouth open and his eyes blinking.

The fish was gone.

Guthrie immediately knew what had happened. He shut his eyes, dropped the rod, and heard it clatter on the deck. For a moment no one spoke. Guthrie let his arms hang limp, not feeling them, unwilling to move or to believe what he knew. A great weariness overcame him with a very real physical sensation, like being slowly submerged in a warm bath, and something mashed against his stomach as if his nerves had been fooled into thinking the rod butt was pressing there. Again, he felt the sun on his hair and along his shoulders.

"Unstrap me, will you, Billy?" he said finally.

"He pulled the hook," said the mate. "At first I thought he'd snapped the leader. Look here where it's frayed from him beating it with his bill."

"I'll look later. Unstrap me," Guthrie said.

Guthrie stood up and felt needles in his legs. Through the muddy glasses, in the glare of the sunlight, he saw Jacob Iles above him at the wheel.

"Sorry, Jake," Guthrie said.

"I saw when he come up he'd about tore the hook loose," said Iles. "I was afraid that'd happen. I hate it as bad as you do, Sam."

"It's a shame, Sam," Senator Rose said.

"That's another thing I don't like about fishing," said Waddy.

"You put in all this work, for God's sake, and you wind up with nothing. It's not a very reasonable pursuit."

Guthrie nodded, tried to smile through lips that felt and tasted like stale biscuits, and went into the cabin. His skin burned from the sun. He tossed his dark glasses onto the table, and for a moment the room got darker, as if they were suddenly passing through a cloud. Feeling nauseous and cold, Guthrie leaned his hands on the table to steady himself. Then he felt back carefully until he found a chair, and lowered himself into it. As the room lightened again, he saw George Washington, the waiter, bending through the door that led down toward the crew quarters. George Washington was struggling with a pole that banged against the walls of the passage and that wedged in the doorway until he pulled it loose. A rope was wrapped three times around his right leg and then trailed off behind, leaving him with a weird limp. The spear end of the pole threatened his face; he kept his neck twisted back from it.

"Where you want this harpoon at, Mr. Guthrie?" the waiter said.

"Forget it."

"Forget it? Mr. Guthrie, this thing has plumb near killed me. It fell me down once, and it tried to stab me."

"Forget it," said Guthrie. "Drop it right there. Get yourself untangled and fix me a scotch in the biggest glass on the boat with the most ice cubes you can find. Then go turn on the shower and find me some clean shorts. Just forget all about that damned harpoon."

"Yessir,"George Washington said, shaking his head as if wondering whether he had gone mad or was merely the victim of a cruel joke. "You real sure you don't need no harpoon?"

"I want a drink!" shouted Guthrie.

Running for the bar, George Washington forgot that his legs were caught in the rope. The crash as he went over jarred a glass from a shelf; the glass fell into the sink and broke. Guthrie shut his eyes again and let exhaustion take him.

In the evening they were dancing in the big room above the dunes. At the curved end of the room, beyond the plateau of the carpet, the dining table had been removed and they danced on a black polished floor. Guthrie's favorite statue turned its wise and suffering visage toward the dancers from its niche in the wall. Music came from hidden speakers; Jane Guthrie had selected thirty records and had fed them into the stereo system. Jane Guthrie danced with Senator Rose, who wore a white suit with the poise that only old men are capable of. The Senator had brushed his long white hair and was aware of the effect of the white against the newly reddened color of his face. Guthrie looked at his wife with the Senator. Rather than collapsing, as he had been about to do earlier, Senator Rose seemed to have got stronger; he danced very well and as if it pleased him, smiling, talking occasionally to Jane, who laughed. Waddy Morris, his cropped red hair in ragged tufts, danced with his wife. His freckled face was set and grim as he concentrated on the music and his steps. Beth Morris wore a flowered cocktail dress and heels that made her three inches taller than her husband. Her blonde hair came down softly onto her bare shoulders. A gold bracelet glinted on her left wrist, the wrist that was casually on Waddy's shoulder.

Guthrie stood by one of the glass doors. Against the plum-colored horizon shone the yellow lights of a freighter, passing slowly. The surf came in to rumble on the beach like far thunder. The wind rubbed itself against the house and stirred the hair of the dunes. Looking out at the humps and mounds in the moonlight, Guthrie remembered how when he was a boy some of the islanders used to fish for coyotes among the dunes. They would bait a heavy fishing rig with a stinking mullet, place the bait in the sand, and wait up in the dunes or in a cabin on the beach. The coyote would gulp the bait and be painfully and solidly hooked. Then the fisherman would play the coyote like a fish, letting it run and jump, howl and pull against the line, until the coyote was exhausted and could be reeled in to be shot or clubbed to death.

In the glass he saw Beth Morris walking toward him, heard her heels on the marble floor, smelled her perfume, saw her golden face appear beside his dark one, felt her long fingers on his arm.

"What do you see out there?" she said.

"Myself," he said.

"You're looking at your own reflection?"

"Sort of."

"Isn't that terribly vain?"

"Sort of."

"Let me look," she said.

"You wouldn't be able to see it."

"Oh, you're looking *outside*," she said. "Well, don't sound contemptuous. You'd be surprised at what I can see sometimes, when there's anything really worth seeing."

"I smelled like shrimp until I was eighteen years old," said Guthrie. "I couldn't get that smell off of me. I practically used to rub my skin off trying to get rid of that smell."

"You're in a strange humor," she laughed. "You haven't said a word about this sun I got today at your request. It *does* look rather becoming."

"You wouldn't have got within ten feet of me when I smelled like shrimp."

"Sam, dear, I *love* shrimp."

"I'll take you over to the freezing plant and show you where they cut off the shrimps' heads. They sell the shrimps for eighty-eight cents a pound," he said.

"Let's dance first."

"There's a lot of gold-bodied flies out there in the dunes, and when they bite it hurts like hell," said Guthrie. "You ever see a man-of-war floating in? It looks like a blown-up rubber, dark purple underneath and with ridges on the top like a Greek helmet and ribbons hanging down that can paralyze you with pain."

"That's fascinating. Let's dance."

"Pretty soon the moonflowers will be blooming on the dunes. They're white and glow at night almost like incandescent lights. Like little moons, I guess. You ever see a rattlesnake bush with purple berries on it? I forget the real name now. I'm forgetting a lot of this stuff."

"Sam," she said.

"I don't know why I'm forgetting it," he said. "I guess my memory is wearing out. Is that possible?"

"All I want to do is dance, for God's sake."

"How many of the oil wells around the channel and the bay does Waddy own?"

"How would I know?"

"Okay. Let's dance then," he said.

They began to shuffle across the floor in a fox trot, the only dance step Guthrie knew. He had progressed in the fox trot from the awkward, arm-pumping stage to his present smooth proficiency; he did the fox trot to all sorts of beats from the waltz to the samba; that, he thought, was enough to know about dancing. He could feel Beth Morris's hair against his face, and her spine beneath his fingers, and her hand with his left hand, but yet she was so oddly light that it was almost like dancing alone. No woman should be that good a dancer, he thought. That took the fun out of it. He wished she'd step on his foot, or fall down just once. The record finished, and they paused beside Jane and the Senator.

"Sam, I don't believe I've ever seen a man look so handsome and distinguished as you do tonight," said the Senator, smiling.

"Cut it out, Senator. People will be talking about us."

Jane Guthrie glanced at Beth Morris and then at Sam with a look that struck him as a warning. The music started again. Jane stepped back, thrust out her rump, and began wriggling her hips.

"Cha cha cha," she said. "Shake it up, Senator."

"Lovely," said Senator Rose.

"Come on," Guthrie said to Beth Morris.

He took her to the long white couch where Waddy sat. Waddy looked up curiously, as if wondering why they were bothering him. Guthrie could feel Beth's eyes on him, and he didn't look at her.

"I need a drink, Guthrie," she said. "Am I supposed to scream for it?"

"How about you, Waddy?"

"Perpetually."

"I'll go see what's the matter with Roger."

"Want me to go?" said Beth.

"He's going to the kitchen, dear," Waddy said. "I'm afraid you wouldn't know how to act in a kitchen."

As Guthrie walked out of the living room he heard Waddy saying, "Well, why don't you ask him to take you outside?" Guthrie went around the corner and pushed through the swinging doors into a large shining kitchen where the pots glistened like a guardsman's buttons. The kitchen was so white and clean and the chrome so bright that it almost hurt to look at it, like a pasture of fresh snow under a noon sun. Two Negro women were putting away the dinner dishes, which they had taken out of the dishwasher. The head man, Roger, and George Washington Simpson, with a Band-Aid over his right eye from the fall on the boat, stood beside the kitchen table talking to Jacob Iles. Guthrie was surprised to see Iles. Under the clear light of the kitchen and without his dark glasses, Iles's face looked more discolored and swollen than Guthrie had remembered it to be. Iles's old blue cap lay on the table beside a bottle of bourbon and a glass. Iles was scratching his bleached hair as he talked to the Negroes, both of whom wore their dinner jackets. Roger and George Washington looked up when they heard Guthrie's voice.

"I got people out there going mad from the drought and you stand in here gossiping," Guthrie said. "If Mrs. and Mr. Morris don't have drinks in thirty seconds, there's going to be two less coons on this island."

"We was only . . ." said George Washington Simpson.

"Shut up and grab these here glasses," Roger said.

The waiters hurried through the door. Guthrie looked at Iles.

"Hope you don't mind, Sam," said Iles, gesturing toward the bottle and the glass. "I had to do some drinking tonight, and I kind of hated to go to the Sporting Life with these decorations on my face. You know, it's one of those nights when a man has to do some drinking."

"I don't mind, Jake."

"I wasn't too sure after today. Thing like that upsets a man. If I'd had that harpoon ready we mighta got him."

"I doubt it."

"Mighta, though."

"Yeah. Mighta."

Guthrie pulled back a chair and sat down.

"I think I'll have me one," Guthrie said.

"Help yourself," said Iles.

Guthrie snapped his fingers and one of the Negro women brought another glass.

"Ice," Guthrie said. "Water. Bottle of scotch."

Guthrie put two cubes into his glass, poured it half full of scotch, and filled the rest of the glass with water from a pitcher. Iles covered the mouth of his own glass with his right hand. Guthrie noticed that the knuckles of the hand were bruised and scabbed.

"You're strictly a scotch man now, huh?" said Iles.

"All of us big shots are scotch men."

"Bloody Marys, beer, scotch."

"That's the routine."

"No more grain alcohol?"

"Not in a long time."

"I remember once we got drunk on grain alcohol," Iles said. "It was in Florida."

"I remember."

"What's the matter, Sam? You look sort of low."

"Nothing. What's the matter with you?"

"Nothing."

They drank in silence for a moment.

"Old lady giving you trouble?" said Guthrie.

"Some. Don't they all?"

"Anything I can do?"

Iles looked squarely at Guthrie and then looked away.

"Probably not," Iles said.

"What is it?"

"Nothing."

"Don't be a stubborn bastard, Jake. We know each other too well."

"Do we?"

"Sure," Guthrie said. "What the hell's the matter with you?"

"Nothing, Sam. Same old crap."

"Kids got Marge upset?"

"Yeah."

"She want to get you away from the water and get a job at a gas station?"

"Naw. She really don't want that."

"She's been wanting to get away from the water for years."

"I know it," said Iles.

"You're a good boat captain, Jake. You ought to stick to what you're good at."

"I ain't so sure I'm a good boat captain after today."

"That wasn't your fault."

Iles shrugged. "I don't know," he said, touching the bruise under his left eye. "It's hard to tell. That's why I like it out there, Sam. The Gulf, you can't cheat it or lie to it or make love to it. It don't listen to your promises or your threats. It don't give a damn about you one way or the other. You get out there and do the best you can, or the worst, and if it breaks you, well, it didn't mean to and it didn't mean not to. You're just a nothing. There can't be nothing phony between it and you. When you're out there you're real, and you're alone, and you don't even have a name. But you feel like you're part of it. That makes me feel good. If I'm religious about anything, I'm religious about that."

"You're talking like I don't know anything about it."

"I'm not talking like anything in particular. That's just the way it is, is all."

"I got tired today, Jake."

"Yeah."

"A year ago it wouldn't have happened."

"We're all getting older," said Iles.

"Older's not it. I got so damned tired that I started thinking about all kinds of damned things. If you'd had the rod, you'd have got him."

"Maybe. I don't know. He wasn't hooked good."

"I had him on for two hours. That was plenty of time to gentle him in. I didn't treat him right. I didn't even think about him right."

"Well," Iles said, "if you want to know the truth you handled him like a blacksmith. You yanked him around like a greedy tourist. I'm surprised he stayed on as long as he did and gave you so many chances. You just plain jacked it off."

Guthrie looked at the thin, muscular man who sat across from him, at the wounded face and hard gray eyes, at the ridge of muscle down the bared chest, at the tattoo on the right forearm: Lone Star and the outline of the state. In the past they had talked with the intimacy of schoolboys, and now Iles was slipping away, becoming a stranger. The words they passed had been considered.

"You're going pretty far, aren't you, Jake?"

"Well, I don't know how you feel about the truth any more."

"Pour me another drink."

"Sam, you got niggers to pour your drinks. But since I'm in your kitchen drinking your whiskey, that makes me your nigger, don't it?"

"I wish I knew what's the matter with you."

"Fire me," said Iles.

"I might."

"Go ahead."

"What for?" Guthrie said.

"It'd make it easier."

"What's wrong, Jake?"

"I ain't gonna ask you for nothing. You ain't the kind of guy a guy can ask. You used to be, but not no more."

"Ask me whatever you want. Is that what's bothering you? Ask me."

"No."

"You're drunk."

"I hope."

"You want more money?"

"Yeah."

"How much?"

"A million dollars."

Guthrie laughed. "What would you do with a million dollars?"

"I'd send all my kids to Texas University and my wife to Paris, France, and then I'd go so far out on the Gulf that there couldn't any sonofabitch find me. I'd never take out another charter. I'd never fish another drunk slob. I'd go out there and just sit until the water swallered me up."

"Jake," Guthrie said, "I'm a little pressed for cash."

"That's all right. Forget it. I didn't ask, anyhow."

"There's a lot of expenses. This business deal I'm in has left me short."

"Sure. I understand."

Iles stood up. He screwed the cap on the bourbon bottle and tucked the bottle under his arm.

"I'm gonna take this bottle with me and drink it," said Iles. "Then I think I'll go down to the Sporting Life and beat the hell out of Captain Sidney R. Burney, who is a old friend of mine."

"How much more money do you want?"

"Name it."

"I ought to throw you out of here."

"You ought to."

"I don't even know what I pay you."

"I figured."

"How about five hundred a year more?"

"Sam, I didn't come in here begging."

"Six hundred then."

"You need me. God knows what would happen around here without me."

"Six hundred, Jake."

"You lose more than that out of your pockets when you change pants."

"A thousand."

"I'll write a letter to your office tomorrow and remind 'em."

"You ought to be fired."

"Sam, you're a good man but you try like hell not to be. I'm going down to the Sporting Life. You want to come with me? I promise we'll get good and drunk and have at least one fight and later we'll lie on the sand and wish we was dead."

"I can't go."

"Okay," Jacob Iles said. "But remember I asked."

He slammed the kitchen door. For the first time Guthrie noticed Roger and George Washington Simpson had returned to the room, and he remembered the two Negro women had been there. All of them had their backs to him. He started to speak. But instead he filled his glass with scotch again and went back into the long room above the dunes.

Jane Guthrie was dancing with Waddy, and the Senator with Beth. Guthrie's wife excused herself and came to him.

"Are you sick, Sam?" she said.

"I feel wonderful," he said. "Why should I be sick? Everthing's great."

He looked at Beth Morris in her tight dress with the red flowers on it, and then down at his wife, at the gray in her hair.

"Listen, Jane, let's dance," he said. "Teach me to do that cha cha thing."

"Is it all right, Waddy?" she said. "It's a rare opportunity for me to get to dance with my own husband."

"We're partners," said Waddy. "We share our assets. Somewhat."

After a few minutes Guthrie gave up trying to learn the cha cha. He couldn't concentrate, and the dance made him feel clumsy. Taking Jane's hand he led her to the glass wall. Below, floodlights shone on the waving dunes. They looked as unreal and artificial as a stage set.

"Jane," he said, "things are changing for us. Today I made the biggest deal I'll ever make in my life. Today, I got a chance to be really rich. Why don't I feel better about it?"

"Are you sure you're measuring it the right way?" she said.

"It's going to be a hell of a ride," Guthrie said. "Hang on to me. I've got to go."

"I love you, Sam," she said.

"Excuse me," said Senator Rose. He spoke quietly. "Sam, I hope you'll forgive my conduct on the boat. I'm afraid I'm an older fool than I sometimes realize. I know how you felt about losing that fish.

My words were hasty and ill-conceived. I thank you for being a gentleman."

"That's all right, Senator," Guthrie said.

The Senator looked at Guthrie as if waiting to hear something else.

"Thank you," the Senator said when he understood there would be nothing else. "Now one last dance with Jane before the old man puts himself to bed. Sam?"

"Go ahead," said Guthrie.

Jane Guthrie stood on her toes and kissed her husband, and he could see in her eyes that he had frightened her. He watched her walk onto the dance floor with the Senator, and then he turned to go and talk with Waddy.

Jacob Iles drove wildly down the twisting road through the dunes. He was listening to the radio, to a station in Corpus Christi, and he whistled and tapped his thumbs on the steering wheel in time to a song by Lefty Frizzell. He slowed as he passed the cutoff to the trailer camp. But he rejected the idea of telling Marge about the raise just yet; that would best be saved for morning, for a new day, for a breakfast unlike the last one they had gone through. Old Marge, he thought, the poor worn-out old shoe. Another thousand dollars would brighten her. It was a hell of a thing to let a thousand dollars make such a difference in somebody's life, but if old Marge felt like she had to have a thousand dollars why then Jacob Iles would go and get it for her. With honor, too, by God. He drank from the bottle. With pride. Guthrie hadn't known how scared Iles was, how ashamed, how close to murderous anger, how filled with dread. It was an important thing for Iles to save his pride, and for a while there he had thought Guthrie wasn't going to let him.

Iles turned onto an asphalt road and drove past a white frame hotel with its sign in the shape of a sail fish, then turned again at the fence and tower of the Coast Guard station, and rumbled down the wide dirt street into town. Neon lights glowed in the windows of the bars, and the plank sidewalks were crowded with tourists who had moved in with the good weather. There would be money for all, and in Port Agness you had to get it when you could. This week, the *Spoon* would be a cinch for charters even at its price of a hundred and fifty dollars a day. That would make Guthrie happy.

If the weather stayed fine, and they could keep the *Spoon* chartered most of the summer, that thousand dollars would be nothing. Guthrie, himself, preferred to fish in the spring or in the fall, when the fishing was the best although very few tourists knew it.

Iles parked the Ford station wagon in front of the Sporting Life and snapped off the headlights. There were cars parked all along that side of the square, where the bars were. Iles thought for a moment, and then took off his cap and dark glasses and left them on the car seat. Let them see his face; by now they all knew how it looked. The stories they had told would probably have it looking worse than it did. Let them see the truth.

With the bourbon bottle under his arm, Iles entered the bar. The noise of the juke box and the bowling and pin ball machines was shattering. He couldn't hear his sneakers on the wooden floor; it made him feel as if he were floating. In the light of the bar everybody looked purple. Iles walked softly, nodding to people, and they spoke to him, looking at him determined not to show curiosity about his face, as people look at a cripple. Iles sat down at a wooden table and ordered a bowl of ice and a pitcher of water. He waved at the owner, a little man named John, who was working behind the bar. John waved back but without enthusiasm, as though he wished Iles hadn't come. Iles laughed. He felt expansive, strong, satisfied with himself. Then standing at the bar he saw a short, squat figure with a pointed red beard and a black cap. Old Burney. Iles squinted at him as Burney turned to look at Iles. Iles searched for marks of combat on Burney's face. Surely there must be more than that one bruise Iles could see on Burney's left cheek and the puffed upper lip. Iles gave the waitress a dollar and told her to keep it. She patted his shoulder.

"Thanks, Jake," she said. "You have a big day?"

"A very big day, Dolly."

Iles poured himself a drink, aware that people were watching from the dark tables around him but that if he turned he would find not an eye on him. He stirred the bourbon and ice with his finger, licked his finger, tasted the drink, and smiled to himself. Then he stood up with the drink in his hand and walked to the bar. Burney looked at him solemnly out of small blue eyes. The men along the bar got quiet.

"What say, Burney," said Iles.

"What say, Jacob," Burney said.

"Can I buy you a drink?"

"Any time."

"John, give old Burney a drink," Iles said.

The owner popped open a can of beer and put it in front of Burney, who sprinkled salt into the triangular holes. Iles tossed John a dollar.

"Things are going good for me, Sidney," said Iles.

"Glad to hear it, Jacob."

"Things have never been better."

"That's nice."

"Never better than they are right this minute."

"That's a good deal, Jacob."

"You bet it is. Drink to it?"

"Sure," Burney said.

Iles raised his glass, and Burney raised his beer can, and they drank.

"How's Marge?" said Burney.

"She's okay."

"That's good. She's not sick or nothing?"

"Nope."

"That's good."

"Drink up, Sidney."

The small blue eyes regarded him doubtfully, then switched down to the beer can. Burney shrugged, lifted the can, and swallowed half the beer before he put down the can. Burney belched. His ears were small and pointed.

"I sure do like them tunes," Iles said.

"What?"

"Them tunes on the juke box. I sure do like 'em."

"I like 'em, too."

"Which one you like best, Sidney?"

"I don't know. Maybe 'Rose of San Antone.'"

"Me too. I like that one," said Iles.

"Me too."

"Let's play it some," Iles said.

"Okay. Want to match for the quarter?"

"Naw. Tonight I'm buying. Things are going good."

Iles called the waitress and gave her a quarter.

"Play 'Rose of San Antone' three times for me and Burney," said Iles.

"That's good," Burney said.

"Sidney, you and me been friends for a long time, ain't we?"

The small blue eyes looked at Iles from beneath the black cap, and a thick right hand went up to the red beard. Iles watched the short, heavy fingers touching the beard.

"Yeah," said Burney.

Iles noticed that the men around them had moved back, leaving a cleared space at the bar.

"Where you guys going?" Iles said. "I'm standing for a beer."

Nobody moved.

"The hell with them," said Iles. "John, give Sidney another beer."

"No more Falstaff in cans," the owner said.

"Bottle's okay," said Burney.

John slid a bottle of beer across the bar to Burney. The music had begun to play:

Deep within my heart
lies a melody
a song of ole San Antone

"Damn, that's pretty," Iles said.

"Sure is," said Burney.

"Know what happened to me today?"

"Nope."

Iles drank off the rest of his glass of bourbon and water and pushed the glass toward John.

"Ice," said Iles.

The small blue eyes were studying the beer bottle.

"Today I run across the biggest blue marlin that's been seen off this island in I don't know how long," Iles said. "It would of went four hundred pounds easy. We got it to the boat, but it wasn't hooked good and Mr. Guthrie lost it."

"Well," said Burney.

"What do you think about that?" Iles said.

"That's good."

"Damn right it's good. Know what that makes you, Sidney?"

"Ain't sure," said Burney.

"A motherfucker," Iles said.

Part Two

AN ARMY OF FROGS

They could see their faces in the black window above the kitchen sink: four blurred faces at various altitudes, like the dics of a mobile. To the host, Harry Danielsen, the tallest of the four, the faces looked foolish, drunkenly crooked, and the fact that the men had their arms around each other made him think of serenading on a sorority house porch. To Jason Hopps the faces blended in fuzzy camaraderie; he tried to think of them as four good old boys singing the good old songs, lifted into innocence as if singing "That Old Gang of Mine" rescued them from their terrible secrets, their silent despairs, their shameful compromises. To Walter Anderson each face he saw anywhere was primarily a voter, and the ones that looked back at him from the window he felt were friends and would vote correctly. To William Sheridan there was only one face worth looking at: his own. Sheridan picked the chords on his guitar, sang tenor, and watched each tilt of his head, each snip of light from his thick black hair that had scratches of gray where it swept from his temples to curl up in what would have been ringlets if he weren't careful about his barbering.

Behind them, although the party had begun less than an hour ago, there was a rabble of voices. Every few minutes the doorbell chimed and Harry's wife, Doris, opened to people who arrived by twos and fours. Most guests carried brown paper sacks which contained bottles of scotch, bourbon, or vodka. It was the procedure in their group for guests to bring their own liquor to parties. Occasionally someone brought a case of beer. The refrigerator was full of beer, the sink was piled with beer and sacks of crushed ice, and now they were stacking the beer on the back porch.

As yet nothing had been broken. There had been no fights, no disappearances involving almost certain adultery, no separations or potential divorces. No cigarette scars had been burned into the floors, rugs, tables, chairs, drainboard, or mantel. No drinks had been overturned. Nobody had vomited into the bathtub or onto the sidewalk or in the back yard. Most of the conversation was still reasonably safe. As yet the evening had been dull. Nobody was singing except Harry and Jason, who had been drinking all afternoon to get into the proper mood for Ben Carpenter's thirtieth birthday party, and Walter Anderson and William Sheridan, who had arrived together.

Gee I get a lonesum feelin
When I hear those church bells chime
Those weddin bells are
Brrreakin up
That ole gang uv miiiiine.

When they got through they grinned at each other and William Sheridan whanged a couple more chords on his guitar. Harry scooped his hand into the sack in the sink and began refilling his glass with ice.

"That was pretty damn good," said Jason.

"It was a little flat," Sheridan said.

"Sounded good to me," said Walter Anderson.

"It was okay," Harry said.

Sheridan bent his head toward the guitar. Harry watched Sheridan's short, brown, manicured fingers tracing imaginary chords. Harry had met William Sheridan only that night, when Sheridan came through the front door with Walter and Chub Anderson, but Harry found that he would very much like to hit him. Sheridan looked up. His face was tanned to a caramel color. He wore heavy black horn-rimmed glasses with shiny lenses. His suit had padded shoulders, and his shirt collar flared into a wide roll as if he wished he could get away with wearing a billow of lace at the neck, like Jean Lafitte. He had a big chin with a dimple in it, and very small feet.

"What business are you in?" said Harry.

"Me?" Sheridan said.

"I've known Jason and Walter for twenty years."

"Oh. Yeah, I suppose you wouldn't be asking them. I'm in public relations."

"Here?" asked Harry.

"In Austin."

"Who do you work for?"

"I have several clients," Sheridan said.

"I see," said Harry. "You're a lobbyist."

"In a manner of speaking," Sheridan said, smiling.

"Are you ashamed of it?"

"No. Of course not."

"Then why don't you say what you are?"

"Public relations is a broad term," said Sheridan. "Lobbyist fits in. I do a lot of things."

"I wonder where's Ben," Walter Anderson said, interrupting.

"He'll be along," said Harry.

"Ben wouldn't miss a party that was given for him," Jason said. "Ben wouldn't miss *any* party."

"That's a tough spot Ben's in," said Walter Anderson. "Way I hear it, he might lose his job if Guthrie wins that proxy fight. Ben should have tried to work something out."

"Ben doesn't see it that way," Harry said. "He's doing what he thinks is right."

"I don't know much about it anyhow," said Walter. "Just what I read in the papers."

"Let's sing," Jason said.

When his wife left him, Jason Hopps thought he might kill himself. Willy moved out suddenly with the two children and left a letter Jason found when he came home from the Oui Oui Club at dusk:

Mr. Rat:

I am deeply ashamed that my two little girls have you for a father and I am going to try to get the court to keep you from ever seeing them again and causing me any more pain and heartaches forever.

("The court?" Jason said to himself as he was reading, and then he understood and he began walking back and forth on the living-room carpet.)

The letter continued:

You are a weak, unfit person. I feel sorry for you, but I can't live with you any longer. I'm tired of fighting with you and of my two daughters hearing you curse when you come home drunk at two o'clock in the morning and fall down trying to get your shoes off. I used to love you, Jason. You could really have been somebody important. When you were in the construction business for yourself I was so proud of you I would want to show everybody what you had built. But when you lost your courage I lost my respect for you.

("That's not fair," Jason said. "Twenty-seven days of rain wiped me out. Was that my fault?")

The letter said:

When you started drinking and staying out late and going around with other women—oh, yes, you thought you fooled me but I am smarter than you think I am, Jason—it broke my heart to see what you had become. Most people think you're clever and witty. I guess you like that. But I know what you really are, Jason, you're a scum of the very earth. If you were only scared and weak I would stick with you and try to take care of you and make you into something. But you're a bad person. It's not right that you can run around with other women night after night and make me pay for it. Last night after you came home I went out and looked in your car and found a pair of panties in the glove compartment and an earring on the floor. I think I know to who they belong. That's the last straw that broke my back. I still have my looks and I'm still young and I can find a man who is better than you who loves me. I'm going to my mother's house. I hate you. Don't ever try to see me or the little girls again. It will be hard on them not to have their daddy but having you is worse than having no daddy at all. If you try to see me or them again I will shoot you. Love, Willy.

"Gumbuckets," Jason said. "She's mad at me, all right."

He dropped the letter on the breakfast counter. Using the pink wall phone that Willy had insisted on having in the kitchen, Jason dialed a number.

"Hello," said Chub Anderson.

"Hi," Jason said. "Walter there?"

"He's watching television. Talk to me, hon."

"Can he hear you?"

"I don't think so."

"Is there a *chance* he can hear you?"

"Yes."

"Laugh like I said something funny," Jason said. He listened to her giggle. That giggle, very young and mirthful and accompanied by a wrinkling of the nose, had been her leitmotif at the University of Texas. "Now I'll really say something funny. Willy left me. You forgot some of your stuff in the car last night."

"I know I did."

"Was that a click?" said Jason. "Did somebody pick up the extension?"

"Of course not. Don't be so jumpy."

"I can't help being jumpy. Willy found that stuff. I don't think she knows it's yours. She says she knows who it belongs to, but she's bluffing. What a fool I am. What a low life. She's taken my little girls away from me. What'll I do?"

"I don't know," Chub said, as if he had asked what movies were playing on Seventh Street.

"Let me talk to Walter."

"What for?"

"I have to have a reason for calling, don't I? You going to tell him I called just to talk to you?"

"I'm not going to tell him anything. I hope you're not."

"All I'm going to tell him is I've been making it with his wife."

"Don't be crude."

"You know I'm not going to tell him."

"It would be mean. We wouldn't want to hurt him."

"Damn it, he might hear you. Put him on."

After a moment he heard Walter's voice: low, pleasant, amiable even though Jason knew he had got Walter up from a Western program. Walter was very fond of eating ice cream and watching Westerns on television.

"Lo, Jason."

"Hey, stud. Did the guy from the church come see you again today?"

"Brother Chunk? Sure did."

"What did he say?"

"Said if I don't get on his team I'm through going to the legislature. Said all the Drys would solid vote against me. From the letters I've been getting, I think everbody in Fort Worth is a hardshell Baptist."

"Anything I can do to help?" Jason said.

"Not right now. Thanks, though. Rand from the convention bureau called me. He kind of hedged around like he wouldn't want to really say anything but he let me know the big shots are saying anybody who tries to dry up the town is finished. Any politician, I mean. We've been losing a lot of conventions, Rand says, on account of the Liquor Control Board raids on the private clubs and our funny drinking laws anyhow. Then Morrison from the bank called me. He sort of let me know if I go with the Drys I can forget about that loan."

"That's tough."

"I've got to have that loan, Jason. I'm putting in two more hamburger joints. The one I got is going great, but I can't make it pay unless I got volume. With three joints I make money. With one, I have to go bust sooner or later."

"I can tell you this, Walter. If you come out for the Drys all the boys at the Oui Oui Club won't like you a bit. Not a bit."

"I told Brother Chunk I was still rassling with the problem. He said if I don't come out for prohibition inside of a week, ever preacher in town will get in the pulpit and tell their flocks I'm a no good antichrist. That's a guy who's against Jesus, isn't it?"

"Sort of."

"That's what I thought. Wow. I wouldn't want to have it come out that I'm against Jesus. Politically speaking, Jason, that wouldn't be very good."

"You could make a speech and say you're not against Jesus, you just don't agree with Brother Chunk."

"But Brother Chunk is a Jesus expert. Everbody knows Brother Chunk is for Jesus. People believe Brother Chunk. I think a couple of the legislators have given up and gone over already."

"Looks like I can quit worrying about the estimate on building that new brewery."

"Looks like it."

"I wouldn't worry too much," Jason said. "The Drys are organized and they do a good job of hollering about the evils of drink, but inside those curtains I think people will vote Wet."

"I wish I thought so. This is the most uncomfortable fence I ever straddled."

"Say, Walter, you still practice law?"

"Some. When I got time."

"I didn't tell Chub, but Willy has left me. I think she's going to court this time."

"Sorry to hear it. I really am. Maybe she'll cool off again."

"I doubt it."

"That sort of thing is out of my line, Jason. I haven't done any of that in years. Byron Williams would be a good man for you, if Willy hasn't already got him."

"I'll call him," Jason said. "Listen, Walter, don't talk it around, huh? I don't want it to get out about me and Willy unless it's absolutely definite. You know what I mean?"

"Yeah. Okay. I really am sorry."

"All right. See you at Ben's party."

"That's Friday night? I'll be there. Won't be any drinking, I hope."

"How could you think such a thing?"

Jason hung up and stared at the kitchen wallpaper. At least Walter didn't know. Jason made himself a cheese sandwich, washed the mayonnaise off the knife, poured a glass of cold milk, and then went out and sat in the patio to eat. The irony of it, he thought, was that this was the earliest he had been home in a week; it was only just now proper suppertime. He looked at the flower garden Willy had labored over. The flowers grew high against the stockade fence. Jason didn't know the names of any of the flowers, although he had helped Willy pull weeds a few times. He could hear crickets from somewhere, and kids yelling over in the next yard, and as it got darker mosquitoes began to bother him. The grass was smooth and thick and neatly clipped around the edges of the flower beds and the flagstone patio. At the rear, through a gap in the hedge, he saw a neighbor appear in the alley and then heard the clang of a garbage can lid. Jason got up and went inside.

He wandered through the house looking at things that had gathered in ten years of marriage: the furniture they had bought on installments, several paintings by Harry Danielsen and some prints from Paris that Jason and Willy had picked up when they were on leave from Germany during Jason's Army duty, an ash tray from the Stork Club, a towel from the Mark Hopkins Hotel, the machete with which he had cut off the head of a copperhead snake at Possum Kingdom Lake, tennis rackets, water skis. Framed on the wall in the den was a color photograph of Jason and Willy standing outside the bullring in Mexico City, both wearing dark glasses, looking gay and sophisticated with the bright posters in the background. It was a honeymoon photograph. Willy was heavier then, and Jason was thinner. Jason examined the things with a vague envy, as if they were relics from the lives of two other people. Then he stuck an anti-acid tablet in his mouth, got his .32-caliber pistol out of a bureau drawer, and put on his coat. He felt used up, like a clown whose shabby tricks no longer amused, who performed to silence. He could sing harmony, imitate half a dozen movie stars, handle a big bass on a light spinning rod, shoot eighty at golf, do a soft shoe, estimate with great accuracy how much it would cost to build a thirty-five story building or a shopping center that covered forty acres (numbers on a pad, he thought: so much for steel, so much for glass, so much for labor, so much for plumbing and wiring, nothing for the wounds of the heart). He felt incapable of ever exposing himself again. And the house was empty.

Jason drove automatically. He went through the stone gates and down the hill past the softball diamonds into Forest Park, whose secret roads he had known since he was fourteen, the park whose trees and shrubbery had hidden the deflowering of so many high school girls that Jason's mind swamped at the thought. He went through patches of canary light from high lamps, beside the dark narrow fork of the Trinity River, past the field where Sunday people flew model airplanes on wires. At the bridge over the river, Jason turned left onto the wide boulevard of University Drive and went up the hill between the dark bluffs where big houses stood as monuments to dearer times. The zoo with its fearful noises and night odors was down below on one side, the golf course of Colonial Country Club down below on the other. He came to Texas Christian University, its yellow brick buildings as comfortably plain and ugly as old shoeboxes, and he drove beyond the university and into a parking space in front of the Oui Oui Club. The Oui Oui Club had a curling red neon sign against a plate-glass window covered by drapes. Jason walked unsteadily because he hadn't slept much the night before, and the tension of the events since he had found Willy's letter was pulling at his eyelids. The pistol hung like a rock in his coat pocket.

The inside of the Oui Oui Club was so familiar that Jason no longer saw it. A few years ago he could have described the rows of beer steins on shelves behind the bar, flanking the mirror, and the beer spigots, and the padded stools, and the cream-colored plaster walls upon which a university student had painted murals of his ideas of Paris streets (a sidewalk cafe with the Eiffel Tower in the background, another sidewalk cafe with the Arc d'Triomphe in the background, a third sidewalk cafe with Sacre Coeur in the background; why, Jason had wondered, hadn't the artist painted Notre Dame and the Louvre with sidewalk cafes in front of them?). But now Jason had been in the Oui Oui Club so often that he had forgot almost every facet of its interior. The noise of the bowling machine came from the rear—a hard chink of bells. Jason sat on a stool in front of the Budweiser spigot, where he could see himself in the mirror, and tapped on the spigot when Harvey, the bartender, approached.

"How's stuff, Jason?" said Harvey, a soft pink man with the smooth complexion of a doctor.

"Nothing new," Jason said.

"Your wife called in here last night. I didn't know what to tell her."

"Doesn't matter," said Jason.

"I told her I'd just come on and that you might have been around and I'd try to remember to get you to call her. Hope that was all right. I'm not very good at lying to women. They see straight through me."

"It doesn't make any difference what you told her," Jason said.

"I've been having lots of trouble with my wife," said Harvey. "She nags hell out of me about being a better man. She wants me to make more money. I get to thanking in another minute I'll either run off to Tokyo, Japan, or make her turn blue. Then she gets so nice and sweet for a couple of days I wouldn't trade places with the Sheik of Arabia."

"That's women."

"I figure she must love me a lot, bad as she hates me."

Harvey scraped the foam off the beer with a tongue depressor.

"I wisht you'd do some of your imitations," Harvey said. "I like the one of Walter Huston singing 'September Song.' That nearly makes me cry. You should of been on the stage, Jason. You got natural talent."

"The catt-le," said Jason. "The catt-le are dyin like flyshe."

"I got it. That was Walter Brennan. Great. Do some more."

"Not tonight."

"You ain't done any in here for a long time. You ain't been in here so much lately."

"I was here this afternoon."

"I didn't come on till six."

"I've been going back to the office and working late."

"I get it," said Harvey, winking.

"Anybody been in?"

"A few guys. Flutebinder and St. Clair and Norman Green are playing the bowling machine. New doll in here I ain't seen before. Setting back there against the wall."

As he turned Jason found himself hoping it would be Willy. But it was a plump blonde woman with a heavy bosom and hair drawn back into a bun so tight that it stretched the skin of her face. She rapped on a glass of orange juice with a swizzle stick as if she were playing drums. A bottle in a sack lay on the table.

"She's drinking screwdrivers," Harvey whispered. "While ago she played both of our Guy Lombardo records three times each. I said give us some Louie and Keely, honey, and she looked at me like I was a nigger. She's an odd one. I don't know if she's waiting for somebody or what. She won't talk to nobody. St. Clair tried to talk to her and she wouldn't even look at him."

"Buncha burglars!" yelled a voice from the bowling machine.

"They've took Green for about fifty bucks," Harvey said.

"He ought to know better," Jason said, and he was glad when Harvey went away to serve another customer.

Jason lit a menthol cigarette and stared at the bubbles in the beer glass. How many nights had he spent exactly like this? How many of these lonely, wasted nights when he couldn't have explained reasonably why he was here and not at home with Willy. Could it be the possibility of adventures that hardly ever happened? Or maybe Willy was right. Maybe he was a scum of the very earth. It used to be better, he remembered. It used to be that it would be Ben, Harry, and Jason, and sometimes Walter Anderson and a few other people. Occasionally they had girls with them, but mostly it was just Jason and his friends sprawled in somebody's car at a drive-in, or drinking beer at a place like the Oui Oui Club. They gambled on the bowling machine or the pinball machine. They sang songs and made big plans. Then later they'd have cheeseburgers and coffee at an all-night cafe, and there would be talks. Ben would get into some kind of serious subject, as Ben always eventually did, and his long face would get very earnest and excited, and he would argue with Harry, red-faced Harry with blond hair that looked as if it had never been combed, and Jason would sink peacefully into the leatherette cushion of the booth and smoke and listen with pleasure to his friends. When they went away to college in Austin, the three of them shared an apartment at the bottom of a hill between a Jewish sorority house and a co-operative dormitory where Jason thought anarchists lived. Across the street was the stone wall of the gardens of Scottish Rite Dormitory, for girls, and Jason recalled how he could sit in the living room of their apartment and look out beyond the wall at crows circling above the trees and know that his friends were close and feel peaceful. In those days Jason had begun going out with Willy, and Ben was seeing Jean, and Harry was dating one girl or another, and everything was fun.

Jason wondered if Ben would share an apartment with him again. He wondered how it would work out. Now that Jean had filed for divorce, and Willy had threatened to do the same, perhaps they could recapture the fun of a decade past. Moving among the same people, except for their Army service, Jason and Ben had each had a wife and two children, but Jason couldn't think of himself as older or different than he had been at nineteen or twenty or twenty-one. Jason did some mental arithmetic. It had been nine years since Ben quit law school to go into the Army. Jason, Ben, and Harry had shared that apartment for three years, until Jason got married. Jason remembered the apartment with more affection than any other home he had ever known.

By God, those had been fine times. Willy used to tell him that he didn't remember them right, that the years had warped his memory, and that he was nostalgic for something that never quite was. But he remembered. He remembered it was only ten feet across from their bedroom windows to the windows of a large sleeping room in the Jewish sorority, and he remembered the wonderful sweet naked girls he had seen. He remembered the night Harry drank a fifth of Jack Daniel's at a party, took a swing at a football player, broke his hand against the cupboard, went to the hospital to have it set and cast, and returned to drink again before the party ended. He remembered their trips to Laredo, and the big football weekends when they would all go to the game to boo Walter Anderson, and the first time he laid Willy on a blanket at a picnic at Barton Springs. He remembered Ben opening a thousand-page government textbook that Ben had never before glanced at. It was two days before the final exam. Ben read the book for thirty consecutive hours, played eighteen holes of golf, and then made an A on the exam. He could still see Ben sitting at the table bent over the book with the light from the gooseneck lamp on Ben's face—a thin face with gaunt cheeks and a straight nose and shaggy pale brown hair—and Ben's shirt hung on the back of the chair, and his wide thin shoulders hunched, and cigarette smoke floating up through the lamplight. That same night, he remembered, Jason had intended to study for a marketing exam but went instead to listen to Dixieland music and came back at six in the morning and found Ben in exactly the same position as if he hadn't moved at all. Cigarette butts had overflowed the ash tray and fallen onto the table; smoke rose from several that smoldered. Jean came in and fixed breakfast. Jean was never very much on cooking, but she could scramble eggs and use a toaster. She was a tall girl and had the reputation of being able to outdrink any man on the campus. Everybody had a good time.

The trouble was, Jason thought, things were always happening that you couldn't do anything about. The Korean War and the draft ruined the life they'd had in the apartment. Jason got scared he was going to be killed, and he rushed out to marry Willy. By the time the three friends returned from the Army they were all married, and things had changed between them just enough for Jason to detect the subtle difference. It was more than a subtle difference with Harry. He was a lot different. He was quieter. He had grown a blond beard while he lived in New York and he came back with a ballet dancer wife and some peculiar ideas. Ben came back married to Jean and started concentrating on law school and finished at the head of his class. Jason went into the construction business and ran into something else he couldn't do anything about: twenty-seven days of rain.

"I don't see why Green bowls with them guys," Harvey said. "They eat him up like pork chops."

"I don't know," said Jason.

"Seen Ben Carpenter lately?"

"Yeah. Some."

"I been reading about him in the papers. About how Ben keeps filing suits and stuff to try to keep that guy Guthrie from taking over that big electronics company in Dallas? I don't understand it all," Harvey said.

"Neither do I."

"But I know one thing. If you're gonna screw with guys like Guthrie you better have a hard pecker. That's big league."

"Ben's working at it."

"Ben's a funny guy," said Harvey. "I seen him come in here and set for hours without speaking to a soul. He'd look like he lost his last friend. Other nights he'll come in here and be the rowdiest sonabitch in town. I guess he's got a lot pressing on him with his old man getting into that trouble and with Ben breaking up with his wife. His wife still in town?"

"She went back to Houston."

"She live there?"

"Her folks live there."

"She's supposed to be rich, ain't she?"

"Her folks have a lot of money. Her daddy owns about nine thousand shoe stores, or something like that."

"Well, it's not so bad then," Harvey said. "What's behind them breaking up? She catch Ben with his head on the wrong pillow? That'd be my guess."

"I don't know."

"Say, remember when you and Ben and Harry Danielsen used to keep them pennies in the beer steins? What was it? You'd each put in one penny for each beer you drank, and then you was gonna take out the pennies at the end of the year and throw a party, wasn't that it?"

"Yeah. That was a long time ago."

"I remember you got about eight hunderd and thirty-six pennies in them steins in a month and then you decided you really didn't want to know how many beers you was drinking and you quit. I think the girl that used to work in here took the money."

"We let her have it," said Jason.

"How come you ain't with Ben much any more?"

"We've both been busy. We don't seem to be free at the same times."

"Harry, he's about quit hanging around these places, ain't he?"

"Looks like it."

"He's better off, if you don't mind me saying so," Harvey said. "Damn, that blonde wants some more orange juice. She's gonna have the sorriest case of indigestion anybody ever had."

The truth was, Jason thought, Ben had dropped him because he wouldn't stop meeting Chub Anderson. "Jason," Ben had said, "I just don't believe in screwing the wife of a friend. If there are degrees to adultery, yours is the worst kind. Evertime you mount that girl, you're helping to kill something. You're doing something that can't ever be undone. I think it's wrong." About then, Ben had started having serious trouble with Jean. Fights in public, a lot of bitterness. Ben never told him what it was all about.

There was one thing Jason was sure of. Chub Anderson wasn't worth what she was costing him. He would get so stricken with remorse that he could hardly look at himself when he was shaving. He would stand under hot water in the shower until the steam made the towels sodden and melted the toilet paper and covered the mirror. But he kept getting further involved and more careless, and now Willy and the kids were gone. He'd lose his house and at least one of his cars, and a big piece of his salary would go to child support. He'd miss his little girls, and he felt very sentimental about old Willy even if she did sometimes have a hard tongue. And there was always the chance Walter Anderson would find out and get a gun and come and murder him. You never knew how a man might react. Yet, Jason thought, Chub might be in love with him; he didn't want to hurt her, either.

Maybe the only sensible thing to do was to kill himself. He was tired anyhow and had a headache. Willy was gone, the little girls were gone, Ben wasn't close to him any more, he had difficulty talking to Harry, he was bored with estimating buildings, and Chub couldn't get out of the house until tomorrow afternoon. By then, Jason might not be around. They could read about him in the papers. It would give them something to talk about. Willy would do plenty of crying, probably, and Chub would feel awful about it. But his poor daughters. The other children would kid them.

The damn thing, Jason told himself, was that he either had to kill himself right now, as soon as the Oui Oui Club closed, or else he had to straighten up and quit seeing Chub and quit drinking and staying out late and messing around. If he could prove to Willy that he wasn't a scum of the very earth, maybe she would come back to him. Willy, Willy, the horrible things he'd done. There was the night he was supposed to take her to a big society dance, and she got dressed up and put on her mink stole, and Jason never did get home to pick her up. He got drunk that afternoon in the Oui Oui Club and when he went home at four in the morning with blood on his overcoat Willy was asleep in a chair in the living room. She looked good. Her hair was in some kind of a French cut, and she wore a red evening dress. He woke her and told her he loved her. She hit him with a china figurine, and then she hit him with an ash tray, and then she called him a name he'd never heard her use before, and then she hit him with a Book-of-the-Month Club novel about the French Revolution, and when he finally went to sleep on the couch he could hear her crying in their bedroom. He was crying too. Willy, Willy, such horrible things.

Chub was a hungrily tender girl to make love to, and she had good flesh. Jason was sorry she was dissatisfied with her own husband. Willy was the kind of woman that you could feel her ribs, uncomfortable to caress, but she was an old horse that had pulled with him for a long time. The idea of being without her gave him a view of his own loneliness that was quickly flooded with sentimentality. He remembered the way old Willy used to wake him up at night and tell him he was strangling. He remembered his daughters in their white dresses at Easter, as fragile and lovely as butterflies.

"What say, Jason," said Walter Flutebinder.

"Nothing much. How bout you?"

"Terrible," the butcher said, wiping his hands on the thighs of his white trousers as if he'd just finished cutting a roast. "I got a sinus infection. You know? Ever had sinus? And I get pains in my heart. I don't think my anal canal is in very good shape, either, but the sinus, phoo! It's terrible."

"I don't have sinus at the moment," said Jason.

"Sinus is the worst thing that can happen to a man," Flutebinder said. "You don't know what trouble is if you never had sinus. Yarf! Those terrible pains behind the eyes! Your face swells up, Jason, I mean it. Your teeth hurt. Your head is full of marbles. You hear these little creekling crackling noises inside your face. Wuh! I gag ever morning and think I'm gonna die."

"His nose drips on the meat," said Norman Green.

"Shut up," Flutebinder said. He blew his nose and looked into his handkerchief. "Aw oh. Blood."

"I've got sinus," said Norman Green. "I've got hay fever, asthma, a bad heart, and scars on my lungs. I've got cavities, neuritis, neuralgia, pink eye, dandruff, bronchitis, sick glands, and bad luck. I'm down on my ass. But you don't hear me complaining."

"Give it a rest," St. Clair said. "Let's bowl."

Jason looked at the three men who had come to the bar to get their beer glasses refilled. Flutebinder was fat, Green was dark and Syrian-looking, St. Clair was tall and lean in a tight suit and Tyrolean hat. To sit and talk to men like these, Jason had spent a great many evenings away from Willy.

"Your bunch going to get that new brewery?" asked St. Clair.

"We're trying," Jason said. "Looks like it might not ever be built."

"It'll be built," said St. Clair. "The city fathers want it. Our town is collapsing, old man, going to sleep. We're an old dog lying in the sunshine. We need new business. I landed the brewery today as one of my accounts. They plan quite a lot of advertising."

"Nice going," Jason said.

"I must say my personal business is doing very well," said St. Clair. "I'm the only executive at Ludlow & Mumm that doesn't have ulcers. There's not another one of them who could stand in here and drink beer all night the way I do. Their stomachs are floating in acid."

"Gar! Mine too," Flutebinder said.

"Seriously, Jason, do you know why I don't have ulcers? It's because I don't care about anything," said St. Clair. "A client can take my brilliant campaigns and scrap them for idiocies his son-in-law thought up, and it doesn't bother me. Why should I worry if they ruin the good things I try to do? People are unjust, ignorant, dishonest, and mean. I recognize that, and I laugh about it. I don't expect them to be different. I don't fight it. I don't care."

"He's lying," Green said. "He cares but there's not anybody who cares whether he cares or not."

"I don't believe I could live without caring," said Jason.

"You know what I say to life?" Green said.

"Who cares?" said St. Clair.

"I care," Green said. "I care plenty about everything. But I say life, up yours, boy."

"There's a lady here," said Harvey.

"I say life, you do it to me. You beat the hell out of me. And boy when you're through you take a long running start and jump up my ass. You can't whip me."

"Let's go back and bowl," Flutebinder said. "It makes my head hurt to listen."

As Jason watched them walk toward the rear, he saw the woman again. She reminded him of a blonde, warm, motherly, sensuous, fleshy milkmaid in a Swedish travel poster. There were dark pockets beneath her eyes, but her skin was smooth and clear as vanilla pudding. She smiled at him, very slightly. He smiled at her and then turned to face the unseen shelves of beer steins.

He wondered what Willy was doing at that moment. Most likely watching television with her father and mother and the little girls. Maybe, though, she was getting dressed to go out. Maybe she'd already found that other man she mentioned in the letter. Maybe she'd found him before she wrote the letter. How did he know what Willy had been doing? She could have lied to him about her bridge games, as Chub had lied to Walter. Movies with a girl friend last week? Shopping all Saturday afternoon? Junior League meetings? A lecture at the Woman's Club? She'd come home from that lecture with liquor on her breath, he thought, although it was hard to tell because he'd had liquor on his breath. One thing Chub had taught him was that you couldn't trust a woman. Maybe this other man already existed. But how could he know? The idea made him nauseous. Willy wasn't the best, and she didn't smell sweet all over as Chub did, but she had been his and he didn't want to share her. He didn't want her saying things into the ear of another man, or being naked with him, or finding out that somebody else could do that physical thing besides Jason and probably better. What flaws in himself that would expose to a woman who'd never known anybody else. Willy, Willy, he thought, you know me with my skin torn off and my sins laid out. Nobody can ever know me as well as you.

Jason got up and went to the telephone in the back, by the men's room. As he walked past the blonde woman's table, she nodded to him. A bob of the yellow hair. Jason went past the bowling machine where St. Clair leaned over the board with his hand on the puck and the other two men watched the lights. Jason put a dime into the phone and dialed Willy's parents.

"Hello," said Willy's mother.

"Hello, Mrs. Poulsen. May I speak to Wilhelmina, please?"

"This is Jason, isn't it?"

"Yes."

"No."

"This is very important, Mrs. Poulsen."

"She's not here."

"Where is she?" Jason said, sinking.

"She *told* me to tell you she isn't here, Jason. That's all she told me to tell you. She doesn't want to talk to you."

"But I want to talk to her."

"I don't know why you kids can't work it out between you," said Mrs. Poulsen. "All I want is for you both to have good lives, Jason. Good clean lives. All I want is for you to be happy. Think of your little daughters, Jason. They need their father. I want all of you to be happy."

"Yes ma'am. So do I. Now can I talk to Willy?"

"No," Mrs. Poulsen said, and hung up.

Jason listened to the heavy silence for a moment and then put the receiver on the hook. Behind him was the door to the men's room. He pushed it open and went in. As he stood there he remembered the dozens of nights he'd had to brace his hands against the wall to support himself. The dozens of nights he'd tried to see himself in the cracked mirror and had hardly recognized the face. He read the signs scratched on the wall. One said: *for a good deal call Gertrude*. Another said: *I am a Nazi don't mess with me*. Another said: *Max is a dirty neo-classicist*. The door opened, and Flutebinder came in.

"My head hurts so bad it keeps me awake," said Flutebinder. "My eyes get puffed up, and all the time creekle crackle inside my face it goes. Creekle crackle. Shifting around. Hanging in my throat and making me sick to my stomach." He blew his nose. "Aargh. That's horrible looking."

"How much you got Green down by?" Jason asked, stepping aside to let Flutebinder in position.

"About sixty-seventy. I don't know where he gets the money. Pore bastard oughta quit."

"Scuse me," said Jason.

Jason himself was the pore bastard that oughta quit, he thought. Shuffle off the mortal coil, and all like that. He was ruining everybody's life—Willy's, his daughters', his own. Perhaps kissing Jean at the Christmas party, when they kept at it too long, had even contributed to Ben's trouble. He was hurting Chub, and Walter Anderson. If he kept up his work he'd somehow hurt Harry and Doris. He'd bring rain down on the bank job and put his company out of business.

He squeezed past Flutebinder and returned to the main room. The juke box was playing a song that made him think of Willy:

"Be My Love," with poor dead Mario Lanza singing it. The song reminded him of Austin and he could see Willy as she was then—bright and clean, unhurt, dancing above the water on the terrace at the Lake Austin Inn, with a nice breeze coming in and the sound of motorboats, and no stretch scars on her belly and no pain in her eyes.

Jason started toward his seat at the bar. Here he went, a scum of the very earth, carrying agony with him like a Santa Claus bag of gifts he handed out to this one and that. The one fine brave thing he could do would be to erase himself, to cut out his scenes from their flickering lives; it would be a surgical operation to remove a spreading illness. A scum of the very . . .

The blonde woman stopped him with her voice.

"Don' yew git tahd of drankin beah all naht?" she said

He looked down at her large teeth and at the huge breasts which lay on the table beside the glass of vodka and orange juice.

"Yeah, sure," he said.

"Set dahn heah an tawk tuh me and hev some vodka."

"I . . ." said Jason.

"Yew lonely, ainch-yew, baby?"

"Yeah. Sort of."

"So'm ah. Anythang yew got tuh dew thet cain't wait?"

"Lord, You made us human," Jason said.

In the next two hours Jason did six imitations of movie stars. Everybody was laughing. Even Norman Green pulled out of his wretchedness to laugh at the conversation between Cary Grant and Gunga Din. Flutebinder pressed his hands beneath his eyes as he laughed, worried that his sinuses might blow up, while Jason, as Jimmy Stewart, invented the Winchester Model 73. A soft shoe and James Cagney singing "Yankee Doodle" got Harvey. Lionel Barrymore was St. Clair's favorite. The blonde woman sat and smiled over her giant bosom and eyed Jason voraciously.

When the Oui Oui Club closed, Jason and the blonde woman got into his car. She slid across the seat and kissed him with such passion that he was both intrigued and frightened.

"Ah hevent hed a man in a long tahm," she whispered. "Thuh nex man tuh git me will thank he hez holt of a tigah."

"We could go to my place," said Jason.

"Honey, hurra up. Ah could splode."

He started the engine as the blonde woman chewed on his ear. Willy, Jason said to himself, Willy I love you I think.

"Party's off to a flying start," Jason said. "There's people sneaking out to the back yard already."

"I'm worried about Ben," said Walter Anderson.

"He'll get here," Harry said. "He had to drive over from Dallas and go change clothes, and he probably stopped to eat."

"Anybody know that song called 'Roving'?" asked Sheridan, who sat on the kitchen table with his short legs crossed at the knees. His eyes peeped up over his black horn-rims, and his tanned forehead wrinkled. "I think I can play it."

"Nobody knows the words," Harry said.

"I know 'em," said Jason.

"Why don't you and Sheridan sing a duet, then?" Harry said.

"Let's get some girls in here to sing," said Walter Anderson.

"That always screws it up," Jason said. "Girls can't sing."

"Yma Sumac can sing," said Walter Anderson.

"Won't you ever forget Yma Sumac?" Jason said. "Is she the only person you saw in New York?"

"She can sure sing," said Walter. "Way up and way down. Boy, what a singer. I don't know any of her songs, though."

"We ought to put our singing on tape," Sheridan said. "You got a tape recorder, Harry?"

"No," said Harry.

"Sure you do," Jason said.

Sheridan swung his small, polished shoes and boosted himself off the table.

"Maybe I'd better leave," said Sheridan. "After all, I wasn't invited."

"I invited you," Walter said.

"We want you here," said Jason. "Tell him we want him here, Harry."

Harry shrugged.

"What's the matter with you, Harry?" Walter Anderson said. "Listen, Bill, you came as my guest. We want you to stay. Harry's just drunk."

"You're our only guitar player," said Jason.

"Well then let's sing," Sheridan said. "How bout 'Four Leaf Clover'?"

When Walter Anderson was the number two right halfback at the University of Texas, life was relatively simple. In the mornings he went to classes and stayed cheerfully awake and took a great many notes. In the afternoons during the autumn and for a period in the spring, he put on a white uniform and practiced football for two or three hours. On Saturdays during the autumn, there was a game. Friday nights the team went to a movie, and later Walter took sleeping pills because he was excited. Saturdays at noon Walter got his ankles taped and put on his game uniform—orange shirt at home, white on the road—and listened to the instructions and studied the circles and X's chalked on the blackboard and, under one coach, knelt to pray that God would help him to hit hard. He ran onto the field for the warmups and watched Chub Robinson, who was a cheerleader, jump up and down and show her underpants. Then he went back into the locker room for more instructions, and again studied the circles and X's and the crinkly line that showed what would be, if all went well, the path of the ball, and listened to the nervous voice of the coach reassuring them that what they were doing was important. Then Walter again ran onto the field, gathered with his comrades in a mobbing huddle, clapped his hands, went to the bench, and stood to watch the kick-off. Walter always got into the game. He played in thirty-two consecutive games, including two bowl games. As a senior he started four games when the number one right halfback had a dislocated shoulder. Walter hardly ever missed an assignment through having forgot what he was supposed to do. He was a good blocker, and he ran straight ahead with some power because he weighed two hundred and eight pounds and he liked to play. He was never fast enough to be a really good halfback, but he was an adequate one. He scored a touchdown in the Cotton Bowl. At some schools he would have been a starter.

After graduation, Walter Anderson entered law school. He flunked out, was drafted, married Chub Robinson, served twenty-one months as a halfback at Fort Sam Houston, was discharged as a sergeant, returned to law school on the GI Bill, and was graduated without any particular distinction. During his final year in law school, Walter campaigned for the state legislature and was elected because he was a halfback, a veteran, and a law student, and he had once had a very good day in the Oklahoma game. His opponent had no point upon which to attack him except a lack of imagination. And that, for Walter, was an asset. Walter charged straight ahead, as if politics were a dive play, and accused his opponent of being neither an athlete nor an Army veteran, but rather something of a smart ass who might even be a socialist if anybody could understand what he was talking about. Walter described himself as a moderate. He was not the tool of big business, although he certainly thought big business had its rights. He was not the lackey of labor, although he certainly thought the working men had their rights. He was for the depletion allowance and against a state income tax. He was for the American Way of Life and against all Foreign Menaces. Chub, who was cute enough to be pleasing but not quite so cute as to make women dislike her, spoke for him at teas and luncheons and midmorning coffee meetings. Walter was elected overwhelmingly, and thereafter he ran for office without serious opposition.

Walter never questioned that Chub loved him. As the years progressed she became more restless and only spasmodically affectionate. But he never did anything to make her not love him; he was a thorough moderate. During legislative sessions they rented a house in Austin and went to all the parties. When the legislature was not in session, they lived at home and Walter tended his various small business enterprises, the latest of which was a hamburger and malt shop. Chub's comings and goings became more and more erratic, and her attitude toward him varied between tender, tolerant, bored, and resentful. But Walter never confronted her for explanations because he never doubted her faithfulness. Walter's life was safe and secure. There was no possibility of a scandal.

The first true complication was the week before Ben Carpenter's birthday. It arrived in the form of a visit from Brother Orval Chunk, pastor of the John The Baptist Church and a very powerful man.

Walter admitted Brother Chunk to the living room and offered to prepare a pot of coffee.

"Isn't Mrs. Anderson at home?" said Brother Chunk.

"She's at a bridge lesson," Walter said. "Gosh, I'm sorry she's not here, Brother Chunk. She enjoys your company so much."

"She's a delightful woman," said Brother Chunk. "A delightful little woman."

"How about that coffee?"

"That would be fine, Walter, very fine, indeed," Brother Chunk said, rubbing his hands together. "But let me go to the kitchen with you while you make it, and we'll sit at the table back there for a good shirtsleeves talk. You never heard of Jesus acting formal."

Walter looked at Brother Chunk, who wore a stiff-collared white shirt, a white silk tie, and a double-breasted, very expensive Navy blue silk suit. Brother Chunk parted his hair in the middle above a glowing face. He had a white linen handkerchief in his breast pocket, and he produced it frequently to wipe his hands or his forehead. Walter was not a suspicious person, but the pinched look of Brother Chunk's white brows and the darting glitter of his blue eyes immediately made Walter wary. He had been in politics long enough to have learned that those who seemed the most innocent were often the most dangerous.

"Good of you to drop by to see me," said Walter. "You ought to do it more. That was a swell sermon you gave Sunday. Very interesting point about Jonah. I'd always taken that story as a sort of allegory."

Brother Chunk smiled as he watched Walter dip coffee out of the can with a plastic measuring spoon and dump it into the electric percolator.

"That's what the Commonists would have us believe," Brother Chunk said. "They come to us and pose as intellectuals, Walter. They talk about allegories and symbolism and patriarchal religions and matriarchal religions and the way the old Hebrews did things. Oh, I know their jargon, don't think I don't. Some of them even teach in our great universities. They write hundreds of books. Books full of the most malicious Commonist lies. But what they're trying to do is destroy America by undermining Christianity. There's no surer way than to make us doubt that the Bible is the literal Word of God. Start doubting that, Walter, and you wind up in confusion, asking all sorts of questions. In confusion, my boy. That's where the Commonists step in. Mind if I sit down?"

"No, no, please do," said Walter.

Brother Chunk took off his coat and hung it over the back of a chair. He was wearing white suspenders and gold cuff links. He sat down and smiled at Walter.

"Confusion, Walter, is what we want to avoid. Why, you cut a man loose to think his own thoughts, and the Devil's got him, boy. The old Devil just reaches right out and grabs him. An ordinary mortal human has no chance against the Devil. The only chance for an ordinary mortal human is to be washed in the Blood of the

Lamb, to read the Word and obey it. Trust and obey. Start trying to think for your ownself and you've got real troubles."

"I see what you mean," Walter said. He was not going to argue with Brother Chunk.

"I'm worried about this great land of ours," said Brother Chunk. "I think I can tell you that. You and I, Walter, we're both in a position of some responsibility. You're the guardian of the laws that guide us through our earthly lives, and I'm the guardian of our souls. A terrible responsibility, Walter, as you can understand. Eternity is a long time. Can you imagine what a long time eternity is? Why, it's *forever!*"

"That's a long time," Walter said.

"We're both being challenged in our duty, Walter. You and me. You with your temporal responsibility, and me with my responsibility for souls wandering through endless eternity. Our people are getting morally soft. I'm worried about us collapsing from within. Our fibers are weakening. That's what the Red heathens are doing to us, brother. With the help of the Devil, they're eating our inner lining. We can't depend on the Lord to appear in the clouds and save us. It's the duty of each citizen to save not only his own self but to save those around him who are in the grip of the Devil. Your duty, Walter, and mine, even more than most."

"Swell idea," said Walter.

Brother Chunk shrugged modestly.

"Any true servant of God would think the same way," he said.

"Sure thing," said Walter.

"Only an atheistic Commonist would think any other way."

"Sure."

"You agree?"

"With what?" Walter said, suddenly feeling he had been trapped.

"That only an atheistic Commonist in the sway of the Beast would want to destroy our great land by weakening its moral fiber and damning its souls."

"What are you getting at, Brother Chunk?"

"There's a big job you can do for the Lord, Walter, to help Him fight the atheistic Commonists."

"I'm always willing to work for the Lord, Brother Chunk," Walter said, without much enthusiasm.

"I knew you would be, brother. I knew it. I've been eager to tell you about this, my boy." Brother Chunk wiped his forehead with the handkerchief and looked at the coffee popping against the glass bubble on top of the percolator. He looked back at Walter. Brother Chunk smelled of perfume, Walter thought, or perhaps it was cologne on the handkerchief. "I've been most eager."

"What can I do?" said Walter.

"We're petitioning for a prohibition election to dry up this city. And then the county and the state. And then the whole country, as our movement gains power from responsible Christian citizens. The Lord wants you to lend us your voice to influence the vote, and to lend us your willing hands to work for us in the legislature. The Lord wants you on His side in this battle, Walter. It's our first positive step toward defeating Commonism. An America that doesn't drink is a healthy America. An America without the corruption of alcohol in its bloodstream is an America more alert, more able to stand and fight. An America with good strong kidneys and livers is an America that says no to Commonism. There," Brother Chunk said, leaning back and smiling, "is our plan."

"The country has tried prohibition before," said Walter, wishing Chub would come home.

"I know what you're thinking, my boy. You're thinking about the evil that prohibition is supposed to have caused. That's Commonist propaganda, Walter. Prohibition was working. The Commonists brought in bootleggers to tempt us, but we were casting them down. Then the Commonists got into power in Washington and caused the repeal of prohibition. They started the propaganda that it had been bad. They've weakened our country by thirty years of steady drinking ever since."

"Well," Walter said.

"Well what?" said Brother Chunk. Looking at him, it occurred to Walter that Brother Chunk had the crafty face of an old chicken thief, and that Walter had been snatched from his roost and was being shoved into a burlap sack.

"What can there be to well about?" Brother Chunk said.

"Cream and sugar?" said Walter, pouring the coffee.

"Both, please." Brother Chunk tipped the cream pitcher and poured half an inch into his coffee cup. He put in two spoonfuls of sugar. He looked up at Walter and drew his brows together. "*What* are you *welling* about?"

"It's gonna take some thinking," Walter said.

Brother Chunk set down his coffee cup so that the saucer rattled.

"Ain't you a Christian, brother?"

"Sure."

"Ain't you a patriot?"

"Sure."

"Ain't you a father?"

"No."

"But if you're a patriot and a Christian, you don't want to see your friends' children grow up under Commonism," said Brother Chunk.

"I wouldn't want to see that," Walter said unhappily.

"Then everbody's got to cut out drinking."

"Everbody?"

"Amen."

"Even beer?"

"Amen."

"How'd you come up with this idea, Brother Chunk?"

"Why, Walter, any man with the brains of a noodle could see what the Commonists are doing to us. I talked it over with all the deacons and then with my fellow ministers around town, and we're united in this here thing."

"All the ministers?"

"All the Baptists," Brother Chunk said, rather ominously.

"Let me do some thinking," said Walter.

"This is the wish of the Lord and of the servants of the Lord."

"You sure it's the right way to fight the Communists?"

"It's the first step, brother, in the struggle for souls."

"Well, let me study over it."

"*Pray* over it, brother."

"I'll do that," Walter said.

Brother Chunk stood up and took his coat off the back of the chair.

"You know," he said, "anybody who's not for the Lord and against the Commonists is not the sort of man we'd want to send to Austin. I've heard, Walter, that you got in mind sometime moving up to the State Senate or even some higher office. The sky's the limit for a good Christian, my boy. You might say heaven's the limit."

"Yeah," Walter said, trying to smile.

"You might pray over that a little bit, too, brother."

"I intend to."

"I'll come see you again tomorrow, Walter. Maybe I'll bring some of the other pastors with me. We'll offer our guidance."

"Thanks. That would be swell."

"These are troubled times, my boy. There's confusion everwhere. The Devil is all around us. He's got to be fought! He's got to be whipped! He's got to be lashed and beaten and driven out and cast down! We just can't set back and let the old Devil have us, can we, boy?"

"No, sir."

"Where'd you say Mrs. Anderson is?"

"Bridge."

"Ah, yes. *Cards,*" Brother Chunk said, looking closely at Walter and shaking his head. "Well, one thing at a time. One thing at a time. Be sure to give her my finest. She's quite a little woman, Walter. May God bless her."

Brother Chunk took a pair of sunglasses out of his pocket and put them on.

"We're announcing our campaign in the papers tomorrow morning," he said. "Within a few days we'll start announcing the people who are on God's team in this *grreat* football game with the Commonist Devil. I hope your name will be counted. I truly hope so, brother."

After Brother Chunk had driven away in his new Buick, Walter made several telephone calls trying to find Chub. Then he gave up and phoned long distance to William Sheridan in Austin. He waited while the call went through Sheridan's secretary, and by the time Sheridan's nasal voice came on, Walter was rapping his fingers against the wall.

"Bill, they're trying to ruin me," Walter said.

"The Dry thing," said Sheridan. "I've heard about it. Don't worry. We'll steamroll 'em."

"Looks like they've got me. I may have to announce for 'em."

"Don't panic, Walter."

"I'd figured you'd say that, you Commonist."

"This isn't funny. Just hang on and stay out of it. We'll take care of you. I'll be there in a day or two. Don't worry about a thing."

Walter hung up the phone and sat down. He wished he weren't alone.

Chub Anderson came into the kitchen with an empty glass. She was a short, plump woman with thin ankles and a pretty face and dark luminous eyes. Using the same wrinkle-nosed smile and giggle that had got her chosen as a beauty queen at the University of Texas, she thrust the glass toward William Sheridan and said, "Lots and lots of scotch and lots of ice." Sheridan had some difficulty reaching around his guitar, which was slung over his neck, to get his hands into the sack of ice. He dropped his guitar pick into the sink. Harry Danielsen grinned. Chub meanwhile took the arms of her husband and Jason and continued to smile. "Wish somebody'd pay attention to me," she said. "I feel left out."

"We been singing," said Walter Anderson.

"Hon, your voice is getting thick."

"I hardly had a drink," Walter said.

"Hi, Jason," said Chub. She kissed his cheek. "You'll pay some attention to me, won't you?"

"You know it," Jason said.

"Not too much though," said Chub. "Willy's sitting in there starting to steam. If you don't get in there and talk to her, she'll leave you again."

"Maybe we ought to circulate," Walter said.

"At least we oughta dance," said Sheridan. "How bout it, Chub."

"Love to."

Sheridan undid himself from the guitar and placed Chub's glass on the drainboard.

"Bring that," Chub said. "All us modern girls can drink and dance at the same time."

Chub and Sheridan went into the living room. Walter stood with his hands in his pockets for a moment, whistling, and then he followed them.

"This the first time you had Willy out since she came back?" asked Harry.

"Second time. We went out to eat the other night," Jason said. "Everthing's been great since she got back, but I don't know if we can stand the pressure of going to a party. When I'm at a party the scum starts rising to the top."

"You let yourself be guided by the group," said Harry. "And that's like following a many-headed monster that doesn't know where it's going anyhow."

"Naw, that's not it," Jason said. "The thing is, I'm about forty per cent scum and when I start drinking this bottled loud-mouth the scum rises to the top. I wish Willy could understand that and take it easy."

"A woman never can reconcile herself to that unless you treat her like something special while you're at it," said Harry. "You can be as scummy as you want to be if you make it clear all the time that you love Willy and you're with Willy and you prefer her to anybody else."

"I wouldn't be a real true life scum if I acted like that," Jason said. "Why don't you grow a beard again?"

"It itches," said Harry.

"I itch, too," Jason said.

In Korea a phosphorous grenade exploded and showered across Lieutenant Harry Danielsen's back, and a few seconds later he was bayoneted in the left thigh. Before he became unconscious he was aware that he was lying face down in a puddle of wet manure deposited by a Chinese soldier who had been shot in the stomach. One Chinese in a quilted uniform stood over him at that moment as if debating whether Harry was worth blowing a few holes in with a grease gun. Undoubtedly, the sight of Harry's back through the charred, smoking shreds of his field jacket was what dissuaded the Chinese. Other Chinese were running through what had been the command post area of what had been Lieutenant Harry Danielsen's infantry company. Harry lay near the entrance to his command bunker, and the offending Chinese, the one who had dumped his bowels, sprawled just above him like a crushed and stinking bundle of dirty clothes that had been thrown on top of a sandbag. There was a great deal of screaming and yelling, and many bursts of submachine-gun fire, and there were quite a lot of grenades going off with tremendous whumps and scattering dirt over everything. Not that Lieutenant Danielsen cared. A man lying with his face in new manure couldn't make himself care about anything except his own predicament. In those last seconds before the blackness came he didn't think at all of his soul's eternal destination, or the loss of his company, or the smell of his burnt flesh, or his friends back home, or what would happen to the United Nations if the Chinese broke through all the way to Pusan. He thought that if he could move his face eight inches to one side or the other he would be the happiest man in the world.

He was never certain how he got to the hospital. There were days of a blurred, euphoric morphine dream, when he was never sure whether he was asleep or awake. But later, in Japan, he had the clarity and the time to think, too much time. The pain in his back was very bad. He tried frequently to pretend the pain in his thigh was worse, to divert his attention. But it was not a successful game. His thigh hardly hurt at all, and his back hurt worse than he had ever imagined anything could hurt. He tried to fall in love with the pelvis of his nurse, which was about all he could see with comfort from his position on his stomach, but he decided that was too Hemingwayish and he suspected the nurse was a Lesbian who enjoyed his agony. Her hips twitched flauntingly in her white uniform, and he occasionally looked down at her white shoes and neat, stockinged legs. Now and then he would roll his eyes until he could see her face; she always had a removed look, as if no one ever again could say or do anything that would affect her in the least. And she had an irritating way of saying, "How are we today?" After a while Harry quit answering her. A doctor came and questioned him to see if Harry had become schizophrenic. "Yes I have," Harry said. "Leave me alone." "Nothing to worry about, then," the doctor said, and went away.

In that barren time, bright with pain, Harry decided he wanted to be an artist. Unlike his closest friend, Ben Carpenter, Harry Danielsen had never set himself a goal. He was majoring in history in an offhanded way, and had minors in English and philosophy, when he and Ben quit school to enter the Army. There was no reason for Harry to resume those studies. He didn't want to teach. He really didn't want to do anything at all. Being an artist, he thought, would be an allowable and semirespectable way for him to bum around. He decided he wanted to be a painter, and to be in love, and to have at least one friend.

After his discharge, Harry enrolled at New York University on the GI Bill. He got himself a room on the second floor of a building on Minetta Street. It was a small, dirty room with pink walls, and it was either cold and damp or hot and damp, depending on the season. He cooked on an electric plate and shared a bath with three girls who lived across the hall and with a Nationalist Chinese student who lived next door and with a lone girl who lived in a tiny room with a TV set on the other side of the Chinese. Harry walked to classes along the gray sidewalks through the refuse of the Village. He took to hanging out at the White Horse and the San Remo and Julius's. He surprised himself by becoming truly interested in painting; he found that he had a talent for it, and the technique fascinated him. He began trying to paint what pain and erotic love were like, and how they were joined in their extreme sensuality. His hair grew long and he grew a beard for the hell of it, and he wore sneakers and fatigue pants. He drank a considerable amount of wine and beer, experimented with marijuana, slept with an astonishing assortment of women of various ages, colors, and nationalities, and wrote letters twice a month to Ben Carpenter. By then Ben was back in Austin with his bride.

> *Fellow Club Member,* wrote Ben in one of the letters Harry kept, *I showed the photograph you sent, and Jean couldn't identify it at first. She studied it under the light at the head of the bed and finally guessed it was a photograph you had copied from a magazine layout about Montmartre. We had just come in from the lake and were a little drunk. It was lovely out there this afternoon. The way those hills changed color as the sun went down. The water was so smooth that it looked frozen. Four couples of us went swimming and water skiing and beer drinking, and at sundown we took off our suits and swam in a little slough by one guy's cabin. Jean is a damned fine girl. I love her. I hadn't realized how really fine looking she is. She has the greatest hips and legs and the most perfect skin I've ever seen.*

Reading the letter, Harry paused to think of Jean. He remembered her as a tall, gawky girl with short black hair, rather too large of tooth, and with brown eyes that had a crazy wildness in them. No breasts, as he recalled. But she was strong, athletic, and she could run and jump and fight and drink. He wondered what you would find if you could dig down and unravel the twisted wires that gave her such frantic energy. But if Ben thought she was fine looking, then as far as Harry was concerned, she was fine looking. Harry waved his cup, and a little Eurasian girl filled it with coffee and then put her head beside his on the propped-up pillow. Through the open window they could see the black framework of the fire escape and hear voices arguing in the street.

We're doing beautifully, the letter said. *We have an apartment with a nice view and trees out back near a little stream. It's a pleasant change from Fort Knox and those bleak buildings and snow falling through the coal smoke. I'm working hard. The town isn't at all the same without you around. Walter Anderson is back in town with his cheerleader wife, and he says he's going to run for the legislature. Can you imagine Walter in the legislature? Sure you can. Three yards up the middle on every issue right down the field. There are quite a few worse than Walter. Jason's in Fort Worth. He writes me that he's going into the construction business with the money his stepfather left him. Willy is pregnant.*

Jean and I are glad to hear you like it there. (Jean and I? thought Harry. Why would Jean be glad to hear anything about me except that I'm a long way off? Tell me what *you're* glad to hear, and let me guess what Jean is glad to hear). *I wish there were some way you could send at least a sketch for me to put on the wall of our apartment. I'd be damned proud to get it. It used to be that when people asked me where you were, I'd tell them you were studying to make a painter. Now I tell them you've turned queer and are running through the Village with a pack of sub-humans. They prefer to hear that.*

It's funny how much easier law school is now than before we went into the army. Concentration does it. I get home in the afternoon, sit down to the books, and don't look up until Jean has supper ready. She's even learned how to cook a little bit. After supper I go at the books again until midnight. We go out to a movie or a party maybe once a week. It sounds dull, but I've settled into the routine and I enjoy it. We don't own a television set. I'm afraid of the things.

I saw my father the other day. He asked about you and was very concerned. He thinks of you as a second son, you know. He's a great old man. I couldn't have picked a better one. Right now he's trying to make the cafes around the university integrate, but I doubt if he can do more than disturb them a little. He wants you to come back to Texas and go to work for him. Says he'll put you in Dallas or Fort Worth or Austin in any one of his outfits. I told him you wouldn't work for an insurance company, even as president. He said okay he'd open an art gallery in Austin and let you run it and paint and have a ready outlet for your own stuff. That's the businessman in him thinking: products and outlets. If you want you could always go out to the ranch or to the lake house at Eagle Mountain and live as long as you want and paint everything you see. Trouble is, my mother would be busting in with her phony poets and writers and neurotic drunks. That ought to give you enough subjects to last all your life. The big thing is, we want you home. This is the way the world ends. Ben.

Harry tossed the letter onto the table by the bed.

"Baby, how would you like to go to Texas?" he said.

"Where's that?" she said.

"Never mind," he said. "I'm not ready anyhow."

It was three years before he was ready. Harry finished at NYU and enrolled at an art school which qualified under his GI Bill. The art school was uptown in a brownstone near Carnegie Hall. He left the Village and moved into an apartment on 57th Street. It was in a drugstore in that neighborhood that he met Doris.

She came in wearing tight denim pants, blue sneakers, a white blouse, and a short jacket. She carried a small leather bag that was partly unzipped, and Harry saw ballet slippers sticking out. Her hair was in a ponytail that hung nearly to her buttocks. Harry observed those buttocks while she was buying cigarettes; they swerved out smartly and the faded denims were so tight that each buttock seemed to be in a separate package. As if she felt his eyes, she turned and looked at him. Afterward Harry told himself there had been an immediate shock, a recognition of the inevitable, as they regarded each other. But that first day she turned and went out of the store as his eyes followed her lithe, muscular, dancer's body with its flat stomach and large thighs. In two days he saw her again in the drugstore. Within a week he found cause to speak to her as they stood at the magazine rack. Within a month they were sleeping together. Within three months they were married. By autumn she was pregnant and they agreed they didn't want to raise their child in New York City. They went to Tulsa, stayed five days with Doris's mother, and then went to Texas. The moment they came into Fort Worth on the train, Harry knew he was home again. Growing up there he had sworn to leave and never come back. Now that he was back, he knew he had never really left and never would.

"It's getting late," Jason said. "Suppose Ben and Cadmus might have run into each other at Colonial or somewhere and got so drunk they can't get here?"

"They'd have phoned," said Harry. "I know Ben'll be here. I'm not so sure about Cadmus."

"Nobody's ever sure about Cadmus," Willy said.

They were sitting in the living room while the party roared around them. Feeding itself, gathering strength, the party was like King Kong sweeping them all into its arms. Sheridan was still dancing with Chub. Jason wandered off to dance with a girl whose long black hair had hypnotized him. She wore a white blouse with a man's button-down collar and a single strand of pearls and a khaki-colored cotton twill skirt. Jason had watched her standing with one knee on the arm of a chair, the skirt gathered close round the soft curve of her hips, and he knew he had to dance with her. Harry studied her with interest, trying to decide what it was that made her unusually attractive, what quality it was he would go after if he were to paint her. The face was rather ordinary, all in perspective, a face that would be difficult to caricature. She was lovely, he thought, because of her large eyes, and the gleaming black hair that she wore with combs, and her grace. And her intensity. She seemed to do things as if they were important. Even when Jason asked her to dance she said yes as if it would be an important and delightful thing to do. Harry couldn't quite place her; she was familiar, as though he recognized certain pieces of her but the major pattern had been altered and reassembled.

"That," said Willy, before he could ask, "is Seton Parry's sister. She came by herself. I wish she had a date and he'd take her home."

"How long's she been back in town?" Harry said.

"I don't know. I just wish she'd leave."

"She's pretty."

"You think so?" said Willy. "Jason thinks so, too. I don't. She looks like a damned Indian squaw. Look at her hair. Nobody wears their hair like that any more, that long and with combs. I think it's phony to brush your hair straight back like that and let it fall down your back. Why didn't she wear a turtleneck sweater and a pair of sandals if she wants to make us think she's writing poetry or something? If I wanted to take that much trouble I could wear my hair like that, too. Any woman could."

"Afraid Jason wouldn't like it?" Harry said.

"Frankly, I don't give a damn what Jason likes. He's not worth it," said Willy. "The only reason I took him back, Harry, is because of the children. That's all. Period. I decided to devote my life to being a good mother and doing for the children and let that scum come and go as he pleases. He's worn me out. He's pathetic. But he does love the children and they love him. How I feel about it doesn't matter. Damn, look at him. The idiot. Who does he think he is, Rubirosa?"

"Scuse me," Harry said. "Somebody's kicked over a drink."

The town of New Hope sat in the middle of a great West Texas wasteland as inconspicuously as another mesquite bush. The highway from Fort Worth to Lubbock passed through New Hope and created its main street. On the highway the speed limit was sixty miles an hour until New Hope appeared through the windshield—a cluster of small buildings huddled together as if to protect each other from the blowing sands. At New Hope, the speed limit abruptly became thirty miles an hour. A police officer in a big hat constantly parked his old Ford with its new radar at one end of town or the other. Before Cadmus Wilkins became known as a prominent young oil operator who was going to succeed where so many others had failed—information that Cadmus, himself, freely passed out—he got three speeding tickets within a week coming into New Hope.

As a town New Hope wasn't much, even for West Texas. It had a gas station that also sold jawbreakers in glass jars, peanut patties, cupcakes, bread, milk, and assorted groceries, and had an ice house attached. There was a general store that sold hardware and clothes, a feed store, a real estate office to which the door had been locked for fifteen years, a larger grocery store, several houses, a Baptist church, and a cafe. The cafe was the center of social life. That was where the policeman in the big hat drank coffee, and where the ranchers gathered when they came to town to buy supplies or to visit. And there was a barber shop. But New Hope's only barber had been dead for nearly two years, and the barber shop was now the home office and headquarters for the Cadmus Wilkins interests.

The letters on the dusty glass window said CADBURN OIL CO. For furniture, other than a barber chair, the Cadburn Oil Company had a desk heaped with maps and well logs and lease agreements, a filing cabinet, a wooden chair, and two army cots. There were three other chairs stacked in the back room in event the Cadburn Oil Company ever had visitors, which it never had. The back room had been the quarters of the deceased barber. But Cadmus Wilkins had shut the door to that room with the finality that the barber's life had closed; Cadmus was not going to sleep in no bed where a man had died.

Cadmus had just finished shaving at the long mirror in the front of the shop, had rinsed his razor in the basin, and had sat down in the barber chair to rest. He put his head back against the cracked leather. He whistled and tapped his knee with a folded telegram which he occasionally reread. The highway and the grocery store across the street and a long bright patch of sky reflected in the mirror. Cadmus kept whistling and smoked a couple of cigarettes and thought about turning on the radio until he saw a yellow Chevrolet convertible pull up at the curb. Cadmus tried to judge from the way Burns got out of the car and walked toward the office what the news was. But he knew that was useless; Burns always walked with his head down, pondering, whether the news was wonderful or disastrous. Cadmus had already prepared himself for the news being disastrous. It would take him a little bit to adjust if the news were wonderful.

Bells tinkled when Burns opened the door.

"One good thing, we won't have to listen to those bells any more," Burns said.

Burns went to the mirror and looked at his face, smeared with dust and sweat, and at his red swollen eyes.

"I haven't slept in a month," said Burns.

"It was a great adventure," Cadmus said, watching Burns's face in the mirror.

"Yeah."

"That's all?"

"Yeah."

"No chance?"

"None. I plugged it."

"Can't offset it or nothing?"

"Offset it?" Burns looked at Cadmus. "Sometimes your ignorance about the oil business is truly amazing."

"Don't make any difference," Cadmus said. "We got no more money anyhow."

"I'm sorry, partner," said Burns.

"How about whipstocking? Ain't there such a term?"

"Yeah. But I'm telling you we can't pour any more money down that hole."

"I said there ain't any more money. Hell, I don't know if whipstocking costs any money or not."

"I'm sorry," Burns said.

"Last night I dreamed I was driving down this very highway," said Cadmus. "It was dark and I was in a hurry to get to this goddamn town for whatever reason I couldn't guess. And suddenly my headlights picked up something on the road. It was a weaving, twisting, hopping mass of something. Looked like it covered the whole goddamn deal. It was coming from over to my right and passing across to my left. Out beyond the lights I could see this mass of something stretched way off. I could see these black thangs twisting and hopping against the sky. I started slowing down but I was going awful fast, as I sometimes do, and I was right in the middle of it before I could stop. You know what it was, Burns?"

"What?"

"It was an army of frogs. Big old bullfrogs and lady frogs and little baby frogs. They had funny, scared looks on their faces, like they were running from something horrible. Like they were moving to another country. And I knew that in their whole goddamn path across the prairie they had left everthing covered with sticky stuff and warts they planted there because they were so scared. They started swarming all over the car and looking at me with their big scared eyes. I could tell they were scared of me, too, and were gonna drown me because they were scared. Man, did they stink. What a goddamn dream. I jumped out of bed and just started running around the room whipping out my hands and stomping my feet to get them frogs offa me."

"Jesus," Burns said.

"They didn't make any real noise that you could tell what it was. Just kind of sweek sweek or something like that. It was more like a noise that you could *feel* instead of hear. What you think them frogs was running from?"

"I don't know. What are frogs scared of?"

"I guess just about everthing. I would be, if I was a frog. But this had to be something special, like it was gonna wipe out ever frog on earth. They were so scared that they were crazy and running over everthing."

"Kind of spooky," said Burns.

"You should of seen their eyes."

"Jesus," Burns said. "A bunch of frogs."

"This hole we dug, is it strictly no show?"

"We couldn't get enough oil out of that hole to fill your cigarette lighter. There's dry holes around here deeper than ours."

"No gas or nothing?"

"Cadmus, how could you have spent your adult life as vice president of the Frontier Oil Company and not have learned a damn thing?"

"I never paid attention."

"I really thought we had it."

"We can sell the rig."

"Every single thing we've got is leased."

"That's what I heard somebody say in a movie once. Sell the rig."

"What's your old man going to say when he finds out you borrowed that money on your producers?"

"He knows about it. We had a talk the other night. He said any son of a bitch who'd go out and wildcat in a place like this is too dumb to belong to him. As of right now, I ain't a vice-president of Frontier Oil Company no more."

"Damn," said Burns.

"Well, now, look here," Cadmus said. "I'm thirty-three years old. Some time in a guy's life he's gonna have to let go of his mamma and daddy and see what he can do for hisself. Just because we come up with a bust here don't mean I'm through living. You're the chief scout for Frontier Oil Company as well as the chief geologist and drill master or whatever you call it. Get out and find us some oil. I'll get out and find some money."

"Your credit is gone."

"Hell it is. Now's when I can operate. Any halfwit can operate when thangs are going good. Don't worry about nothing, Burns. I'm still the president and chairman of the board of this here company. You're just a junior podnoo. You find us some oil."

"I have a few ideas," Burns said.

"Get back to Midland and cash a check," said Cadmus. "We got some kind of dollars left. Get a hotel room and take a bath and sleep. I'm going to a birthday party. I'll see you next week."

"I'm starting to feel a little better."

"Sure. Don't let it get you."

"Okay, partner."

"Don't despair, use your . . . I forget how that used to go," Cadmus said.

The bells on the door tinkled as Burns went out. The yellow Chevrolet convertible drove out of the mirror frame. Cadmus looked down at the telegram in his hand.

"Old Ben," he said. "Old Ben's birthday. I better go cheer him up. Old Ben needs me."

Upstairs, Jason found Chub Anderson and William Sheridan under the bed.

Jason was on his way into the bathroom when he saw a man's foot sticking out from beneath the guest bed. It was a small foot inside a brilliantly polished shoe. Since he had been drinking a great deal by then, Jason assumed someone had died. He bent, grabbed the foot, and pulled. The foot jerked. There was the clatter of a head knocking against a bed slat, and a curse. Jason lay down on his stomach and turned his face sideways to look under the bed. He saw Chub and Sheridan peering back at him like animals looking out of a cave.

"Hi," Jason said.

"Hi, Jason," said Chub, her voice muffled.

"Hi you all," Jason said.

"Go the hell off," said Sheridan.

"Did you lose a collar button?" Jason said.

"Collar button?" said Sheridan. "Nobody wears collar buttons any more."

"I thought maybe you'd lost a collar button," Jason said. "How bout a cuff link? Is that what you lost?"

"I didn't lose a cuff link," said Sheridan.

"What you see under there?" Jason said.

"You," said Sheridan.

"Hey, Chub," Jason said.

"What, hon?"

"Hey, girl," Jason said.

"What?" she said.

"That's old Chub under that bed," Jason said. He laughed as if he had discovered something really delicious. "Hi, Chub."

"Hi, Jason."

"Son of a gun," Jason said. "Maybe you lost your VFW pin?"

"No," said Sheridan.

"They can roll into funny places," Jason said.

"I don't belong to the VFW," said Sheridan.

"You proud of that?" said Jason. "Lot of good guys in the VFW."

"I think I've lost my mind," Sheridan said.

"I would help you look for it, but I have to go to the bathroom," Jason said.

"I want you to go away," said Sheridan.

"Chub? You want me to go away?"

"It might be better, hon."

"Hey, Sheridan, you're a pretty good singer," Jason said. "Where'd you learn to play the guitar like that?"

"In the Navy," said Sheridan, looking out at Jason.

"He was a lieutenant junior grade," said Chub.

"Hey, that's swell," Jason said. "I was a corporal myself."

"Bill shot a cannon," said Chub.

"Did it hurt your ears?" Jason said.

"Sometimes," said Sheridan. He cursed. "Why are we talking to this man?"

"I don't know what else to do," Chub said. "He's sort of out there, and we're sort of under here."

"That's a nice, analytical summary of the situation," Jason said. "Very clear cut. Very concise."

"Go away," said Sheridan.

"Chub likes me," Jason said.

"I'm starting to hate you," said Sheridan.

"Don't you like me, Chub? You told me you did."

"I like you, hon, you know that."

"Damn it, go away," said Sheridan.

"You sure are touchy," Jason said.

"Just go the hell off."

For a while nobody spoke. Then Sheridan said:

"Are you gonna leave?"

"I suppose I will eventually. I *said* I have to go to the bathroom, didn't I?"

"Jason, dear, I hope you don't misunderstand this," said Chub.

"I'm trying not to," Jason said.

"I mean I hope you don't get the wrong idea," she said. "I mean I know it looks sort of strange."

"I'm keeping a perfectly open mind," Jason said.

He lay there and looked at them.

"Oh Christ," said Sheridan.

Sheridan struggled to crawl out, and he rapped his head on a bed slat again.

"Oh Christ," said Sheridan.

"I'd be awful interested to see how you got under there and how you were going to do what you were going to do," Jason said.

"We weren't going to do anything," said Chub. "Don't be mad at me, hon."

"I wasn't mad," Jason said. "It's not my place to be mad."

"Gahdammit quit looking at us then," said Sheridan.

"Okay," Jason said.

Jason stood up, stepped to the bed, and climbed atop it. Standing on the bed he spread his arms like a trampolinist and began to jump up and down. He hadn't jumped up and down on a bed since he was a child. It was very satisfying. Below, he heard Sheridan's head banging against the slats and Sheridan saying, "Oh Christ."

Jason started singing as he jumped up and down.

"Valencia!" he sang.

Squaang squaang went the bed springs. Clack! went Sheridan's head.

"In mah dreams . . ."

Squaang squaang Clack!

"It *al*ways seems . . ."

Squaang Clack! Clack!

"Ah hear yew . . ."

When Jason saw Sheridan's large, curly head appear, glasses dangling from one ear, Jason leaped over the head and onto the bedroom floor. Sheridan was halfway out from under the bed now. He was tangled in Chub's skirt and was pulling himself forward like a dog with two broken hind legs. Jason saw violence in Sheridan's face.

"I'm going down to have a drink with my friend Walter," Jason said.

"Gahdam you," said Sheridan.

In the living room things had begun to happen. A woman had lifted the heavy coat tree and, brandishing it like a spear, had pinned her husband into the corner where he had been talking to another woman. Harry and Walter leaned against the mantel and observed. The room flowed with people. Several had on paper hats and were blowing noisemakers. Willy stood at the dining-room table scraping potato chips through a bowl of bean dip and trying to look as if she weren't searching for Jason. Doris had thrown her mop, broom and dust pan onto the back porch and had given up the idea of making small repairs. She was dancing the mambo with an interior decorator; a crowd had circled them and was applauding. The interior decorator was yelling "*Ole!*" Somebody else was yelling "Holey!" One man sat on the couch looking as if he were at the edge of tears. Harry saw Jason come downstairs laughing and go into the kitchen. In a moment Jason came into the dining room, saw Willy, and put his arm around her. She elbowed him in the ribs. Jason left her at the bean dip and joined Harry and Walter.

"I've been looking all over for Brother Chunk, but he's not here," Jason said. "We forget to invite him?"

"Surely he wouldn't show up," Walter said seriously.

"He might be peeking through the window," said Jason.

Sheridan came down the stairs, his coat wrinkled and his tie askew, and looked around wildly. When he saw Jason talking to Walter, Sheridan paused, straightened his tie, stared at them as if trying to read their lips, and then went into the kitchen. Harry lit a cigarette and kept watching the stairway. After a pause, Chub came down. She looked at Jason and Walter, and followed Sheridan into the kitchen. Harry glanced at Walter, who had noticed nothing but was talking earnestly to Jason about Brother Chunk and hamburgers.

"I wonder where Chub is?" Walter said, as though he had suddenly sensed her.

"Last time I saw her she was sitting out in the kitchen talking to somebody," said Harry. "That friend of yours from Austin, I think."

"Sheridan? He's a hell of a guy. Listen, Harry, I could tell you didn't take to him," Walter said. "But he's a hell of an operator. He's done a lot for this state. Sometimes by helping himself, a lobbyist can help everbody."

"How's that?" Harry said.

"You know, explaining legislation and stuff."

"He seems like a sharp guy," said Jason. "That's how he strikes me."

"He's a close friend of mine," Walter said. "When we're in Austin, Bill is over at the house all the time."

"Zat right?" said Jason, frowning.

"He's got plenty of influence, too, boy, don't think he hasn't," Walter said.

"He's pretty smooth," said Jason.

"Damn right," Walter said. "I guess I better go in the kitchen and find 'em. I wouldn't want to leave Sheridan stuck with Chub all night. There's some girls here he could hustle."

As Walter went into the kitchen, Jason laughed.

"What else could I expect?" said Jason. He looked at Harry. "You see 'em come down? I was hoping Walter wouldn't."

"I saw 'em," Harry said.

"Funny," said Jason. "Funniest damn thing."

"Walter wouldn't think it was so funny. No matter who it was, Jason."

"You don't understand," Jason said.

"I guess I don't."

The front door banged open and six more people rushed through as if they were chasing a thief. The three men carried paper sacks, and one had a carton of soda. Harry saw the black-haired girl, Seton Parry's sister, looking through the stack of record albums.

"More than a hundred here now," said Jason. "Ben's got lots of friends."

"That must be it," Harry said. "I saw you dancing with Seton's sister. What's the story on her?"

"I don't know. She's been off to school or in Europe or somewhere. I'm in love with her."

"She anything like Seton?"

"Hell no. She's a nice girl."

Two policemen arrived. Harry went to talk to them. A girl snatched a policeman's cap and ran around the room with it on her head. The police regarded her somberly. People laughed. Harry retrieved the hat and gave it back to the policeman.

"You got one going," the policeman said.

"I'll try to hold 'em down," said Harry. "This is Ben Carpenter's birthday party."

"I should have known Ben was connected with it somehow," the policeman said. "We've already had one complaint from the lady across the street, and she's deaf."

"I'll do the best I can, Luther," said Harry.

"Let's beat it," the other officer said.

"Couple of drinks to take with you?" said Harry.

"Are you crazy?" Luther said. "This bunch would fink on us right off. We'll change clothes and come back for one at two o'clock."

Harry and Jason walked outside with them. Jason shut the door but the noise still assaulted the street. The policeman named Luther shook his head.

"I hope those nuns down at the end of the block don't start complaining," he said. "Captain McChesney is a Catholic."

A blue Cadillac convertible with the top up came around the corner between the two rows of parked cars. The Cadillac slammed to a stop, and its horn began honking.

"Tell 'em bout it!" a voice yelled from inside the Cadillac.

"Ratchit," screamed a girl's voice.

"Wherem I gonna park this mother?" the man's voice yelled.

"Ratchit, who cares?" screamed the girl.

"The law got 'em!" the man yelled. "Hold on, boys, till I park this mother! Don't say a word!"

"Come on, let's get out of here before we have some trouble," the other officer said to Luther.

"Ratchit!" the girl yelled as the Cadillac drove on. "Ratchit on the police!"

"Thanks, Luther," said Harry. "We'll be going strong at two."

"I'll bet," said Luther.

The police got into their car and left quickly.

"Ain't Luther the one that was with you in Korea?" Jason said.

"Yeah," said Harry. "We drink beer together."

By then the Cadillac had parked and two people were staggering up the sidewalk in the speckled light of the street lamps. One was a very tall, bulky, blond-haired man in a checked sport coat. The other, who clung to him, was a girl with silver hair.

"I hoped Cadmus would make it," Harry said.

"Where'd the law go to," said Cadmus, grinning and showing his slightly crooked upper front teeth. His face swayed above them. "We come to give you boys help."

"We're clean," Jason said, looking at the girl. She leaned against Cadmus as if he were a tree and smiled drunkenly. Her silver hair glittered and she had an impressive cleavage. Her yellow dress was so tight that she had to hobble on her extremely high heels.

"This here is Blossom," said Cadmus. "Tellem bout it, Blossom."

"Ratchit," the girl said.

"She has a limited vocabulary," said Harry.

"Blossom knows a lot of other words," Cadmus said, grinning and touching his crooked teeth with his tongue. "But she's kind of stuck on that one. She's an awful smart girl. She went to Harvard, didn't you, honey pot?"

"Damn good," said Blossom.

"I'm a Harvard man my own self," Cadmus said. "That's how come we get along so well. Driving down here we been having a long talk about the country's socioeconomic problems and how they tie in with our geopolitic and contribute to our general moral decay. Tellem what we decided, Blossom."

"We decided it's a buncha ratchit," said the girl.

"We're drawing up a report to send to the President," Cadmus said. "He's just folks. Us Harvard people understand each other."

"Whoo," said the girl. "Whooee."

"Where's ole Ben?" Cadmus said.

"Not here yet," said Jason.

"I got a surprise for him," Cadmus said. "This'll be one birthday party he won't never forget. Jason, take ole Blossom to the bar and supply her with strong drank before she goes wild. Us Harvard graduates can't stand to be thirsty."

"Where'd you find her?" said Harry as Jason went up the steps with Blossom clutching his arm and mincing along in her high heels.

"Wichita Falls," Cadmus said. "Sweet girl."

"You ought to marry her."

"I'll tell you, Harry. She's an exceptional person. Good swimmer, good tennis player, good companion, hell of a dranker, spectacular looking, fine cook, very affectionate. Don't complain, don't talk too much. She'll do anything I tell her to do. Loves to get naked in public. And she don't give a damn if I live or die."

Harry laughed. "Everthing going all right?" he said.

"Couldn't be better," said Cadmus. "I'm on top of the world, son. Problems are something you got to make up for your own self, and I just don't care to do it."

"You're lucky," Harry said.

"Why sure I'm lucky," said Cadmus. "I'm here, ain't I?"

Part Three

WITH STAMMERIN LIPS
AN ANOTHER TONGUE

It was a two-story white frame house with blue slatted shutters, and it stood among elms on a quiet narrow street with broken sidewalks. The street was on a bluff in a high part of the city. Looking down to the west between the trees and the dark houses Ben Carpenter could see the tumbled blackness of the woods below, and beyond, where the earth slowly rose again from the turgid river, lights spread like Christmas ornaments against the purple night. Sunset Ridge was slightly more than a block long; it swung off a crowded boulevard and curved to the west past a grassy park, then turned south along the edge of the bluff for two hundred yards before it dropped abruptly down and was lost in the parking lot of a church above an expressway.

Fifty years earlier Sunset Ridge had been a place of stables and crystal chandeliers, of unthreatened elegance, a secret shaded street where the houses turned masks toward the world. The house in whose yard Ben Carpenter stood had been an estate; down the terrace behind it, almost lost in the trees, was the ruin of a dairy barn that had somehow stopped in the act of toppling sideways and had hung for years looking as if a child could push it over with his foot. The expanding city had surrounded and isolated Sunset Ridge and had moved on, carrying the descendants of Sunset Ridge's old rich into new stone and glass show windows to the west. Carmelite nuns had arrived to occupy a white brick mansion on the forehead of the bluff near the curve at the park, and had walled themselves in with their mystery. One of the old houses had been remodeled into seven apartments, although it was done discreetly and without disturbing the quiet of the street. In a tall stone house next door to where Ben Carpenter stood, an old lady lived alone and played her television loudly on the second floor, bending toward it to hear; her yard, in the spring, blossomed miraculously with flowers; the flowers were plastic and were simply stuck into the ground. But her father had been a settler of Sunset Ridge, and her eccentricity had helped the street to keep its character. Sunset Ridge was a refuge, a silence where lamps reflected off the pavement through the shadows of the leaves, where crickets were, where the memory of hoofs and carriage wheels still lay among the elms.

Under the lamps gleamed the chrome of cars parked along both sides of the street. Ben Carpenter had driven his Mercedes sedan with great difficulty between the rows until he found a parking place in an empty lot near where he now stood. He would have given up and gone away when he saw how many cars there were, but it was his birthday and he was already four hours late for his own party.

He leaned against an elm and looked at the white house. The house slanted at the right front corner, as if it had shifted on a crumbling foundation, and there was a crack in the concrete at the flower bed. Ben saw people moving in the two big front windows, heard them yelling and singing, heard music. He wanted to slide down against the tree, to sink into the soft grass, to sleep. But he pushed himself away and staggered into the street, aware that he was very drunk, that the lights of the house were blurred, that he was trying to go toward the front porch but was swerving instead toward the driveway, toward the dark tunnel between houses. He was confused as to the location of his feet. They walked along without his consent, crossing themselves, taking erratic steps, going off in one direction and then reversing to another, carrying his lurching body with them. He heard his shoes on gravel and saw the black cavern of the garage door. That would be a silly place to wind up, he thought, piled in there with the dusty cardboard boxes and the lawnmower and the coiled hose. He tried to turn himself to the left. He demanded that his feet stop and it cost his balance; he fell into a hedge. Mumbling, Ben crawled out of the hedge, mashed his hands into the gravel drive until he could thrust himself up again, and stumbled into a gate. He heard a picket ripping his coat. Carefully he unsnagged his coat from the picket, undid the latch, pulled the gate open, and fell on his back in the driveway. After a moment Ben rolled over, scrambled up onto his knees, lowered his hands again, and crawled through the gate. Arf arf, he said to himself, here come faithful Sandy, ready as ever to be man's bes frin if any man could be a frin to him. But a terror to his enemies.

When he awoke, a hand was on his shoulder, experimentally

nudging. Ben opened his eyes, trying to remember into what foul predicament he had got himself, and looked up at the sky between tree branches. The hand nudged again. He saw the dark shape of a girl bending over him.

"Frins," he said. "I need frins."

"Are you all right, Ben?" said the girl. The hand lifted from his shoulder but the girl still bent over him; he saw the black of her hair and the white of her face and arms, as ghostly white as those of lost Ophelia, and for an instant it frightened him. Could this be death? Ben grabbed the girl's ankle. She felt real.

"D'y'know me?" he said.

"Yes," the girl laughed.

"D'know yew?"

"Yes. I'm Pippa Parry."

"Don' mean a thing."

"I'm Seton's sister."

"Seton who?"

"Seton Parry."

"Seton Parry! Songun. D'know him?"

"Yes, you know him very well."

"D'yew know him?"

"He's my *brother.*"

"I didn' know that."

"You're not trying."

"D'I vomit?"

"Yes."

"Am I in it?"

"Pretty close."

"Suthin smells turble. Zit me?"

"Yes, I think it is."

"Go way," Ben said.

"Let me help you."

"Go way. I'm shame. Don' wan yew see me smellin bad. Lissen, I got to piss."

The girl didn't answer.

"Hear?" Ben said.

"I heard you."

"Don' yew see I cain git up? Howm I gonna? Lissen."

"I don't know," she said.

"Portan to me. Very portan."

"I could help you up."

"Lissen, will yew gim shower? Will yew take off m'nasty close and turn cole water on me an soap filthy nasty off me? Listen, will yew? Could make big diffrins in our lasheship."

"I'll go get Harry," the girl said.

"Use garn hose. S'okay."

"I'd better go get Harry."

"Don' leave me. Please. I need frins."

"I won't leave you," the girl said. "I'll just go get Harry."

"Good old Harry. He won' leave me. I love ole Harry."

The back door slammed, and Ben knew she was gone.

The clouds moved in the upper wind like curtains billowing. As Ben watched, feeling helpless and paralytic and unsure whether he might vomit again, the white lace blew away and a blackness tumbled across the sky, blotting the stars. The blackness took shape: it became a giant manta ray with a gray underbelly, its wings outstretched and its black tail dragging the sky. Stars popped through to glitter in its head like eyes. The manta ray swam slowly far above, its eyes looking down—an apparition that stirred a cold wet wind against the grass and shook the leaves. Around the edges of the shape glowed an odd lime-colored light.

"Hey there," Ben said aloud. "Th sign of th Son of Man in heaven. Woop. Then shall all th tribes of th earth mourn."

The wind rippled the manta ray, made its wings move, and the eyes burned downward as if searching for Ben beneath his feeble shelter of tree branches. The Son of Man coming in the clouds of heaven with power and great glory. This is no way to find me, Ben thought, drunk in the grass, enraptured by my own small and ignoble wounds. Ought to get up. Hoo boy. Not so easy. Have to take me as I am, ole buddy.

"Gim the word," Ben said. "Talk t'me so I can hear yew an unnerstan. Yew sit up ther smug an quiet an try scare me t'death. I hurt. It hurts t'be me. Tell me bout truth an good, faith an love, the meanin of th word. Woop. Almost throwed up again."

The eyes found him. Fascinated, Ben looked up at them feeling as if he were to be granted some tremendous discovery, some great revelation.

"Th word," he said, looking at the hard white eyes. "C'mon, gim a sign. Which? C'mon, cut me in. I'll tella restum."

The manta ray swam silently through a black sea. And then the eyes that had been about to burn through to Ben's soul left him. The manta ray began to diffuse in the high far winds, and the lace curtains floated back across the dark window between the branches until all impression of the manta ray and its outflung wings and terrifying tail had vanished. Ben found himself looking at the squashed and idiotic face of the moon and at the iced light of the stars. He realized that he was trembling.

"Up there," he said. "Comin up there wif yew."

By the time the girl returned with Harry, Ben had managed to stand up, his head rolling, arms hanging, absurd and angry, his feet uncertainly trying to prop themselves against the grass.

"That's a swell box step you're doing," Harry said. "I didn't know you could dance so good."

"M'not dancin. M'stanin."

"I could whistle 'Darktown Strutters' Ball' and you'd be right in tempo," said Harry. "Do 'Tea for Two' for us."

"M'sick, Harry, ole frin."

"You look like you've been rassling a gorilla."

"Don' laugh at me, Harry, sumbitch. M'sick. Hear? Need frins. Yew m'frin or not?"

"Put your arm around my neck."

"Oh no! Not till getta answer. Yew m'frin or not, damn it?"

"I'm your friend."

"Sarda tell ese days. Phony sumbitches, Harry. Phony sumbitches."

"Always has been," Harry said. "Put your arm around my neck."

Ben put his arm around Harry's neck, and felt Harry's arm around his waist.

"Whur's girl?"

"Right here," said the girl.

"Don' leave me."

"I won't leave you," she said.

"She gone gim shower," Ben said, and he smirked.

"You can work that out later," said Harry. "Right now I'm gone gim you a shower."

Harry Danielsen helped Ben up the back steps, across the screened porch, and into the kitchen. The sudden light made Ben throw up one hand to shield his face as if saying no photographs please. He heard laughter, and he heard his name, and he wanted to spit at them but he remembered it was Harry's floor, and he wanted to fight but he knew if Harry released him he would fall. Clinging to Harry, he tottered through the living room as helpless as the last surviving Civil War veteran, feeling senile and deteriorated, thinking there should be urine spots on the front of his pants and not at all sure that there weren't. As they reached the stairs he heard Doris's voice and felt a new pressure against his other arm. Then they were going up, stumbling, clumsy, sounding like cattle on the stairs, with Ben slipping and clutching and being dragged. Below he could still hear laughter and the loud thrumming of the bass tones of the stereo.

In the upstairs bathroom Ben sat on the commode while Harry and Doris pulled off his clothes. Ben grinned foolishly as he watched them unbutton his shirt, unhitch his belt, peel down his socks, tug at his pants legs. It was a delicious sensation, like being a child again.

"Don' let Dors view m'nudity," Ben said.

"The hell with your nudity," said Harry.

"She might leave yew, Harry, ole frin, if she views m'nudity."

"I've viewed your nudity before and I'm not much impressed," Doris said.

"Zat yew, Dors? Sumbitch."

Ben tried to stand up. He fell sideways off the commode onto the tile floor.

"Woop," he said.

"Man, you're out of it," Harry said.

"Dors, don' look down here at m'nudity."

"I'm just staring at it every minute," she said.

"Intrustin little devil, ain it?" said Ben.

"First one I ever saw," Doris said.

"Zat right? Sumbitch. Hey lissen Harry, show her yours."

"Okay, Ben," Harry said as they took his arms and lifted him. "We're going into the shower."

"Yew'n me bofe?"

"Only you."

"Whur Dors goin mah close?"

"She ought to throw 'em away. They smell like a wino's blanket."

Ben stumbled toward the door, but Harry held him.

"Hey Dors don' thow way mah close," Ben said.

He heard people laughing again, this time in the upstairs hall.

Harry led him to the shower, and then Ben felt water hitting him in the face.

"Cole," he said. "Sumbitch. S'cole Harry. Yew sure yew m'frin?"

Harry closed the shower curtain. In a few seconds it was yanked open again and Doris looked in at him. She smiled. He saw the black beauty spot beneath her right eye, and he looked at her bony nose and her brown hair. He decided he was in love with her.

"Here," she said. "Sit on this."

She put a white three-legged wooden stool into the shower and helped him balance himself on it.

"Keep sitting there until we come for you," said Doris.

"Dors I love yew."

"You say that to everybody's wife. Now you sit there and we'll bring some coffee."

"Dors yew don' care bout me."

"Ben, I love you. Sit there and get wet."

"M'freezin."

Doris adjusted the shower handles until the water was warm and then gave him a bar of soap.

"Dors I member suthin. While waz layin out there parlized somebody come an yurnate on me. Findim killim."

"Happy birthday, Ben," she said, and closed the shower curtain.

For twenty minutes Ben sat in the shower and stared at the green shower curtain and tried to remember the words to a song that was hung in his mind: *I wish you bluebirds* is all that he could remember. He kept singing it and belching and smirking. Ladies and gentlemen of the jury I come before you today a seriouser and wiser man, my heart full of love for all my wonderful frins and loathing for my enemies, to say I wish you bluebirds. Yes I truly do. Ain't that nice? I come to you as a stranger in your country, in *mah* country, as another sort of creature, to defend my own self against these here noxious charges that I am anxious and full of dread. To these here charges I say hoo hah and whoo whoo and sometimes chugga chugga chugga. The problem, gentlemen, is can a locomotive find true love? I mean outside of all that coupling and uncoupling that a locomotive has got to do or else there wouldn't be no train. The problem is not how to love or even how to keep from loving, but how to abide love. You do see, don't you? To put it more basically, in universal language, hoo hah and whoo whoo. I wish you bluebirds. What do you wish me? He shut his eyes and let the water beat on his face, humming the piece of song. I *sit* here before you, ladies and gentlemen of the jury, sort of, well, entirely, naked, to accept your judgment and to beg your passion. My self assurance is broke. It sure hurt when it broke, too, gentlemen and ladies, and how can we put it back together again? Oh yes I am aware of myself. My own self. I know my bonds. Bounds. I don't care if you look at my genitals, but don't do it unless you love me, don't bother unless you want to join up with me in this here great short floundering time that we got. I wish you bluebirds. Uniquely. That's better than nothing. I maintain, with yawl's indulgence, that I am a sociable man with nice manners and very little tolerance who has been invaded and jumped up and down on. They have scattered my forces, dear frins, put my ignorant armies to rout, and then made these here noxious charges that I am restless and flipflopping around and guilty of shameful conduct. To you I say *bluebirds.* To them I say—I forget what it is I say to them. But it'll come to me. I have a finely keened legal tune, or something of that nature.

The curtain opened and Doris thrust a glass of cold milk at Ben. "Drink," she said.

He drank it and belched. She gave him a cup of coffee. The coffee burned his lips as he drank it, and the water from the shower sprayed the cup. Doris took the cup and shut the curtain.

Hoo hah. Whoo whoo. Hear me shuffling along? Happy birthday to yew, happy birthday to yew, happy birthday, Ben Car . . .

Harry stuck another cup of coffee at him. Ben drank it automatically as a patient accepting medication from his doctor, not questioning that it was the best possible thing to do and that he was being cared for. What else was that about bluebirds? *There'll be bluebirds over the white cliffs of Dover. . . .* Hoo hah. The cliffs, amazingly enough, were white, all right, but he hadn't seen any bluebirds there. Just some mangy-looking gulls flapping around the barges and tugs. There'll be mangy gulls over the white cliffs of Dover. That sounded better. I wish you mangy gulls, Sam Guthrie.

"What are you saying?" Harry said.

"I'm preparing my defense."

"You said something about mangy gulls."

"Couldn't have."

"Drink the coffee. Does your head hurt?"

"More than a little."

"How's your stomach?"

"It despises me. We haven't been frins for months."

"When did you eat last?"

"What's today?"

"Damn," Harry said. He took the coffee cup and shut the curtain.

Ben began to soap himself. Sitting on the stool, as at a Japanese bathhouse, he soaped himself carefully all over and then soaped his hair. He slid the stool forward to get the full flow of the shower. His head was clearing, and as it did an awful remembrance began coming to him. Several awful remembrances. A man with only one awful remembrance was a man without experience of life, he thought, an uneducated man. Hoo hah. Get back in there you awful remembrances. Don't bother me on my birthday. Don't you want me to have any fun at all?

As he pushed the button in the elevator to come down from the law office that afternoon, Ben Carpenter had noticed that his hand was trembling. He lifted his attaché case and held it with both hands and mashed it against his stomach. He looked up at the lighted numbers moving across the panel above the elevator door. Down from 32, dropping quickly, with the feeling that there may be no bottom, the lights popping across the panel and music softly playing, and the elevator falling as if this would be the final descent, and he realized that his feet were pushing hard against the carpet as though trying to drive the elevator down faster.

The bright steel door slid back quietly. Ben walked into the lobby of the office building and went past the cigarette counter and the stacks of newspapers and shoved the revolving door and found himself spun onto the street. In the heat of the early May afternoon he went around the corner and into the parking garage, still holding the attaché case awkwardly to his stomach like a woman with a sack of groceries. He gave his car ticket to a woman inside a glass booth and watched her read the number of the ticket into a microphone, and then saw that she was looking at him oddly. She raised a forefinger and motioned to him. He bent his head so that he could talk to her through the round porthole in the glass.

"Seventy-five cents, sir," she said.

"Oh," Ben said. "I'm sorry. I was thinking about something else."

"Yes sir," she said, as if everyone who came in there told her that.

A young Negro in a khaki uniform drove Ben's black Mercedes

down a curving concrete ramp, stopped the car sharply so that the tires squealed, opened the door, and leaped out. Ben tipped him fifteen cents, got in, and laid the attaché case on the seat beside him. He looked at his hands on the steering wheel. The trembling had stopped, but now his stomach felt as if he had swallowed a mouthful of orange seeds. He was sweating.

"You kay?" said the young Negro.

"Fine," Ben said.

"Tough night?"

"They all are," Ben said.

The Negro laughed. Ben put the Mercedes into gear and pulled into the downtown traffic. He moved slowly across town for five blocks, turned left onto Commerce Street, and edged with the jammed mass of cars and buses along the narrow defile between the cliffs of buildings, between the hotels and the shops, past the plain square gray Neiman-Marcus building, past the walls of glass of the new hotels which had put potted plants on the sidewalks in an effort to restore some of the trees the merchants had cleared away to build Dallas. With a tree at least there was some kind of a sense of history but nobody had thought of that until it was too late and now they had no history except the records of their inventories.

Ben turned the Mercedes left onto the North Central Expressway, found a place in an inside lane, and began to move north. In a few minutes he had cleared downtown and then he was going sixty miles an hour between motels and office buildings and residential districts, past the red brick campus of Southern Methodist University, and then out into the rolling plain of North Dallas. It was an area that fascinated him—miles of low brick houses on straight bare streets, miles of houses of which each looked like the other and where sixty thousand dollars was a very common price for a very ordinary stack of bricks placed behind a couple of scrubby hedges on a plot of plowed dirt with perhaps a tree. Off to the left was a more hilly area, stuck in the plain by some geologic accident, where water lay in the creek beds and where someone had neglected to chop down the trees and thus had created a comforting place for a vast housing project of the very rich. In there, Ben knew, among the elms and oaks and hackberrys, sung to by mockingbirds and observed by squirrels, lived Sam Guthrie.

There was once, Ben remembered, when he had gone to Guthrie's home with Edward Simmons, the president of Ramco. They had gone to see if the war could be avoided and they had found that like most wars it could not because it was rooted in greed. The moment he drove through the gates of Guthrie's estate Ben had given up the idea of not having to fight. The house was a Bavarian castle with a gate house and guest house that had turrets and battlements. Behind the house glistened the water of a small lake. They had found Guthrie sitting beside his swimming pool. Guthrie was reading the sports section of *The Dallas Morning News* and hardly bothered to look up. Guthrie's lawyer asked Ben and Simmons to sit down at the white iron table, and in a moment Guthrie folded the paper and dropped it onto the grass. Guthrie listened to Simmons's offer of three seats on the board of Ramco, and then Guthrie laughed.

"That's not what I want," Guthrie said.

"What do you want?" said Simmons.

"Ramco," Guthrie said.

Guthrie glanced at his lawyer.

"I told you this was useless," said Guthrie. "Now I'm going to play golf. If you gentlemen should reconsider you know where to find me. Otherwise, it's time for the kickoff."

That afternoon Ben had driven back to his office to begin preparing the first of the injunctions that he knew would be both unsuccessful and annoying. The courts would refuse to order Guthrie to quit buying Ramco stock, but at least the legal quibbling would delay him and divert some of his energy.

Thinking about Guthrie, Ben pushed down on the accelerator and fled through the pear-light of the plain and came to the high cyclone wire fences of Ramco. At the gate he showed his pass with the photograph and the SECRET stamp. He parked his Mercedes in the executive lot where the whitewashed spaces were filled with Cadillacs and Lincolns. A hawk drifted above the trees beyond the fence. The Ramco plant was as silent as an abandoned barn in its pasture. Behind the yellow brick walls were several hundred people, but no signal of life came out. He showed his pass again to a guard at the door of the plant and walked down a long hall and showed his pass again at the doorway to the executive offices. The hall and the offices were bright with hidden light. In Ramco there were no windows and no shadows.

At Simmons's office the receptionist smiled at Ben and spoke into the machine on her desk and while he waited he wondered if they were going to let him in or if Simmons, too, was part of what had happened. But the receptionist nodded and Simmons's secretary appeared, also smiling and nodding—for to them in this war there had never been anything at stake, most likely not even their jobs—and Ben was led into Simmons's inner office.

Simmons sat behind a wide curving plank of mahogany that he used for a desk. He looked up and smiled, but his smile was painful, as if he had slammed a drawer on his finger and was trying to deny that it had hurt.

"Ben," he said, "I hadn't expected you until four. But sit down. Would you like some coffee?"

"Please," said Ben. He sat down in the leather chair across from Simmons's desk. Simmons pushed a button and the secretary was there.

"Coffee for Mr. Carpenter. Black, I believe." Simmons waited for contradiction, his blue pupils looking at Ben from out of their yellowed mountings. "Yes, black. Bring me a glass of buttermilk, please, dear."

Simmons took a cigarette from a silver box on the desk, studied it for a moment, and then put it back into the box.

"I'm cutting down," Simmons said. "The way I do it is I refuse myself three times in a row. Sometimes I lose count."

Simmons leaned back and clasped his hands behind his head. The gold of his watchband peeked from beyond his shirt cuffs. The coat of his gray silk suit hung from a rack in the corner. Along the wall by the rack were signed photographs of Simmons shaking hands with various senators, admirals, generals, and one President. On the opposite wall were photographs of Simmons in the uniform of an Air Force colonel standing on the wing of a World War II fighter plane, of Simmons in leather flying cap and puttees standing beside a World War I fighter plane, of Simmons wearing a steel helmet and standing beside a missile. A large color photograph of the Ramco plant and grounds, looking very much like a prison, covered the wall behind Simmons.

"My doctor has been telling me to cut down for twenty years," Simmons said. "And then the other day I was suddenly sixty-three. Sixty never sounded bad. Sixty-one sounded mature. Sixty-two I forgot about because we were busy that year. But then suddenly I was sixty-three and I thought about dying. I decided to cut down."

Simmons came forward, dropped his hands, and took a cigarette out of the silver box.

"But it's silly to try to hang on to anything," he said. "Nothing lasts. As long as I'm going to die anyhow, I might as well die smoking."

Simmons snapped a silver lighter in front of his cigarette. He looked at Ben. Simmons's hair was white and cropped short and lay flat on his skull, as though after he stepped out of the shower in the morning he never combed his hair but let it dry however the water had left it. His face wrinkled as he squinted and blew out smoke. He was tanned but his left hand was very white from having worn a golf glove.

"Something funny happened to me while ago," Ben said. "That's why I'm here early. Johnson wouldn't let me in his office."

The secretary brought in the coffee and the glass of buttermilk and then went out with a swishing of hose. Simmons raised the buttermilk, said "Cheers," drank, licked the buttermilk off his lips, and made a face.

"I really don't like that stuff," Simmons said. "The doctor again."

"Johnson wouldn't see me," said Ben. "Something's wrong over there. It scares me. After what I found out this morning, there's plenty of reason for us to be scared even without Johnson acting funny."

"What did you find out?" Simmons said.

He sounded tired and for a moment Ben wondered whether Simmons really cared what he had found out.

"Last night Guthrie's people mailed out what they called Simmons Dollars," said Ben. "They're little replicas of dollar bills about the size of postage stamps. Each one is in a money clip to make it look smaller and more ridiculous. And each one has a letter about Ramco profits being down and about the cut in dividends. They sent out thousands of those Simmons Dollars and money clips. Stockholders all over the country are getting them today."

"I got one," Simmons said. "Clever idea."

"Yeah but that's not what's worrying me," said Ben. "You remember a couple of weeks ago when we got Thurlowe to switch his thousand shares to us?"

"Nice piece of work. Must have cost you an awful hangover."

"Thurlowe's gone back to Guthrie, and he did it in hiding," Ben said. "You know that whenever you switch a proxy you have to register it. Well, Thurlowe has switched back without registering it. He postdated it. Guthrie's got his proxy and it's dated next Wednesday when it'd be too late for us to do anything about it. God-damn him, we would have walked into that stockholders meeting thinking we had Thurlowe's proxy tied up and they'd have pulled that postdated one on us and made us look like idiots. They'd have registered it right before the meeting."

"How do you know Thurlowe did that?"

"A pretty good source," Ben said. "I've been dating Thurlowe's secretary. She told me this morning after she heard Thurlowe talking on the phone to one of Guthrie's people."

"Disloyal girl," said Simmons.

"It's lucky for us that she decided she didn't have to be loyal to a lying son of a bitch," Ben said. "What I'm wondering now is how many others like Thurlowe there are. Our latest counts and projections show we've got a good chance. The Simmons Dollars will hurt us some, but we've been going great. We're picking up momentum. When we announce that new contract in the Sunday papers we ought to just about wipe out any damage from the Simmons Dollars. But our counts and surveys are based on a lot of guys like Thurlowe. He's proved that our counts are soft. Until his secretary told me that this morning I really thought we had it won. Now I see that's what Guthrie wanted us to think, and then he was going to kill us in places where we thought we were safe."

Ben tossed the cardboard cup into the wastebasket.

"What I want to do is start right now and go back over all the stockholders we can," Ben said. "We won't have time to make them all, but we can make the bigger ones. Chances are, Guthrie wouldn't have bothered trying this with the smaller ones. Close as it is, a few Thurlowes could cut us. Our guys in the field working on the uncommitted proxies I want to leave alone. I want to round up another crew and get them to check on the ones that we think are already committed. I can make quite a few of the bigger ones myself before the stockholders meeting. We might seduce a few Guthrie thinks he has cinched. But it's going to cost money, and I want your approval."

"You've worked very hard on this," said Simmons.

"I've tried," Ben said. "But I guess I haven't been dirty enough. I let Guthrie slip up behind us. But while he's back there I want to trap him. I'm going to turn these postdated proxies around on him and either get them with us again or get the whole thing confused and shoved into court until we can get time to straighten it out. First, though, we have to have an idea whether Thurlowe is the only one or whether we might have dozens of guys to tackle. That'll take money and a lot of people and we'll have to start the minute you authorize the expense."

Simmons had listened with his eyes squinted and looking at the wall beside the coat rack as if trying to make out who that man was in those pictures. When Ben paused, Simmons turned and stubbed his cigarette in an ash tray mounted on a model of a missile for which Ramco had built several component parts of the guidance system.

"Why did you go see Johnson?" said Simmons.

"Naturally he's the number one man," Ben said. "His block of proxies is worth two dozen Thurlowes."

"I know that. Why did you go see him?"

"I made it a social call. Keeping up team spirit. I was going to tell him that we had it won, and reassure him, and get in a few personal licks at Guthrie. And see if I could get a hint whether Johnson was still solid."

"I would think," said Simmons, "that would be in my scope of operations. You know Johnson is a very close friend of mine. He's like a dear nephew. I almost raised that boy. He was married to my daughter for a while. Insufferable bitch. If Johnson was going to defect on us, he'd tell me. And if we suspected him of treachery, I'd be the man to take up the matter with him."

"I wasn't going to take it up with him," Ben said. "It was a morale visit. Probably as much for my morale as for his. It would have been nice, the way I was feeling about Thurlowe, to be reassured that the biggest single stockholder on our side was still on our side."

Simmons got up from his chair and walked around the office with his hands in his pockets, looking at the floor as if he had dropped something but couldn't remember what it was or if he was in fact searching in the right room. For the first time Ben noticed that Simmons had a bit of a paunch; usually Simmons stood erect, as if he were still a colonel and proud of it, but now his shoulders had fallen and as he wandered around his own office he let his stomach shove against his alligator belt. It seemed somehow to mean the end of discipline, to mean that Simmons had given himself up to age. Ben had admired Simmons, had fought for him as fiercely as he had fought for his own father, and now Ben began to wonder with alarm if Simmons were ill, if there had been some menace of more significance than cutting down on cigarettes.

"I had dinner last night with Rosco Morrison," Simmons said. He stopped in front of the big color photograph of Ramco and looked at Ben. "The senior member of your law firm has quit threatening to throw you out on the street. Rosco was very angry at you for a long while. He blamed you for talking me into this proxy fight. Rosco was all in favor of surrendering to Guthrie as soon as Guthrie turned down our offer."

"Mr. Morrison made that clear to me," said Ben.

"Rosco is happy now. I told him last night we had this fight won and he decided maybe you weren't trying to wreck the company after all and he told me how glad he was that we had fought Guthrie."

"That's nice," Ben said.

"No, it's not nice," said Simmons. "It's something but it's not nice. Tell me, if we had lost this proxy fight, or rather if we lose it, do you really think Morrison will fire you?"

"I'm a very junior member. We wouldn't have got into this merely on my authority. But you know Mr. Morrison better than I do."

"I think he would fire you. I'm sure of it."

"So am I."

"Is that why you've worked so hard? You really didn't talk me into this, you know. I was for fighting all along. But you did help me talk the rest of the board into it when they were ready to surrender. If Guthrie wins, he won't keep your firm and you'll be out of work. Why didn't you want an appeasement like the others?"

"Because I think Guthrie is a bastard," Ben said.

"There must be more to it than that?"

"He's a grabber," said Ben. "He calls himself a builder, but he's just a grabber. I don't like him. I don't like anything about him. I don't like his Bavarian castle or those phony speeches he makes about doing good for the city. I don't even like his golf swing. And to put it on a strictly human basis, I don't want to see Guthrie get bigger at your expense. You built this company."

"I thought there might be something personal in it. I appreciate that," Simmons said. He smiled and sat down again and the smile went away. "But this is merely a business, I suppose. It's been much of my life. But as I said nothing lasts—not Ramco in the form we know it, and not my life in the form I know it, and not even Guthrie will last forever, thank God. I have to tell you something, Ben. I'm not supposed to tell you this, but I wouldn't consider myself a man if I didn't. I have done a lot of wicked things in my time. All men have. You don't build up a business the size of Ramco and stay pure. You don't, unfortunately, live to be sixty-three and stay pure. But one crime I have never been guilty of is treachery. You've been sincere with me. In the last few months you've been closer than a son to me. I wouldn't be surprised if the time you've devoted to me hadn't been partly a cause of your domestic problems. So I can't sell you out without a warning."

Simmons took another cigarette out of the silver box and lit it.

"I'm not refusing myself this one," he said. He looked at Ben again and his face seemed to have become older in the minutes Ben had been in the office. "You, my boy, are in a jam. The reason Johnson wouldn't see you is because Johnson has gone over to Guthrie with seventeen per cent of the stock in Ramco. Johnson is not going to postdate his proxies, but he's not going to register the switch until Wednesday. He did, of course, telephone me this morning to tell me. He wouldn't do anything like that without telling me."

"But why?" Ben said.

"Because Waddy Morris, Jr., called Johnson from Guthrie's fishing boat and told him we would be much better off if Guthrie took over Ramco. So you see, the fight is lost."

That was it. When Johnson had refused to admit him, Ben had suspected disaster. And the blow had been struck, more smashingly than he could have guessed. For a minute Ben sat silently. There was nothing for him to say. It was finished, and more than likely he was finished as a junior member of the firm of Morrison, Karl, Lewis and Gilliland. That his job was probably gone didn't seem as important as the look on Simmons's face; to Ben it mattered more that Simmons was out of the business that he had put his life into. It was for Ben another step along an odd corridor of circumstance. He looked at his hands, and they were steady. There was no use in trembling now.

"If I see Guthrie today I'll kill him," Ben said quietly.

"I wouldn't bother to give this matter that dignity," said Simmons. "It's nothing. These things happen frequently. As for myself, there's no worry. Waddy promised Acey that in return for Acey's proxies

I will be kept on as president of Ramco and that after Guthrie effects the merger I will have a seat on the board of the new corporation."

"Do you believe that?"

"No," Simmons said. "But it's of no importance whether I believe it. They'll live up to their word as long as it's convenient and then they'll cut my throat. But I'm taken care of. I would be retiring in a few years. This way I'll simply be retired earlier. I can get my golf game polished." He held up his white left hand and smiled the painful smile. "I haven't been exactly neglecting golf, which may have something to do with the fix we're in, but now I'll get my game sharp and win the senior championship at the club for the next ten years in succession."

"But damn it, you can't let them do that. Johnson is your friend. Appeal to him," said Ben.

"It's not a clean case of friendship versus power," Simmons said. "Waddy Morris, Jr., is convinced the eventual merger is the best thing, so Johnson is also convinced. It makes sense."

"You're not convinced."

"Certainly not. But Acey is. He thinks he's doing right for me and for himself. I'm not going to beg him to do otherwise. I don't beg anybody to do anything for me."

"How did Waddy Morris get into this?" said Ben.

"I don't know. Some devious path or other. But I think it's quite interesting. I'll be curious to see Waddy's influence in the future of the new corporation. I'd be very surprised if Waddy has less than four seats on the new board. I think Guthrie has taken on a more formidable partner than Guthrie realizes."

"And you're going to let them do it."

"I have no choice."

"I'm disappointed," Ben said. He picked up his attaché case and pushed back his chair. "If you're not a fighter in this, I can't be."

"Ben," said Simmons. "Ben, I'm sorry. You know how grateful I am to you and how much I like you and what this means to me. But what could I do?"

"You could go to Johnson and change his mind for him. You could sell Ramco to him. You could tell him what a bastard Guthrie is. You could remind Johnson of your association with him. You could forget your pride and start fighting. You didn't build Ramco by being weak, but you're losing it by being weak. I care what happens to you. You've been honest with me but you're not being honest with yourself, and if you're not honest with yourself then pretty soon you won't be honest with anybody. For a man like you, Mr. Simmons, that's suicide. You won't be able to live with yourself."

"Trying to convince Acey that I'm a better judge of this than Waddy Morris would be impossible."

"I don't give a damn about Waddy Morris. You shouldn't give a damn about him. You can persuade Johnson to do what you want him to. And if you can't, then you'll know what kind of guy Johnson is."

"Ben, this isn't easy for me. This isn't easy for me at all. But I think I had best accept their terms. I know when the fight is lost."

When Simmons said that, Ben felt anger burst in him like a winter pipe.

"Then so do I," Ben said. "I'm through with fighting. Let Guthrie have this damned company. Or let Waddy Morris have it. Give it to any son of a bitch you want to give it to. Just sit there and worry about your golf game and stroke your belly and let them take Ramco and run off with it. Why should I give a damn? I haven't been fighting for anything except losing causes lately, and I'm sick of it. I'm sick of fighting for you or for me or for anybody else."

Ben threw the attaché case at the color photograph of Ramco. The leather case slapped against the picture and papers fluttered out as it dropped to the floor.

"This belongs to you now," Ben said. "It's stuffed full of counts and surveys and reports that you might want to wipe your ass with."

"There's no profit acting like a barbarian," said Simmons. He jumped up from his desk and glared at Ben, his blue eyes squinting from yellowish slits. "Who the hell do you think you're talking to, young man? You can't come into my office and act like a pig."

"You've got it right," Ben said. "That's what I am now, a barbarian. I'm disgusted with all this formalized legalized structuralized whoring. As a barbarian, I'll talk to you any damned way I want to. But the thing is, I don't want to talk to you or to anybody else like you. I just want you bastards to leave me alone from now on. Go play with Guthrie. Bend over and let him enjoy you. If you're not a man, let's quit kidding about it."

Simmons came around the desk as Ben went to the door.

"By God, I could go see Johnson if I chose to and maybe get

him back and I might do it, but I'm not going to have you talking to me like that," yelled Simmons.

"I don't care whether you go see Johnson. I'm through. I'm sick of being crapped on. The hell with it," Ben said.

Going out, Ben tried to slam the door. But the architects of Ramco had seen to it that the doors would not slam. Ben was denied that pleasure.

The curtains opened again and Harry turned off the water. Ben stood up and sloshed across the slippery floor of the shower. Doris wrapped him in a beach towel and rubbed him briskly. When Ben was dry, Harry plugged in an electric razor and rapidly buzzed it down Ben's cheeks and along his jaw and chin and upper lip. Harry stepped back and looked at him professionally.

"Good enough," Harry said. "Not beautiful but good enough."

Harry poured out a handful of shaving lotion and slapped it onto Ben's face.

"I wish you bluebirds," said Ben. "Some folks I wish bluebirds and some I wish mangy gulls."

"I knew you said something about mangy gulls," Harry said.

"Not mangy gulls. *Mangy* gulls. Show emotion."

"You mean like you did dancing on the grass? What was that, *Midsummer Night's Dream?*"

With the towel hanging around him like a toga, Ben followed Harry into the bedroom and sat on the bed. Doris made him drink two Alka-Seltzers and a bowl of hot soup and another glass of milk and cup of coffee. By then Ben was fully aware of where he was and how he got there, and when he thought of his entrance into the house he shuddered. Harry sat at the dressing table and watched him. Ben kept licking the roof of his mouth; the soup and coffee had burned his tongue, and his cigarette tasted like a spider web. Through the window Ben could see the top of an elm whispering against the house. Ben looked around. Doris and Harry had brought him into their own room, and he was thankful. He had thought they might have taken him into the room they had originally made into a nursery. After the baby had died, they had repainted the walls and moved in a desk and had intended to use the room as an office, but neither Harry nor Doris went into the room much.

"Doris is cleaning your shoes," Harry said.

"Don't let her do that. I'll go barefoot."

"They'll have to be cleaned. What did you do to 'em besides wade around in vomit?"

"Don't remind me. Just stop her."

"She'll be through with 'em in a minute."

"Harry to the rescue," Ben said. "Again and again and again."

"You've rescued me plenty," said Harry.

"Not lately though."

"We don't have to keep books on it."

"I am properly grateful for that."

"You're the guest of honor," Harry said. "Think you can make it downstairs?"

"In a minute. Did they all see you bring me in?"

"Most of 'em."

"Nothing I can do about it now. I don't care anyhow."

"Where you been all day?"

"Practicing up on being dissolute."

"I guess any man's got a right to be dissolute on his thirtieth birthday," said Harry. "It's a big occasion."

"I got a better excuse than that. Another double cross today."

"Jean?"

"Not Jean. In the proxy fight. A big stockholder who'd promised he was with us suddenly went over to Guthrie and left me with my foolishness showing. Bam. Just like that. One minute he was with me, and the next minute I was completely whipped. I went hustling into his office this afternoon with an armful of intrigues and battle plans and enthusiasms, and he wouldn't see me. Sent out a message for me to go away. I went to see my client and he told me we'd been sold out.

"Must have had a reason."

"Damn reasons."

"But something happened."

"Yeah, something happened. Guthrie got to the guy through Waddy Morris, Jr."

"I've heard of him. At least it was an elegant screwing."

"It left me and my law firm with nothing to do but empty chamberpots and march off to our cells and tremble," Ben said. "Our heads get lopped off. At the minimum, mine does. Ramco was a very big client. If there's a chance of keeping even a little piece of work after Guthrie takes over, and Guthrie can be satisfied with a human sacrifice, you are looking at the bleating lamb."

"What good would it do Guthrie to get you fired?"

"I don't like him. He doesn't like anybody who doesn't like him. I've said a few things to him and done a few things to him that he won't forget. Anyhow, after I left my former client I went over to the University Club and drank scotch until I almost fell down the stairs, and then I drove out to Gordo's and drank beer with Gordo and ordered a pizza to go, which I dropped in the parking lot, and then I drove over to Fort Worth. First thing I did when I got here was stop at Masseys and drink some more beer and look at those dogs they got on the wallpaper and try to figure out which one of 'em was supposed to be me. I ordered an open hot steak but I didn't eat it because I decided I absolutely had to go to the Oui Oui Club immediately. Searching for my youth, I guess. The bartender pushed me out of there and demanded I go to my birthday party. Jason had told him. I invited the bartender and some guys playing the bowling machine and a blonde-headed woman who seems to know Jason. They're all my good comrades. I'm raising a rabble army to march on Dallas."

"I wish there was something I could do," Harry said.

Ben looked at his friend. Harry's blond hair was cut short and brushed straight forward onto his forehead like a Roman senator's, and he had a red face and a prominent Adam's apple. His big hands were clasped in his lap and he sat hunched forward, big-boned, looking up through gray-blue eyes.

"I know you do," said Ben.

"It's been tough. All this crap with your daddy and Jean and then what happened today."

"It's been difficult. It's what I would call trying."

"You could go crazy if you let it get to you."

"What I want is not to think," Ben said.

"Looks like what you want is to destroy yourself, the way you've been acting."

"I'm being scourged."

"That's one word for it. How about the proxy fight? Is it dead? No chance the guy who switched to Guthrie will switch back to you? We could go bend his arm a little bit and then keep him tied in the closet until the stockholders' meeting."

"A noble thought. A pleasurable thought. I guess there is a very slight chance that my client could get back in it, but I told him the hell with it and that's what I meant. I've been a fighting man, and I've been a drinking and singing man, and being a drinking and singing man is better. I'm going to treat my soul to some awful wallowing. The only time I'll ever be a fighting man again is if I get an opportunity to work on Guthrie with a hammer."

"You might need a big hammer from the looks of him. That day you pointed out Guthrie to me over at the golf tournament, he looked like he could tear legs off of people."

"Then one of these days he will have to tear mine off. I have become a vindictive man, Harry. There is murder in my heart. But there is so much murder that ought to be done that it defeats me, and thus I sublimate it and it gives my eyes this lively sparkle and my feet this comely stagger."

"I thought you'd sobered up," Harry said, grinning.

"The friends thou hast, grapple them to thy soul with hooks of steel."

"Yes sir, the man got drunk on soup and coffee."

"In my ugly little ways," said Ben, "I've managed to make myself unloved. When I think about not being with her any more, not living with her any more, her not loving me any more, it's more than I can take. I can't accept it. I just can't think about it."

"How about some more coffee?" Harry said.

"I'm okay now."

"All the sudden you're talking about Jean. Last time you told me you were through talking about Jean. You said she was out of your mind."

"I say a lot of things."

"Want to get dressed?"

"Isn't this a costume ball?"

Harry went to the closet and tossed Ben a pair of slacks. From the dresser, Harry produced a clean shirt and underwear. Ben folded the beach towel, laid it on the bed, and began to dress. Harry's clothes were a proper fit in length, although the waist of the pants was a bit too large. Harry found Ben's own belt, and Ben cinched up the pants.

"Maybe I'm just a loser," Ben said.

"You never were before."

"Maybe I've always been a loser and didn't know it until my

father showed me. There are some guys who are just losers. They get to thinking they're winners, but it's an illusion."

"You've had some bad luck lately," said Harry.

"I caused most of it myself. That's the loser's syndrome."

Ben sat down on the bed and lit another cigarette.

"I don't believe in divorce," Ben said.

"You used to believe in it."

"That was when Jean and I were having those fights before we split up. That was when we weren't being tolerant of each other or keeping the faith. I guess I do believe in divorce in extreme cases. If she was really in love with somebody else, or if I was, maybe. But you know how it is, Harry. You see some girl and you get aroused and think you've got to have her, and mostly it's because she's sort of unobtainable. So you smash up everthing to make her obtainable, and it's a great sensation, and then pretty soon you find out she's not so hot after all, that what you had spent years building up is a lot better than this new thing. Even if what you'd spent years building up isn't exactly smoldering with passion and throwing off deliriums of wild orgasm. Old friends are best. You usually don't learn that until you've lost 'em. That's why I'm against divorce."

"That's not necessarily true."

"I'm just talking. Hell, I'm babbling, ain't I?"

"Talk," Harry said. "I've got ears."

"That last night, the night I left," said Ben. "I think about that a lot. Jean and I'd had another big scene and had said things to each other that we couldn't take back. She started telling me to get out. So I went and got out. I packed and she went into the den and slammed the door and then I went upstairs to the kids' room and sat on Julie's bed. The kids were asleep, of course, you know, with their arms and legs all sprawled out and breathing loud and with these sweet expressions on their faces. I looked at Julie and I looked over at little Elaine, and I was doing all right. I was thinking how sorry I was and how sad it was that I wouldn't be there to watch 'em grow up ever day, and thinking about the little things we are going to miss from each other, and wondering if they could ever understand how sorry I was. I was a long way from being happy, you understand, but it was a relief to think about no more loud arguments and Jean and I not tearing each other up all the time, and I was doing all right. Then I looked at the head of

Julie's bed. She had three Indian faces put up there with Scotch tape. Just three damn Indian faces she had drawn and cut out of that yellow art paper kids use. They were round faces with big eyes and feathers coming out of the top of their heads. And they were smiling. I think it was the smiling that got me. Anyhow, those faces cracked me. I fell apart. I got this big sudden rush of what I guess you'd call agony or something, got it in the chest, hard. I ran out of there and grabbed my suitcase and got in the car. I was crying like a woman. I drove my car into a ditch and sat there and cried until I didn't think I could ever cry again."

"That toughen you up?" Harry said.

"I don't want to get tough like that. It scares me to think I might get that tough. Anyhow, after a while I quit crying and went to a motel. I unpacked. I was thinking how funny it was that I could pack eight years of married life in one suitcase. Then I started noticing the kind of things I'd packed. A few shirts, a few socks, two suits, no ties, no belts. Some underwear. My hand vibrator machine. All my bathroom stuff except my toothbrush. A picture of Jean and the kids. An envelope that had my birth certificate and passport and smallpox shot record in it. That picture you took of the sailfish I caught that time we all went to Acapulco. Our household ledger. A cotton bathrobe. Three golf balls. An extra pack of cigarettes. I must have thought I was going to jail or something. I packed a letter Jean wrote me in February when I was in Chicago. The key to our lake cabin in Austin. A paperback copy of *Notes from Underground*. And a letter I had written to her once. In that letter I said evertime I left her I was afraid it might be the last. I said looking at her made me aware how little time we had together, and I didn't ever want to be away from her. I didn't know how little time I really meant. It was quite a letter. I wrote it last year. It was like something you'd have expected me to write when we were first married. But I didn't feel that much when we were first married."

"You felt pretty much when you were first married."

"But not as much as I did later, that's the point. Oh, crap, there's no use talking about this."

"You're in a hell of a mental state," Harry said. "From all I'd heard, you'd turned into a gay young scoundrel without a heavy thought in the world. I've heard about you being out with fifty different women in the past few weeks, and being drunk in all the better places."

"People talk."

"Most of 'em got nothing else to do."

"They make up a lot of things that they like to believe because their own lives are so empty."

"They can get vicious," Harry said. "If you're not doing what they're doing, they slice you up. I've heard some stories about your conduct lately that weren't very flattering."

"They were probably true."

"Probably," Harry said, grinning.

"Think you can support me for a while after I get fired? I'll sleep on that old cot out in your studio. I'll mow your lawn, haul the garbage, paint the woodwork, serve the drinks, let old massa beat me with a rope."

"Why don't you hang out your own shingle?"

"I don't have the guts for it any more, Harry. I've had about all I can take."

"I'm not going to try to tell you what to do," said Harry. "You've always got a place here."

"I'll tell you something odd," Ben said. "That first betrayal, or whatever you want to call it, with my father, hurt so much I kind of enjoyed it. I enjoyed walking around hurting. I felt noble. You know what I mean? Raised in my pain to nobility. I could see these wrinkles coming into my face and feel my hair growing gray and I felt like people were looking at me and thinking there's a man who's suffered and ain't he got dignity? But all this crap that happened afterwards, it just beat me down, knocked me down, twisted my brains. It was sure a passing nobility."

"Aren't you getting awful involved with yourself?" said Harry.

"I suppose," Ben said. He picked up the socks Harry had given him and then dropped them on the floor. "I'm going barefoot. As an expression of my personality. My new humble, unworldly personality. I wish I had a big shaggy beard with cockleburrs in it."

"How come you didn't bring a girl tonight?"

"I didn't want to mess with it. It's a lot of trouble to have to go pick up a girl, and act like you're interested in what she's saying, and then take her home afterward. I'll have a few drinks and find me a girl downstairs."

"What do you intend to do about the man she's with?"

"I'll hold him, and you hit him."

"I'd better start moving the furniture."

"You promised my mother you'd take care of me."

"I've been doing it since you were this high," Harry said, placing his palm two feet off the floor. "It was a sacred promise."

"You've done a rotten job."

"You're not the easiest person in the world to take care of."

"Let's go down and see what a great party I'm having," said Ben.

They left the bedroom, walked past the guest room where Ben's shoes sat polished in the doorway, and went down the carpeted stairs, ducking as their heads cleared the top of the landing. The living room was a large room with walls paneled in dark oak. The mantel above the fireplace was lined with drinks, each leaving a wet ring since the party had advanced enough that coasters and napkins had been discarded. Someone had opened the front door for ventilation, but smoke still hung in the overhead lights. People stood in bunches, like islands, leaving canals for passage between. Many of the faces Ben didn't recognize; there were quite a few, he was sure, who were the friends of friends of friends, and who had never met him. There were other faces he remembered but couldn't attach names to. And quite a lot who were acquaintances from as far back as fifteen or twenty years. At the other end of the room, by a bay window covered with louvres, people stood around the stereo and sang. Several were dancing. Until he became accustomed to it, the noise was painful, like a dock at departure time with a band playing and people waving; many of them, he thought, seemed to be shouting goodbye. To him? Feet shuffled on the oak floor. A girl's voice battered its way through the orchestration on the record. Ben shook hands with a dozen people, accepted a drink, and looked around nodding and smiling and being what he called political. Three lovely girls, all with purple eyelids and high packed hair, smiled at him from the couch beside the fireplace. He listened to people laughing about his previous entrance, and he smiled and said things he was hardly aware of saying. He pushed through the crowd, weaved between the dancers—saying scuse me, pardon me, woops, scuse me, hi, what say—and stopped to look at a sign draped on the wall above the kitchen door: *BEN IS THIRTY.*

"I was thirty once myself," a voice said. "Seems like almost three months ago."

"Lo, Walter," said Ben.

"Happy birthday," Walter said, shaking hands with Ben. "Have you seen Chub?"

"I just got here."

"Yeah. Yeah, I heard. I thought you might have seen her somewhere."

"Walter, in my condition I couldn't see anybody."

"I guess she's slipped off with one of my constituents."

"I doubt it."

"I was joking. You didn't think I meant it, did you?" Walter said. "Hey, congratulations on making thirty. I didn't think you'd ever get there."

"There was some doubt."

"Sad to leave your twenties," said Walter.

"Sad to leave anything important," Ben said. "I understand the Baptists have got you around the neck."

Walter Anderson smiled, and Ben studied his round, bland face for an indication of anxiety. But the face merely looked back at him, as impassive as a pumpkin, small brown eyes undisturbed, mouth slightly open and turned up in a healthy smile. It was the poker-playing face that Walter had achieved in college, an expression he could maintain through hours of joy or despair.

"I'm learning to sing hymns," said Walter. "I'm getting good at 'Bringing in the Sheaves' and 'Washed in the Blood,' but 'Little Brown Church in the Wildwood' is kind of tricky."

"So is Brother Chunk."

"He's a man of conviction," Walter said. "Yes sir, a man of conviction. Them's the kind that's tough to deal with. Say, Ben, how'd you like to invest in a chain of hamburger joints? I'll let you come in with me, for friendship's sake. Sure fire deal."

"Invest what? I don't have enough money left now to keep myself in bubble gum."

"Court got it, huh?"

"That wasn't my money. That was my father's money."

"It would have been yours though."

"Look, Walter . . ."

"Yeah, okay, I'll change the subject. But you could go to the bank. They'd loan you the money. Just don't mention my name."

"I'm not buying," Ben said.

"All right," said Walter. He sighed. "All right. I thought I'd ask.

It's a sure fire deal. Hey, here comes somebody I want you to meet. Friend of mine from Austin. He's a guy you ought to know."

Ben shook hands with William Sheridan.

"How bout singing a song with us," Sheridan said.

Ben looked down at a smudge of lipstick on Sheridan's collar and shook his head. "Maybe later," said Ben.

"Who's gonna win the proxy fight?" Sheridan said.

"The side with the most votes," said Ben.

"Couldn't give me a little advance prediction? This is big news," Sheridan said. "If Guthrie wins, that stock's liable to go booming. No offense to your team, Ben."

"No defense to my team, either," said Ben. He started to break away from them but Chub Anderson came through the kitchen door, jumped up, and kissed him wetly on the cheek. Awkwardly he tried to react, to hug her as she slid down, and his elbow mashed into her bosom. Once there had been nights when Ben couldn't sleep for waking dreams of making love to her. In college she was peachish and virginal and her breasts looked swollen, as if one touch would bring forth a showering of love juices that a man could drown in. Ben had watched her lead cheers, her skirt flapping and the various parts of her bouncing, until he'd had to jolt himself and look away. In half a dozen dates with her in college he hadn't got anywhere, put off always by that wrinkle-nosed giggle and by conversation that enchanted him with its surrealism. Chub was plumper now and not so strainingly ripe, gone more hippy and bosomy although her legs had stayed thin, and she was certainly no longer virginal, but he still remembered her as the ideal bedwarmer, as a curiously impersonal loving machine.

"Walter, hon, get me a drink?" Chub said.

"Sure," said Walter. Sheridan followed him into the kitchen.

"Ben, you look marvelous," Chub said. "I'd expected to see you looking all pale and skinny and ghastly."

"They like to keep us victims healthy," he said.

"Hon, you just look marvelous," she said, giggling. She glanced over her shoulder and then looked back at Ben. She put one finger into his shirt pocket and pulled him toward her, raising up meanwhile to bring their faces together, and Ben thought she was going to kiss him. "Ben, I'm worried," she said.

"What about?"

"I don't think Jason cares for me any more. I think he's mad at me."

Ben stared at her soft lips and innocent face.

"Don't say that to me," he said. "You don't have any right to tell me that."

She leaned her head back and wrinkled her nose, but without giggling.

"Why look who's being high and mighty," she said.

"Chub, don't."

"Now you look at me. Damn you anyway, Ben Carpenter. You don't know anything about what a beast Walter is. You don't know what I go through."

"I don't want to hear it," he said.

"You sure are smug. Aren't you smug? *You* don't have any right. I've heard about you in those motels with those girls."

"That's different," Ben said. "That's biology."

"And what Jason and I've been doing isn't biology?"

"Naw," he said. "It's adultery."

"What would it be if your precious Jean had been doing it?"

"That's all," he said. "That's all I want to hear."

"Wait a minute. Dance with me."

"You're ten years too late."

"Go ahead then, Mr. Smug. Go ahead and act like that. Don't give a person a chance."

Ben looked at her. Was she going to cry? Her nose had wrinkled, but her lips sagged and trembled, a very unattractive expression. She dropped her arms, and suddenly Ben wanted to comfort her. Then she smiled and reached out her hand. Walter was back with the drink.

"Thanks, hon," she said, looking at Walter with what would have passed as love in the view of witnesses. "Didn't you get one for the birthday boy?"

"I forgot," Walter said.

"Never mind," said Ben. "I'll get my own. I want to see what's happening in the kitchen."

As Ben left them, Walter began dancing with Chub, holding her close, a tender scene of mutual care triumphant. Ben went into the kitchen and leaned against the doorway. Cadmus was sitting on the window ledge. When he saw Ben he grinned and stood up to his improbable height and started across the room. Cadmus had the face of a dissipated undergraduate: dark-mooned eyes, blond hair combed into a low pompadour that had drooped forward until it jutted out, flesh beginning to be loose beneath his chin, red cheeks, crooked upper front teeth that his lips rode over when he smiled. At the kitchen table sat Jason: smaller and quicker, handsome, with fast puppyish brown eyes and black hair that looked as if it had been dabbed lightly once on top with a powder puff. Cadmus's girl, Blossom, sat beside Jason at the table. Her legs were crossed above her spiked shoes, her bosom bulged over the restraint of her dress. Blossom's face was alight with a baffled ignorant smile, and her fingers patted her silver hair as if to be sure it had not come undone. Jason's wife, Willy, sat at the end of the table laughing at something Cadmus had said. Fifteen or twenty people had arranged themselves in a standing semicircle around the table, as though they were in an amphitheater and Cadmus was on the stage.

Cadmus shambled forward, big as a bear, and held out a bottle half full of clear liquid.

"Buenos goddamn noches, amigo," Cadmus said. "I have brung fruits of the native country."

"We been drinking tequila," said Blossom.

"Dranking," Cadmus said.

"Dranking," said Blossom. "I didn't know how to drank it before."

"Goddamn native fruits," Cadmus said, examining the bottle. "What they do is take a goddamn cactus and whop off the spiny needles, some of 'em, and have eight or ten Meskins jump up and down on it until it gets to where they can put it into a bottle. Here, Ben, have a drank."

Ben poured salt onto his wrist, licked it, swigged the tequila, and mashed half a lime against his lips. The salt and the lime stung his lips and tongue; the tequila was hot deep inside, like indigestion.

"Whoo," he said.

"Good, hah?" said Cadmus.

"You ever drink any pulque?" Ben said.

"Drank," said Cadmus.

"You ever drank any pulque?"

"I drank most everthang known to man and some unknown. I like dranking and heart-rending experiences. How bout you, Blossom?"

"Damn good," she said.

Cadmus looked at Willy. The severity of boarding with Jason showed in her face; she had begun to wilt like a cornflower.

"Little mother, you got to have a good time," said Cadmus.

"I am," Willy said. "Don't pick on me."

Harry entered through the dining-room door.

"Harry!" shouted Cadmus. "I brung fruits of the native country!"

"Pass 'em over," Harry said.

As they were drinking, Cadmus began to notice a girl in the crowd. She was very young and wore a white skirt and pink blouse. She laughed nervously and clung to her escort's elbow.

"Who that lurking back thur?" Cadmus said, shading his eyes as if peering into a forest. "Step out here, sweet thang, and let us look at you. We ain't gonna hurt you. We white gods that just swum ashore."

The girl looked at her escort to ask his approval.

"She thanks we're Borneo pirates," Cadmus said.

The girl walked out of the crowd and stood uncertainly by the kitchen table, glancing at her escort and then looking up at Cadmus as he grinned at her.

"I bet your daddy is king of this here island," Cadmus said, putting his arm round the girl and pulling her head against his armpit. "Take me to him, little princess. Show me where your idols is at with the rubies in they foreheads."

"I don't know," she said, laughing.

Cadmus swung the girl around.

"Goddamn I wisht I could play the banjo," he said. "We all friends, we all love each other—ain't that right, little princess?—we all in good health and about half dronk, and it's a beautiful night and it's ole Ben's birthday. This is what we like!"

"Are you a millionaire?" the girl asked.

"Why of a certainty, little princess. I'm a millionaire zillionaire. Matter of fact just the other day I bought controlling interest in God. Now I'm God. Did I tell you that, Ben? I thank it slipped my mind."

"Give me a drink," said Ben.

"Drank," Cadmus said. He handed Ben the bottle. "You thank I ain't God, little princess? Why not? Because I fall down and throw up? Hyeh! Hyeh! How bout earthquakes and wars and goddamn ovens? Hyeh! Hyeh!"

"What's this hyeh hyeh?" Harry said.

"That's how God laughs," said Cadmus. "Yes sir, I fall down and throw up and we have goddamn earthquakes and whatever else I said it was. Hyeh! Hyeh! Gimme that native fruit back, Ben."

"If you're really God, do something large," the girl said.

"God can put up with a little doubting and a little argument, but go easy on the challenging," said Cadmus, frowning. "I got thunderbolts. I whop down them unbelievers. I point my fanger and go Whop! Hyeh! Hyeh! Now I put you here to have joy, little princess, not to get your mind all troubled with thanking."

"How come you made sharks?" Harry asked.

"To gobble up the unbelievers that gets under the water where I can't whop 'em with my thunderbolts."

"Why do people have to die?" said the girl.

"You ain't gonna die," Cadmus said. "Ain't you paid attention? You ain't gonna die. You're ee-mortal and ee-ternal. Forever and always. I am ee-mortal and ee-ternal, and I make everbody ee-mortal and ee-ternal. I pass it around. There ain't nothing small and cheap about God. There ain't nothing small and cheap about nobody once you get down to it, but it's kinda hard to get down to it."

Dragging the girl with him, Cadmus bent and kissed Blossom's silver hair.

"Even you," he said, "are ee-mortal and ee-ternal." He straightened up, nearly pulling the girl off her feet. "Course I got to cause a little grief and anguish now and then so you won't be so regretful when it come your time to join me upstairs. How bout it, little princess? What to join me upstairs?"

"I think he's a myth," Harry said.

"Be easy," said Cadmus. "God love everbody but don't push it. Don't ask me for nothing."

"I'd like to ask you, respectfully, sir, for a drink of that native fruit," Jason said.

"Drank," said Cadmus, passing the bottle to Jason. "Harry, somebody, get me a banjo. Just brang me a banjo and let me play till everbody dances and they hearts leap up. Harry, get Doris to put on her long black underwear and dance like she used to in the ballet. Play that record about the ducks that she dances to."

"Swans," Harry said.

Cadmus released the girl.

"Go, little princess, till I call you," he said. "Look at her. Sweet youth and innocence. I was like that oncet, I recall. Gimme that native fruit, Jason, you filthy curmudgeon."

Ben leaned against the drainboard. He could not feel the tequila yet, but he had regard for the assault that was coming. Cadmus grabbed Willy's thin wrist and pulled her toward the living room to dance, leaving the bottle with Ben. Blossom sat smiling and weaving a bit in her chair. Jason, seeing the crowd in the kitchen about to disperse with the exit of Cadmus, stood up.

"I got a new one," Jason said.

"Jason's got a new one," somebody said.

"Ben, I got a new routine," said Jason.

Ben nodded, drank from the bottle, and looked at Jason. Unbuttoning his collar and loosening his tie, Jason moved his hands in quick sharp gestures. He jabbed his forefingers out, his eyes flicking under heavy brows at the people who had stopped to listen. Jason stood slightly knock-kneed, patches of talcum white on his face like make-up. He was assuming a role, getting into character. People grinned and whispered and nudged each other.

"You heard these preachers on the radio from Del Rio?" said Jason.

Heads bobbed. People laughed.

Jason thumped an unseen microphone and adjusted it to his height. He spread his arms, fingers clawing at the air.

"Oh frins ah *laid on* mah face las nat and cried fer ars an ars," Jason shouted. "Thuh angels of thuh *Lord* come tuh visit me rat ther in mah bedroom! Oh frins ah rassled with *thim,* ah tried tuh git up, ah waz sore afraid! Thuh three of thim stood at thuh foot of mah bed an *played* their *trumpits.* Their garmints was white as thuh noonday sun, it dazzled mah eyeballs tuh look upon thim! And thuh Lord God uv Hosts come an stood ahind mah bed so as not tuh *blind* me with His holy light and he saith untuh me: Brother, yew go on thuh raddio an yew do Mah good works untuh thuh people! Untuh thuh people He saith, oh Lord!"

"The true messenger!" somebody yelled.

Jason's voice rose into a chant.

"Don' yew move! Oh don' *nobody* move! Oh yew got to *hyer* His holy words! An his voice was lak thuh soundin brass an frins oh ah tell *yew* ah was afraid an thuh angels played their trumpits an ah laid an wept! Ah waz give thuh gift uv tongues'. Ohhh geeerawlee-wowwowowow! Who shall *He* teach knowledge and who shall *He* make tuh unnerstan doctrine? Them that is *weaned* from thuh milk an *drawn* from thuh breasts! Fer precep mus be upon precep, precep upon precep, line upon line, line upon line, hyer a little an thur a little. Fer with stammerin lips an another tongue will He speak tuh His people! Tuh who He said this is thuh *res* that may cause thuh *weary* tuh res! An this is thuh *refreshin!* Yet they would not hyer! But thuh Word uv thuh Lord waz untuh them precep upon precep, line upon line, hyer a little an thur a little, that they might *go* an fall *backward* an be *broke* an *snared* an *took!*"

Ben walked to the big window and looked into the back yard. The kitchen lights shone in a long rectangle on the rock fish pond and the iron furniture and a bronze nude that Harry had sculpted and cast.

"Brothers, thurs a frin of mahn, a pore sinner down in Georgie that wrote me a letter an said he had been vistid by thuh Lord an thuh Lord had tole him not tuh give me no money tuh holp me do His good works! Frins thet waz a *hallucination!* Thet waz thuh Devil! Oh he is wily, he is clever, he comes tuh us in many guises. Thuh Lord *wants* yew tuh holp me, an ah have been give thuh power uv prophecy an thuh gift uv healin tuh save thuh pore lost souls."

Cadmus appeared, grinning and filling the kitchen doorway, with the sallow Willy frowning in front of him.

"*Stay* yourselfs an wonder, *cry* yet out, an cry, they are drunken but not with *wine,* they *stagger,* but not with strong *drank,* fer thuh Lord hath pored out upon *yew* thuh spirit uv deep sleep an hath *shet* yer eyes! Even thuh spirit uv thuh truth thu worl cann-ot receive because it *seeth* Him not, neither knowth Him!"

"That's what I always say," yelled Cadmus.

"Fer thuh Lord shall rise *up* as in Mount Perazim, He shall be *wroth* as in thuh valley uv Gideon, thet He may do His work, His *strange* work, an brang tuh pass His *ack,* His *strange* ack! Now thurfore be ye not mockers les yur bands be made strong! Fer ah have heard from thuh Lord God uv Hosts a *consumption* even upon thuh whole earth! From thuh beginnin He walked an talked with Adam an Eve! Then sin entered an His fellership was broke! An then man had to *seek* after God tuh *know* Him! If yew profess tuh know God an yew don' have no vital *sperience* with Him, *yur* God mus be dead!"

In the dining-room doorway Ben noticed a girl. He hadn't seen her before at the party, but it seemed that he had seen her somewhere, in another time. As he watched, her head turned and her eyes examined the crowd. Her eyebrows were arched, her lids were smudged, her eyes large and grave as the eyes of a doe that had stepped cautiously into a clearing. Her eyes came round to him and stopped. She smiled at him briefly and then looked again at Jason. Ben kept staring at her, and he knew she was aware of it, but she wouldn't look at him.

"Trade off yur false Gods!" Jason shouted hoarsely, banging a fist on the kitchen table. "Repent *yur* sins an turn from yur wickidniss! Behole ye despiser an wonder an perish! God shall work a work which yew shall in no wise believe though a man shall tell it tuh yew! After thuh way which they calls hairysee worship ah thuh God uv mah fathers *believin* all thangs!"

He lifted his hands.

"Oh sinners *hyer* me! Hyer me before a turble vistation vistid upon yew!"

Jason pretended to reach into a sack at his feet and pick up an object.

"Ah got hyer a pitcher, a beautiful pitcher uv Lord Jesus Christ they *glows* in thuh dark! See how Our Lord's eyes is shet cep in thuh dark? Ah have *laid* mah hands upon it an *blessd* it! Sinners is saved when they *look* upon it! A lady in Kerrville got ex-zeema, ah cured her! A lady in Tyler got dishwarter hans, ah cured her! Pore lil feller over in Harlingen got polio, ah cured *him!* God is *speakin* tuh me! Ohhhh geeeerawleewowowowow! Speak up, Lord! Yes *thank* yew, Jesus, just a little louder! Much oblige tuh yew, Jesus! Ther is twenty people in this hyer crowd thet got ten dollars apiece to buy these hyer blessd plates an holp me tuh do thuh work uv thuh Lord! Jesus *says* they is. Is they a man would call Him *wrong?* Now step forth mah frins!"

Jason paused for breath and saw the bartender, Harvey, from the Oui Oui Club, had come into the kitchen with Green, Flutebinder, St. Clair, and the blonde woman who wore her hair in a bun. Jason made a little noise, sort of a choking cry. Flutebinder blew his nose and looked sorrowfully into his handkerchief. The blonde woman smiled and started toward Jason. People were laughing and applauding. "Jason, do the one about the rat-eating boy," someone yelled, and there was more applause. The blonde woman, the tiger, eyed him ravenously. Jason ducked quickly toward the living-room door, collided with Cadmus, looked at Willy, scrambled around Cadmus, and lost himself in the living room. Behind him people were yelling, "Do Walter Brennan . . . do the rat-eating boy . . . do *High Noon*."

Ben drank another mouthful of tequila and, sucking on a lime, began moving through the crowd. The oak boards of the living-room floor were smooth and cool against Ben's feet and he hopped around nimbly to avoid being stepped on. He stopped beside the stereo with his hands on his hips, braced for a new attack of exhaustion. Cadmus brought Blossom in and began to dance. Ben saw Doris in the corner talking to several people he didn't know, and he saw Jason going out the front door. The three purple-lidded girls with piled-up hair still sat on the couch, posed brightly as a flower arrangement, long legs crossed, feet turned properly as if for a photograph of a shoe advertisement, chins up, smiles carved and immobile. Walter Anderson was brushing something off the lapels of his blue suit and telling the girls a story. Ben went over to the couch. The three purple-lidded girls smiled up at him. "Hey Ben," said Walter Anderson. Ben studied the three girls and then pointed toward the one in the middle.

"You," Ben said. "Come with me."

"Where we going?" she said.

"Haven't decided yet. Come on," he said.

"It's his birthday," said Walter Anderson.

The girl smiled at the others, stood up and smoothed her sheath cocktail dress. She had red hair and a slight underbite. Ben walked to the dance floor, and she followed him.

"Kick off your shoes," he said. "I don't want you tromping on my feet."

"All right, honey," she said. "You always order people around like that?"

"Just when I don't feel like being polite."

"I kind of like it."

"Where's your husband?"

"In the kitchen."

"Drunk?"

"Yes."

"Passed out?"

"He will be."

"Fine," Ben said. "Name?"

"Wanda."

"My name's Ben."

"I know who you are. Your daddy's a big man."

"My daddy is a pathetic broken old hypocrite."

Ben was immediately angry at himself for saying that. He kissed the girl.

"Why, honey, what if your wife's watching?"

"You know damn well my wife's not watching."

"Do you hate everbody?" the girl said.

"Only certain ones."

"I love everbody."

"Swell."

"Maybe you just haven't done it right."

"I've done it right and wrong, and it has wore me out."

"Where *is* your wife?" the girl said.

"Promise me you won't tell?"

"Not a word."

"She's gone to her reward."

"Oh, honey, I'm sorry."

"She was okay. She was all right. I used to love her some."

"When did she pass on?"

"She's not dead, bless her heart," said Ben. "Except as far as I'm concerned."

"You're the strangest man."

"I don't like to be crapped," he said. "Ask me some questions you don't already know the answers to."

As they were dancing, Ben saw Seton Parry come through the front door, glance at his gold wrist watch, brush back his hair, and look around, sucking his lips and scowling as if unsure he was in the correct house. Seton waved at several people and said, "Well hi." Then with swaying hips and a scuffing walk he traveled across the room toward the kitchen, where the bar always was. Seton stopped and wiggled his fingers at Ben. "Well hi," Seton said.

"I'm incognito," said Ben. "Play like you don't recognize my feet."

"Fool," Seton said, laughing. "Foolish boy. I'd know those feet anywhere. They were the only feet in junior high that I could outrun."

Seton went into the kitchen.

"That was a malicious lie," Ben said. "He outran me once when I had cut my foot on a piece of broken glass. It's a good thing for him he outran me, because I had ever intention of hanging his pants on the flagpole. That's like Seton. He remembers he outran me, but he's forgot all the details."

"Who is he?" the girl asked.

"Fullback for the Green Bay Packers."

"He's kind of small to be a fullback."

"Tough as a rattlesnake," Ben said.

"He walks like a fairy."

"If I told him you said that, he'd scratch your eyes out."

The music ended. Cadmus and Blossom wound up beside Ben and the purple-lidded girl.

"Ole Seton's in a sweat about something," said Cadmus. "Let's go give ole Seton a drank of the native fruits."

"Listen, Wanda," Ben said, "you put on your shoes and in thirty minutes I'll meet you in that black Mercedes parked down the street."

"I can't do that. What about my husband?"

"Suit yourself," Ben said, shrugging.

"Thirty minutes?"

"Or so," said Ben as he started toward the kitchen with Cadmus and Blossom.

The kitchen crowd had lessened somewhat after Jason's sudden departure. Willy, Chub, and Harry sat at the table beside the big window listening to Seton Parry. Seton talked excitedly, snapping off his words, his voice climbing to a nasal whine. Seton had a sickly pallor, as if he'd never had enough sleep, exercise, fresh air, or sunlight.

"They're going to get me, I tell you," Seton said. "The sons of bitches. They're all out to get me. I'm disturbed from fighting them. I'm utterly disturbed."

"Who's them?" said Willy.

Seton glared at her, wondering at her authority to question him.

"Them!" he said. "All the sons of bitches! Insurance salesmen, mortgage loan companies, PTA presidents, members of the school board, anybody who is the parent of one of those fourteen-year-old gangsters in my classes, druggists, people who write civics books, politicians, policemen, soldiers, doctors, lawyers, dentists. And more. There's more sons of bitches. They're all out to get me."

"Ole Seton," said Cadmus. "He thinks the whole world was

created just to infuriate him. Have a drank of the native fruits, Seton."

"No thanks. But I would like a glass of milk. It's my ulcer," Seton said. "Sonofabitching doctors. Liars, thieves, murderers. I suppose they'll want to cut me open and take my stomach out. They'd like that. They get their kicks cutting people open, sticking knives into people, taking things out of people that they can put in glass jars and look at. Like jars of jams and jellies. They like to get people naked and helpless and then cut them open. Sons of bitches. They *like* to make you drink chalk. They *like* to shoot you full of radiation."

Seton opened the refrigerator door.

"Candy," he said. "I'm dying for some chocolate candy." He poured a glass of milk, went over to the bread box, found some cookies, and began eating. "What I wouldn't give for some chocolate candy with coconut inside. And almonds. Well hi, Doris. Wonderful party. Do you have any candy? No, I guess not. Nobody keeps candy around the house any more except me."

"Seton," said Walter Anderson, "I want you to meet a friend of mine. William Sheridan, from Austin."

Sheridan stuck out his hand. Seton ignored the hand, nodded to Sheridan, and went on eating.

"I don't shake hands with strangers," Seton said. "Shake hands! God, I *hate* to shake hands with strangers. Shaking hands is so erotic. Touching palms. Sensitive flesh against sensitive flesh. To shake hands with a stranger is raw, open, crude, vulgar sensuality. No thank you, Sheridan. Let us merely say how do you do."

"How do you do then," said Sheridan.

"Not worth a damn," Seton said. "We had one of those open houses at school today. All the stupid mothers and fathers came to see how their stupid children spend their days, and I had to shake hands with every one of those monsters. I was a trembling, quivering wreck by four o'clock. I went back to my apartment and ate a whole box of chocolate-covered cherries. Then I cleaned up my apartment and ironed some shirts and watched a play on television. In the play everybody kept shaking hands. It was a nightmare. God, all people do any more is go around shaking hands. It's a great public orgy of palm touching."

"I never did see the deeper significance of shaking hands before," said Cadmus. "Damn if I'll ever shake another hand."

"I don't think there's anything wrong with shaking hands," Walter said.

"You wouldn't," said Seton.

"What's that supposed to mean?" Walter said. "Are you calling me dumb?"

"Look at him," said Seton, chewing cookies. "Ready to brawl. Get over being a football hero, will you, Walter?"

"What were you ever a hero at?" Walter said.

"I have been heroic about not being a hero," said Seton. "Well hi, Pippa, you had a good time?"

"I've had a fine time," the girl said.

When he heard the name, Ben remembered. From some musty wing of his mind the pieces came out and arranged themselves: Pippa Parry, Seton's sister, the girl who had awakened him in the back yard. Seton kissed her. She saw Ben and smiled at him. Seton drank the rest of his milk and put the glass on the drainboard.

"Ben, you remember my sister, Pippa, don't you?" said Seton.

"Tell her to take me back where she found me and let me start over," Ben said.

"What's that? I don't understand. Everybody in this house is crazy," said Seton.

"All that hand shaking got 'em," Cadmus said.

"How do you feel now?" the girl said.

"Miserable," said Ben. "These kind of deals are rough on a guy like me who doesn't smoke or drink or attend parties."

"Your eyes are red," she said.

Seton opened the refrigerator door, took out the milk carton, and filled his glass again. Then he began taking out bologna, cheese, lettuce, tomatoes, and a jar of sandwich spread.

"I'm starving," Seton said. "I'm sorry everyone, but I'm simply starving. Doris, the bread? God, it's smoky in here." He coughed. "Cigarettes are going to kill me. Cigarettes are going to kill everyone of us. But I love to smoke. I really do love to smoke. The only reason I eat is because it makes smoking taste so good. I'd die if I couldn't smoke. The doctors tell me not to smoke. It agitates my stomach. I tell them to go screw. I really do." Seton piled the bologna, cheese, tomatoes, and lettuce on a piece of bread while Doris smeared the relish on another piece. Seton drank half his glass of milk. Cadmus watched him, grinning, fascinated, licking his crooked teeth. "God, Doris, I wish you had some tuna fish," Seton said. "I adore tuna fish. I fall down on my knees and worship tuna fish. At my apartment I always have a big bowl of tuna fish salad. I have to eat a lot to keep my stomach full."

"That's about the best reason I ever heard," said Cadmus.

"Let's step out on the back porch and breathe," Ben said to the girl. "No, Seton, I mean your sister and me."

The girl looked at Seton.

"I'll be right back," she said.

"All right, but look out for that man," Seton said. He bit into the sandwich. "That man is dangerous around young girls."

"Be careful not to let him shake your hand," said Cadmus.

Ben took her by the arm and pushed open the screen door. They walked across the concrete floor of the back porch, opened another screen door, and stepped into the soft clean night. The elm leaves moved in a faint breeze. Ben guided the girl toward a white iron bench beside the fish pond beneath the trees, and they sat down. He lit her cigarette and then his own, and for a while they didn't speak. Ben looked up to see if his personal apparition, his manta ray, had returned, but the sky was clear and empty. The moon was hidden behind the house.

"I'm thinking about Seton Parry's sister," he said finally. "The last I heard of her she was living in Paris and had got engaged to a Frenchman. Or Frenchwoman. I forget which."

"He was an American student," she said.

"That's right. And you were going to the Sorbonne."

"I was supposed to be."

"And you were hanging around in the cafes on the Boulevard St.-Michel and going dancing over in Montmartre. You were too hip to go to the Sélect or the Dôme or the Rotonde or the Deux Magots."

"I went to them a lot. They're still all right. I don't think you should ever get so hip that you keep yourself from going to a good place just because it's popular."

"The American student. Did you marry him?"

"No. He stole my clock radio. And a hundred and eighty-five dollars cash."

"Terrible rat. I've known his kind."

Ben turned to study the gray light and shadows on her face.

"I haven't seen you in five or six years. Until tonight," he said.

"You've seen me several times. I've been back from Europe nearly a year. I've seen you at three dances at the club, at one New Year's Eve party and one Christmas party."

"I was drunk all those times."

"You certainly were."

"I was loud-mouthed and obnoxious and on the make and accompanied by my former wife, Jean, who has a beautiful soul."

"Yes."

"Save me," he said.

"From what?"

"The ravages. All the ravages. If you save me I'll love you forever and forever."

"You'd just be grateful."

"Grateful isn't bad. That's as good an emotion as any. Hold still a moment." He took a handkerchief out of his pocket and wiped her face with it. "Nope. I'll need a washcloth."

"Is my face dirty?"

"I'm trying to see if that's powder or if you're really so pale."

"I'm afraid I haven't got my color back," she said. "I was sick for a while this spring."

"Would you fight hard if I started trying to make love to you?"

"I'd scream for my brother."

"Okay, but don't leave me. You left me once tonight." He stood up from the bench and lay down on the grass with his hands behind his head, looking up at her. "Now, I can admire your ankles. You have very nice ankles. Talk to me. What happened to you since the last time I remember seeing you five or six years ago when you were going to school at Texas and were wearing baggy sweaters and tennis shoes?"

"I left Texas and went to graduate school at Columbia."

"That's a bad start. Texas girls should never ought to go off to New York. We need Texas girls to stay at home."

"I quit Columbia to go to Paris."

"Why?"

"To see Paris."

"I mean *why*."

"I was engaged to a man who was working on his doctorate at Yale. We became very unhappy with each other."

"Broke up on the rocks of a New Haven weekend."

"Good guess."

"I'm aware about Yale men. Personally, I can't tolerate 'em. They talk grand and they act like rats. Only kind of women fit for Yale men are those long-haired girls with sinusy voices and rich daddies and hair on the insides of their thighs. They don't care what a nowhere phony their man is as long as he can make martinis and look bored at horse shows."

"I didn't think Yale was like that."

"I know about Yale. Only good man Yale ever turned out was Mabel Dodge."

"Mabel Dodge is a woman."

"You think so? You really think so?"

"You're drunk again."

"No I'm not. I'm tired. I've had a hard day. Ever notice how some days are hard just to get through? Some days are like that. Go on with your story."

"That's all," she said.

"That's all?"

"I left Europe and came home. That's all."

"You're leaving a lot of gaps. You went to Columbia, broke up with a Yale man, went to Paris, broke up with an American student, and then came home, and that covers five or six years? Must have been something in between that was of interest."

"It does seem that there should have been."

"Shame you've never been married. All my friends have been married at least once, just about. Cadmus has been married three times. He claims he never learned any of their names. He says he loves all women and can't stand to be attached to just one at a time. One of his wives tried to kill herself. I don't think she tried very hard. She cut her wrists and bled all over the carpet. She was mad because he wouldn't buy her a new car. She was his third wife, I believe. She turned him in to the Internal Revenue Service. He got out of it, but he divorced her for that. Just and sufficient cause. Any jury could understand it."

"Seton told me you're getting a divorce."

"Oh? I didn't realize anybody knew," he said.

She laughed. "As a matter of fact I've heard it from at least thirty or forty people."

"There's a leak somewhere, Anyhow, Seton had his terminology mixed. I'm not getting a divorce. She's getting a divorce. I have acted harshly, cruelly, and with intemperance. I have caused her distress and anguish. That's what it says. I like that word anguish.

Now there's a word that says something. That word is fraught with meaning. Fraught as hell. Damned fraught."

"Did you?"

"Did I what?"

"Cause her anguish."

"Sure, I guess so. When two people get close enough they always cause each other anguish. That's why the word is so fraught with meaning. You've got to be close to somebody to cause him anguish. Somebody you're not close to, you can make him mad or hurt him physically or cheat him, but you can't cause him anguish. Very fraught."

"You're going to get chiggers lying in the grass," she said.

"They don't cause anguish."

But when she said that his neck began to itch. The grass tickled his ears, and he could feel the coolness of it through his shirt. He looked at Pippa's long legs and then up at her face. It was not a classic face. The bridge of the nose had a small knot, as if from an old blow that never healed. There was a definite parenthesis on either side of her mouth when she smiled. But the eyes and the high forehead and the quickly revealed emotions of the mouth gave the face warmth and intelligence, and the bump on the nose gave it honesty. It was a face that deserved looking at. And the long black shining hair framed it like a portrait.

"I think two busted engagements ought to count for one marriage," Ben said. "You must have had some anguish."

"I had a little."

"Not that you always have anguish in marriage. Some people can be married for fifty years, or go through one marriage after another, and never know what anguish is. But they don't care. I'll bet you cared."

"Not exactly the way you mean."

"You're fraught, you know that? You're a romantic incapable."

"Why do you say that?"

"Because you must be about twenty-four years old and not married."

"I'm not incapable of love."

"I'm going to sit on the bench," he said. "I'll get chiggers in the grass."

He got up and brushed the scraps of grass out of his hair. His back was tingling. She moved over, and he sat beside her. He looked down at his bare feet. His feet were white with long toes. He looked at the curly brown hair on the backs of his hands. How could a beast with long toes and curly brown hair on his hands ever sit and weep? That was what made man the most absurd of creatures. Other beasts with long toes didn't weep. They hung from trees.

He turned and kissed Pippa.

At first her lips were dry and hard and she held herself rigid. Ben put his arms around her and pulled her against him; he mashed his teeth against her lips until her mouth opened and he felt her gasp for breath. She began to relax. He kissed her as he always kissed girls he barely knew: with a great show of passion, and with a certain skill, and she began to respond. But he was as always, his mind coldly set apart, observing himself with this girl, deliberately planning move and countermove, wondering if her responses were true or as artificial as his own. He kissed her on the ear and then got the lobe of her ear between his lips, and when she moved her head he kissed her on the neck. She murmured something he didn't understand. He slid his lips through her hair and onto the curve of her neck and then to her mouth again, letting his left hand fall onto her thigh, judging her attitude from the noises she made and from the feel of her fingers on his back. He timed his pauses for breath so that he had her smothered in his most intense outpouring of emotion as his left hand crept up her thigh, lingered at her pelvis, and crawled up against her right breast. He cupped her breast, considering the solidity of it, until she shook her head and removed his hand. He found himself wishing it weren't quite so simple. He was playing the game by the same old rules and winning; her checks were the ones he anticipated, and his jumps were delicately ahead of her.

She broke away from him once and looked at him with her magnificent brown eyes and said, "Ben, it's been so long."

Those were the words Jean had said to him on a night a few months ago. At least this girl had the taste to use an evocative line. By now her lips were wet and her tongue was probing; he could feel her ribs under his fingers. He had his left hand between her legs, between her soft inner thighs which were moist with perspiration. It occurred to him how foolish they would look in sober examination: her smooth thighs squeezing his hand to halt its advance, their mouths planted together, both of them breathing as if they had climbed six flights of stairs, making little sucking noises, and he was panting like an excited dog while he strained to touch her flesh, and she was fighting herself as much as him to keep him from it. Do we think we're originals? he wondered. Or do we think we're children? What's the sweating about? If we can't go ahead and do that ridiculous thing, that animal interlocking, then let's quit wrestling. And yet oddly he was hoping that she wouldn't yield. Was he that tired? Or was it that he was wanting her to be something more than ordinary, something uncalculated, something beyond the regimented push and pull of the past weeks. Maybe, he thought, he was wanting all this to mean something again, to be able to lose himself in it without trying to deceive himself that this was Jean and that he was more than a mechanical toy that you wound up and it drearily, laboriously asserted its manhood. He was weary of cheating, and he was surprised to discover that he didn't want to cheat this girl.

Ben released her. He looked at her for a moment, still breathing hard. Her lipstick had disappeared. Wisps of hair were hanging in her face. On the bench he saw one of her combs, and he handed it to her.

"Let's smoke a cigarette," he said. "Do you have any?"

She dug a package out of her purse. He lit two cigarettes and gave her one.

"That was automatic with you, wasn't it?" she said.

"What was automatic?"

"You know what I mean."

"All this kissing?"

"I wish you'd tell me. I know you're trying to make out, and I don't blame you. But I wish you'd tell me if I'm just another girl or if you, well, feel anything."

"Oh Christ," he said, "let's don't do a lot of talking about it. If you talk about these things they turn into smoke. I wish someday I'd find a woman who didn't want to talk about everthing."

"I'm sorry. Don't be angry."

"Up till now you've been pretty straight," he said. "Let's keep it that way. If I could find a woman who was straight and who didn't want to talk about everthing, I'd run off with her."

"Is that all you want in a woman?"

Ben stood up and rubbed his feet in the damp grass. In the kitchen window he could see the party raging. A man appeared to be standing in the window in his underwear; then he vanished. The back door slammed. A dark figure came out and walked around the corner of the house, and they could hear someone urinating into the hedges.

"I want about the same thing ever man wants," Ben said. "What I want is a woman who's an extension of myself. Somebody who doesn't give me a hard time and who thinks I'm great. I want a woman that I can feel like it's you and me against the world, baby, and screw all them people out there. I don't want a lover. I'm all burnt out on that. I want something better. A companion. A partner. A helper. I don't know what you'd call it. Somebody who won't argue about ever damned thing and act like she's having a rotten time. That's all I want. But where you gonna find a woman like that? They quit making 'em about fifty years ago."

"You could probably find one," she said. "But I don't know if you'd like it."

"Are you serious? Ever woman says she's one of those and they all think they mean it for a while. But it doesn't take long for them to decide their man ain't the king but is some kind of semiarticulate fool that's supposed to go to the PTA meetings and keep his mouth shut and not insist on too much lovemaking or any dirty stuff in bed and keep his eyes off other women and be a humble cowardly father who pays all the bills and hurries home from work so the television can blast his brains out and the kids can jump up and down on him and he can carry out the garbage and cut the grass and trim the petunias. He's got to be home so his loving wife will have a target to bounce her complaints off of and can tell him what an utter disappointment he's turned out to be and ask him what's happened to their perfect burning love. Love. Piss on it."

"Jean wasn't like that."

"No, Jean really wasn't like that. How'd you know?"

"I'm Seton's little sister. I know a lot about all of you."

"Well, most women are like that."

"Most women don't know how to love," she said. "You mind if I say something else?"

"Go ahead."

"You don't know how to love either. You may have the capacity for it, but you haven't learned how to do it."

"You don't have to learn how. You just have to hang on."

"No, you have to learn how. The right kind of love takes knowledge. And that first thing you mentioned, about a woman who's an extension of yourself, that's not love. You're more of a person than to want that. A great love is a union that includes conflict. You're hurt and you're striking out in all directions."

"I'm tired and ungracious," he said.

"You're lonely."

"That's the root of all love, anyhow, isn't it? That's how come it's necessary to love. So maybe I'll love you."

"Don't," she said, and laughed. "I don't know if I could take it. I used to have a tremendous thing for you when I was a little girl. You'd come over to the house to see Seton and you'd never see me, but I'd be looking at you. When Seton was going out, and he was going to be with you, I'd be terribly jealous. I had a room upstairs. I'd lie on my bed and look out at the roof of the house next door and think how cruel everything was. I'd hear the horn honk, if some of you came by to pick him up, and I'd think you might be in that car and maybe something grand would happen, like a flat tire. When the car would drive away I'd be so desolated I'd want to jump out the window. Even when I was older and was dating, I'd pester Seton to find out what you were doing. But your crowd had dropped him by then."

"We never did drop Seton."

"Yes you did. It was because of what he did one summer at the lake. Or what he tried to do. With Harry. Seton told me about it. We used to be very close. It nearly ruined Seton. He wanted to die. He kept saying if he'd just kept it out of the group."

"That wasn't it. We all went away to school, and Seton stayed here at TCU. You drift apart."

"Why do you think Seton stayed here?"

"Let's don't discuss Seton," Ben said. "Let's discuss how you used to be in love with me."

"I didn't say I was in love with you. I said I had this thing for you, whatever it was. I had it until I was seventeen. Then something happened to make me forget it."

"What happened?"

"Something."

"You were made love to by the quarterback."

"Nothing like that."

"What was it?" he said.

"I'd rather not say."

"What *was* it?"

"You'll probably laugh."

"See those pickets? I'm going to stick one of them in my throat and hang there like a side of beef if I laugh."

"I had a mystic experience."

He laughed.

"I lose," he said. "I wasn't looking for anything like that."

"It's all right. I haven't told many people about it, but everybody I told laughed except Seton. He got mad because he hadn't had one, too."

"Well, what happened? I mean did God come and tell you to put the Dauphin on the throne of France, or convert the Russians? Did you heal a leper? What happened?"

"Ben," she said, "I'd rather not talk about it. Please accept that it's very serious to me, and then let's don't talk about it. Can you?"

"Sure. Hell, I know how Seton felt. I wish I'd had one."

He sat down on the grass with his back against her legs. He leaned his neck against her knees and let his head drop back awkwardly and looked up at the dark rustling cover of the elms.

"Pippa," he said, "if there was any way. I mean if you could possibly be. I need somebody. Oh crap I don't know what I mean. Listen, put your hands on my face, will you? Just touch me."

Her fingers touched his cheek and lightly began to stroke his forehead.

"Do you know Sam Guthrie?" he said.

"No."

"Thank God for that," he said, and then he shut his eyes.

Part Four

THE ONLY FERRY BOAT

At Agua Verda, in the long white room above the dunes, Waddy Morris had just proposed a toast when Roger, the houseman, suddenly appeared at Sam Guthrie's shoulder as quietly as if he had materialized from the carpet. Bowing and clearing his throat until Guthrie turned, Roger said there was a telephone call for Mr. Guthrie. Waddy Morris looked at him, annoyed to have had his toast interrupted before the finish, which was, of course, the drinking. The toast had been to the prosperity of Guthrie-Ramco Electronics Inc., with a rider to the additional prosperity of Waddy Morris. And with some few words about a power source that would heat and cool every building in the world and would operate every engine. Jane Guthrie and Beth Morris were not aware of what Waddy meant about a power source, but by then anything seemed worth drinking to. Senator Rose had gone off to bed after first walking squarely into one of the glass walls and bloodying his nose.

"Who's it from?" said Guthrie.

"Ah doan know, sir. But they said it wuz important."

"It better be important for them to call me at midnight," Guthrie said. "Excuse me, Waddy."

"Drink up first," said Waddy. "It's bad luck not to carry through a toast."

Guthrie drank, and then went to an ivory telephone beside an armchair. Beyond the glass wall the sand hills sat in the floodlights with black shadow valleys between, and past the edge of the light lay the dark mounds that led to the cannonading of the water along the beach.

"Mr. Guthrie?" the voice said on the telephone. "This is John. John Tibbs. I own the Sporting Life Bar in town. I hate to bother you this time of night, but I figured you'd wanta know."

"Yes?" said Guthrie. He listened for a moment, asked several questions, and hung up the phone without saying either good night or thank you. He stood by the phone, leaning over a bit with his hand still on the receiver. Jane Guthrie saw that her husband was frowning, and she came to him.

"What's wrong?" she said.

"It's Jake."

"Something happen to the boat?"

"I mean it's *about* Jake," said Guthrie. "I've got to go into Corpus."

"Is he in trouble?"

"He's hurt. Roger, get me a car."

"Capn Jake taken the station wagon. Alls we got is the pickup truck and the jeep," Roger said.

"The pickup truck then. Hurry."

Guthrie walked swiftly through the enclosed courtyard, past the rock garden of cactus and flowers, and down the stone steps to the garage. Roger had called ahead, and the pickup truck had been backed out and was waiting with the engine running. Sand whirled from the wheels as Guthrie skidded along the twisting road through the dunes, honking at the curves, sand drifting through the headlights. Two eyes glittered like burning cigarettes in the headlights; a jackrabbit bounded away as the front wheels reached it. The ferry boat operator, who had been notified, was waiting when Guthrie drove up to the landing. As the ferry went across, Guthrie sat in the cab of the truck with the windows rolled down and looked at the moon in the black water. The ferry rumbled and sloshed across the channel. Guthrie smelled the salt and oil and dead fish odor as the ferry slowly plowed ahead. Once Guthrie said aloud: "This is stupid." On the mainland Guthrie turned onto the highway toward the city and pushed the pickup along at seventy miles an hour, cursing because it would not go faster. The dark fields and telephone poles flew past, and then roadside taverns and houses and stores, and then he was at the high bridge that soared above a neck of the bay. The bridge always made Guthrie feel as though his car had taken flight and was carrying him helpless into the air. The bridge frightened him, made him think that one night he would remove his hands from the wheel to answer whatever it was that pulled him upward, and he would go through the rail. The furrowed water of the bay was so far below that he did not want to look at it.

The pickup dropped down the far arc of the bridge and came onto a boulevard beside a row of motels along the beach. Guthrie drove into a curving street past palms and white buildings that overlooked the bay. He parked the pickup in front of the hospital. Inside, Guthrie checked at the desk and took the elevator to the second floor. A deputy sheriff met him in the hall. Guthrie had seen the deputy before around the island; he was a fat man who wore a Sam Browne belt and had a gold whistle on a chain that looped out of his shirt pocket, as if he had never got over being a first sergeant.

The deputy was folding up his notebook as Guthrie approached. Sticking the notebook into his left hip pocket, the deputy nodded.

"Howdy, Mist Guthrie," the deputy said.

"How is he?"

"Looks like yore boy ain't doin too good."

The deputy pulled a cigar out of his pocket, scratched a kitchen match on the wall, and didn't say anything else until the cigar was puffing and glowing. The deputy flicked the match toward the No Smoking sign at the end of the hall.

"Son of a gun I wisht ole Jake hadn't of did that," said the deputy. "But I knowed he was gonna sooner or later. He couldn't of let it alone."

"How'd it happen?" Guthrie said.

"Jake and ole Sidney Burney—you know him?—had theirselfs a little scrap thuther night and Jake come out on the short end. So Jake went back to the Sportin Life while ago, and there was ole Burney again, big as life. John Tibbs, he's the owner, called me right off cause he knowed there'd be trouble. But I didn't get there in time."

The deputy grinned, enjoying his story. Guthrie waited impatiently, knowing there was no use trying to hurry him.

"If it had of all been set fair up, I might of bet on Jake this time," said the deputy. "Jake's a wiry son of a gun. But Jake never give hisself a chance. I'd of thought he'd of knowed better. Jake stood up there to the bar and called Burney a fightin word while Burney had a full beer bottle in his hand. Jake knows bettern that. Burney cracked Jake acrosst the head with that bottle and laid his skull wide open. Gettin hit with a full beer bottle, why that's like gettin hit with a iron pipe. Burney fetched him a good lick. That first lick ended the fight right there. But ole Jake, he got more guts than a cornered bobcat. He snatched that busted bottle outta Burney's hand and shoved it in Burney's face and give it a good twist. My, my, you oughta see Burney. If he don't look like somethin the dogs been chewin on? He's in this here hospital right now tryin to get his face put back together, but I don't see how they ever spect to do it."

The deputy puffed on his cigar and thought about the looks of Burney's face.

"Then," he said, "Burney knocked Jake down, or maybe Jake just fell down from gettin hit with that bottle in the first place. They was both all covered with blood so they couldn't see. Burney must of been plumb mad by then. Way I get it, he jumped up and come down on Jake with both feet. Give him the boot real good. That's when I got there. When I come in Burney was bleedin like a hawg and I figured he'd lost that fight for sure till I seen what it was he was kickin like a football. It was ole Jake's head. Why, I had to hit Burney mahself, behind the ear kind of, with my slapjack, to make him quit kickin Jake. Them guys was pretty good friends, too. People do funny thangs, don't they, Mist Guthrie?"

"Yeah," Guthrie said.

"There gonna be any charges you spose?"

"Charges?"

"I sure hope not. Just make a lotta paperwork. Way I see it, wasn't nothin but a fight."

"There won't be any charges," said Guthrie.

"Thas good," the deputy said, grinning. "I'll tell 'em to send ole Burney home when they get thew sowin him up, if they got enough thread to ever get thew. We started foolin with charges on all these here fights, it'd shore cut into our sleepin."

"How is Jake?" said Guthrie.

"Yonder comes the doctor. You ast him. Jake don't look too good to me. I could see clean down into his head thew that hole in it, and *I* thank when you can see a feller's brains that feller ain't in too good shape."

The deputy nodded to the doctor and then nodded again to Guthrie and waddled off down the hall, his gold whistle bouncing on his chest and his leaded leather slapstick protruding from his right hip pocket behind the pistol that hung in a holster from his Sam Browne belt.

"Mr. Guthrie?" the doctor said.

"Can I see him?"

"For a few minutes, I suppose. He's very ill. Skull fracture, broken ribs, internal injuries. Anybody but you, we'd keep out. Terrible, these brawls. Terrible. They've already taken more than a hundred stitches in that other man's face."

"Jake's wife been here yet?"

"Mr. Iles's wife? Not that I know of."

"Is he going to die?" Guthrie said.

The doctor shrugged.

"We like to be optimistic," said the doctor.

"Tell me the truth."

"I could only tell you what my opinion is."

"What's your opinion?"

The doctor took off his steel-rimmed glasses and polished them on his white smock. He looked nearsightedly at Guthrie through narrowed eyes.

"My opinion is that there's cause for some very, very cautious optimism, although not much."

"In other words, you think he'll probably die."

"I didn't say that, I *have* seen people I thought were closer to death than Mr. Iles pull through. With care and patience, we might be able to keep him with us. He's a very strong man with a very tough constitution, and so much in these cases depends on how badly the patient wants to live. There may be surgery, of course."

"Why hasn't there already been surgery?" Guthrie said.

"The proper men for these kind of jobs don't roam around hospitals at midnight, Mr. Guthrie. We're doing as we think best. As they say, Mr. Guthrie, *we're* the doctors."

"All right. I'm going in now."

"Uh, one more thing," said the doctor. "If Mr. Iles . . . or, rather, in order for Mr. Iles to recover, it will be a rather long and, uh, costly process. They told us he's your yacht captain and so we, uh, put him in a private room thinking you probably would . . . uh, that is, you would want to, uh . . . if you wish we can have him moved to a ward. He had no record of insurance in his wallet, and we, uh, naturally assumed . . ."

"I'll pay all the bills," Guthrie said.

The doctor smiled. "Very well," he said.

Inside the room the thing that struck Guthrie was that Jacob Iles wasn't breathing, that he had died. There was no movement beneath the sheet that was pulled up to Iles's chin. A plastic tube led down from a hanging bottle into Iles's left arm, and another into his right. The light from a table lamp fell across Iles's face; his left eye was a monstrous purple hump, much worse than it had been when Iles met the plane at the airport. A white bandage wrapped around Iles's head from where the eyebrows should have been, like a gauze helmet. It was a bare room with one bed, one table, one chair, and a painting of The Last Supper. Not the sort of room to make anybody want to get well, Guthrie thought. But Iles would be too sick to notice.

Guthrie glanced at the nurse who stood beside the bed.

"I want you to stay here," he said. "I don't want you to leave him for a second."

"I have to make rounds," she said.

"I'll fix that," said Guthrie. "You'll be paid for staying here."

That seemed to satisfy her. "I think he's conscious," she said. "We've pumped a whole drugstore into him, but he won't let himself go all the way out."

Guthrie went to the bed and looked down. Iles's right eye was open, a slice of a red eye peeping from between pus-colored lids. The eye seemed to have no man behind it; a tiny blank window that looked into nothing and out at nothing, as if the man behind it had gone off somewhere and had left this red slice of an eye and this battered face and this body that could not find enough breath in it to move a sheet. But then the split and swollen upper lip trembled as if trying to form a smile. The mouth opened.

"Tried t'push too far," Iles said thickly through smashed lips. His voice was whispery and his words indistinct; his tongue could not touch the proper places to manufacture speech.

"Don't talk if it hurts too bad," said Guthrie.

"Shudda come w'me."

"I wish I had of, Jake."

"Doan ever push too far Sam. Thas what I did."

"Why'd you have to do this?" Guthrie said. "Why'd you have to go down there and jump on Burney again? You crazy son of a bitch."

"How Burn'?"

"His face is cut to pieces, if that makes you feel better. But I don't care how Burney is."

"He m'frin."

"So am I your friend."

The red slitted eye regarded Guthrie.

"Use be Sam. Doan know now."

"I wouldn't be here if I wasn't your friend," Guthrie said.

"Sure y'ould. F'ole times. Make believe. Big shot now. How you like that? Lotta lies now."

"Damn it, I'm paying your hospital bill," said Guthrie.

Iles tried to smile again. The lip twitched like a piece of raw flesh with its nerves jumping from pain. The thin red eye took on a flicker of life.

"Hanks," Iles said.

"I didn't mean to say that," said Guthrie. "You made me mad. Let me take that back, Jake."

"Hanks," the whispery voice repeated. "Doan make ussha t'me but Marge'll be happy."

The nurse touched Guthrie's arm.

"He shouldn't be talking so much," she said. "I don't know how he can do it."

"I've got to go," said Guthrie. "You gonna be okay?"

"Sure. Too tough t'kick off."

"Don't worry about anything. Just get well."

"Hanks, Sam. 'Member doan push too far."

Iles looked very small in the bed, much smaller than Guthrie had ever thought him to be. He looked shrunken and grotesque with the purple lumpy face beneath the white bandage.

"'Member," Iles said.

"I'll remember," said Guthrie. "You get well, you hear?"

The red slit shut. The eye disappeared in a pulpy fold. The mouth stayed open and Guthrie could hear air hissing through it. Guthrie looked at the nurse, who watched Iles with her lips tightly together. The figures of The Last Supper, faded behind dirty glass in a tarnished gold frame, stared down at them. The nurse leaned over the foot of the bed, her hands on the pipe.

As Guthrie closed the door he heard Marge's house slippers flapping along the tile floor of the hall. She walked with her hands supporting her pregnant belly, her purse strap hooked over one arm so that the purse dangled from an elbow. Her red hair was frazzled, as though she had mashed her head hard against the pillow as she slept but had twisted often. She had put on a wrinkled cotton maternity dress.

"How is he?" she said.

"Beat up pretty bad, Marge, but he'll be okay," said Guthrie.

Her tired eyes slid toward the door of Iles's room, then back to Guthrie's face. He was surprised at how ugly she had become. She had let go all at once, he thought. In his mind she had been a tall, red-haired woman with a sprinkling of freckles. Even her freckles seemed to have got larger. He wondered how long it had been since he had really looked at her, if he ever had.

"I would of been here quicker but I was trying to find somebody to stay with the kids," she said. "Miz Guthrie come down to stay with 'em. Roger brought her in the jeep. That sure was nice of her. Billy drove me here in his car. He's downstairs."

"I should have thought of that, Marge. When I heard about Jake, I drove straight here without thinking about anything."

"That's all right. I wouldn't expect you to. You don't need to get tied up with this, Mr. Guthrie. I'm sorry it happened. I don't want to ruin your party. Jake's a drunken fool. He makes trouble for everbody."

"I don't call it making trouble when he's bad hurt."

"Well, I do, Mr. Guthrie. I'll swear, I don't know how much of this I can take. If I could just get him away from the water he might be okay. If I could just get him to go inland somewheres that we could live like ordinary folks."

"If you took Jake away from the Gulf, he'd die," Guthrie said.

"He'll die anyhow. He'll break hisself, and he'll kill me with him if I let him. Listen, Mr. Guthrie, I sure preciate everthing you've did for us all these years. You go on back to your party. I'll look after Jacob."

"Did he tell you about the raise?"

"No," she said. "I ain't seen him since breakfast."

"Jake got a good raise last night. I thought he'd earned it. I guess he was celebrating."

She shook her head. "That man's a fool," she said. Then quickly she reached down and took Guthrie's hand and kissed it. Startled and embarrassed, he jerked his hand away from her rough lips.

"Thank you," she said. "God, we needed that money."

"I should have given it to him a long time ago."

"Mr. Guthrie," she said, "would you put him to work up in Dallas? He wouldn't ask, but I'm asking."

"Why?"

"We gotta get away from here."

"I don't think it'd be right, Marge. Jake's a good boat captain."

"Well," she said. She looked at the door again. "Mr. Guthrie, you spose there's any kind of job up there I could get? After the baby comes? Jacob may think this is some kind of a Garden of Eden down here, but I don't. I can't take it down here much longer."

"We'll talk about it later, Marge."

"I could work in your house, do your laundry, anything you say. Jacob could send us a little money, too. Just so I could live in a little house somewheres and get out of that trailer."

"I don't know," said Guthrie.

"I'd be awful grateful, Mr. Guthrie. I'd do anything you say. After I get rested up, I won't look so bad. I used to be pretty. If I was happy I could be pretty."

"I don't know, Marge. We'll talk about it after Jake gets well."

"I could do any kind of job. I could work in a factory. I'm a good waitress."

"You wouldn't want to leave Jake," Guthrie said.

A tear appeared on her cheek and began to edge down through the freckles, leaving a trail of moisture behind it.

"You'n him," she said. "It always used to be you'n him."

"Marge, I've got to go back. I'll have one of the boys bring you some clothes and stuff up here. Jake's asleep now. Don't worry about the kids."

He took a twenty-dollar bill out of his silver money clip and put it in her hand. Hesitating, he then pulled another twenty from the clip and put it over the first one in her palm. She didn't look at the money; her eyes were on his face, and there were tears on both cheeks now.

"That's for breakfast, or whatever," he said. "I'll check back with you."

"Thanks," she said.

Billy, the mate, was waiting for the elevator when Guthrie got off at the lobby.

"Stopped down to see how cut up Burney is," said Billy. "Man, man. They're trying to keep him in the hospital but his wife come to get him and he's leaving."

Billy jerked his head. Guthrie looked down the hall toward the emergency room. A tall woman wearing a blue shirt and a pair of floppy blue denims stood outside the emergency room smoking a cigarette.

"Jake gonna be okay?" said Billy.

"It'll be close."

"That way, huh? I tried to make him forget it, but he was spoiling for it. He couldn't let anybody get the best of him. I wish he'd at least of waited till he could see better."

Guthrie drove back to the island and stopped at the Iles trailer. The other trailers were dark, but from Iles's trailer planks of light came through the middle windows and the open door to slant across the white picket fence and the bougainvillea and the small plot of grass. Guthrie pushed through the gate, stepped up on the concrete block porch, and went in. Jane sat at the kitchen table drinking coffee. She had been crying. A wet diaper lay in a sodden gray lump on the floor. The inside of the trailer smelled like stale urine. Clothes were scattered around. A toy fire truck with its ladder snapped in half was upside down by the table, and pieces of a child's building set were strewn across the linoleum. A cracked window had been patched with tape. In her white cocktail dress, bare shoulders, and gold necklace, Jane looked absurdly out of place.

"You look like you started to the Idlewild Ball and wound up in the back of a pool hall," Guthrie said.

"Sam, this is awful," she said.

"Are the kids asleep?"

"Yes. They didn't wake up."

"Come on. We'll go up to the house and send one of the maids down here to stay with 'em."

"Sam, how could they live here? I was going to clean up the place for Marge, but when I really looked around I started crying. How could they live like this? Marge must have completely quit."

"The maid'll clean it up. Come on."

"It's not right for them to have to live like this when we live the way we do."

"They don't have to live like this. Marge is lazy."

"Nobody should have to live like this."

"We worked hard to live the way we live. If Marge worked hard this place would be all right."

"How's Jacob?"

"Bad."

"What would happen to Marge and the kids without him?"

"I guess Marge would ask me for handouts."

"Don't sound angry about it, Sam."

"Okay."

"You know Jacob would never ask for a handout," she said. "He's proud."

"I can see why he'd rather go to the Sportin Life than come home."

"Couldn't we move them up to our house?"

"Where, for Chrissake? Have four kids running all over the house? Have Marge walking around in slippers and a housecoat in front of our guests?"

"They could be caretakers."

"Honey, we got caretakers up there. We got full-time servants. Jake's a boat captain. He ain't a caretaker. Jake wants to live in a trailer because we move the boat around."

"But the boat's been here for a year," she said. "We could build them a house so Marge would have it to live in when Jacob is away."

"He used to like for Marge to go with him."

"She can't go with him any more."

"I'm on my way back to the house," Guthrie said. "You coming?"

When Guthrie arose at seven, after not quite four hours' sleep, a hard wind was blowing in from the Gulf. Guthrie couldn't see out for the salt spray that covered the glass door in the bedroom. His wife had burrowed beneath the sheet with her back to him and her hair against his shoulder. He slipped out of bed and stood under the shower until he began to feel awake. While he was shaving he called the kitchen and had a maid bring coffee and a sweet roll.

"Any of the others up yet?" he asked her.

"No sir."

"If they get up and ask, tell 'em I've gone for a walk."

Guthrie took the telephone into the bathroom with him so he wouldn't disturb his wife. He poured a cup of coffee out of the small silver pot and bit off a piece of the roll. He phoned the hospital. There was no change in Iles; they still called his condition critical. It was undecided about surgery. There would be more X rays that afternoon. Guthrie put on sneakers, khakis, a golf shirt, and a windbreaker. He dialed Roger, the houseman, on the intercom.

"Roger, I want you to go down to Captain Iles's trailer and make sure that girl we sent there has got it clean. I want it fixed up nice.

Stop at the grocery store and make sure that trailer is stocked. Get a painter over there, and a carpenter if you need one. The girl is to stay over there as long as they need her. Might be a month. If we need another girl up here, get one. Understand? Tell Charlie I don't know yet when we'll fly out of here but to be ready. Okay?"

He hung up, walked out of the bathroom, looked again at his sleeping wife, quietly slid the glass door, and went down the back steps into the dunes.

It took him ten minutes to climb through the dunes and get to the low sand cliff that crumbled off to the beach. He stood for a while at the edge of the cliff, breathing deeply from the exertion, and listened to the booming of the surf. The water was gray-green, and oily, and it came in frothing ridges to crash against the beach. As each wave withdrew, leaving matted brown grass or a piece of gleaming black wood or a bottle or a stranded man-of-war, sandpipers raced into the wake and pecked at tiny holes in the sand. Guthrie had sat for hours watching sandpipers and had never seen one get wet. They stayed always at the very edge of the water and darted back when a new wave washed in.

The greasy yellow sky hung low and heavy, a dull frosting. Wind tore at the sand. Far to the left Guthrie could see the public fishing pier with waves climbing its brown rails, and black figures out at the end five hundred feet from shore. People slept out there at the end of the pier in sleeping bags or wrapped in shelter halves and blankets, and they fished all night. Guthrie had done it. He'd caught a six-hundred-pound hammerhead shark out there on a cable with a hook the size of a small anchor. When the shark took the hunk of horse meat they were using for bait, they snubbed the cable around a piling and waited to see which would crack first—the pier or the shark. Eventually it was the shark. Guthrie and Iles got the cable off the piling with difficulty, for the cable had sawed into the wood, and, working before dawn by lantern light, lifted the cable onto a pulley mounted on the pier. Guthrie's hands bled through his torn gloves. With the help of several other fishermen, they hoisted the shark out of the water where it hung like a great black sledge while Iles shot bullets into it with a .30-06 rifle. The bullets made slapping noises. As they swung the shark onto the pier, Iles ripped his left forearm against the sandpaper hide. They hung the beast from a crossbar and sat back to smoke and drink brandy and watch the flashlights bob along the pier as people came to admire their catch.

Then it occurred to Guthrie: What have I done this for? Guthrie got sand in his shoes as he skidded down the low cliff. He walked along the beach with his hands in the pockets of his windbreaker. He stepped around the puffed, purplish men-of-war with their violet streamers laid out in the wet sand. The recent bad weather had littered the beach with the discards of the Gulf. As a child Guthrie had roamed this beach hoping the Gulf would deliver him some marvelous gift: a treasure chest, a yacht, a whale, a bottle with a genii in it. Instead the Gulf gave him tin cans, weeds, driftwood, shells. The only thing of any value he ever found was a lifeboat which had lost whatever passengers it might have had, and someone had taken the lifeboat away from him.

Guthrie fell over a piece of driftwood and went down, hands and knees sinking into the sand. A wave splashed him. The water covered his wrists and then began curling back, leaving a man-of-war a few inches in front of him. The ugly balloon had several small fish trapped inside. Guthrie jumped up, grabbed a stick, and poked at the man-of-war until he saw that its streamers had wrapped around the stick and had come very close to his hands. He dropped the stick and walked back along the beach toward the house.

The others were eating breakfast beside the pool. Inside the courtyard, cut off from the wind, it was warm. The sun had begun to burn through the yellow overcast. Roger and George Washington were serving food on glass-topped tables that had been placed at the edge of the pool. The guests were in bathing suits. Beth Morris had changed from her bikini into a more conservative one-piece suit and had put on a wide straw hat. She sat with Jane and the Senator. Waddy was at another table, grinning, in dark glasses, leaning back in the chair with one hand on his thin, naked, hairless chest. A telephone was on the chair beside him.

"By God, the Ancient Mariner," Waddy said. "Come sit with me, old man, and tell me your wondrous story. You've been days clinging to a spar. Was it hard?"

"Tough," said Guthrie.

"You're supposed to say, 'Was it not.' Then you're supposed to stoppeth one of three. Go on. Stoppeth one."

"All right," Guthrie said. "Roger, get me a Bloody Mary."

"Two," said Waddy.

"Three," Senator Rose said.

"Worked out just right," said Waddy. "How about that, Beth?"

"Four," she said.

"Beth really doesn't want one," said Waddy. "She just wants to ruin the symmetry."

"You *shouldn't* want one," Beth said. "How many have you had already?"

"I can handle the concern for my own alcoholic intake," said Waddy.

"Oh, God," said Beth. "There's the first indication that Waddy is going to be smashed before noon."

Guthrie sat down at the table with Waddy. He ordered breakfast—scrambled eggs, sausage, toast, milk, coffee. He took off his windbreaker and gave it to Roger. Guthrie's ankles were crusted with sand. The colored tiles in the pool made the water look green; it flashed with sun.

"Glorious morning," Senator Rose said. "Utterly glorious. A day or so down here puts me at my peak, Sam. I feel like a college boy. This is the way to live. A nice swim, a good breakfast, a soothing drink, grand companions, beautiful women, God's own gentle sun on my flesh."

The Senator stretched his skinny arms and legs and then patted his belly. On his chest was the purple bruise left by the rod butt.

"Ah me," said Senator Rose. "Ah me. Paradise."

"Jane told us what happened to your skipper," Waddy said. "Too bad. He picked on the wrong guy. A man should be careful who he picks on."

"Jake's got more guts than sense," said Guthrie.

Guthrie sipped his Bloody Mary. Beth Morris pushed back her plate and began to smoke a cigarette, her hand, with cigarette, disappearing under the dark canopy of her hat. The Senator turned his face up to the sun with his eyes shut; the patches of broken blood vessels in his cheeks gave him a ruddy, vigorous look.

"I've got a call in to Bob Francis," Waddy said. "I'll get him to nose around and see if he can find out what the attitude of the Justice Department would be toward the merger. Forewarned, you know."

"Good," said Guthrie.

"Are you listening to me?" Waddy said.

"Sure."

"Worried about your skipper?"

"I was thinking about him."

"He'll be okay. These boat captains beat each other to a blob and the next day they go out and help each other find fish. They're indestructible. Guy I used to have in Florida, he'd be on the radio all day talking to other skippers, trading information on spotting fish, and that night he'd be knocking their teeth out in some saloon. That's kind of like politics, isn't it, Senator?"

"Somewhat," said Senator Rose, smiling into the sunlight.

"I thought we were going to Mexico, for God's sake," Beth Morris said.

"What time you want to leave?" Guthrie said.

"I've had about *enough* sun," said Beth.

"Sam, we can't leave with Jacob so badly hurt," Jane Guthrie said.

"What more can we do for Jake?" said Guthrie. "I ain't his doctor."

"But he's hurt," she said.

"Roger, tell Charlie we'll want to leave right after lunch," said Guthrie. "Have the car ready to take us to the airport at one-thirty."

Beth Morris stood up, walked over to one of the collapsible aluminum chairs, took off her straw hat, shook out her long blonde hair, and sat down. The chair tilted back. She kicked off her sandals and arched her feet at the end of the chair. She wiggled her toes.

"Fascinating business," Senator Rose said, his eyes still shut. "Fascinating business, electronics. The contracts, Lord, the millions and millions and millions in contracts being passed out every day. The most incredible things. When I was a young man we never dreamed of any of these things. Radios so tiny you can barely see them. Transistors. Guidance systems. Television pictures of the *moon*. When I was a young man, rockets were for the Fourth of July. Sometimes I'm glad I won't be around in another thirty years. I don't think I could bear to see what the world will become. The world has already changed too much for me."

"From reading the papers, it looks like nobody will be around in another thirty years," said Beth Morris.

"War? I think not, my dear," the Senator said. "Not the big, final war. It's too hideous, simply too hideous for man to turn it loose upon himself. There will be dangers, but I must believe man is too intelligent and basically too good ever to release the big bombs. A nuclear war would be perversion. I don't believe man is perverted. I don't believe man has turned against himself and desires his own destruction. I believe in God and the goodness of man."

"Where's your bomb shelter?" said Waddy.

"I'm too old to have a bomb shelter," the Senator said, half-turning in his chair and squinting toward Waddy and Guthrie.

"I'm too smart not to," said Waddy.

"You're rather cynical, Mr. Morris," Senator Rose said.

"That's your word for it, Senator. My word is realistic. I don't believe in man's inherent goodness. I believe in his inherent avarice, stupidity, and lust. I've made quite a few deals successful by counting on avarice and lust in the people I was dealing with."

"Tell me, Mr. Morris," said the Senator. "If you believe we are bound to deposit these horrible bombs on each other, why do you go on with your grand business schemes? Why do you worry about mergers and the Justice Department?"

"What do you want me to do, go sit down and die?" Waddy said. "I think the bomb will probably come, but I don't know when. And I can't do any more about it than Roger over there can do. In my world, bombs go off all the time. Personal bombs. An associate of mine got caught in a squeeze a couple of years ago and shot himself in the head. That was the same as a bomb for him. But instead of worrying about the big bomb, I keep working and keep developing and keep making money. It's what I do, like what you do is serve in the Senate and what Roger does is serve the Bloody Marys. It's my life. I'm not going to panic and give up my life."

"Why don't you go to Brazil and develop down there?" said Senator Rose. "You could have your pleasure and your assured survival as well."

"Survival is never assured, Senator. And anyway I like this place. I like this state. I belong here. I know if the bomb catches me in Dallas I'm dead, shelter or no shelter. If the bomb comes while I'm at my ranch in Mexico or somewhere like that, I might survive. And if I do survive, the first thing I'll do is start building this state up again. Whatever's left of it."

"How much do you think you'd be worth if this state were blown to ashes?" the Senator said.

"Senator, nobody knows what my family's worth right now," said Waddy. He raised his dark glasses onto his freckled forehead. "Anything you might hear, even if you heard it from me, would be no better than an educated guess. But if all of it was gone, if it was all gone overnight, I'd still be an individual. I'd still be worth something as an individual. I'd still have a brain and courage and I could start building all over again, and I'd make a hell of a lot of money again. I'll tell you something about money, Senator. People who don't have it think there's something mysterious about the people who do. But money's easy to make if you think about money. If you concentrate on money, you'll make it."

"Begging your indulgence, I'd like to point out that you began life with a considerable quantity of money," said Senator Rose.

"That helped," Waddy said, grinning. "I wouldn't deny that it helped. But I'd have made money. What you really need to make money is the temperament. Suppose I concentrated on golf and spent all my time thinking about it and working at it. I could be a par shooter in two or three years. I could never be a great tennis player because I don't have the speed and reactions, and I could never be a great football player because I'm too little. But I have the concentration to be a good golfer. I could be a great racing car driver. I've got the temperament. Money, itself, doesn't mean too much once you've got whatever pleasure it can give you. There's a limit to what it can do in that way. You hit that limit without having millions. But if you have the temperament you go on making it because it's fun. It really is fun, Senator. You move on from just making money into controlling things, manipulating, moving. You pull this string to see how that thing over there reacts. You see something you don't have, and you go get it. That's the biggest pleasure in life. It's like playing a big deadly game of chess. If I somehow today lost every penny, everybody would drop me. Beth wouldn't stay with me ten minutes. Sam'd throw me out of his house."

"Wait a minute," Guthrie said.

"It's true," said Waddy. "Don't ever think any different. But it's all right. My relationship with you, Guthrie, and yours with me, has a practical basis. You want me because I have money and power and besides what I can do for you you're queer for money and power. I want you because you can help me do things I want to do. What's wrong with that? That's fine. But what I was saying is that if I lost all my money, I'd start down the same track because building it up is what I enjoy. It's not work. It's my life."

"Waddy, for God's sake, you're drinking too much," Beth said.

"Look at Sam there," said Waddy. "He started off with nothing, and now he's got a lot and he's trying to catch me."

"I don't see how I could catch you," Guthrie said.

"I don't either," said Waddy.

"The tax laws are fixed so nobody can catch you," Guthrie said.

"It's not the tax laws. There are ways. The reason you won't catch me is I've got a finer temperament. The only thing that bothers me about you is I feel like there's something in you, some block, pulling at you."

"You talk like Sam is your hobby," said Jane Guthrie.

"Pretty expensive for a hobby," Waddy said. "No, Sam can help me and I can help Sam. We can help each other. I like things that pay off."

"God!" said Beth. "You're such a bore when you talk that way, Waddy."

"It's not aristocratic, is it?" Waddy said. "Beth's an aristocrat. Her whole damn family hasn't got enough money to keep one of our airplanes in gas, but they got their money in the right place and at the right time. I'm not a blueblood, Sam. You're a hell of a long way from being a blueblood. Beth's family wouldn't like you because you were dumb enough to have a poor drowned fisherman for a father."

They were silent. Guthrie inspected the rim of his glass.

"Waddy," Beth said after a moment, "if you're going to carry on like this all weekend, I don't believe I'll go to Mexico."

"I don't think I'll go either," said Jane Guthrie. "Excuse me, please."

She went around the edge of the pool and through the door that led to their bedroom. Guthrie watched her go, listening to the anger in the clap of her sandals on the terrazzo.

"She mad at me?" Waddy said. "What did I do?"

"Oh, why don't you swim or something?" said Beth.

"Hey, Senator, how about a race?" Waddy said. "Senator? What the hell, are you asleep?"

"Huh?" said Senator Rose, his head jerking up and his eyes blinking.

"How could you go to sleep when I was talking about all this vital stuff?" Waddy said.

"I wasn't asleep. It's this beautiful warm sunshine. What were you saying?"

"I'll go off and talk to myself," said Waddy.

"How far off?" Beth said.

"Sam, don't ever marry an aristocrat," said Waddy. "They've got something sick in their blood."

"I better go see if I can mend a fence," Guthrie said.

He found his wife sitting on their bed looking out the glass wall toward the Gulf. The maid had been in; the bed was made and the night's spray had been wiped off the windows. Jane, in aqua shorts and a white blouse, sat on the yellow silk spread with her short legs folded. Guthrie came around and stood in front of her. She kept looking straight ahead, as though she could see through his chest.

"What's the matter?" he said.

"Nothing."

"Waddy didn't mean anything by what he said. Several Bloody Marys before breakfast will do that."

"This has nothing to do with Waddy. I'm not going to Mexico, that's all."

Guthrie sat down beside her and put his arm around her. She did not move.

"Somebody ought to stay here in case Jacob needs something," she said. "You go to Mexico with your friends and have a lot of fun this weekend. I'll stay. I don't mind."

"What are you trying to do? There's nothing we can do for Jake that we haven't already done. You can't pull out on me now. I need you."

"What for?" she said.

"Look, Waddy's helped me, but he could still change his mind. This is an important weekend. He likes you. Don't break up the party."

"It's just wonderful the way you put that, Sam. It really moves me."

"Don't let me down."

"You're letting down Jacob," she said.

"He's got doctors. He's got a special nurse. What does he need me for, to hold his hand?"

"It might help," she said. She slipped out from under his arm and went to the glass wall. It was white and burnished out there now, impossibly bright. "Are you scared to go to Mexico without me? Are you afraid of Beth Morris? You can forget her, lover. She wouldn't let you wash her underwear."

"Don't be stupid," said Guthrie.

"You're being stupid. Don't you see what's happening?"

"Baby, I need you. Please, just this weekend. After I get this merger business finished and after Waddy and I get going on our other deal, I promise I'll ease off. I'll relax. I'll be like I used to be. We'll take a vacation."

"I'd like to believe that," she said.

"We'll go to Europe. We'll stay six months. We'll ball it up all the time. Just hang on a while longer. Stay with me through this. Let's don't let anything blow us away."

He went to her and leaned down and kissed her eyes and then her mouth and then her eyes again.

"All right," she said. "But you'd better be telling me the truth, Sam."

"We'll only be in Mexico until tomorrow evening. If Jake isn't out of the woods by then, I'll try to come back here for a day and see what else I can do."

"For a day? That would be kind."

"You know what I've got coming up next week."

"I said all right. I'll go tell the cook what to put on the plane."

"I'm glad you're going," Guthrie said. "Waddy had his heart set on going to Mexico, and I wouldn't have wanted to go without you."

"You know what I think? I think you're the one who wants to go to Mexico more than Waddy."

"Waddy likes these fiestas."

"Will you do me a favor? Will you, in our private conversations, quit talking about Waddy Morris?"

Waddy Morris was floating on a rubber mattress in the pool and drinking a Bloody Mary through a straw. When the mattress touched the side of the pool he would put a foot against the drain and give himself a push toward the other side. His dark glasses turned toward Guthrie as he entered the court. Senator Rose had dragged another mattress to the edge of the pool and lay on it asleep. Beth Morris had put on her bathing cap and stood on the diving board as if she had accidentally found herself up there and was undecided what to do about it. She seemed to be considering jumping on top of Waddy and sinking him, a possibility which he was not ignoring in his crossings of the pool. Guthrie went to the table where he had left his own Bloody Mary. The glass was warm, the ice was melted, the drink tasted acid and peppery.

"I told George Washington to bring a big cold pitcher of vodka and apple juice," Waddy said. "George Washington is a wonderful man. You can scare him."

"Waddy yelled at him," said Beth.

"I'm watching you," Waddy said. "You stay right where you are."

Waddy's mattress bumped against concrete. He reached back with his free hand and pushed.

"The Senator got mad," said Waddy. "I tried to throw him in the pool and he told me he was a United States Senator and you don't throw United States Senators in pools and not being from Texas he didn't give a damn whether I liked it or not. I like the Senator. He turns red when he gets mad. Then he gets tired and goes to sleep."

"I think I *will* jump, for God's sake," Beth said.

"Hell, I'm not just from Texas," said Waddy. "I'm a true American. I have interests everywhere. I'm a citizen of the world. Right this minute, for example, I have the only ferry boat that operates regularly back and forth across this pool."

Beth jumped. The wave barely rocked Waddy's mattress, but the splash showered him. Water trickled down his dark glasses. Calmly he waited until she appeared, laughing, water streaming from her face and shoulders, and then he threw the contents of his glass at her. Tomato juice and ice cubes sloshed in front of her. She laughed and swam with long strokes to the end of the pool. She climbed up the ladder, the wet suit clinging to her hips and giving the illusion that flesh could be seen. Waddy frowned.

"Now my drink is gone," he said. "Tempestuous action never gets a man anyplace."

Waddy rolled off the mattress, flutter-kicked on his back to the side of the pool, and crawled out. He put his empty glass on the table and sat down beside Guthrie.

"I forgot to tell you," said Waddy. "I talked to A. C. Johnson this morning while you were communing with nature. You'll like this story. That young lawyer, whatshisname, who was running the proxy fight for Simmons?"

"Carpenter," Guthrie said.

"Yeah. I guess. Well, he went to see Johnson yesterday. Except my phone call beat him there by a few hours. Johnson wouldn't let him in the office. One of Johnson's girls said that guy—Carpenter?—had been telling them they had the proxy fight won, and then when Johnson wouldn't even see him, they said the guy's face fell all over his shoes. Johnson is expecting a visit from Simmons this morning. Conditional surrender."

"Good," said Guthrie.

"Carpenter. Carpenter. He any kin to B. L. Carpenter, the guy who got in trouble?"

"Son."

"Huh. The old man was pretty smart," Waddy said. "But very unlucky. Is the boy as smart as the old man was?"

"The boy is dumb."

"That happens," said Waddy. "That does happen."

Senator Rose groaned and turned over.

"Hey, Senator, I want you to help me run a pipeline across your state," Waddy said.

The Senator snored.

"Unimpressed," said Waddy. "What are you doing with him, anyway?"

"He's a friend," Guthrie said.

"Sure."

"Waddy," said Beth. "Waddy, darling, bring me that sun tan oil."

"Damn aristocrat," Waddy said.

Beth had sprawled on her back on another mattress, her long legs smooth and clear as ivory, her toenails red, her nose and chin as perfect as the features of a bust dug up from Iona, her voice imperious as a spoiled child's.

"Where do you want me to rub it?" he said.

"All over, darling."

Waddy took the tube of ointment to where she lay, squeezed a green worm of it onto each thigh, and began massaging it in. He knelt beside her. Looking at Waddy's flat, hard stomach, Guthrie unconsciously began to rub his own.

"Dear, don't be such a bore any more about money," Beth said. "Everybody knows you have it, and how powerful you are, and all that. Don't be dull about it, for God's sake."

Waddy's small lips pinched together. With one finger he pushed on the bridge of his glasses. Guthrie waited for Waddy to chill her with a word as he had done when she had made him angry with her story about the Secretary of the Navy.

Instead, Waddy's dark glasses swung toward Guthrie.

"Guthrie," he said, "go find that nigger and get me a drink."

Part Five

NEKKID BRIDGE

Ben Carpenter awoke with a wild lurch, falling forward onto the grass and then quickly rolling up onto one elbow. He looked at the white house where the lights glowed, and looked up at the trees, and wondered why they had put him out here. He *had* been in there, hadn't he? Then he heard soft laughter behind him and, turning, he saw the girl sitting on the iron bench. He shook his head and patted his shirt pocket. The girl's hand reached out to him with the orange tip of a cigarette, and he took it. Ben breathed deeply, as if he had just come up from nearly drowning. His lungs felt like prunes. From way off down the alley he heard a dog barking. Another dog, closer, began to bark. A third took up the alarm. Several houses away a voice started yelling for the dogs to shut up.

"I shouldn't have laughed, but you looked so funny," the girl said. "As if you had to wake up dodging. Do you think someone is going to murder you in your sleep?"

"I forgot you were here to protect me," said Ben. "How long did I sleep?"

"About twenty minutes."

"Something cozy about this back yard. That's twice tonight I've slept out here."

"Maybe you used to be a Boy Scout."

"Still am. I'm working on my Merit Badge in debauchery."

She sat in the shadow of the trees but he could see the white of her teeth and eyes and the softer gray of her face and arms, and the long black flow of her hair. She leaned forward with her knees primly together, the forefinger of her left hand hooked in her strand of pearls.

"You remember me, don't you?" she said.

"I think so."

"I hoped you would."

"Help me up."

She laughed and held his hand while he struggled to his feet. He released her and brushed the grass off his pants and slapped at the grass on the back of his shirt.

"It wouldn't do at all to go inside the house with grass on my back," he said. "People'd think I'm a pervert."

"I wouldn't think so."

"Scratch my back. I got some grass down my shirt. There, between the shoulder blades."

Her fingernails scraped against his back. He allowed his shoulders to drop and the tension to ease in his neck. Facing Harry's house he could see people moving in the windows and hear loud music. The houses on either side were dark, but the dogs were barking. Somewhere down the alley a garbage can fell off its rack with a whanging clatter. The dogs were frantic. A voice kept yelling for them to shut up.

"Must be a cat prowling in the cans," Ben said.

"Is it keeping you awake?"

"I'm trying to remember if I'm in love with you."

"You didn't make it clear," she said. "But I finally decided you're not."

"Why?"

"Because you didn't make it clear. If you were in love with me, it'd be clear enough."

"Are you always clear when you're in love with somebody?"

"I think so."

"Not me. I'm the kind of guy that it doesn't show what I'm feeling. I never let myself look like I've gone overboard about anything."

"Oh, Ben," she said.

"What?"

"That's not true. There's pain in your face and in every gesture you make."

"Does it look noble?"

"No."

"Then it's not pain. It's only self-disgust."

"It's pain. And probably self-pity."

"Self-pity and showing your emotions is pure vanity. Me, I got no vanity. I'm absolutely without vanity of any sort."

"You're as vain as a Brazilian general," she said.

"Stop scratching my back. I'm not sure I like you if you're going to argue with me. I hate arguments."

"So do I."

"Arguments are pure vanity. I'd rather hurt people."

"But you don't."

"Oh yes I do. Not all's I'd like to, though."

"Tell me about all of it."

"All of what?" he said.

"Everything that's bothering you."

"Some other time, some other country."

"Don't pull away."

"I don't like to be probed."

"You're a bunch of raw nerves."

"Notice the twitch in my left eye? Whattaya call it? A tic? Here, look."

He turned and as she lifted her eyes he kissed her. Her body arched against his, and he could tell from the way she trembled that she was feeling it somewhere and liking it.

"Let's go upstairs and lock the door," he said.

"No."

"Now damn it, you can't say that."

"Let's go inside," she said. "To your birthday party."

"You're crazy."

"I don't really know you. Maybe you're not who I think you are. Maybe you never were the boy I thought you were. Give me time to find out."

"You'll have another mystic vision and hoo hah I'm out again."

"I thought you weren't going to joke about that."

"All right," he said. "You're pretty. No, not pretty. You're beautiful. You're odd beautiful. I've seen that hair on high-born ladies in old Castile. Do you have two maids to brush it for you at night when it hangs over the back of the chair at your dressing table? Do you put gardenias in it?"

"Would you like for me to cut it?"

"Absolutely not. You're an Aztec priestess. You've got those eyes that look into a man's soul when you're getting ready to bend him over a stone and tear his heart out with a flint knife. I can see you in a long white robe. Where'd you have this mystic experience, Mexico?"

"We're not going to talk about it."

"How'd I guess that?"

"Seton must have told you a long time ago."

"You don't look like Seton. You don't have the same facial structure. Seton looks like a coyote."

"We didn't have the same mother. Seton's mother died when he was a baby."

"Sure, I knew that."

"Ben, what's the matter with you?"

"Needles and pins," he said. "Needles and pins."

The dog next door was barking and whining and clawing at the back fence. "Shut up! They'll hear me!" a voice said.

"Now I'm having a mystic experience," Ben said. "That sounded like Jason."

"*Hsssssssst!*"

"Don't say a word," Ben said. "That couldn't be Jason out in the alley going *hsssssssst.*"

"*Hsssssssst!* Ben!" the voice said in an urgent stage whisper.

The dog next door began to howl from frustration at not being able to get at the mysterious, irritating figure on the other side of the fence.

"*Hsssssssst!* Ben! For God's sake!"

The back gate opened and a dark head appeared. Not above the gate but in the middle, peeking around, crouching. The head became a body that crept through the gate, shutting it afterward, and then scuttled across to the rock fish pond and went out of sight. In a moment the dark head appeared again, from round the edge of the fish pond wall, in a splotch of moonlight.

"*Hsssssssst!* Pippa!"

"What is it?" Pippa said.

"*Shhhh!* Not so loud!"

"What is it, Jason?" Pippa whispered, trying to make herself heard above the barking dogs.

"Is Ben drunk?"

"Not very."

"Ask him to come here, please."

"Ben, would you please go over there behind the fish pond? Someone wants to talk to you."

"Damn it, dog, shut up!" Jason yelled.

The dog moaned and hurled itself at the fence.

"I won't go," Ben said. "Why should I go?"

"*Hsssssssst!*"

"You have to go," said Pippa. "That dog will hurt itself."

Jason knelt behind the fish pond wall as if it were a battlement. There was a black smear on his chin. His tie was pulled loose, and his coat was unbuttoned.

"Thank Heaven you've come," Jason said. "Scuse my pants. A garbage can fell on me."

"Olee olee ahhsenfee, all that's out can come in free," said Ben. "That's what we used to yell when we played hide and seek, I think."

"You've got to help me," Jason said.

"Let's lie down here with him," said Ben.

"That wouldn't help," Jason said. "That would make me nervous."

"What can we do?" said Pippa.

"It's that blonde-haired woman, Ben. The one that came with Harvey? You got to get her out of here. Is Willy mad at me?"

"Willy's usually mad at you."

"Well, you got to get that blonde-haired woman out of here. She thinks I'm divorced. I told her my wife had gone off with a bongo player and lives in San Francisco. On North Beach, I told her. I was pretty explicit about it. If she sees me, she'll rape me. Willy wouldn't like that."

"One of these days, Jason, you'll go too far," Ben said.

"I know. I know. Won't we all."

"This is my fault in a way," said Ben. "I'll go tell Harvey to get that woman out of the house. Bartenders know how to handle these situations."

"I'll stay here," Jason said. "When she's gone you signal me from the window. Pull the shade up and down three times."

"There's not a shade on that window," said Ben. "I'll blink you a message with my infrared flashlight."

"I'll come out and get you," Pippa said.

"That won't do. Willy would see us come in together. Willy sees everthing."

"I'll stand in the window and wiggle my ears," said Ben.

"Just stand in the window and wave. Be casual about it," Jason said.

"How could I wave casually out into a dark yard?"

"We have to think of something," said Jason.

"When she's gone, I'll stand in the window," Pippa said.

"Great. Great idea," said Jason. "Will you marry me second from next?"

"What will you tell Willy about the dirt on your face and the garbage on your pants?" Pippa said.

"I'll tell her . . ." said Jason. "I'll tell her . . . I'll tell her I love her and maybe she won't notice. Naw, she'd notice. I'll tell her I fell out the second-floor window and laid unconscious until a barking dog woke me up. I'll try for sympathy."

"Come on," Ben said.

Ben and Pippa walked across the yard and up the back steps and onto the screened porch. He was careful not to get splinters in his bare feet on the wooden steps. When he opened the kitchen door into the party, it was like walking into the inferno.

Six people sat at the kitchen table in various stages of undress. Cadmus, wearing shorts, shoes and socks, was dealing from a deck of cards. The flesh on his chest was pink and sagging around the breasts, and his belly rolled over the elastic waistband of his shorts. He looked up through dark-circled eyes and showed his crooked teeth. Blossom sat at his left in a wooden chair, wearing a brassiere and half-slip, hose and shoes, her stomach flat and her shoulders smooth and golden. Chub Anderson, fully clothed except for her shoes, sat beside Blossom. A young man Ben knew only as Chink sat beside Chub. Chink wore nothing but his shorts; his vaguely Oriental face with its swelling cheekbones was turned steadily toward the cards in Cadmus's hand. The last person at the table was Chink's wife, who had covered herself with a large dish towel so that Ben couldn't tell what else she had on. Harry, in shirt and trousers but barefooted, stood at the end of the table. Seton sat on a beer case in the corner, smoking and watching the game with a satisfied smile, as if it had now been proved to him that the world was lunatic.

A few others stood at the drainboard or in the two inside doorways and watched.

"You getting up a basketball team, Cadmus?" said Ben.

"Ole Ben!" Cadmus said. "I wisht you coulda got into the game, son, but it's too late now. Hell of a scientific game. Takes all the skill and know-how I developed up at Harvard for me to keep from publicly exposing my handsome scrotum."

"Ratchit. Deal," said Blossom.

"Strip poker?" Ben said.

"Naw, strip poker is old-timey. They played that in Hugh Walpole's apartment," Cadmus said. "This here is a new game that I just invented. It's called Nekkid Bridge."

"Damn good. Deal," said Blossom.

"Blossom here thanks the one that gets nekkid is the winner. I can't splain to her," Cadmus said.

"What he does, he deals around the table and the low card has to take off an article of clothing," said Chub. "All jewelry counts as one, shoes count as one, hose count as one. It's a nice game. Very complicated."

"Pardon me," Pippa said.

"Where you going?" said Ben.

"The living room."

"Mr. and Mrs. Chink's had a bad run of luck," Cadmus said. "You can see they ain't broke no bank."

To get into the living room, Pippa had to step over the body of a girl who had passed out in the doorway on the kitchen floor. She lay peacefully sleeping with her head on a sack of crushed ice. Her arms were outflung, hands and forearms resting on the linoleum as though it were a mattress. The front of her dress was wet, and an overturned glass lay beside her right hand. Ben recognized her as the girl Cadmus had called Little Princess.

"The cards, the cards," said Chink.

"Wait once, son," Cadmus said. "We gotta have suspense in this here game."

"Ben, this is so much fun," said Chub.

"I'm trying to learn the strategy," Harry said. "I never was much good at honor count and all that."

"Where's Walter?" said Ben.

"In the living room," Chub said. "He refused to have anything to do with this game. It's terribly risqué."

"It ain't risqué," said Cadmus. "It's goddamn downright filthy."

"Nothing dirty about the human body," Chink said.

"You deviate," said Chink's wife, tucking the dish towel tightly around her.

"You don't have to play," Chink said. "I told you you didn't have to play."

"And I told you the next time you did anything like this I was going to do it too," she said. She looked at Ben, her lips turning down. "I thought that would make him quit. Lot I knew."

"Don't make cracks," said Chink.

"Needa drank," Blossom said.

"Get the little girl a drank, Ben," said Cadmus. "She barely speaks Anglish."

"Gimme drank," Blossom said, looking up at Ben.

Ben stared at her breasts bulging against the brassiere as she reached up with her glass, and she giggled and shook her silvery hair. He noticed her hair had spangles in it, on top, where it was like spun silver, like the angel hair that was used to decorate Christmas trees. Beneath the half-slip he saw the outline of her legs and her garter belt with its snaps sitting like bugs under the nylon slip on her firm thighs. She poked the glass into Ben's stomach and looked at him fuzzily and opened her mouth and then swung her head suddenly to look at Cadmus, her head bobbing as if her neck were a coil spring. Chink took his eyes off the cards for a moment to look at her. Ben carried the glass to the sink, scooped ice out of the melting puddle inside a sack, and sloshed the glass half full of scotch from somebody's bottle. At that hour, it no longer mattered whose bottle anyone used; very few ever put name tags on the bottles to identify them. By that time most of the bottles on the drainboard were usually empty and it became a search to find the bottles the sly ones had hidden behind canned goods in the pantry or on the shelves of dishes. Ben had once found a bottle someone had hidden in Harry's kitchen behind a framed painting that was hung on the whitewashed wall; the bottle was a half-pint and had been stuck behind the wooden frame. When Ben gave Blossom her drink, Cadmus started to deal.

"Hod dawg, five of clubs, Blossom," Cadmus said.

"Hep me git this thang off hon," said Blossom, looking at Ben and shrugging her shoulders to indicate the brassiere.

"You ain't lost yet," Cadmus said.

Blossom scooted back her chair, stood up, and fell against Ben. Using him for support, she pulled off her half-slip. She threw the half-slip away. It landed on the sleeping Little Princess. Blossom stood there, holding Ben's arm, in her brassiere and garter belt and hose and white nylon panties through which a dark fluff was visible. She giggled. Her head, as though the weight had shifted in it, flopped around again to look down at Cadmus.

"I can't splain to her," said Cadmus.

"Ratchit," Blossom said, and abruptly sat down.

Pippa came into the kitchen. She stepped over the Little Princess, looked questioningly at the half-slip, glanced at Ben, and went and stood in the big window so Jason, from his hiding place, could see her. To Ben her mouth formed words: they're gone. Pippa stood there briefly and then returned to the living room. Her long black hair bounced as she walked.

Cadmus dealt an ace to Chub Anderson.

"No way we can rob you of any garmints," he said. "Course, I could cheat if you'd like me to. I'd hate to do it though. I got Harvard principles."

"I'd rather everone else lost," said Chub.

"Magine," Cadmus said, and flipped a six of spades to Chink.

Chink leaned back in his chair. He looked disappointed.

To Chink's wife, Cadmus dealt a four of hearts.

"You low so far, honey pot," said Cadmus.

Chink's wife glared at the card and crushed out her cigarette.

"Here go, Harry, ole buddy," Cadmus said.

Harry got a jack.

"Now it's mine," said Cadmus. "You sweating it, Mrs. Chink?"

All the eyes followed Cadmus's fingers as he slowly lifted the top card from the deck, looked at it, grinned, and dropped it onto the table. "Son of a gun," he said. "How bout that?"

Cadmus had drawn a ten of diamonds.

Chink's wife looked at the card as the realization gradually came into her face that she had lost. Her eyes widened. She bit her lip and looked at each of them.

"I won't do it," she said.

"You will," said Chink. "You wanted to play. Be a sport."

"Sport, hell," she said. "You told me if I'd go in the bathroom and come out in just this dish towel I wouldn't have to take off anything else."

"That's what *you* said. I didn't say that," said Chink. "This way you got an extra turn."

"You *want* your wife running around naked in front of all these men?" she said.

"A game's a game," said Chink. "Winners win and losers lose."

"I won't do it," she said, pulling the dish towel tight again to reassure herself and folding her arms across her breasts. "Do I have to, Cadmus?"

"I spose not, honey pot."

"You told me you didn't ever want anybody to see me naked except you," Chink's wife said to her husband.

"That was a long time ago," he said.

"Well, I'm not going to do it."

"You're embarrassing me," said Chink. "You're humiliating me. I don't want us to be bad sports."

She began to cry.

"It ain't worth all this," Cadmus said. "Lemme deal again."

"Naw, we lost," said Chink. "We gotta pay."

He arose and yanked off his shorts. He put his hands on his hips and looked down at his wife, who had covered her face but was looking between her fingers. "Now what does *this* prove?" Chink said. Chub wrinkled her nose and giggled. Blossom smiled foggily, unsure what was happening but pleased by it. Harry grinned. Seton said, "Oh my God," and got up from the beer case. Jason came in from the back door, looked at the scene at the table, started to go out again, stopped, and looked back; the portent of it was bewildering. Cadmus sighed as if he regretted ever having started the game.

From the drainboard someone yelled, "Chink's nekkid!" Both inside doorways were quickly full of people who laughed and pointed. Chink walked around the edge of the table with admirable dignity. His wife wept. "I think it's disgusting," a woman said. "Don't look then," said someone else.

"I'm going to run to the corner and back," Chink said.

"Don't, baby, you'll go to jail," said his wife.

"I've been to jail before," Chink said proudly.

"I don't know if you oughta do that," said Cadmus.

"Is it all right with you, Harry? It's your house," Chink said.

"Is this my house?" said Harry.

Chink walked toward the doorway. He was tanned and not so fat and obviously didn't mind being naked in the crowd; he seemed rather to enjoy it. The crowd parted in the living room doorway to open him a path. "Don't touch him," a man said to his wife. "Touch'm iffwanna," said the wife. Chink held his head up and his shoulders back, pacing as slowly and erectly as a guard at the Palace of St. James. Chink's wife leaped up and ran after him, clutching the dish towel around her.

"Stop him!" she shouted. "Don't let him do it!"

Chink and his wife went through the crowd. Ben could hear shrieks of laughter from the living room.

"The cops are in there," Harry said, remembering. "They're off duty, but I don't know *how* off duty. I better go talk to Luther."

Cadmus put down the cards, walked to the drainboard, and began to fix himself a drink. From the rear, it was more obvious how the fat around his middle rolled out, and that he was knock-kneed, and that his legs were very long.

"Is the game over?" said Chub.

"We had a loser," Cadmus said. "Or winner, by Blossom's book."

"I thought we played till everbody lost," said Chub.

"Honey pot, everbody has done lost," Cadmus said. "If you want to, shuck off your close. Won't make a hell of a lot of difference."

"Ben, wasn't that funny?" said Chub. "I'm surprised you stayed to watch it, being so high and mighty. That got down-right human, didn't it?"

Ben pushed his way into the living room. The stereo played at full volume; the sound bounced off the walls and attacked the crowd like a swarm of hornets. People stood in mists of smoke. Doris was opening the front door again. The crowd gave no sign of the passage of Mr. and Mrs. Chink; in the paroxysm of mass drunkenness the nudity of Chink had been hardly more than a fleeting diversion, and unreal, at that; a comic and unlikely vision that appeared and vanished and left the observer wondering if it had been seen at all—would leave him wondering for days afterward, would leave him asking other veterans of the party if they had truly seen a naked man walking through a crowded living room at an hour nearing dawn on a Saturday at Harry Danielsen's house on the occasion of Ben Carpenter being—how old was it?—thirty or something? The banner that said *BEN IS THIRTY* had fallen off the wall above the kitchen door and was crumpled and trampled on the dance floor.

Ben saw Pippa through curls of smoke sitting on the couch with Walter Anderson and Willy. Jason had joined them and was explaining something, jabbing his hands, laughing—as if to say, well, it was the *damnedest* thing—and Willy was frowning, not believing anything Jason said. The right knee of Jason's pants was badly blotched and baggy, and there was a foul stain on his coat. Ben wriggled between the dancers and started toward the couch.

For an instant he was blinded. His cheek stung, he heard the slap. Tears came into his eyes as the palm of a hand glanced off his nose after it smacked against his cheek.

"You bastard," said the purple-lidded girl. "I waited."

"Pardon?" Ben said.

"I waited in the damned car. I thought maybe I had the wrong car."

"What'd you hit me for?"

"You were gonna meet me. In thirty minutes."

"Oh. Did you see a nude man go past?"

"He went upstairs. Him and his wife. Listen, it's too late now to apologize."

"I wasn't apologizing," Ben said. He looked at Pippa. She had seen the slap and was staring at him.

"My husband is upstairs sick and wants to go home. You missed your chance," said the purple-lidded girl.

"Pity," said Ben.

"Serves you right. I waited a long time. You must think you're a pretty big deal to keep a girl waiting like that."

"I'm the humblest man you ever met."

"Will you call me? Roy plays golf tomorrow afternoon."

"You mean Saturday?"

"This is Saturday already. I mean Sunday."

"Who is Roy?"

"Ain't you humorous?" said the girl.

"I'm a one-man band."

"The way you act, no wonder your wife left you."

"That's right, hon. You're an excellent judge of flesh."

Ben walked away from the girl, motioned to Pippa, and went to the front porch. He stopped beside a thin window adjoining the oak door to light a cigarette. Then he stepped onto the porch. The street lamps were off. It was quiet except for the sound of a truck passing down below to the left on the expressway, and for the clamor of the party behind him. Across the street, at the stone house where plastic flowers grew, the windows were black: was the old lady looking at the party from her upstairs bedroom and wishing she could hear? To the right the Carmelite nunnery was serene behind its yellow brick wall, the red slate tiles of its roof wrinkled in the moonlight, the nunnery shut off from the world that Ben stood in. The nuns inside, what were they doing? Waiting for another sunrise in a very limited progression of sunrises? How did they wait? Ben wondered. Confidently? Sadly? Eagerly? He felt Pippa's hand fumbling for his.

"What do nuns do?" Ben said.

"They work and they pray," she said.

"They must lie there by themselves in their beds and debate whether they made the right choice," said Ben.

"Maybe some of them do. I don't know. The Carmelites take the vow of silence."

"That sounds like a lonely life."

"They have something to sustain them," she said,

"Tough being a nun."

"Is it tougher to be a nun than it is to be you?"

"I never thought of that," he said.

"Sometimes I think I should have been a nun."

"You a Catholic?"

"Convert."

"Hoo boy," Ben said. "A Catholic convert and a mystic. Worst combination I can think of. I'll try to overlook it. I want to show you something."

Ben moved aside to let out eight people who were leaving the party. They made a weaving course down the sidewalk, bumping against the black trunks of the elms and yelling at each other. Ben waited until their car doors slammed and their engines started and their cars roared away, somehow not hitting anything.

With the girl beside him, Ben went across the street and up a gravel driveway and then down an uneven stone path between two houses. There were trees along the path. Ben turned down a low, narrow tunnel hung with trumpet vines on a lattice. Pippa stumbled in the blackness. Ben knocked his head against an old carriage lantern that had been wired and dangled from the lattice. Ducking, they came out on a grassy slope, and suddenly they were on a ledge above the city. Below was the black shape of the half-toppled dairy barn; the forest began there and went down the great hill to the river valley. Farther down shone the top of a metal water tank that looked like a pond in the moonlight. The valley passed on in darkness, and beyond the ground rose in the west and the lights of the city glittered as if shaken out of a jewel box, red and white and yellow and green. The ribbon of the expressway, glowing with lamps, led off to the west. Ben and the girl sat down on the rock wall of the terrace. A mockingbird sang in a tree above them; a twig snapped off and fell at their feet.

"We shouldn't be here," Pippa said.

"This is an apartment house now," he said. "Nobody knows who belongs. A friend of Jean's used to live here, and I found out what a fine place this is to sit at night."

"You can see everything from up here."

"You can see the west side, all right. You can see the lights all the way out at TCU stadium when they're having a night game, and you can hear the airplane engines out at Carswell and Convair. And on that hill out in front you can see the Will Rogers Coliseum. On Sunday nights you can hear Negroes singing at their little church down in the valley. It always smells good up here. It always smells clean, and there's a breeze. But the big thing is if you sit here long enough and sort of, well, clear the rubbish out of your mind and just be alone with yourself and not be thinking about what's coming up or worrying about what's past, then pretty soon you get to feeling like an Indian must have felt up on this hill a long time before any of these lights or houses were here. You start feeling like you *belong* here, like you're really part of this. Like the woods down there are you, and that big sky is you. And you start feeling like the forest is all around, and the forest is full of bears and panthers and deer and you're naked and one of them. You know?"

He laughed. "If you really have a good night," he said, "you go back past man, and you can hear a dinosaur thrashing around in the trees and hear some huge bird scream."

"That sounds frightening," she said.

"Yeah. But not really. It's peaceful, really. I've tried to go back past that, but I've never made it. I get impatient. But I like it up here. Tonight, with you, is the first time I've been up here since I moved over to Dallas. I've been back here to see Harry a lot, but somehow I never took the time to walk across the street."

"It's strange how different Fort Worth and Dallas are," she said.

"It's historical, I think. Fort Worth started out as an Army post and a stopoff on a cattle trail. There was a good Indian fight down on that river. But the Indian forts moved out farther west as the frontier pushed on, and the railroad came, and the cattlemen started driving their cattle here to be shipped or slaughtered. Dallas had no reason for being at all. No genuine reason to exist. Maybe that's what's wrong with the place. No foundation. Dallas didn't have a Spanish mission heritage like San Antonio and wasn't a seaport like Houston. So Dallas developed strictly on a mercantile basis. Banking and finance and selling. A place to get money and to store money and to buy things. A place where you've got to hustle and run fast and stay ahead so the whole thing won't collapse. That's why Dallas has this frantic compulsion to get bigger and build taller buildings and show off, so you won't ever look down and ask what you're doing there. Dallas doesn't have any patience with people who want to stop and examine the values to see if they're real. In Dallas those uncomfortable people are losers, and there's no sympathy for losers. That's why Dallas is so terrified and hysterically conservative in its politics, because it's built purely on materialism and is greedy and is ashamed to be asked about it. It's a city of salesmen—well dressed, well fed, swallowing everthing, selling everthing, clothes, electronics, services, money, insurance, food, housing, selling to each other and to everbody else. A salesman has to be at least a little phony or he won't be successful, and in Dallas to be successful is the only reason to exist. But a phony doesn't want anybody around pointing out that he's phony. It's a place to cooperate and conform. If you're not like that, it'll try to break you. Fort Worth is like a tired old leathery-faced rancher who's set in his ways and doesn't much care. Dallas is like a post-debutante, painted up and wearing mink and diamonds and wondering what you can do for her."

"Why haven't you left Dallas?" Pippa asked.

"Now, that's an interesting point. I have . . . *had* . . . a very promising job with a very respected law firm, and I . . . thought . . . *felt* like . . . Dallas needed me. Until today. I thought that when I used to have vanity."

"You and Jean must have sat out here," she said.

"A few times. Never during a party, though. We usually fought at parties. We left torn and bleeding fragments of each other at an awful lot of parties. Especially those last few months."

"Tell me about your father."

"Seton must have told you. Or you read it in the papers."

"I know the general story," she said, "but I want to know your side."

Ben got up and stood on the terrace ledge. Below, a drop of six feet, was another grass terrace before the woods tumbled off down the hill. The shadow of the raised iron grill of the barbecue pit looked like a jail window on the lime grass of the lower terrace. At the left was a tool shed that had been made into an apartment; at its bedroom window, clinging like a carbuncle, an old water-cooled fan whirred and dripped, and the puddle beneath the window had caught a gem of moonlight.

"My side?" Ben said. "My side now is the legal side, I guess. Did you ever meet my father?"

"No," she said. "I saw him a few times at church before I was converted. Before I became a Catholic, I mean. But Seton talked about him a lot. Seton used to wonder why our father couldn't be like yours. Of course our father couldn't be home much. Doctors never can be."

"You would have seen him at church whenever you went," said Ben. "He was a deacon, or whatever you call it. One of those guys who carry the little trays of crackers and glasses of grape juice. He enjoyed doing that. But he was never a hellfire Christian. He was what I thought a real Christian ought to be—gentle, kind, understanding, tolerant, loving. Persuaded he was right in what he believed, but not beating you over the head with it. There never was a finer gentleman, a more noble man. No, there never was. You can imagine how a little kid like me looked up to him."

Ben paused. "You sure you want to hear this?" he said.

"Yes. Are you sure you can tell it?"

"I never tried before. I couldn't for a long time, I know."

"Here," she said, and lit him a cigarette.

"My father's family made a lot of money out of cotton," Ben said. "He went to school at Yale, and then to the University of Texas for his law degree. He got a Doctor of Laws, and he had a master's degree in philosophy, and he spent years writing a thesis in economics. But he never finished it. I don't guess he ever will now. His family lost most of its money in some bad speculations while he was in school, but he didn't care about that. He married my mother, who was nutty with her poets' groups and marathon talkers. He must have seen something in her that I never could see. Maybe I came along too late to see whatever it was good she had. He started off in corporate law, and he was the best. You could tell as soon as you saw him that he was the best. He was tall and had a long nose and a hard jaw and soft white hair and wonderful eyes. His eyes had little crinkles at the corners from smiling. I can remember that from twenty-five years ago, when he was in his early thirties. He wore string ties, and on him they looked good. A little Southern aristocratic, maybe, but good and right.

"My mother was about half butch or something. For a man like him, she was like having a crazy sister locked up in the attic. But he was kind and gentle to her and let her bring her idiot friends over and let her run off to Europe with 'em for as much as a year at a time. He let her have seminars and teas at the house. I remember one night when I was in high school she got mad at him because he wouldn't let some of her pals smoke hashish in the house. One of 'em had brought it from Morocco. But he gave her money to put out a little literary magazine so she and her friends could edit it and write essays about each other. They were always analyzing him and making fun of him and laughing behind his back. It used to make me mad. If she wasn't my mother I'd have knocked the hell out of her. I hit one of her friends one afternoon for something I heard him say about my father. Knocked him off the porch into the rose bushes. My mother tried to get my car taken away from me for that, but I think my father understood what it was about and nothing ever happened. When I was younger and saw that going on, I couldn't do anything except cry. As a kid I was a great one for crying. I'd see a poor little dog or something, or a kid without a daddy, and I'd cry. I remember when I was real little, not more than five or six, I saw the milkman whipping his horse and I ran out crying and started kicking him in the shins, and the milkman slapped me, and my father came out of the house and got that guy up against the side of the milk wagon and beat the crap out of him. Must have broken three or four crates of milk bottles, and I kept crying and kicking the milkman on the shins, and my mother woke up and started screaming for the police. But my father, he didn't need my crying. He stood way up above all those people. I loved him so much that I could just look at him and start crying. You ever feel that way about a man?"

"No," she said.

"Finally," he said, "I got to thinking that it was good for my father to have a wife like he had because it left him free to use his emotional energy on himself. He didn't have to use any of it on her. She wouldn't have it. How I got born is what I can't understand. I can't imagine them ever in bed together. They never slept in the same room that I can remember. But if he ran around with other women, I didn't know it. A man's got to have some outlet for that sort of thing, but he was so discreet about it that even my mother didn't accuse him of having other women, and she accused him of plenty.

"He did some great things. He started a charity hospital for crippled children and raised all the money himself and organized the board and got it running. He set up several scholarships. He started a school lunch fund for poor kids and saw to it they got the dole without being embarrassed. He was always getting parks built, or working to help the migrant laborers. Stuff like that. He never had any big hits in oil, but his insurance company did damned well and had offices in five cities. He got to where he was too busy to practice law, and he let his partners take over most of that. Then when his trial was coming up, they wouldn't defend him. That almost killed him right there, both personally and in the eyes of the court and the public. So of course he decided to defend himself. He had been the best there was at that kind of complicated corporate law. And I helped him."

Ben shook his head. The ruined dairy barn creaked as its timbers shifted. Ben looked down at Pippa, who sat on the rock ledge, her long black hair hanging down her back.

"I never went into anything with such zeal," he said. "All my life I'd done nothing but work to get his approval. He hadn't had too much time for me, but whenever he'd look my way I made sure he liked what he saw and I'd go into a song and dance to impress him. I wanted to be him. I felt like he wanted me to be him. I went at preparing the briefs for that law case like it was the Crusades. I had a holy purpose. For those guys to claim he'd swindled 'em on that industrial development was a crime in itself. I was so fired up and tear-blinded and fighting so hard that the trial was half over before I realized they were right. He was a thief."

Ben sat down. He flipped away his cigarette and watched the burning tip arch onto the grass of the lower terrace where it died.

"We never had a chance," he said. "When it was over he had lost everthing he owned except his homestead, and he was lucky not to go to jail. There had been an oil venture that I hadn't known about that had taken half a million dollars, and he was into a salt water conversion process that failed for almost a million. But he had enough left for the court to make restitution and pay damages.

Almost enough to handle it all. I sold the stocks and bonds he had put away for me and paid that money to take care of the rest. I should have kept some of it for my own kids, but then Jean and I didn't know we were about to split and she agreed with me about selling the stocks and bonds.

"I don't know how a man as intelligent as he was could have been stupid enough to think he could get away with that swindle. The morality of it is hard enough to understand, but the stupidity of it is impossible. He'd gotten away with it, though, for a couple of years. I won't bore you with explaining how. But you know what he did after the verdict? He came and looked at me with those wonderful eyes and told me he was innocent. I knew better, but I almost believed him. If he'd just admitted he was guilty, I think I could have taken it and I know I could have forgiven him. But he still says he's innocent, and he turns those eyes on me, and I want to run for the womb and yell God take me back.

"I went off and got drunk for a while. Then Jean and I started having trouble. We'd been shaky, but we got shakier, and I got in bad shape. I got to where I'd lie awake at night and be scared, and yell out. In the morning I couldn't decide which side of my teeth to brush first. Should I start right or left, up or down? I couldn't decide which sleeve to put on first, or which pants leg. Those decisions would paralyze me. I'd be driving to work along the route I'd taken for years, and suddenly I'd be lost. I wouldn't recognize anything. I'd look at a familiar word I'd always spelled automatically, and I would think it was spelled wrong and wouldn't be sure what it meant. I said things I didn't listen to and thought it was somebody else talking. I kept thinking I was having heart attacks. Jean and I were both drinking a lot and going to parties. It was the season for parties. And then we were finished.

"After a time I pulled myself together, somewhat, and started fighting Guthrie. You might have heard about that from Seton or seen it in the papers. I got mean, wanted to hurt people because they're human like I am. I didn't have to fight Guthrie. My office didn't want to. But I wanted to, for a lot of reasons, because I can't stand power grabbing son of a bitches like him, because I think he's basically wrong and corrupt and destructive and I wanted to be right for once. The president of the company Guthrie is trying to . . . is taking . . . over is a nice old guy and I didn't want Guthrie to kill him. My motives are all mixed, all tangled.

Maybe I went after Guthrie so hard because I was feeling mean and he looked too strong and invulnerable. Anyhow, he crushed me. He swatted me like a fly. Life's absurd, isn't it? It's either absurd, or it's rotten. I go from one idea to the other."

"Where's your father?" she said.

"He's here. He lives on his ranch west of town. He has plenty of money to get by on until he dies. I think he still plays golf, except the men he used to play with at Colonial or River Crest or Shady Oaks won't speak to him any more, and he plays in Weatherford. Mother stays in Austin most of the time with her literary pals. They couldn't ever forgive him being a wealthy businessman, and now they can't forgive him being a thief." Ben laughed. "The literary magazine," he said, "is defunct."

"Your father is alone out there?"

"He has people around him. There's some tenants on the place, and some hired hands, and he still gets invited out occasionally. He's talking about starting a law practice in Weatherford. He wasn't disbarred. I plan to go see him a couple of times a year."

"If you're not afraid to love him," she said, "you'll forgive him."

"He hasn't asked me to forgive him. He's innocent."

"He can't ask you."

"Don't start analyzing it to me. You don't even know him. Damn it, that's what Jean used to do. Analyze everthing. Only, she was a chaotic personality herself, and a person in chaos can't straighten out anybody else."

Pippa looked at her watch. "It's nearly four," she said. "They'll be wondering what happened to us."

"So am I," said Ben. "I brought you over here to hug and kiss, and instead I started hollering at the moon."

He reached for her, and she put out her hands and stopped him. "Not now," she said. "Let's go back."

There were ten of them left, and they sat in the living room and looked at the wreckage. They were in a sort of daze, their lungs aching with smoke, their minds weary but unwilling to give up the possibility that perhaps if they kept drinking and smoking and awake something else would happen.

"I'd estimate fifty cigarettes stomped out on the floor, but only a couple of bad burns," Jason said. "Pretty good. Two broken ash trays that I've seen, at least six broken glasses, one broken chair leg. Chink did that after he got dressed and tried to show us how he used to be a hurdler."

"Dressed? He had on Harry's jockey strap," said Doris.

"One broken record," Jason said. "Another record ruined when that girl mashed the phonograph arm down on it. Who brought that girl? Don't they have automatic changing phonographs where she comes from? Four or five throwups but no stains."

"One stain," said Doris. "On the guest room bedspread."

"A guy threw up in the bathtub and his wife made him clean it," Harry said.

"Probably two or three divorces," said Jason.

"Are you counting your own?" Willy said.

"Aw, honey."

"You still haven't told me where you disappeared to for an hour," she said.

"Four separations," said Jason. "No fist fights."

"Boring party," Cadmus said. "I figured we'd have a wild one for ole Ben."

"Where is Ben?" said Doris.

"Out yonder," Cadmus said, waving his arm. "Out there in the darkness. He's all right. He got a girl with him." He looked at Willy. "Whyn't you call Jean and tell her that? Tell her ole Ben got a girl with him."

"I wouldn't tell her," said Willy.

"You told her a bunch of other stuff, honey pot," Cadmus said.

"Anybody want breakfast?" said Doris.

"Don't Doris look beautiful in that black underwear?" Cadmus said.

"I wish you'd quit saying this is black underwear. These are leotards," said Doris.

"It sure looks beautiful," Cadmus said.

"I want some eggs," said Sheridan. He stood up and looked angrily down at Jason. Sheridan's glasses were set at a slant; the last time he put them on one of the earpieces hadn't quite connected with the ear.

"Let's go out and eat," Walter Anderson said. "Get off my lap, baby, you're hurting my leg."

Chub moved over and sat in Jason's lap. He didn't look at Willy, and he was careful where he placed his hands.

"Let's have another drink," said Harry.

"We gotta do as the host says," Cadmus said. "Besides, the party ain't over yet. I got a surprise coming."

"At four A.M.?" said Doris.

"Four A.M. is early for a party. I wanted my surprise to wait until we got rid of the quitters and didn't have nobody left but the stayers. Quitters don't deserve nothing good."

"I wonder what Ben's doing to my sister?" Seton said.

"Talking her ear off, most likely," said Cadmus. "I always knew ole Ben would make a good lawyer because he's a good talker. Knew it when he was a little feller."

"You didn't know Ben when he was little," said Seton.

"Come on and get a drank of milk, Seton, and eat a few dozen aigs," Cadmus said. "You got to eat to keep your stomach full."

Cadmus, Harry, and Seton followed Doris into the kitchen. The Little Princess still lay in the doorway with her head against what had once been a sack of ice but had melted so that her hair was in a pool of water and mushy brown paper. Her dress had somehow got pulled up to her waist, probably by her own movements. She lay with one knee up and the other leg stretched out.

"Where's her date?" said Harry. "Anybody know who she came with?"

"I remember the guy," Cadmus said. "I thank I saw him carried out about two."

"Wake her up, Doris, and find out who she is," said Harry. "I'll call a cab."

Cadmus dipped ice into two glasses and began shaking bottles to find one still operable. He looked down at the Little Princess.

"Goddamn," he said. "I sure hate to see youth and innocence laid out that way. Is they any virtue left? Sure is, friends." He clapped himself on the heart. "Right here in this noble breast."

When they woke the girl she began crying. Doris took her upstairs and washed her face and combed her hair and found her purse. Harry phoned for a cab. Cadmus went back into the living room with his drink. Seton returned with a glass of milk and sat on the arm of the couch where Blossom slept. The front door opened. Ben and Pippa came in. Grinning, Ben walked straight to the chair where Cadmus had sprawled. Cadmus rubbed his crooked upper front teeth with a forefinger and looked up at Ben.

"You've got to be behind this," Ben said. "It couldn't be anybody else."

"What's that, son?" said Cadmus.

"You know what I mean," Ben said. "The bus. There's a bus parked out front with a sign on it that says Ole Ben's Happy Time Minstrels. It has to be yours."

It took Cadmus five minutes to explain to them why it was a good idea that they should all go to Nuevo Laredo, Mexico, in the Frontier Oil Company bus for the Cinco de Mayo fiesta and to see a bullfight. The drive would be a little more than eight hours; if they left within the hour they could be across the border by early afternoon. They could then depart from Mexico after the bullfight Sunday and be back in Fort Worth in time for work on Monday morning. The bus had two couches that made into double beds—Cadmus explained, leaning forward and waving his hands and sloshing scotch on his clothes—and a kitchen and a shower and a record player and a television set and a dependable driver, and a bar, and Cadmus has already wired for reservations to his goddamn good amigo at the Gran Hotel Reforma right slap there on Avenida Guerrero, and beside it was ole Ben's *birthday*, not just no ordinary day, and they ought to show ole Ben a great time, and they owed it to their own selfs as well. While Cadmus talked, Jason glanced at Willy and read the expression on her face and then began to explore the corners of the room with his inner struggle. Harry and Doris were ready at once. Chub wanted to go, Walter was doubtful, Sheridan sat and looked through his slanted glasses and wondered if he was losing his vision. Cadmus wasn't sure if he had intended to invite Sheridan, but he figured that his own heart was big enough to include everbody. Ben was whispering urgently to Pippa, who nodded and smiled, and Seton sat back sniffing as if he could smell the Mexican streets that undoubtedly had assassins lurking in alleys.

"We got toothbrushes and pajamas, for them that needs 'em, and stuff like that on the bus," Cadmus said.

"I'm going home," said Willy.

"I think I better go to Mexico," Jason said unhappily.

"You have a family," said Willy.

"They'll be here when I get back," Jason said.

"Don't be too damned sure," said Willy. "Give me the car keys."

"Willy," Jason said.

"Jason," said Willy.

Jason looked at all of them. He suffered. He wrestled with his personal devil—now the devil on top, now Jason with a headlock, now the devil in a propeller spin, now Jason with a full nelson, now the devil with a body slam, while Willy and the little girls in their white Easter dresses sat on the front row and looked at the two wrestlers on the mat under the white light—and sweat broke out on Jason's face as he held the keys in his right hand, torturing himself with ideas of a frolic on the border as opposed to the simple sweetness of sitting on his flagstone patio with his daughters and his steadfast wife.

"Give me the car keys," Willy said.

"Oh," said Jason, in pain.

"The keys," Willy said.

"Good night everbody," said Jason suddenly and walked out the door.

Willy allowed a quick, quiet smile of triumph to crack her thin face. She told them good night with more grace and affection than she had shown the rest of the evening, and gave Ben a happy birthday kiss on the forehead, brushing aside the hair that had flopped there, and she left.

"A upset," Cadmus said.

"I don't know about this," Walter was saying.

"It will give you a good excuse not to see Brother Chunk over the weekend," said Chub. "You don't *want* to see him, do you, hon? Course not. We can get somebody to call and tell him we had to go out of town and we're sorry we won't be in church Sunday."

"What do you think, Bill?" Walter Anderson said.

"Sounds like fun to me," said Sheridan, trying to look slyly at Chub and seeing, instead, a black rim of his glasses. His high rolled collar was mangled, as if it had been crushed in a fist, and his left shoe was scuffed from having got under someone's much larger foot. Fifteen minutes of tedious combing had not quite repaired the damage to his coiffure done by rapping his head against the bed slats; little tufts stuck out here and there like tiny horns, and some had looped into curls.

"Please, Seton, I'd love to go to Mexico again," Pippa said, grasping her brother's right hand in both of hers.

"This isn't Mexico," said Seton. "It's only just across the border. It stinks there. It's crowded. It's full of Mexicans. God knows what kind of diseases they'll try to give us. God knows what their food will do to my stomach. Their milk is impure."

"We'll stop and buy you three of four gallons of milk," Cadmus said.

"Please, Seton," she said.

"You go," said Seton.

"I couldn't go without you," she said.

"Observing proprieties, are we?" said Seton. "Was it proper that you stayed outside with Ben half the night?"

"Crap, Seton, come off of it," Ben said.

"Oh crap, Seton, come off of it," repeated Seton. "This is my sister, Ben. This isn't one of your hot pillow girls. This is my *little* sister. I know, I know, I know. I've known you for years and years, and you've done me certain favors, and we're old friends. That's why I don't know."

"I'm going," Pippa said.

"Without me?" said Seton. Pippa didn't answer. "I'll go then. But I don't like it. Bullfight, God! They stick them with swords or something, don't they? They bleed. We'll probably be jammed in with thousands of Mexicans, breathing all over us. We'll probably get typhoid. We'll all die of typhoid because we let Cadmus drag us to Mexico. I'll get hot peppers in my stomach and start hemorrhaging and be hundreds of miles from medical attention."

"Where you think we're going, the Matto Grassy jungle?" Cadmus said. "They got doctors in Mexico. Their milk ain't too bad. Their food is great if you knock the flies off of it."

"Flies! God!" said Seton.

"Seton wants to go. I can tell," Cadmus said. "He just don't like to agree to anything without a fuss. He thanks it's a sign of weakness not to get offended all the time."

"It looks like we're going, too," said Walter Anderson, still dubious. "Chub wants to run home and stick some things in a suitcase."

"So do I," Pippa said.

"Thirty minutes," said Cadmus. "Everbody be back in thirty minutes."

With a show of unwillingness, Seton let Pippa take him along. Chub, Walter, and Sheridan went to their car. Doris started a pot of coffee and went upstairs to pack for herself, Harry, and Ben. Blossom raised her silver head from the couch. "Whuz?" she said.

"We going to Mexico," said Cadmus.

"Damn good," she said, and her head dropped again.

"Ben, ole son," Cadmus said after the room had got quiet, "this is gonna be the best birthday you ever had. Everthang's on me down in Mexico 'cept whores and maybe them too if you ain't greedy. Man gets to be thirty, he gotta have a big splash. Thirty is a dividing point. Cuts manhood off from boyhood. Thirty's about halfway. When you gotta stop and take stock and see what you done and where you going at. That's how come so many people have such big changes in they lives at thirty, whether they know it or not."

"How'd you get the bus?" said Ben.

"Sort of took it," Cadmus said.

"Your dad know?"

"He'll know soon enough."

"This has already been a considerable party," said Ben. He kicked a cushion over in front of the fireplace and sat down. He wrapped his arms around his knees and noticed that his bare feet were dirty. Cadmus drained his drink, poked a finger around in the ice, and shut his dark-smudged eyes for a moment, thinking.

"Everbody at this party," Cadmus said, opening his eyes, "was right about at the edge of cracking up. You see that? It's like somebody blew a whistle and told 'em all to shift partners. Kind of like they all looked inside theyselfs just for a second, long as they could take it, and then got frantic as all hell never to look in there again. Because they didn't *see* nothing. I tell you they's trouble all around like black smoke and way out there you can hear the Angel's wings beating and the path upward is enlaid with diabolical traps and if a man don't watch it his heart can get heavy as a brass cat."

"Want some coffee?" said Ben.

"Might be a good change of pace," Cadmus said, getting up to that height that was always a bit of a shock after he had been sitting for a while, and glancing down at the sleeping Blossom.

They walked toward the kitchen, through the living room that now seemed so utterly quiet after the cascading explosions of noise and activity of the past nine hours. Blossom's gentle snoring was the only sound in the room except for their footsteps. The red bulb on the record player glowed, and Cadmus bent to snap off the knob. One of the partitioned bay windows had been opened; a sweet breeze stirred a cellophane cigarette package wrapping in an ash tray on the window ledge. Outside an elm shone blackly, and a leaf skittered a few inches on the broken sidewalk before it hung against a crack in the concrete. There was a patch of yellow-apple light on the pavement of the street. Behind its high brick wall the nunnery was silent, and elms and oak branches guarded its roof and windows. Beyond the nunnery through gaps in the trees and notches in the hill were the prickling lights of the city. Over it all now had begun the first faint wash of intruding day; still dark purplish and barely creeping. The heavy oak flooring of the living room—the old and irreplaceable oak that was no longer put into houses—was scuffed and marked by dancing shoes; there were even the black gashes of rubber heels. Cadmus sighed and picked up the trampled banner that said *BEN IS THIRTY*. He folded the banner and laid it across a chair. It would be a good thing to take on the bus.

In the kitchen, Ben had poured two cups of coffee and had sat down at the white table by the big window. The window faced east. The sky there was pink above the rooftops, growing into blue and then into purple and then into black. They could see stars, but the back yard had started to take the curious violet light of dawn; the shadows were long from the hedge beside the rear fence, and from the rock fish pond and the bronze sculpture and the iron furniture. Ben looked at the tree he had lain under, and at the bench where he had sat with Pippa. That seemed years ago, somehow, separated from the present by a bleary veil—far back and unreal, and yet left him with an uneasy eagerness that was almost like a feeling of discovery, a sense of finding the unexpected and of not being certain whether it was good or bad, only that it was new and for that reason, perhaps for that reason alone, appealing. This girl had come to him. He had known her always but had never seen her, and then she had come to him, as if she had intended for years to come to him and tell him something he had wanted to know without realizing it, to unlock some hidden part of him that he had never known how, or ever quite dared, explore. He was in no way sure how he felt about her except that she was unsettling to think of, and that he *was* thinking of her at this instant and not of Jean, which he regretted and knew he should regret and which made him sad. He had been thinking so steadily of Jean and with such vividness that he had felt that if he turned he would see her in the room, had been thinking of Jean when he first went out to the iron bench with the girl, Pippa, and then for a while later had hardly thought of Jean at all.

Cadmus lowered himself into the same chair he had sat in during the Nekkid Bridge game. In the early light his face looked puffy. His blond hair was in disarray from the pulling off and pulling on of his undershirt; strands of hair that he usually brushed back dangled over his left ear.

"It's like some disease took hold of everbody," Cadmus said, sipping coffee. "They awful anxious. Like everthang's been done wrong and there ain't no way they can straighten it out. But you're the one I'm worried about, son."

"Why me?" said Ben.

"You didn't use to be really in all this," Cadmus said. "You used to get drunkern fourteen Frenchmen on Bastille Day and fight with ole Jean sometimes and vomit on your shoes and hustle women. You used to do that as good as anybody. But you was always a way back off from all this crap even when you was at your lowest. Like you was down there wallering but you was still sitting back looking and you knew you could step right out. You used to have you some dignity, ole son. Right now you ain't got enough dignity to be a men's room attendant in a queer night club."

"They cut my nuts out, Cadmus."

"Lotta crap. You had some tough speriences. Who the hell ain't? That was bad about your daddy. But you was putting too much on him anyhow. You're in a perfect position right now if you take advantage of it. You're standing on your own two feet. By your own self. Bad trouble can either break you or make you strong. It'll always do one or the other. It's up to you. There ain't no heaven gonna open up and send down no golden babies with wings on they backs to take care of you. All you got is the fact that you're here, and you got to make out of that whatever you can with whatever you got inside. You act like you can't understand why all this crap been done to you. That's because you all wrapped up in it. Take a good look at your own self and see what you got inside before you go whooping and yelling and crying about what's outside. Learn to get along with your own self. Man, this coffee is black, ain't it?"

"Want some cream?"

"Naw. Let me tell you what you're here for. On this earth. You're here to have joy. And joy ain't all this flap-doodle. Joy is really being alive. Now look at ole Walter. You thank he knows what being alive is? Nothing ever shook him into it. Jason got a little inkling but he don't go about it right. Chub ain't found out, but she'd like to know. Harry, he's got an idea. That Pippa, she's got an idea.

You can see it in her face. She lights up. She's interstid. I know you got an idea. Cut loose on it, son. I can't splain how. They never taught me that much at Harvard. But when you find it you'll know. Thang is, you got to look."

"Are you an example of joy?" said Ben.

"I hate to put mahself up as an example of anything, but I'm better off than you are."

Harry came in, clapping his hands and grinning. His face was bright with after-shave lotion, and his hair was wet. He had put on khakis and a white tee-shirt and white tennis sneakers.

"This is great," Harry said. "This is great. Goddamn it, this is great."

"Where's Doris?" said Cadmus.

"In the shower."

"I said we got a shower on the bus."

"She doesn't trust you," Harry said. "I don't trust you. I just love you, that's all. You've got that big shiny bus out there, and we're going to Mexico, and I love you."

"I been trying to cheer up ole Ben."

Harry brought the chrome-plated coffeepot and refilled their cups. He poured one for himself.

"Ben got double-crossed again today. Yesterday. Did he tell you?" said Harry. "On the Guthrie deal."

"He didn't have to tell me. It's bleeding out of his heart. Hell, so what? What'd he expect? Way ole Guthrie probably looks at it there wasn't no double cross. Just hard business. I don't know nothing about it, but I know right now Ben couldn't wash Guthrie's feet. Guthrie's got a aim, and Ben's been fighting him out of spite."

"That's not true," Ben said.

"How come then? Just cause it was your job?"

"It's more than that."

"Good," Cadmus said. He grinned. "Then go get him. Don't set around and blubber to a girl and try to make her feel sorry for you. I saw you mooning around at that Pippa, and I'm betting you didn't screw her, so you must of told her the whole sad story of how cruel the world is to Ben Carpenter."

"I ought to hit you right in your crooked goddamn teeth," said Ben.

"Go ahead on. But it ain't me you ought to hit. It's Guthrie, if he means so much."

"He's beaten me, damn it," Ben said. "If you'd ever learned anything about business instead of playing all your life you'd understand that."

"I ain't learned about business," said Cadmus. "But I know you're never beaten unless you give up. You're trying to give up. The size of your guilt makes this room crowded. Take it easy on yourself about that, and get to be a man again. Go find Guthrie and pull his ears. Hell, do *something*."

"Cadmus makes everthing pretty basic," Harry said.

"Everthang is basic," said Cadmus. "Everthang is basic if you can understand it. My brother Waldo used to tell me that."

"I didn't know you had a brother," Harry said.

"I got two brothers. Waldo, and good for nothing Oscar Lawrence. Waldo used to say life came down to two thangs. One of 'em is 'Some thangs is playing and some thangs is serious and you shouldn't confuse 'em.' And the other is, 'You can go anywhere and do anythang and say anythang and that's all.' My good-for-nothing brother Oscar Lawrence took both them thangs all wrong. Oscar Lawrence is thirty-one years old and he's been married seven times. He's married to a Turkish belly dancer right now out in Los Angeles. He sure is a trial to my mamma and daddy."

They packed quickly, first at Seton's apartment and then at their father's house, where Pippa lived. Seton wrote his father a note and left it on the breakfast table. He was nervous until Pippa came out with her bag. He felt like a stranger in that house. He watched his sister come quietly down the long hall, coming on tiptoes past the room where their father, twice a widower within twenty years, slept alone. Looking at his sister moved Seton to a kind of pride he never felt for anything else. She was the only person, the only thing, he had ever referred to as being beautiful. The faults in her construction were faults he did not see. Where someone else might have seen only brown eyes, Seton saw eyes that were as deeply brown and opaque as Apache tears, the desert stones. Her long glinting hair, crow-black, to him was majestic. Her walk, to him, was of indescribable grace. He was disturbed by her recent paleness, but he thought it set off her eyes and hair more dramatically. Seton had scarcely even tolerated Pippa's mother, and had never known his own.

Seton took her bag and tossed it into the back seat of his car.

Driving past the quiet corners where newspaper boys waited for their bundles, Seton kept looking at his sister.

"You're not falling for Ben Carpenter, are you?" he said, finally, mashing in the cigarette lighter on the dashboard.

"I really just met him," she said.

"Don't be carried away by this childhood dream you used to have," said Seton.

"I'm not. That was a long time ago."

"I wish you wouldn't fall for him. Do you know why his wife left him?"

"He said they weren't getting along."

"He wasn't a very nice person," Seton said. "He wasn't very nice at all. Jean put up with him a lot longer than I would have. But I shouldn't say that. He did something for me this spring. Did he tell you?"

"No."

"I got into trouble. I got into some trouble at a place downtown. Well, you can guess what kind of trouble. It was very messy. It was while you were working in Austin. No, it was while you were sick. I didn't want to bother you with it. But Ben heard about it from one of his law school friends who's in the District Attorney's office, and he came over and took care of it for me. I don't know what he did exactly. He just took care of it. It would have been bad. I would have lost my job. But Ben took care of it, and he wouldn't let me pay him."

"That was very kind of him."

"No it wasn't. Not at all. When I tried to go see him afterward he wouldn't talk to me. He looked at me with, well, with cold disgust. I'll never forget that look. He didn't have to do that. What does he think he is?"

"He might have been involved with some problems of his own," said Pippa.

"Oh yes, but he didn't have to look at me that way. I don't think I owe him anything. That look canceled it out. I don't want you to fall for him."

"I haven't fallen for him."

"Catholics can't fool around with divorced people, can they?"

"Seton . . ."

"I see how you could fall for him. He's attractive. He has that appearance of good breeding that his father has."

"Seton, I wish you'd mind your own business just this once," she said.

"Don't be rough with me, dear."

"I'm not. I'm sorry I said that."

The lighter had popped out and gone untended. Seton pushed it in again.

"I want you to look out, is all," said Seton. "I want you to look out what sort of feelings you get mixed up with him. He's not very stable right now."

"I'll be careful."

Seton turned the corner onto Sunset Ridge. They saw the bus parked at the curb, and people around it.

"That's all I can ask," Seton said.

While Walter Anderson carried the bags to the car, William Sheridan caught Chub Anderson in the hall. He put a small hand on one of her breasts and with his fingers stroked the bunched brassiere cloth until he could feel the nipple getting hard. He kissed her on the ear.

"Baby," he said, "I've gotta have you quick."

"Quit," she said, without moving away.

"I'm good to you," he whispered. "Have you ever had anybody like me before?"

He was getting very male then, and he pressed against her.

"Don't," she said. "Don't."

She began to rub herself against him.

"Touch me," he said.

"I can feel it."

"Have you ever had anybody like me before?"

"We can't be doing this here," she said, putting her arms around his waist and squeezing him against her.

"Have you ever?" he whispered.

"No. Nobody."

"Is it good?"

"Walter will be coming back."

"Is it good?"

"Yes. Yes."

"I've gotta have you quick."

"Yes, yes, me too," she said.

They heard the trunk lid bang shut. Sheridan stepped back.

Chub's eyes were out of focus as she looked at him, and she was trying very hard to get herself under control.

"Better go," Walter Anderson said from the door. "Brother Chunk's liable to show up with a delegation and want me to make a speech."

"Don't worry about Brother Chunk," said Sheridan.

"Not much," Walter said. "All he can do is knock me out of the legislature."

"We'll take care of you. We need you in the legislature."

"You don't know Brother Chunk."

"I know his type. We'll handle him. There's not anybody who can't be handled if you know how."

"He'll wonder where I am this weekend," said Walter.

"Forget him. Relax and enjoy the trip," Sheridan said. "We'll handle Chunk when we get back."

Chub brushed between them and walked toward the car. She had changed into toreador pants, and both men watched her buttocks as she walked.

The bus driver was a fat Negro named Damon. His neck overflowed his white collar as he shoved the bags into the undercompartment. He straightened slowly, as though his spine might crack from the weight of his belly. He had polished the brass buttons on his black uniform, and the leather bill of his black cap gleamed like his shoes and his black plastic bow tie.

"Shoo boy, Mist Wilkins," he said. "We gotta nuff stuff for two whole months it peers."

"Get all the whiskey on board?" said Cadmus.

"Yessuh. Case scotch, case bourbon, five cases beer, lotta ice, soda, Cokes, cigarettes. Got records for the record player, TV's workin again. Got cards an soap an towels an toofbrushes an some extra razors an peejamas. Got fried chicken an cole cuts. An ahm plumb wore out."

"Toilet paper and Kleenex?"

"Yessuh," Damon said, hurt that Cadmus would think he needed to ask.

"Let's roll," said Cadmus.

Cadmus got into the bus and hunched over as he walked toward the rear. He bent past the card tables, each of which had four armchairs, and then past the shower and toilet, and into the back of the bus where the couches were being occupied. Blossom slept on one of them. Seton fiddled with the television set, although it was too early for programs. Pippa and Ben tried to start the phonograph. Harry popped open two cans of beer. The others sat around grinning and waiting. Cadmus refused to think what would happen when his father returned from Los Angeles and found out Cadmus had bluffed the business manager of Frontier Oil Company into letting him have the bus; that would be a scene that made even Cadmus hesitate to anticipate it. As he doubled over to take a seat beside Doris, Cadmus looked out one of the blue-tinted windows and saw a car swerve around the corner. Cadmus laughed.

"Wait a minute, Damon," Cadmus yelled.

The car sped past the nunnery and grew larger until it was about to crash into the bus. Then the car stopped, the door flew open, and Jason got out running with a bag in his hand. They heard the air whish as Damon opened the bus door. Jason came down the aisle. He was sweating and he hadn't got his shirt tucked in, but his eyes flicked happily around the interior of the bus. He put one hand on his stomach and panted.

"Afraid I'd miss you," Jason said.

"Couldn't stand it, hah?" said Cadmus.

"Scum came to the top," Jason said. He leaned against the bar and heaved for breath. "Poor old Willy wanted to come at the last minute but we couldn't get a baby sitter. Besides, if she came I wouldn't have as good a time. I better have a good time because I ain't gonna have a good time Monday when I get back."

Cadmus took one of the beers from Harry.

"Here we go, Damon!" Cadmus yelled.

Up front, Damon put his shoe on the accelerator, and the elms began to move past the windows.

"Driving off into obscurity," said Harry.

"Naw, son," Cadmus said, raising his beer can. "This here is the Good Ship Lollipop."

Part Six

CINCO DE MAYO

It was the softest of spring mornings, a day as calm and new as a sleeping child. With Damon driving and nipping from a Thermos of gin, the bus went south out of Fort Worth along an expressway. Dreary thickets of suburban houses rolled past, and the final hazy sight of downtown buildings was wiped away. In the rear of the bus, the passengers dozed. Damon glanced back at them, shook his Thermos, and smiled at the sloshing sound. He bit off the tip of a cigar and spat out the window. Then he squirmed until his heavy body had crackled into, and around, the leather seat. He propped the Thermos against the wall, grabbed the wheel, pushed on the accelerator pedal until the speedometer needle rose to eighty, and stared at the road and hummed as he drove.

As the light broke along the highway, swatches of bluebonnets looked purple against the green of the fields. Smaller patches of pimento and yellow Indian blankets wove in with another flower as delicately pink as lingerie. The bus came across dozens of hidden meadows, each as green and clipped as a golf course, with low hills climbing slowly beyond against a fine clear sky. There were hundreds of ponds, very still, some newly dug with red dirt around their lips, others quiet beneath shading umbrellas of trees. Oaks and pecans grew along the road, where gashes of red clay mixed with the black earth. Young green corn stood in the fields. The bus passed a wood that had long ago burned—the trees gray and dead as cemetery monuments—and then rocketed around a farmer who was creeping down the highway in an old pickup truck. A cow looked over the slats in the back of the truck and watched the bus roar past.

Occasionally Damon saw oil wells pumping: black arms steadily and rhythmically reaching into the earth. In the middle of a field he saw another well being drilled, the derrick tall and black with a red light on top, the bit below screwing downward. He clucked as he looked at the old white farmhouse in a meadow. Behind the house, in a pasture, were two oil wells. Beside the old wooden house stood a new brick house with an Oldsmobile in the driveway. Three cows chewed on the grass of the front yard. Blocks of hay were stacked in the barn.

And always there were the signs on the highway:

HONOR ALL

and

THE KINGDOM OF GOD IS AT HAND

and

EL RENO MOTEL 87 MILES

and

BURMA SHAVE

and

IF YOU DRIVE, DON'T DRINK

Damon chuckled and sucked on his cigar and sipped from his Thermos.

The new highway avoided most of the towns. Where once the highway had gone through Main Streets, and watching the traffic had been a civic amusement, and it had taken some agility not to get run over by the big cars speeding through, the towns were now nothing but placards on the highway and cut-offs that seemed to lead to nowhere. The little towns had been abandoned in the rush and were left for dead. The highway stretched on, a hard bright path flowing south. Lulled by the road, Damon began to get sleepy. The speedometer needle fell to fifty. Damon would shake his head, raise the needle again to eighty, and let it drift back down toward fifty. It was three and a half hours before Damon realized Cadmus was standing at his shoulder telling him something.

"Austin," he heard Cadmus say. "You know it, that big motel on the right. We wanta get some breakfast."

Damon swung the bus onto the access road and parked it at the curb in front of the Villa Capri coffee shop. The motel sprawled across three blocks of cliff dwellings and surrounded two swimming pools. Bellhops rode in electric carts among the maze of courtyards and narrow drives. People coming out of the coffee shop stopped and stared at the bus as Ben, Cadmus, Harry, and Sheridan got off. The banners that said *OLE BEN'S HAPPY TIME MINSTRELS* were still secure on either side. The four men stood for a moment at the corner and looked down the street that dropped toward the university. At the bottom of the hill were the football and baseball stadiums and a stream that trickled over rocks or lay in clear pools beneath the trees. The red tile roofs of the campus held the early sunlight. The great dun sword of the university tower rose above the buildings; by its clock the time was nearly eight-thirty. To the left, above the trees and rooftops, squatted the dome of the State Capitol, looking like the spiked helmet of Kaiser Wilhelm. The morning was flushed with light and hung with silence, as though a dry lethargic heat would soon descend.

The four men entered the coffee shop, leaving the other passengers asleep on the bus. Sheridan telephoned a cab, explaining that he would pack a bag and return. The eyes in his caramel face were red and his hair curled down over his shirt collar, but he marched out of the coffee shop with determination.

"I hope he doesn't come back," Harry said.

"Don't be uncharitable," said Cadmus. "Hate will destroy you."

"Cadmus is going to give everbody a psychic enema today," Ben said.

The three of them took a table by the large front window that looked out at the bus. When the waitress came Cadmus ordered scrambled eggs, a breakfast steak, fried potatoes, coffee, and four glasses of milk. He insisted Ben and Harry order the same. Harry, leaning forward, hair brushed onto his forehead, hoarse from the eighty cigarettes of the past twenty-four hours, protested but surrendered. Ben scratched the bristle on his chin and shrugged.

"Gotta lay a base for that border food and tequila," said Cadmus. "Eat ever bite of this healthful vitamin-enriched, sanitary-packaged American food. It'll keep you going, and then I got these here little green pills to keep you up after that."

Ben looked out at the sunlight streaking from the chrome of the bus, and he grinned.

"This town got a lot of memories for you guys, don't it?" Cadmus said. "I like this town. I was always sorry I didn't go to school down here."

"You went everwhere else," said Harry.

"Naw. Only to SMU, Oklahoma, Texas Tech, Colorado, and TCU," Cadmus said. "I could of made a few more if I'd wanted to get a degree. But why would I need a degree?"

"Austin is a good town," said Harry.

"I'd live here if it wasn't for all my vast holdings being out in West Texas," Cadmus said. "I got associations here. My brother Waldo used to hang out over at the Scholz Beer Garden. Waldo skinned many an elbow on them wooden tables under the trees out back. I like it best over by the lake up in them mountains. People call 'em hills, but a West Texas boy oughta know a mountain when he sees one. You get up in them mountains and it's like being in Southern California. Without ever leaving the borders of this here state you can be in New Mexico desert or Mexico mountains or Maryland countryside or Louisiana swamps or Georgia pine forests or Kansas prairies. I guess that's how come I like it here so much, because it's big enough for me. That West Texas out there that they make the movies about the tumbleweeds and sagebrush and miles of nothing, nobody ever goes there. Except me. I drill holes right through that useless dirt."

"How's your discovery well coming along?" said Ben.

"Couldn't be better," Cadmus said. "Why, I got prospects of being richer'n Waddy Morris or Clint Murchison or H. L. Hunt or Bob Smith or any of them bobos. The Cadburn Oil Company is a force to be reckoned with, son."

"You going to swallow up Waddy Morris?" said Harry.

"He's a mouthful," Cadmus said. "He's one of the big five in the state. He'll run up into the hundreds of millions. The corporations he controls will run into the billions. Waddy Junior, hisself, probably worth sixty million or so. Junior knows how to spend it, too, bless him. He ain't a tightwad like a lot of 'em. Except his clothes look like he bought 'em at the Good Will Industries and they never fit. He'll come to a party wearing what looks like a fifty-dollar suit and an eight-dollar pair of shoes and a two-ninety-eight sport shirt, and you know he don't give a damn what you think about it. Of course I don't know Waddy Junior very well. We speak, is about all. He's smart, I'll tell you that. He'll be at one of them big society parties, and everbody in the room knows he could gobble most of 'em before breakfast and he might elect to do it."

Cadmus raised a glass of milk in each hand and drank both glasses before he began to saw his steak. He soaked the eggs, steak, and fried potatoes in catsup and doused them with salt and pepper.

"Those big guys, they got a hell of an organization," said Cadmus. "They know everthang that happens before it happens, and there ain't much they don't have a fanger in. Woodrow Morris might of built this road we been driving on, and own this motel, and make this ketchup, and sell us our gas, and the animal this steak come off of might of ate grass at one of the Morris ranches. But you'd never realize any of it, it's so complicated."

Cadmus stirred his fork in the catsup until he found a blob of egg, and he stuck it into his mouth and drank milk. He glanced at Ben, who was eating slowly and looking out the window.

"I hear Waddy Junior been running around some with your pal Guthrie. You hear that?" Cadmus said.

"They got together on the Ramco proxy fight," said Ben.

"Oh, that was what you were moping about," Cadmus said. "Yeah, that's a tough combination. It's plenty of reason for you to tuck your tail and run. Now don't look mean at me, son. This here is your birthday party, and I won't say nothing else."

"You're right," Ben said. "It's a tough combination. I don't guess I could have expected my client . . . ex-client . . . to do anything except what he did."

Cadmus smothered a belch behind his napkin.

"Wish we had time," said Cadmus. "I'd go show you Waldo's house. He still owns it. It's one of them old gingerbread houses with the cake icing all over it and the funny-looking little kew . . . kew . . . what's that word?"

"Cupolas?" Harry said.

"I guess. It looks like a house where you expect to see a guy with a handlebar mustache come down the driveway on a bicycle with a big front wheel. Waldo ain't lived here for quite a while. Did I ever tell you about him?" Cadmus lit a cigarette. "Well, he was my smart brother. He's nearly seven years older than me, which would make him going on forty. He went to school down here for years and years and studied everthang they got to study. There wasn't nothing he didn't know about, but mostly he knew about philosophy. I thank it was awful painful for him to come home Christmas and set around the table and talk to the old man and mother and good-for-nothing Oscar Lawrence and me. But Waldo never did let on. He'd talk to us like we could understand what he was saying. The old man would give him suspicious looks, and Mother would smile and nod and not hear a word, and Oscar Lawrence would say yeah man yeah man I dig when there was reason to believe he really didn't dig nothing. Later on Waldo thought he might of helped to be the ruin of Oscar Lawrence. Oscar Lawrence listened to just enough that he could use it to do whatever he wanted to do and then he went down and bought a new Cadillac and took off with a lady high-wire walker. But I kind of admire Oscar Lawrence even if he is awful and does abuse people something fierce.

"Waldo disappeared. He was gone for several years and we didn't hear from him except a postcard ever now and then from places all over South America and he sent a ex-wife of mine a shrunken head for her birthday. One day he turned up again, at his house in Austin. He called up his friends, had a big party for 'em at Scholz's, and then he went to bed in his bedroom on the second floor of that gingerbread house. People would come to see him, thanking he was sick. But he wasn't sick. He just wouldn't got out of bed. They got to thanking he was despondent. But he was happy as a bluebird. He laid there for three years. We got him a housekeeper. He wouldn't hardly read a book or nothing. He said he was like the angels. He just laid there. I thank he was laying there getting stupid on purpose. He'd say things like 'It's not this and it's not that,' and then he'd laugh till he cried. My, how he used to whistle and sang. Songs that didn't have any real words. Just dum diddle dum. My mother sent a preacher up to talk to him and Waldo told him there ain't no flies on Jesus. Finally my old man decided Waldo was crazy. He shipped Waldo off to a place my old man got in the mountains around Red River, New Mexico. All Waldo does now is chase goats."

"Here comes Sheridan," said Harry.

"No use being unhappy about it," Cadmus said. "Man's got to bear his thorns in this here life. The lucky man is the one that gets to choose his own thorns."

The bus rolled through the hill country. Between Austin and San Marcos they passed the giant caveman that stood beside the road inviting customers to visit Wonder Cave, and they went along the San Marcos River and passed the yellow Van Gogh fields and the long low bluffs outside San Antonio. Damon thought he felt the engine missing, and he stopped at a service station to check the plugs. In a tavern adjoining the service station, Cadmus found a sign which he brought Harry and Ben to see. The sign said:

No Credit, Please
Bad Pay——Kill Him

They passed San Antonio and Natalia and Devine, where the green had begun to fade from the land and cactus appeared along the road. The earth flattened out. There was a big sky. They went through Hondo and Yancey, where a sign pointed off toward Big Foot. Along the road were shoulder-high scrub oaks and mesquite and cactus. In the town of Pearsall, in front of the Chamber of Commerce office, was a huge statue of a peanut and a sign saying Pearsall had the biggest peanut in the world.

A two-lane concrete bridge carried them over the Frio River, a thin sluggish water path that wandered through a dirt field in a funnel of trees. A deserted wooden bridge was off to the left. Beyond the Frio the fields were deep dark red and brown, very flat, with windmills and farmhouses and red ponds. A railroad track ran beside the highway for a while. Telephone poles rose above the mesquite. They came to a sign that said SEE THE WORLD'S BIGGEST WATERMELON IN DILLEY. A few palm trees had begun to grow along the road, and there were Mexican adobe and stucco houses in pastel colors. In the town of Dilley red trucks parked on the street, and a farmer in overalls and a straw hat sat in front of the red brick Dilley Hotel. By then the bus passengers were awake; they watched for the World's Biggest Watermelon but failed to see it.

While Ben and Seton were playing gin rummy at one of the two card tables in the front of the bus, Pippa went back to turn over the records on the phonograph. Sheridan was sitting on a couch in the rear talking to Chub, who blinked and yawned, and to Blossom, who looked dazedly at him as if he were trying to teach her Latin. When Sheridan saw Pippa stop at the phonograph, he excused himself and went to her. Bracing himself against the wall as Damon rocked the bus around a tank truck, Sheridan leaned his face close to Pippa's. She looked around at him and then turned again to the phonograph.

"I'm glad you came," he said. "I've been wanting to talk to you."

"Really?" she said. "I must have been out when you called. I've only been at home day and night for two solid months."

"You know what I mean."

"I know exactly what you mean, Bill. I never saw anybody clearer in my life."

"Aw," Sheridan said. "Come on, Pippa. What's been done has been done. You can't stay mad at me forever."

"I'm not mad at you," said Pippa. "I'm beyond that. But I want you to stay away from me, Bill. I want you to leave me alone. I'm going to forget that you ever existed, or that I ever knew you. Now please step back."

"Listen, Pippa," he said.

"No," she said. "I won't listen."

She pushed past him and went down the swaying corridor toward the card tables. Sheridan looked at her. He pulled up his shirt collar and fluffed it. He sat down on the couch between Chub and Blossom."

"What did you say to her?" said Chub.

"Just small talk," Sheridan said.

The abandoned railroad station of Gardendale sat among mesquite across from a pile of slab rock in a gravel shoulder of the road. A long silver gas tank, like a torpedo, lay in a field protected by a cyclone fence. Coming into Cotulla was a sign FREE COLD ARTESIAN WATER. The sky was clean and pigeon blue with no clouds to mute the sun. It was going to be a very hot day.

They pulled into Laredo, on the Texas side, and Cadmus went up front to direct Damon. The bus squeezed through the cluttered traffic of the narrow streets, where people overflowed the sidewalks and fell into the gutters. Near the white stucco building of the Cactus Inn hotel, with its wide veranda hung with rattling vines, they turned left with the heavier flow of cars, pedestrians, and bicycles. Damon managed to steer the bus onto the International Bridge above the muddy Rio Grande without hitting anything. Damon kept blasting with his horn. The air-conditioning hummed inside the bus, but outside the sun was white against the straw hats and bare brown arms. Dogs lay panting in scant shade.

There was a dispute over what toll fee should be charged the bus entering Mexico. Clearly, it was neither a commercial vehicle nor a private automobile. Cadmus got out and discussed the matter with an officer under the shed at the customs office while the officer studied Cadmus's height and smoked a cigarette as if he found the whole business terribly boring. Cadmus returned, laughing and cursing, and squatted beside Damon to guide the bus to the Gran Hotel Reforma in Nuevo Laredo. It was Saturday afternoon of the fiesta of Cinco de Mayo, and cars were piled up for blocks as the drivers honked and shouted at each other. Even the people on bicycles were having a hard time getting through. Men rushed out from the money changers' shops to hammer on the sides of the bus. Peddlers weaved through the traffic with stacks of sombreros, buckskin jackets, purses, whips.

Avenida Guerrero was white, baking, stinking. A legless old woman sat on a corner selling postcards. An Indian woman with a shawl over her head came to the door of the bus, crying and holding up her baby toward Cadmus, begging for money. Cadmus frowned and opened the door and tossed her a dollar, which she protected by angry kicks at the children who swarmed around her. Dozens of ragged little boys roamed the sidewalks with wooden shoeshine boxes. Young girls paraded arm in arm, plump and big-hipped and short, with short skirts. They came under the scrutiny of the young boys, who were lean and sharp-faced with long black hair and with their shirttails out. There were many farmers in town for the fiesta, their hard brown faces still sober under their wide hats, their overalls or khakis newly washed. Heat came up like steam from the cracked sidewalks.

In the difficult few blocks to the Gran Hotel Reforma the passengers of the bus drank beer in the purr of air-conditioning and looked through the blue-tinted windows at the shops: *zapaterías, farmicias,* souvenirs. Many of the open front shops had straw hats and leather sandals hanging on the walls. Inside small openings in the stucco walls, sweating men in undershirts fried tortillas. A butcher-shop window displayed *cabrito,* skinned and split open with gelatinous guts showing, ribs prominent, hanging by upraised front feet in rows of gaunt bodies.

Cadmus pointed toward the *cabrito.* "Looks like roll call at Dachau," he said.

"I'm getting sick," said Seton Parry.

The bus passed two plazas on the left. The bases of the palm trees had been painted white, and tents and stalls were set up beneath them. People posed for pictures on burros. Balloons floated in bright bubble clusters. Black clouds of birds moved in the trees.

Police in khaki uniforms pushed through the crowds. Women peddled tortillas and baskets of strawberries.

"This here is romantic Mexico," Cadmus said.

After twenty minutes the bus wedged to a stop in front of the Gran Hotel Reforma, an old building at a corner of a plaza. Cadmus opened the door and bounded out into the heat and began shouting for bellhops to come and divest the bus of its luggage. Motorists screamed and honked as they tried to get around the bus. Cadmus stood on the sidewalk and yelled back at them and gestured with his fist. The passengers hurried off the bus and into the dark lobby of the hotel. They clacked across the tile floor to the registration desk and looked out at Cadmus through the broad, open door. Cadmus gave five dollars to a hunchback who agreed to guide the bus to a place of storage. The hunchback got onto the bus grinning. Damon sat with his Thermos in his fat hand. Cadmus yelled at the motorists who edged past in the wake of the bus, and they yelled and threatened him. Cadmus was yelling: "Hooray for Harvard!" and making it sound vile. After an obscene motion with his right arm, Cadmus whirled and marched into the lobby where the passengers were waiting.

"Everbody gets two hours off to rest up or take a bath or whatever, and then we meet in the dining room for a banquet and then go out and see thangs," Cadmus said. He looked at the bellhops and pointed to the luggage. "Hola, hombres, pronto sumbitches, get them bags upstairs!"

Ben had a room by himself on the third floor. A barefoot maid was mopping the hall as Ben got off the elevator with the bellhop, a thin Mexican boy in a white shirt with the sleeves rolled up.

—good afternoon, Ben said to the maid as the bellhop was opening the door to Ben's room.

—good afternoon, sir, the maid said. She was an Indian woman with a dark face and black eyes that shone like lacquer.

—you speak spanish? the boy said, putting Ben's bag on the bed.

—a little, Ben said.

—not many tourists do, the boy said.

The bellhop cranked open the windows. Ben's room looked down on an alley and a small courtyard which was shared by two mud-colored brick houses. Children in the courtyard played beneath laundry that hung on a line. Opening onto the courtyard was the toilet for both houses. The toilet had no door, and there was no seat on the commode. Above the roofs of the houses were other buildings, masses of dirty concrete and exposed brick, and through a tangle of rooftops and hanging laundry Ben saw another courtyard. They heard church bells tolling the hour.

—it is better not to have a room on the plaza, the boy said. —everybody will be drunk down there for two days.

—I will be among them, Ben said.

Ben sat on the double bed. It was lumpy and the springs creaked, but the linens looked clean. Other than the bed, the room had a bureau with a mirror, two chairs, and a lamp. Ben got up and walked into the bathroom. The pink tiles were stained, but there were towels on the rack and a bar of soap in the dish. Ben cranked open the bathroom window inside the shower stall and looked down at the small courtyard. One of the little girls who had been playing in the courtyard was now using the commode. Ben turned back and walked into the bedroom where the boy was waiting.

"There is no shower curtain," Ben said in English.

"It must have been stolen. People steal from hotels."

"Have the woman bring me a shower curtain. You bring me six bottles of Dos Xeches in a bucket of ice. What's the price of this room?"

"Forty pesos," the boy said. "Is it too much?"

"It's enough," said Ben.

"The rooms on the plaza are seventy pesos. I myself would not pay that to listen to drunk people holler all night. You have the best room."

"Forty pesos is all right if I can have a shower curtain and a radio and those Dos Xeches."

Ben gave the boy a dollar.

"Si, señor," the boy said, and left.

Ben was hanging his clothes in the closet when the Indian woman entered with his shower curtain. She smiled shyly.

—one needs a shower curtain, Ben said.

—if one does not wish to wet the floor, the woman said and laughed.

She went into the bathroom. The boy brought the beer and the radio, and Ben paid him. Harry came in. Harry had been drinking steadily for the last two hours of the bus ride, and his face looked as if he were blushing. He wore white canvas sneakers, khaki pants without a belt, and a white tee-shirt. Ben opened two of the dark bottles of beer. Harry looked into the bathroom and saw the woman.

"You speak English?" Harry asked.

The woman shook her head.

"Does she speak English?" asked Harry.

"I guess not," Ben said, handing a bottle of beer to Harry.

Harry drank from the bottle and smiled. "I remember the last time we drank this stuff," he said. "At the bar at the Fronton Mexico. That big long bar downstairs from the room where they fling that ball around. Remember that? The day we won all the money betting on the *jai alai.*"

"Eight hundred pesos," said Ben.

"Seemed like a lot. Terrible disappointment to find out it was only about sixty dollars."

"We put it to use," Ben said.

"We should have gone back. We knew the system. Bet on the guys who are behind."

"It's a good system."

"Simple, too. A good system has got to be simple. But not so simple that you can't understand it." Harry went to the window and looked out. "Those people don't have any door on their toilet."

"I noticed that."

"There's not a lid on that thing, either."

"Sure isn't."

"What do they do?"

"The best they can."

"Must be very uncomfortable."

"They're probably used to it."

"My room looks out on the plaza," Harry said. "They shot off some skyrockets a few minutes ago."

Harry turned around and sat on the window ledge.

"I like that *jai alai,*" said Harry. "You think they really break their wrists all the time like they say they do?"

"I don't know."

"They throw that ball awful hard."

"Yeah."

"Sometimes I think they throw it too hard for their own good."

"Could be."

"Man wasn't meant to wear a basket on his wrist."

"Comes in handy, though."

"It does if you're a *jai-alai* player," Harry said. "That seems like ten years ago when we went to the Fronton Mexico. When was it? Two years ago? No, last summer. The four of us. Then we went to Acapulco and you caught the sailfish that danced on its tail and the bait boy was drunk and nearly cut his thumb off stripping a mackerel and Jean made everbody else look silly on water skis."

"She was good at that."

"Lot's happened since last summer," said Harry.

"Quite a bit."

"I've got a confession to make to you," Harry said. "I never mentioned it before because there was so damn much going on, and I figured you had enough to worry about, and I knew you'd heard it a thousand times anyhow. Jean came to see Doris and me one night a couple of months ago. She started telling us what a bad deal you had become. She said you couldn't talk to her any more, and you weren't home very much, and she thought you were running around on her, and you were isolating yourself from her. She said you were in a bad temper and were acting funny, and to her that meant another girl. It made me mad. I told her if it was so bad she ought to get a divorce. She said that's what I'd wanted all along. She was really mad when she left. Pretty soon, she filed. I felt bad about it."

"Don't worry about it. Your advice isn't what made her file. She was determined to do it. She was convinced it was a hopeless situation."

"I didn't want her to file," Harry said. "I just wanted her to quit complaining. I thought she might go home and help out or something. Jean's got a lot of love to give somebody. At least, that's what she told me. She said she had more love to give than you could ever take."

"Who'd refuse love?" said Ben.

"I don't know. I don't think you or Jean either one knew what was happening to you."

"I loved her."

"I guess so. I know you needed her. Let's don't talk about it. It makes me sad. Open two more beers."

Ben opened the beers, passed one to Harry, and sat in one of the wooden chairs.

"I sold three paintings last month," Harry said. "People came to the house."

"That's great."

Harry grinned. "Yeah, it's good. That makes eight this year. Doris wants me to quit my job. But I don't think I should yet. I don't mind doing commercial art work. I'm good at it, and I do an honest job. I don't feel like I'm a sell-out. Do you think I'm a sell-out?"

"Not as long as you keep painting the way you want to paint."

"I'll keep doing that. But what I mean is doing the commercial art work doesn't make me tense. It doesn't hang me up. Having the money coming in relaxes me. I don't like to be broke and live dirty. I've tried that, and I never got anything done that way because I was depressed a lot. I don't kid myself. I'm not Michelangelo. But I try hard and do as well as I can. That's all I can do."

The Indian woman came out of the bathroom.

—the shower curtain has been put up, she said.

—thank you, Ben said.

Ben gave her a dollar and she bowed and smiled and thanked him.

"Tell her I love her," Harry said.

The maid looked at Ben.

—the gentleman is drinking, the woman said.

"What'd she say?" said Harry.

"She says you're the handsome prince she's always dreamed would come down from the North and carry her away," Ben said.

"She say all that in those short little words?"

—the gentleman wants to know if you would go to texas and live with him, Ben said.

—i would have to take my husband and four children, the maid said. She laughed and looked at Harry.

"She wants you to murder her husband," Ben said. "He beats her and he always has a knife in his belt."

"I don't go for that. I'm scared of husbands."

"He's a little guy."

"Nobody with a knife is a little guy."

"You could creep up on him in the dark."

"Mexicans can see in the dark. They're like pumas."

"You don't know anything about pumas."

"I know enough not to creep up on one," said Harry.

—the gentleman says he will give your husband very much money and send him to brazil, Ben said.

The maid giggled.

"I heard you say something about money and Brazil," said Harry. "I never said anything about money and Brazil."

—tell the gentleman I wish he could meet my daughter who is beautiful, the maid said.

—daughter? Ben said.

—my oldest daughter is twenty-three.

—you're making a joke.

—i am nearly forty, señor.

"She's sixty-eight," Ben said to Harry. "These Indian women hold their ages."

"Tell her I love old women. I got this thing for my mother."

—the gentleman says regardless of the difference in your ages he loves you madly. the gentleman has the brains of a ten year old, but the heart of a giant. i can attest, Ben said.

"Tell her there's no life hereafter," said Harry.

"What?" Ben said.

"Go on. Tell her."

"I'm not going to tell her that."

"I'll get Doris then. Doris can tell her. Doris studied Spanish at Tulsa."

The maid looked at Ben and smiled.

—the gentleman says he wants you to run off with him at once, Ben said.

—the gentleman has impulses, the woman said.

"Did you tell her?" said Harry.

"No," said Ben.

"Go on and tell her. Tell her there's no final compensation for the miserable life she's living. What do you think she'd do if she knew that?" said Harry.

"She'd start off by cutting your throat."

"Oh," said Harry. He looked at the maid, whose black eyes glittered at him above her yellow smile. "Better not tell her, then."

"This woman is an Indian, not a Catholic. She probably doesn't go for the hereafter very big anyhow. The Indians are still Aztecs down deep. They believe in some kind of rejuvenation of nature where when they die they become part of the earth and the sky and all that. They believe something of that sort. I'm not sure what. I think most Mexicans are still Aztecs down deep," said Ben.

—i don't understand you, the woman said.

—the gentleman is a catholic. he is waiting for his wife to die, Ben said.

—ah, that is the catholic way for husband and wife to part. i think it can be done more simply, the woman said.

—it certainly can, Ben said.

—in your country, is it easy for husband and wife to part?

—very easy. too easy, Ben said.

"I don't like all this talk," said Harry. "What're you getting me into?"

"She says she will go with you, after all."

"Tell her I changed my mind."

"She won't like that. It'll hurt her pride. The Indians are keen on revenge against people who hurt their pride."

"I wonder what Doris would think about me having an Indian mistress?" said Harry.

"She'll take care of Doris."

"I about halfway believe you," said Harry. "Discourage her. Tell her the mumps went down on me. Tell her I'm wanted for murder and I was lying about the money. I don't have a penny."

"Murder?" the woman said in English. Then in Spanish she said —i understand that word.

—the gentleman says his wife will murder him if he brings you home with him, Ben said.

—ah, but not as quickly as my husband would murder me. i must go back to my work, the woman said.

—thank you for the shower curtain, Ben said.

—for nothing. tell the gentleman he is pretty. i like his big red face and his yellow hair and his big adam's apple.

—if i tell him he will have great conceit, Ben said.

The maid laughed, looked at Harry, and padded out of the room.

"Did she take it okay?" said Harry.

"She offered her sympathy."

"She's a nice woman. I'm glad you didn't tell her about the hereafter."

"What made you think of that?"

"It seemed like something she ought to know. I want to get a public address truck and drive through every city and tell people." Harry rose from the window ledge, finished the second bottle of beer, and yawned. "This Two Exes is gonna put me to sleep. I think I'll run down to the Plaza and make some sketches."

"Maybe a few nudes of Blossom."

"Why not? That girl can't keep her clothes on any more than Doris would take hers off. But you know, I sort of like Blossom. Cadmus told me she is a very moral girl in her own way. With her, it's one man at a time. No more than one. She's faithful to whoever's paying the check."

"She's a hooker?" Ben asked.

"No, no, nothing like that. I mean she's faithful to whoever she's dating as long as he's showing her a good time and spending his money. She's not like Chub. Chub has the morals of a cocker spaniel. I think she'll lie down and roll over for anybody who'll scratch her ears and say nice doggy."

"Chub told me Walter is a beast."

"Yeah? Well, she ought to leave him then instead of making a fool out of him. That's not very nice."

"Is there somebody besides Jason?"

"There was a little incident at the party before you got there . . . But I don't know. I shouldn't say. I don't know anything about it." Harry looked at his watch. "I think I'll forget the sketches and take a nap. Cadmus will have us up all night at three or four wild joints. Say, I was going to ask. You getting sweet on Pippa?"

"I like her."

"I like her, too. There's something odd about her. But I like her. You could sure do a lot worse."

"I've done worse," Ben said. "I've done worse and worse and worse. But I'm taking my ride through hell for all that I've done, and I don't want to hurt Pippa with it. I've hurt enough people."

"No reason to think you'd hurt her. You don't have to hurt her."

"I hurt people. I've been thinking about what Cadmus said this morning, and I know I hurt Mr. Simmons when it could have been avoided. I shouldn't have done that. He's a good man, but they had him."

"People hurt themselves," said Harry. "Thing is, you react to it. You shouldn't let it get you so much. But I suppose if you didn't let it get you so much then you'd be somebody different. I don't think you realize how much everbody admires you and wants your approval."

"Like Jean, for example."

"Jean admires you."

"That's what she kept telling me over and over. Honey, I admire you. You drove your car through my geraniums. You missed supper eight nights in a row. You put your pants on backward and tried to shampoo your hair with toothpaste. You cry in your sleep. I sure do admire you and I'll miss you when you're gone."

"All right," Harry said.

"I'm going to call Simmons and apologize to him."

"You ought to. At least you always think of the decent thing, even if you don't always do it." Harry yawned. "I'd better get that nap. I want to be rested when the fighting starts."

"You expecting trouble?"

"We're carrying the seeds of it," said Harry.

While the bellhop was unzipping the luggage and coat bags and helping to hang up Beth Morris's dresses, Waddy Morris sat down in the living room of Suite 508–10 on the top floor of the Cactus Inn. Beth Morris got the dresses into the closet neatly in their plastic wrappers and then frowned at the smudge of dust on her fingers.

"Are you *sure* this is the best hotel in Laredo, for God's sake?" she said.

"Yes ma'am," said the bellhop. "It's as good as any. They's some nice new motels though."

"I don't want to stay at a motel."

"Yes ma'am."

"I like prompt room service."

"Yes ma'am."

"Is there a private club in the hotel?"

"A what?"

"A private club. Where we can get a drink."

"I'll fetch you up a bottle, ma'am."

"I don't want a bottle, damn it. I'd like to have a martini."

"That's kind of a mixed drink, ain't it?"

"Of course it is."

"They sell mixed drinks over across the river on the Mexican side. We can't sell 'em here. It's against the law."

"I know what the law is, for God's sake. That's why I asked about a private club."

"Yes ma'am."

"Bring us up a bottle of gin and a bottle of vermouth."

"A bottle of gin and a bottle of what?"

"Oh for God's sake."

Beth went into the living room, where Waddy sat at the desk talking into the telephone and twisting the cord of the Venetian blinds. "That's right, operator," Waddy said. He glanced at Beth. "Swell place."

"Can you explain to that man what vermouth is?" she said.

"Write it down for him," said Waddy. "I've got a call."

"You always have a call."

"This is Johnson," Waddy said. "I'd picked up the phone to call Sam's room and the operator said I had a call from Johnson."

"That won't get me a bottle of vermouth."

"Write it down. Can you spell it?"

"I don't know why you wanted to come on this trip for God's sake."

"So you could spend the weekend flirting with Guthrie."

"Are you kidding?"

"Do you think I'm kidding?"

"Certainly."

"I'm kidding," he said.

"Guthrie doesn't appeal to me."

"What a pretty face you have."

"Well, he doesn't."

"Remember that," Waddy said. Then into the telephone: "Hello? Yeah. Hello, Acey. What's up?"

The bellhop came out of the bedroom.

"Vermouth," Beth said. "Vermouth. Go to the liquor store and say vermouth. They'll know what you're talking about."

"Shut up," said Waddy. "Listen, Acey, tell me that again. I'm sure I didn't hear you right. There's a lot of noise in this room."

The bellhop went out. Beth Morris sat down on the yellow plastic cushions of the couch and looked at her husband. Waddy stared at the telephone as if it had stung him. He listened to Johnson with an expression of incredulity. He began to rub his chin as though trying to decide whether he needed a shave. Bars of slatted light bent across his face. Beth started looking for the thermostat to turn up the air-conditioning; the room seemed warm and dusty and in need of having clean air washed through it. She found the thermostat almost hidden by the rump of a bucking horse on the wallpaper above the light switch beside the hall door. She glanced at Waddy again. He was scowling into the phone and pinching his chin.

"You can't do that, Acey," he said. "You gave me your word . . . Yeah, I know what Simmons has done for you, but that's past. Simmons is finished and his company is finished if we don't take it over . . . I don't give a damn about a new contract. I know about that new contract. It won't save Ramco . . . Acey, look, I'm involved in this. I'm not doing this as any favor to Guthrie . . . All right, do you want to make money out of your Ramco stock or not? If you hang on with the old bunch and they win that proxy fight your stock won't go anywhere . . . Don't make it sound like a moral problem. If you think you owe Simmons something, then you ought to want to do what's the right thing for him. The right thing for him is a merger with Guthrie . . . I told you we'd take care of Simmons . . . So what if he doesn't believe me? You believe me, don't you, Acey? . . . Let him get mad at you for a few days. He'll see in the end that you're his friend . . . Goddamn, Acey, don't be an idiot. Simmons wouldn't do that . . . He'd never do that. . . ."

Beth Morris went into the bathroom and turned on the water in the tub. She looked at herself in the mirror for a while, turned her face so that she could examine it from different angles, opened her mouth and studied her teeth, smiled at herself, opened her mouth again and looked at her tongue and down her throat, dug a piece of tobacco from between her teeth with a fingernail, and made a silent expulsion of gas. She pulled at the flesh of her throat to reassure herself that it was not loose. She tore some Kleenex out of the holder on the wall and blew her nose. She looked down at the tub, which was still less than half full, and took off the coat of her gray linen suit. She unsnapped the skirt, took it off, walked into the bedroom in her slip, dropped the suit on the bed, lit another cigarette, and walked into the living room.

". . . I'll call Simmons myself, Acey," Waddy was saying. ". . . Sure, I see what a spot you're in. Sure, I appreciate it. But don't think for a minute that I'm going to let you take this proxy fight out of my hands . . . A threat? Take it however you want it, Acey. But I haven't started getting tough about it. I don't want to do that . . . Look, I'll call Simmons . . . Well, where *is* he? . . . Okay, I'll call him later this evening at home and then I'll call you back . . . Where will you be tonight? . . . Fine. I'll call you at the Cipango."

Waddy banged the phone down and cursed steadily for thirty

seconds. Then he picked up the phone and asked the hotel operator for Guthrie's room.

"Sam," he said, "come down here for a minute. I'm in 508. Sure it's important. Hurry up."

Waddy put down the phone and looked at Beth.

"Trouble, darling?" she said.

"An irritation," said Waddy.

Beth returned to the bathroom. The water was six inches below the rim of the tub. She turned off both handles. Beth pulled the straps of her slip off her shoulders, pulled down the slip, and kicked it aside. She removed her brassiere and girdle and hose and dropped them on the floor. Standing at the mirror she rubbed her face with cleansing cream, wiped it with tissues, and applied skin freshener lotion with a cotton pad. It was a process she enjoyed because she was never tired of looking at herself. From the living room came the sound of Guthrie's voice. Beth got into the tub and stood while the water burned her feet and ankles and calves. Then when it no longer burned she lowered herself slowly with hands on the sides of the tub and sat down. Gradually she straightened her legs and lay back in the water. Her shoulders touched the cool porcelain and she slid down until the water crept up to her chin. From the living room she could hear Guthrie's heavy voice yelling about something, and Waddy's higher voice talking above him. She smiled and shut her eyes. Out on the street it was hot and dirty, and in the living room there was some sort of angry discussion, but here, where she was, with only her head and knees rising from the envelope of warm water, there was reason to smile.

Waddy shut the door that led into the bedroom and turned to look at Guthrie. With Guthrie had come the bellhop with a bottle of gin, a bottle of Vermont Apple Cider, and a bucket of ice. Waddy tipped the bellhop a dollar and waited until the bellhop was gone before he looked again at Guthrie.

"Can we win this proxy fight without Johnson?" Waddy said.

"Without him?"

"That's what I said."

"Maybe. But why?"

"Tell me exactly what the chances are without Johnson."

"Good, I'd say. I've got a few tricks the Simmons bunch doesn't know about. I think I can win without Johnson, but ever last proxy would have to be counted. What's this all about?"

"Drink?"

"Not right now."

Guthrie rubbed his stomach and frowned and looked at Waddy. "Isn't Johnson with me any more?" Guthrie said.

"He's still with us whether he knows it or not," said Waddy. "But he's being irksome about it. Simmons came to see him this afternoon and made speeches about their long friendship and about how we were going to boot poor old Simmons in the ass regardless of what we promised and about how Ramco's new contract is going to save them and how we're going to get buried in anti-trust suits, and a bunch of other nonsense. He must have got Johnson to feeling sentimental. Johnson says he's not going to switch to us any more."

"How did Simmons find out about the switch?" said Guthrie.

"Johnson told him. I knew he'd do that. But I figured Simmons would fold up and agree to what we'd offered him. Simmons told Johnson he'd had a long talk with that young lawyer . . ."

"Carpenter?" Guthrie said loudly.

". . . I guess. And Simmons had decided we were a pile of liars and raiders and he could do a better job of running Ramco than we could and he didn't like the idea of a merger and he was going to fight us to the death. Or something like that. Simmons must have got pretty dramatic about it. Johnson even got the idea Simmons might kill himself if he loses. That's rubbish of course. But Johnson's got a lot of feeling for the old man."

"Carpenter!" yelled Guthrie. "He's behind this. He stung Simmons into this. That bastard. I'm going to smash him."

"Don't holler," Waddy said. "If anybody's going to holler around here, I'll holler. I don't know whether that lawyer talked Simmons into going to see Johnson, and neither do you. That doesn't make any difference."

"It makes a difference to me. I'm up to here with him."

"I asked you not to holler. Have a drink."

"I don't want a drink. I ought to get back to Dallas and go to work."

"What do you think you would do in Dallas on Saturday night? Go look up all the stockholders and sing lullabies? Don't show signs of panic, Sam. That's disturbing. I don't like that."

"It's not panic. I'm mad."

"Sit down," said Waddy.

Guthrie sat down on the yellow plastic cushions. He looked at the bottles on the coffee table as if he wanted to throw them through the window.

"Our deal's still on," Waddy said.

Guthrie looked up.

"There's no change," said Waddy. "I still want in, and I still don't like the idea of having to count proxies. The promises you made still hold."

"Those promises depended on you delivering Johnson."

Waddy looked at Guthrie's dark face for a moment, and then he laughed.

"You're in a terrible hurry, aren't you, Sam?" Waddy said. "I would suggest that you sit there quietly and reflect. We talked about a lot more than just this proxy fight. Now you think about it a little bit, and if you want to call off the whole deal, why we'll call it off and you can rush back to the wars and start butting heads with Simmons all you please. You can go into that stockholders meeting and torture yourself for days while they count proxies, if that's what you want to do. I can get along pretty well without having a goddamn thing to do with you, if that's what you want. Think about it."

"I lost my temper," said Guthrie.

Guthrie picked up the bottle of Vermont Apple Cider and poured out a glass of it. "The deal's still on," he said.

"All right, then it's still on as far as I'm concerned, too," Waddy said. "All of it. As for this first little matter, here's what I'm going to do. I'm going to call Simmons myself and try to talk him into giving up. I think that will work. If it doesn't, I'll have to get out a bludgeon and use it on Acey. I don't want to, but I won't hesitate to do it."

"What can you do to Johnson?" Guthrie said.

"Several things," said Waddy. He sat down at the desk and smiled as if pleased with himself and faintly surprised at the thoughts he was having. "Several things. It wouldn't be discreet for me to mention them unless it's necessary for them to be done. But I'll fix him if I have to, Sam. And for educational purposes I'll let you watch me."

Waddy stood up and walked over to the coffee table. He looked at the cider bottle in Guthrie's hand and then looked at the closed door to the bedroom and smiled as if hugely amused.

Ben let the shower run until the rust went out of the water and adjusted the velocity so that the pipes quit groaning. Then he soaped himself and stood under the spray for a long while looking down from the window at the children playing in front of the doorless toilet and at a woman in a shapeless cotton dress who was taking her wash off the line in the courtyard. It was a good shower with a spray of needles, and when he turned it off and stepped out he felt as if he had managed to get his circulation started once more. The hot and cold water at the basin came from different spigots. There was no plug for the drain. Ben turned on the hot water in a smoking trickle and jabbed his razor at it as he shaved. The razor burned him, but when he was through it was pleasant. He patted a few drops of the hot water on his face, splashed his face with the tepid water that was supposed to be cold, and spanked his face with after-shave lotion. He came out of the bathroom and walked naked across the linoleum floor and opened another beer. The floor had looked clean until his wet feet touched it, but the tracks he left were muddy. He lay on the lumpy bed smoking and drinking and looking up at the spinning blades of the ceiling fan that squeaked as if someone were feeding it mice. He heard the elevator door bang and footsteps in the hall, but the footsteps went past his door and it was quiet again. In the silence he began to think of Jean, and then to think of Pippa, and nothing was clear any more. He had barely snubbed out his cigarette before he was asleep.

The knocking woke him up. He pulled the sheet over himself and said, "Come in."

"Were you asleep?" said Pippa.

"No. It's too hot."

"I couldn't sleep, either."

"Any more beer in that bucket?"

"One," she said. "It feels hot."

"I'll split it with you," he said.

She snapped off the bottle cap and went toward the bathroom.

"We don't need a glass," he said. "Come sit by me on the bed."

"Mr. Carpenter, you are still technically a married man."

"All right, I'll come over there."

"Are you dressed?"

"Not a bit."

"I'd better come over there, then."

The springs creaked as she sat beside him on the bed. He drank from the bottle and accepted a cigarette she lit for him. The beer was warm and tasted malty. Pippa was wearing a cocktail dress. There were pearls of sweat on her bare shoulders. Her black hair had been parted on the right and swept down across her left eyebrow before it curved back up and was pinned by a comb. Another comb was above her right ear. The bright black hair flowed down her back. As she leaned forward to take the bottle from him, a locket on a gold chain swung out from her breast. Her wide deer-eyes seemed curious and a little afraid as she looked at him. He reached up with his right forefinger and touched the small bump on the bridge of her nose. She smiled, twisted her head, and kissed the finger.

"What will we do tonight?" she said.

"Get drunk."

"What else?"

"There's more?"

"Don't play games with me. You're not all that interested in drinking. What else will we do?"

"Go to a couple of joints. Watch the whores parade."

"I don't like that word," she said.

"Whores? Why not?"

"It sounds dirty. It's a bad word with a dirty sound to it."

"Whores are all right. You know where you stand with them."

She picked up an ash tray off the floor and put it on Ben's stomach, which was covered by the sheet. She brushed a few droppings of ashes off his chest. He looked past her at the white sky above the tile rooftops. When he looked at her again, her eyes were on him.

"Are you still in love with your wife?" she said.

"Of course not," he said.

"Tell me the truth."

"I can't," he said. "I wouldn't know the truth any more if it bit me on the ankle. Besides, how could I think whether I'm in love with her or not when you're sitting on my bed this close to me."

"It wasn't a fair question, was it?"

"It was a fair question but not fairly asked. Now you answer a question. Why are you scared of me?"

"I wouldn't be sitting here if I were scared of you," she said.

"You might."

"I might," she said.

He pulled her down beside him.

"Don't," she said. "My hair."

"Forget about your hair."

"I thought you were going to give me time to find out about you."

"I didn't promise anything."

She sat up.

"That may be the trouble with you," she said.

"Don't tell me riddles. Just lie down here."

"No."

"I'll promise anything you want."

"Would you?" she said, smiling.

"Blithely."

"And mean it?"

"To the best of my ability," he said.

"Promise me you'll forgive your father."

He frowned at her, and then started grinning.

"You say the most amazing things," he said.

"You promised."

"Okay. He's forgiven," he said, snapping his fingers, "just like that."

"You can't do it that easily."

"I know it. Lie down here."

"I'll get my dress wrinkled."

"Take it off."

She looked at him and then stood up. She unzipped the back of her white dress down to her hips, shrugged off the dress, and stepped out of it. She went to the closet and hung up the dress. Coming back, she stopped and took off her white high-heeled shoes. He looked at her standing with one hand against the blue plaster wall of the hotel room. She wore a strapless brassiere, a half-slip, and a panty girdle. She came back and sat on the bed.

"If I ever start thinking I can outguess you, please correct me," he said.

"You didn't think I'd do that."

"No," he said. "No, I certainly didn't."

He put his left hand on the back of her neck, his fingers in her hair, and brought her down on him and began to kiss her. With his right hand he reached up and pulled down on the brassiere, and then he felt her breasts come out of it. Her mouth opened, and her tongue began to probe. With thumb and forefinger he massaged her nipples.

"I've never felt quite like this," she whispered into his ear.

With his left hand under her buttocks he rolled her over on top of him and lay holding her there and kissing her. She moved against him. The locket dug into his chest.

"Take off the panty girdle," he said.

"No."

"I said take it off."

"I don't want to do that. Don't be angry. I just want to lie here."

He put his hand down and began to rub her.

"Please don't," she said.

"I can't quit now. You've got me into this shape."

"How do you think I feel?"

"Get up," he said. "Get up and get us another cigarette."

"You're angry."

"Yes, I'm angry."

He watched her go to her purse. The brassiere was around her waist. She came back.

"We've turned over the ash tray," she said.

As she bent and scraped the cigarette butts into her hand the locket dangled out. He began to massage her breasts again.

"You're persistent," she said, smiling. The right comb had come loose and her hair hung in her face.

"You absolutely won't?" he said.

"You don't love me."

"Has everbody you've been to bed with been in love with you?"

"No." The deer-eyes looked at him. "But I wanted to think they were."

"Do you love me?" he said.

"Perhaps I do."

"I could tell you I love you. How about that?"

"You should go back to your wife."

"That's funny," he said, as she lit the cigarette, handed it to him, and sat down.

"It's not very funny."

"What's the matter with you?"

"I wouldn't want anything to be wrong," she said.

"Suppose I propose to you?"

"I don't mean that. I don't want to have to explain everything that's involved in this. There's a lot involved in it that you don't understand. But I'll tell you something about me. I've never had an orgasm."

"I wouldn't have thought it," Ben said. "Usually you can tell the ones who can't make it. There's a look about them. But you don't look that way."

"Well, it's true," she said. "And it's too important to be wasted."

"Those things are never wasted."

"Yes they are. They usually are. It's even more important for me. Sometime maybe you'll understand how I am."

"How many guys have tried?" he said.

"Why?"

"How many?" he said.

She took the cigarette from him, inhaled, and blew a strand of smoke that was torn away by the ceiling fan.

"Five," she said. "One in high school, pretty often. One in college, my steady date. The man at Yale. The boy in Paris. A British colonel on the boat. I thought he would, but he didn't."

"Why'd you think he would?"

"He was so big."

"But he flunked, too?"

"He was the worst one of all," she said. "He was very proud of himself. He thought he was doing me a favor."

"And that's all of them?" he said.

She hesitated. "There was . . ." she said. "There was a boy in junior high when I was thirteen and had that mad desire for you. But that was such a clumsy affair that I don't count it."

"Did you tell all of these guys?"

"I told the man at Yale and the boy in Paris. I had pretended to have it with them. It made them happy to think so. But when the man at Yale found out the truth he was terribly embarrassed and we didn't last long after that. I don't think the boy in Paris cared much, but he stole my clock radio and the money. They were the only ones I told. The boy in high school and the boy in college wouldn't have known the difference. The colonel never considered the possibility that I wouldn't. I almost told him. Men resent that, don't they?"

"Some of them do. And now you've told me."

"I thought you should know it."

"Are you afraid of it?" he said.

"I think that's . . ." she said, with the deer-eyes on him. "I'm very confused about it."

"What were you going to say?"

"Nothing."

"Give me the cigarette," he said.

"The boy in Paris," she said, "did everything there is to do, I think. He worked very hard after I'd told him."

Ben mashed out the cigarette in the ash tray and put the ash tray on the floor. He kicked the sheet off of himself, put his arms around Pippa and drew her down beside him. Her flesh was warm and damp. She began crying as she kissed him. He got his fingers beneath the elastic of her panty girdle and started pushing it down. She helped him. She was crying harder now, and laughing, and kissing his chest.

"Look down there," Walter Anderson said. "Somebody's trying to climb one of those palm trees and a cop's got him by the leg. Come look."

"I don't want to see it," said Chub Anderson.

"The cop yanked him down. He fell right on his head."

"You shouldn't be standing at the window in your shorts."

"I'm covered."

"Walter, come over here and talk to me for a minute."

"I can hear you. I want to watch what they're doing. They're dragging the guy off."

"Do you think anybody could ever really care for me?"

"What do you mean?"

"I mean don't you think a person needs to feel wanted?"

"Why, sure, baby."

"Come over here and get in bed with me."

"Right now? In this heat? We'd get sweaty."

"You really don't care for me, do you, Walter?"

"Why, sure I do, baby. Hey, look. The guy got loose. He's running."

"I mean do you love me?"

"Sure. Sure I do. They got him again. Look at that. He should have known better."

"Why?" said Doris Danielsen.

"Why what?" Harry Danielsen said.

"Why do you think it's good that Ben seems to be fond of Pippa?"

"To get his mind off Jean."

"He doesn't want to get his mind off Jean."

"But he's going to have to."

"Maybe not. I think Ben and Jean love each other."

"That's not the point. The point is they've done too much to each other and they're going to have to move on. You can't go back and you can't stand still."

"Do that some more."

"That?"

"Yes. That feels good."

"You already owe me ten minutes of neck rubbing."

"I'll pay you tonight."

"That's what you told me Wednesday."

"Harry?"

"What?"

"I don't think it's a good idea. We don't know anything about Pippa."

"She's Seton's sister."

"But other than that."

"She's pretty."

"She does have beautiful hair."

"Good body, too."

"You would notice that."

"When I quit noticing things like that you'll know I'm sick."

"Jean has a good body."

"Ben always thought so. I never could get aroused looking at her."

"She says you never liked her."

"I liked her a lot of the time."

"She says you were jealous of her."

"We don't have to believe everthing she says, do we? I liked her most of the time. But I didn't like her a bit those last few months. When she saw Ben starting to crack, she kicked him. But he won't crack. He feels like ever bad thing anybody in the world has ever done is his fault, but he still won't crack. I think Jean will come back, but I hope when she does it's too late for her."

"That's a cruel thing to say."

"She's earned it."

"Did you tell Ben that?"

"No."

"Why not?"

"Because maybe he loves her."

"You know he loves her."

"I know he loves his kids. The rest might be remorse."

"Harry, let's have another baby."

While Pippa was in the bathroom, Ben placed a long-distance telephone call to a number he had come to know very well in the past few months. Ben had got dressed except for his shoes and he sat on the edge of the rumpled bed and smoked and listened to the confusion of the telephone operators and to the water running behind the bathroom door. The windows were copper in the late sun. Then he heard the operator ask the identifying question, and he heard the familiar voice.

"Mr. Simmons, this is Ben Carpenter," he said.

"Ben! Where are you?" said Simmons.

"In Mexico," Ben said. "It's my birthday party. I mean yesterday was my birthday. We came to Mexico."

"To Mexico?" said Simmons.

"It's kind of hard to explain. But the reason I called is I've been thinking about what I said to you and I shouldn't . . ."

"Don't bother to apologize," Simmons said.

"No, listen, I didn't have any right to talk to you that way. I know what kind of trap you were in and I shouldn't have blamed . . ."

"What you said was exactly correct," said Simmons.

"But I didn't need to say that. You'd done all you could. I wish you'd accept my apology so we can break as friends."

"I won't accept your apology," Simmons said.

"Then at least I want you to know that I do regret . . ."

"Ben, I won't accept your apology because no apology is necessary. After you left my office yesterday I was so damned mad that I wanted to jump in my car and find you and drum the hell out of you. I picked up that attaché case and those papers and walked around the office in a rage, and then I realized what it was that I was really mad at. What you said about me was the truth. So I went to see Johnson."

"You what?" said Ben.

Behind him the bathroom door opened and Pippa came out adjusting the combs in her hair.

"I went to see Johnson, and I put it to him as you had suggested, and I think I swung him back."

Pippa came over to the chair beside the bed and sat down and crossed her legs. Watching Ben, she picked up one of her white high-heeled shoes and began to put it on, arching her nylon foot and sliding a forefinger down the inside of the heel.

"Ben? Did you hear what I said? I think I swung him back."

"Yes. Yes, I heard," Ben said. "That's great."

"When can you be in Dallas?"

"Mr. Simmons, I remember that I said . . ."

"I don't suppose it would do any good for you to come back tonight," said Simmons.

"I couldn't do that," Ben said, looking at Pippa. "I think it's great that you went to see Johnson, but I remember telling you that I had quit."

"Surely you don't mean that."

"I don't know. I meant it when I said it."

"Ben, I meant it when I told you that I had given up to them. But you showed me I was wrong. This is still a frontier. We're crude and blunt and we make a lot of mistakes, but we need people who will keep trying to tell us what is right."

Ben looked at Pippa, who had put on her other shoe and was lighting a cigarette.

"I couldn't come back tonight," Ben said. "But maybe I could get a plane early in the morning."

Pippa blew out smoke and looked toward the window.

"I know you won't let me down," said Simmons. "But there's no use rushing back. Let me tell you the rest of it. Johnson called Waddy Morris and told him. Waddy and Guthrie are in Mexico, too. Where are you? Monterrey?"

"No. Just in Nuevo Laredo."

"You might run into Guthrie then. He's staying across the river in Laredo." Simmons laughed. "I shouldn't have told you that. Don't go looking for him. It wouldn't help a bit for you to knock his teeth out."

"I can't promise what I might do if I see him. But what about Waddy Morris?"

"Waddy tried to talk Johnson into changing his mind again, but

Acey wouldn't do it," said Simmons. "So Waddy called me. Just a few minutes ago. Waddy promised me absolutely on his personal word that I'd stay as president of Ramco until after the merger and then that I'd have a lifetime seat on the board if I'd release Acey from what Waddy called an odious bond. I heard Waddy once tell Guthrie to be quiet. Waddy told me what a grand thing the merger would be. He flattered me about how important I would be to the big new corporation. It was quite enjoyable. I've been smoking one cigarette after another ever since I hung up. He even talked as if they might make me president of the new corporation. He was very convincing."

"What did you tell him?" Ben said.

"I told him to go dump in his hat."

Ben smiled. "I wish I could have heard that," he said.

"It made me feel good, but it didn't strengthen our position. Waddy threatened me. He said he's going to get Johnson no matter whether I release him or not and that if he has to do that, I'm out. I don't doubt that he can do it, Ben. But we still have breath. Waddy gave me until tomorrow morning to change my mind. He's going to call Acey again tonight, and I gather Waddy will put tremendous pressure on him. So there's no reason for you to hurry back. We won't know anything for certain until we see how Acey reacts, and that will probably be tomorrow."

"Mr. Simmons, I haven't said I'd come back. I told you how I felt."

"I don't honor your resignation. I didn't hear a word you said about quitting. What I heard you say was you didn't want Guthrie to get Ramco. Have you changed your mind about that?"

"No," Ben said.

"Then remember this, Ben. A proxy fight is never over. This one may be over for me by tomorrow, but next spring always comes, and there'll always be somebody to challenge him."

"If you've got Johnson back, this one won't be over for you tomorrow," said Ben.

"My hopes are not extremely high. Personally, I will refuse to crowd Acey any further. I've made my gesture of defiance, Ben, and it has been at Acey's expense. If Waddy breaks him after this, I'll have to let Waddy break him. I won't damage Acey any worse. I *am* fond of him. I don't want to force him to stand up to Waddy if the pressure is too much. I hate to force Acey to betray me, Ben, but that's probably what I've done, and if he has to betray me I don't want to make him suffer for it any more than necessary. This is a hard thing to do to a friend. I won't talk to Acey again until tomorrow, when he will have made his decision. If he goes over to Waddy and Guthrie it will be because that was what he had to do, and I'll let him know I don't hold it against him. In a way, I've forgiven him in advance, and I'm sorry that I will have made him do something to be forgiven for. But, at least, Ben, you and I will have fought to the end. That's better than what I was prepared to do yesterday."

"I ought to be there. I shouldn't have left," Ben said.

"Not at all. Not a bit. Enjoy your birthday. And don't try to call me tonight. I can't take the suspense, so I'm going to knock myself out with some sleeping pills. When do you plan to come back to Dallas?"

"Late tomorrow night."

"That's time enough," said Simmons. "By Monday morning if we still have Acey we're still in the fight and we can go to work on the Thurlowes as you wanted to. If we don't have Acey, there is no fight. The stockholders meeting will be an Appomattox. There's not a thing you can do to affect Acey's decision. To tell you the truth, Ben, it's really because of you that I forced him to make a decision. You're the one who made me mad enough at myself to take it out on Acey. And now, good night. I'm going to smoke one more cigarette and turn myself in. My wife is gone for the weekend, and I'll get a nice long quiet sleep. This excitement has tired me."

"Good night," Ben said. "I'll call you tomorrow evening."

"Good night," said Simmons.

Ben hung up the phone.

"That was my client," Ben said.

"When I heard you on the phone, I was afraid it might have been your wife," said Pippa.

Cadmus had ordered several tables pushed together to make one large table in the hotel dining room, which was also the hotel bar. Eight waiters arranged themselves in formation on the brown and white linoleum squares of the floor, and three bartenders watched from behind the brown wooden bar. The television on the wall had been turned off at Cadmus's demand, even though it meant cutting out Dizzy Dean broadcasting the baseball game of the day. There was only one other table of diners in the room, and it was behind a pillar. Two men sat at the bar drinking Madero brandy from a bottle and watching Cadmus and shaking their heads at his commands in unusual Spanish and profane English. A thin young man in a green double-breasted suit stood at the end of the bar and looked at Cadmus through dark glasses as big as goggles. On the mint tablecloths were plates of nachos—small crisp tortillas spread with melted cheese and green peppers. When Ben and Pippa came in all of Cadmus's guests were eating nachos and drinking Carta Blanca. All except Seton, who was neither eating nor drinking but was staring straight ahead as if an eye wandering past the green peppers would rip a hole in the lining of his stomach and cause him instant death. "Murder," Seton kept saying. "Pure murder. Foul and horrible murder." Seton's face was the color of concrete.

When Pippa sat down beside Seton he wouldn't allow himself to look at her. He kept mumbling that it was murder. Ben pulled out one of the wooden chairs with a brown cloth back and sat down between Pippa and Jason. Already quite drunk, Jason smiled and put his elbow into a plate of nachos. Blossom had revived; her silver hair sparkled with sequins, and her black dress dipped between her breasts. Chub Anderson sat between Sheridan and her husband, munching nachos and washing down the peppers with Carta Blanca. Harry was eating and drinking with both hands. Doris watched Cadmus and smiled as Cadmus stood up and called for silence.

"Hey, hombre," Cadmus said to a waiter, "set us up a pronto round of tequila sours. I'm gonna make some toasts."

In a white linen sport coat, a red sport shirt with an open collar, and canary yellow pants, Cadmus looked huge. The tequila sours had already been prepared at his request, and the eight waiters hurriedly passed them around the table. Cadmus grinned and licked his crooked teeth. He raised the martini glass of cloudy liquid.

"This here's just to get us going before the rest of the meal comes," Cadmus said.

"Damn good," said Blossom.

"Seton, you ain't dranking," said Cadmus.

"I am not," Seton said.

"Anyhow, I'm gonna make some toasts," said Cadmus.

Seton glanced at his sister, scowled, and jerked his eyes away.

"Where is your locket?" Seton said.

Pippa touched her breast, and then felt around her neck.

"It must have broken off," she said.

"I thank we oughta have some attention paid to these here toasts," said Cadmus.

Harry made Jason move his elbow so he could get at the plate of nachos. Jason smiled at him.

"I'm gonna toast," Cadmus said, "to the Good Ship Lollipop, Father Flanagan, Pete Rozelle, and Mickey Mantle."

The waiters stared at Cadmus. One of the bartenders, a man with a bushy mustache, put on his dark glasses and stared at Cadmus. The boy in the green suit stared at Cadmus. With a flourish, Cadmus drank his tequila sour. Cadmus waited until the others had at least tasted theirs, and he signaled for another round. The drinks were promptly set out, but the waiters and the mustached bartender and the boy in the green suit kept looking at Cadmus.

"Now," said Cadmus, "I want to drank to Arturo Godoy, Wilma Rudolph, and Arthur Schlesinger, Junior. Arturo and me and Wilma Rudolph was classmates at Harvard. Then I want to drank to Blossom, everbody at this here table, to Ben's birthday, to love, virtue, and charity, to nekkid swimming, nekkid bridge and nekkid polo and Admiral Rickover that used to dandle me on his knee. I want to drank to all the men that are home making love to their wives, and to all unborn children that are coming from God knows where into God knows what."

Cadmus drained his tequila sour, wiped his mouth, and stuck out his hand for another drink. Nobody else was ready.

"And last I want to drank to all the free spirits in the world. Of which I am one of the very few," Cadmus said, turning up the glass and sinking into his chair.

The waiters began serving the food. Cadmus had ordered enchiladas, chicken tacos, refried rice, refried beans, carne asada, chili con queso, soft tortillas, chalupas, guacamole salad, beef tacos, tamales, and a broiled steak for Seton. The waiters scuttled in and out of the kitchen door with platters of food. The two men drinking brandy at the bar laughed and shook their heads. Cadmus heaped something from each dish onto his plate and doused the mixture with salt, pepper, and green pepper sauce. Seton began to eat with his head down, shielding his eyes with one hand.

The waiter in dark glasses bent over and whispered to Ben.

"Does he truly know Mickey Mantle?" said the waiter.

—he truly does, Ben said.

—he truly knows mickey mantle well? the waiter said.

—they are like brothers, Ben said.

"Ah," the waiter said, nodding to the bartender. "And he knows the others?"

"Some well, and some not so well," said Ben.

"Ah," the waiter said. He went to whisper to the bartender. The bartender stared at Cadmus. "Ah," the bartender said. The boy in the green suit listened to them and looked at Cadmus.

"Why did you tell him that?" said Pippa.

"It was what he wanted to hear," Ben said. "That's how things are done in Mexico."

"Who is Mickey Mantle?" said Seton without looking up.

"A baseball player," Pippa said.

"He plays for the Cincinnati Cubs," said Harry.

"Is that supposed to make him important?" Seton said. "God, they have twelve men on a team or something, don't they?"

"At least," said Ben.

"I hate baseball," Seton said. "I don't keep up with it. The only baseball player I remember is George Keller. They called him Pie Head or something. He played for the New York Yankees?"

"He must have," said Ben.

"Ben's kidding you," Pippa said.

Seton peeked around at Ben from beneath his hand. There were moments when Seton's eyes suddenly shone with hatred, when he had the eyes of a jealous mistress. Then Seton laughed.

"So what?" said Seton. "So what about baseball? Ben might as well have his fun with me."

"Everybody's after you, aren't they?" said Sheridan, who had been listening.

"I wasn't talking to you," Seton said.

"Pardon me," said Sheridan.

"Go screw," Seton said. "Just go screw."

"You ought to try it some time," said Sheridan.

"You sonofabitch," Seton said. "Nobody invited you on this trip. You pushed your way in because you're trying to get in Chub's pants."

"Seton!" said Pippa.

"Hey now," Walter Anderson said.

Sheridan jumped up.

"It's a good thing for you your sister's here," said Sheridan, glaring through his black-rimmed glasses. Sheridan clenched his small fists, and thrust forward his dimpled chin.

Seton lifted his eyes to look at Sheridan and raised his steak knife.

"If you try to hit me, I'll kill you," Seton said.

Nobody moved.

"Try to hit me," said Seton.

Sheridan looked around the table.

"Well, try to hit him," Harry said.

Sheridan sat down.

"Damn good," said Blossom.

"Seton, you're acting like a fool," Pippa said.

"So are you," said Seton.

"Everbody having a good time?" Cadmus yelled.

"You shouldn't talk that way, Seton," said Walter Anderson.

"Go screw," Seton said.

After dinner Cadmus paid the bill and signed autographs for the waiters and bartenders. Harry awoke Jason. They all got up from the table and waited for Cadmus to finish with the autographs.

"Tell Señor Mantle we wish him luck and that he hits seventy quadrangulars," said the waiter.

Cadmus promised to tell Mickey Mantle exactly that, the waiters and bartender grinned a display of gold and lead, and Cadmus shepherded his flock onto the street. They walked along the crowded sidewalk in the hot evening. Fireworks burst and showered above the plaza. Lights burned from the palms. Cadmus stopped in a drugstore and came out stuffing bottles into his pockets. He opened one of the bottles and gave each of his guests a green heart-shaped pill. Cadmus, himself, took three pills and Jason took two. "Zoom zoom," said Cadmus.

"What are these?" Pippa said.

"Heart medicine, honey pot. Swaller it," said Cadmus. "Won't hurt you none."

—pardon me, señor, but do you speak spanish?

The boy in the green double-breasted suit had followed them from the Gran Hotel Reforma bar. He looked up at Cadmus through heavy dark glasses with black plastic rims that curved above his ears. Cadmus looked back suspiciously. With one thin hand the boy pushed back his black hair and pulled a pencil and pad from the breast pocket of his coat.

"Deal with him, Ben," Cadmus said.

The boy in the green suit looked at Ben.

—my english is not so very good, the boy said.

—nor is my spanish, Ben said.

—but you speak it well. my name is alonso guzman. i am a columnist for *Nuevo Laredo Hoy.* i write what you call the gossip. i wish you would tell me some information about this truly magnificent person, the boy said and gestured toward Cadmus.

—i will translate, Ben said.

Alonso Guzman glanced at Blossom and then looked again at Cadmus.

—i have your name from the hotel register, señor wilkins. i wish to know about this remarkable bus you arrived in. does it belong to you?

Ben translated the question.

"It belongs to the Harvard track team," said Cadmus. "They loaned it to us on account of my close association with Wilma Rudolph."

—he says the bus belongs to his father's oil company and we have borrowed it for the weekend to come to this fiesta. we are celebrating freedom, Ben said.

—but that is not what he said. i understand much. he said you brought wilma rudolph here in it.

—all right. put it down then.

—where is miss rudolph?

Ben translated.

"Taking laps," said Cadmus.

—i don't get that, Alonso Guzman said.

—we have misplaced her, Ben said.

—that is terrible, the boy said.

—it is unfortunate. it is an awful loss to our nation.

"Ben, what is this?" said Pippa.

"We're being interviewed."

"The others are walking on."

"Stick with me for a minute."

"Tell him to hurry up with his questions. We got a lot to do," said Cadmus.

—are you extremely wealthy? Alonso Guzman said.

"Sometimes more so than other times," said Cadmus. "I have built an oil empire in the town of New Hope, Texas, but I have turned all that money over to establishing a Katherine Dunham Chair of Dance at the University of Alabama. At the moment I am giving my assets a piercing reappraisal. But not so piercing as to cause me mental unrest. Now, translate that, Ben."

—he says yeah he's pretty rich, Ben said.

—i would like to go to texas and work for a big newspaper. maybe some of your rich friends will see my article and will like it, Alonso Guzman said.

—one can never be sure of the future, Ben said.

—truly. but i must go to my office and prepare my column.

—you haven't received much information.

—but i have. i learned much at the hotel. i can prepare a great column from this, the boy said.

"See if he wants to know about my childhood," said Cadmus. "I had an interesting childhood. I was under the care of a kindly old nanny who was also a pipe fitter in East Texas. I was fourteen before my daddy ever spoke to me. Then one day he walked in to my room and said, 'Why the hell ain't you in college?' It was hard to splain to him about how I was supposed to finish high school first because he hadn't done nothing except dig post holes and bust horses and ride fence when he was a boy. But when he finally understood he shipped me off to military school. Don't that sound like an interesting story? I could give him some sensational material about the sex life in military schools."

—he says his father was a cowboy who became an oil man, Ben said.

—i will note that. but i must hurry to my office. i will see you around town later tonight. please allow me to offer that if there is any affair with the police you should call for me, as my father is in the government.

—many thanks, Ben said.

—for nothing. my thanks to you.

Alonso Guzman nodded to Blossom and Pippa, shook hands with Cadmus and Ben, and hurried off through the crowd.

"I wonder how much of that he really understood," Cadmus said.

"I think he was telling the truth about his English," said Ben.

"It's kind of fun to be interviewed, ain't it, honey pot?" Cadmus said.

"Damn good," said Blossom.

"Sure would make my daddy happy to see all that stuff in the paper," Cadmus said.

"I bet he's already delighted that you took the bus," said Ben.

"I'll work it out," Cadmus said. "I'm one of them guys that naturally stays on top. I just won't let it be any other way."

Jason had wandered across the street to a candy-striped tent at the edge of the plaza. In front of the tent, in the white arc of a floodlight, stood a dreary, mouse-colored burro. A man in a flowered vest, blue denims and leather sandals was urging people to have their pictures made riding the burro. Propped against the tent was the backdrop—a crudely painted canvas of a cactus, a purple mountain, and a cloudless sky. A woman dressed like a gypsy grabbed Jason's arm and pulled him to the burro. The others came across the street to watch him. The man in the flowered vest stuck a sombrero on Jason's head and helped him mount the burro. Jason lay for a moment hanging across the burro on his stomach like a sack of meal. As the man in the flowered vest reached for Jason's foot to give him a boost, Jason kicked out, hit the man in the chest, and knocked him backward. The planting of his foot provided enough push to throw Jason over the other side of the burro. Jason got up dizzily, clinging to the backdrop. The peak of the sombrero was crushed. The man in the flowered vest muttered several curses. He and the gypsy woman lifted Jason between them and dumped him onto the burro, which had neither moved nor looked around. Rubbing his chest, the man in the flowered vest walked over to his box camera which was mounted on a tripod, pulled the black hood over his head, and picked up the switch that would flick the shutter. Jason grinned, snatched off the sombrero and waved it above his head. He raked his heels against the burro as if he were fanning the flanks of a bucking bronc. The man in the flowered vest clicked his camera just as Jason toppled off the burro again.

Cadmus decided he wanted to be next. Doris led Jason away and examined the bump on Jason's head. Cadmus jammed the smashed sombrero onto his blond hair, swung a long leg over the burro, and sat down. Sitting on the burro, Cadmus squatted a bit and his feet were flat on the grass of the plaza. Then it was Blossom's turn. She sat sidesaddle on the burro and crossed her legs with her skirt above her knees. The man in the flowered vest stayed for a long while beneath his black hood, as if the camera needed a great deal of careful focusing. The gypsy woman poked him on the arm.

"You want a picture?" Ben asked Pippa.

"No," she said. "I feel sorry for that burro."

"You all right?"

She looked up at him. A thin mustache of sweat glistened on her upper lip, and there were dark smudges beneath her eyes. The two of them stood just outside the rim of the floodlight. Her face looked very pale against the black of her hair.

"I'm fine," she said. "I was wondering where I lost my locket. In your room, I suppose."

"I'm sorry about this afternoon," he said.

"Don't be sorry. I'd warned you."

"I don't know what made me think I'd be the one."

"The male ego," she said.

"That's such a general category. Besides, I told you I have no vanity."

She smiled. "It was the closest I've ever been," she said.

"Truthfully?"

"Of course truthfully."

"Have you ever said that to anybody else?"

"Yes," she said, "and it was always true."

By the time they were through with the picture taking, and the pictures were developed and given to Cadmus in wet prints mounted on cardboard, the sun had died behind the rooftops and the last pink of dusk had gone with it. More lights went on in the plaza. Rockets exploded above and streaking arms of yellow, white, and red reached for the sky and then faded. The plaza bustled with noise: the shouts of men, the screaming laughter of children, the scolding voices of mothers, the singing of drunks, music playing from loudspeakers in the palms. Children with ice cream cones raced around the statue in the center of the plaza. Police with nightsticks and pistols hung on their belts moved through the crowd.

Cadmus took his group back across the street and herded them down the sidewalk of Avenida Guerrero toward the International Bridge. The stalls and shops along the sidewalk were bright and open. Thousands of comic books were clipped by clothespins to racks in the newsstands. People stood in lines in the liquor stores. Little boys tugged at the pants and skirts of Cadmus's guests and begged them to buy a box of Chiclets or get their shoes shined. At the corner a man sold toy fighting cocks. He wound them up and their feathers bristled as they hopped about. Beside him was a woman who had green baby parrots in a cage. The parrots sat with unblinking eyes above their curved yellow beaks. On open counters lay stacks of fried pies and sugar-frosted pastries that seemed to be dotted with raisins until occasionally a vendor would wave his hand and some of the raisins would fly away. Harry stopped to look at a piece of painted statuary in a shop window: it was a bleeding Christ. The shopkeeper saw that Harry was interested and began to demonstrate. When the shopkeeper squeezed a bulb behind the statue, blood flowed from the wounds of Christ. Pippa hurried on, taking Ben and Seton with her. Harry sighed and shook his head. The shopkeeper looked disappointed.

Ben, Pippa, and Seton waited beside a *zapatería* for the others to catch up with them. The shop smelled of new leather. A man came past dragging a cage in a wagon. The cage was full of Chihuahua puppies. A woman pleaded with them to buy the blankets, shawls, or vests beneath which her barefoot children staggered.

A man touched Ben's shoulder and Ben turned around. The man wore a white, short-sleeved sports shirt and had a black case hung on his chest with straps that went up around his neck. The man opened the lid of the case, and a light came on to show its contents.

"Knives, reengs, bracelets," the man said, indicating the case. He lifted with one finger a turquoise necklace and glanced at Pippa. "For the pretty lady?"

"No," said Ben.

The man moved himself around so that he was between Ben and Pippa and had his back to her. He grinned at Ben. "Sponeesh fly?" he said.

"No," said Ben.

"Peectures?"

"Creo que no."

"Hokaye," the man said, shrugging. He nodded toward Seton, who was looking at leather bullwhips in the window of the *zapatería*. "Heem?"

"Ask him."

The man went over to Seton. Seton looked at him as if he were crawling with snakes.

"Hey, mon, you like the wheeps?" the man said.

"I beg your pardon?"

"I got some good bondage peectures for you."

"Oh God," said Seton.

Cadmus and the others arrived.

"Knives, reengs, bracelets?" the man said, opening his case and turning on the light. Then without pausing he said: "Peectures?"

"Anybody want any dirty pictures?" said Cadmus.

"Damn good," Blossom said.

"I'd like some," said Chub.

Walter blushed. "Come on, honey," he said.

"But I've never seen any," she said.

For three dollars Walter bought a packet of photographs which he put in his coat pocket. Walter was embarrassed. Cadmus led them down the sidewalk past more shops, peddlers, celebrators, and police. Jason plodded along in the rear, grinning foolishly and saying, "Scum of the very earth."

The sidewalk was worn and gray and smelled like hot corn meal. They came to a bar named the New Shamrock which had green neon shamrocks chasing each other across the sign above the door and had pictures of girls in the windows. One girl was dressed in high heels and a sort of bikini with a skirt tagged on behind which she held up like the wings of a butterfly. The poster called her: *Lucy Gonzáles Beautiful Dancer*. Cadmus took them inside. Indirect lighting gave the place a purplish look. A walkway went past a small pond and waterfall and tanks of tropical fish and then opened onto the tables and the dance floor. Jason stepped off the walkway into the pond, sloshed through water up to his knees, stepped back onto the walkway, and went to the table with his creaking shoes leaving puddles on the floor. He sat down beside Chub, put a hand beneath her chin, turned her face toward him, and kissed her. He smiled happily at Walter, lowered his head into the ash tray, and said, "Kizzum."

Cadmus had the waiter bring a round of tequila sours. Another waiter came with a rag to mop up Jason's puddles. On a small platform beyond the dance floor a band was playing: bongo, piano, drums, flute, saxophone, snare drums, and marimbas. The music made Ben think of Rome.

"Ain't this grand?" Cadmus said. He put his arm around Blossom. "I love you, Blossom. I always fall in love when I hear pretty music and I'm about half drunk. I look around and the first pretty girl I see I fall in love with her. That's what I call Clang Clang Love. The bell rings, see, like it does in the movies, and the lightning cracks and the thunder goes boom and I thank I'd swim the oceans and climb the mountains because I'm so much in love. I'm Gene Kelly in a white dinner jacket and I'm dancing with a gorgeous woman and my breath don't stink and she ain't got warts and these here phony clouds are floating behind us. It's wonderful, long as you don't get confused and thank it's gonna be permanent. That's one place where it comes in handy to know the difference between playing and serious. When you get 'em mixed up, wow, boy, you're heading for grief."

"Since I'm not the pretty girl you happened to see, I'd like to go dance with somebody," said Doris. "Seton, you know all these Latin dances, don't you?"

"I love to dance," Seton said, getting up and pulling back Doris's chair.

They danced very well and inspired the musicians. Doris was smooth and professional and subtly muscular in her dancing, but hardly better than Seton whose shuffling awkwardness disappeared on the dance floor. Of his customary movements only the hip-swaying remained, and that was perfect for what they were doing. The tables of the New Shamrock had begun to fill. Other people went to the dance floor. Jason took his head out of the ash tray, lit two cigarettes, and sat contentedly smoking and drinking his tequila sour. Walter and Sheridan switched to beer. Chub, her eyes wide and her mouth wet and red, watched the dancers with envy until Sheridan invited her to dance. She leaped up and went with him to the dance floor.

"This is great," Harry said. "This is great. We ought to move to Mexico."

"We live close enough to it," said Cadmus.

"We could move to Mexico and get away from the bomb," Harry said. "It'd be great. We could dance all the time."

"That's playing," said Cadmus. "*Tahr*some, too."

"Pippa, what does the Pope tell you about the bomb?" Harry said.

"I don't know," she said.

"But you're a Catholic," said Harry.

"I don't get into arguments about it," she said. "If I thought it had to be defended, then I wouldn't think it was worth believing in."

"Who's arguing?" said Harry. "I'm discussing. Don't you think it's worth talking about? We have to live with the thought that at any moment our entire culture can become pits of ashes and steaming water, and there's nothing we can do about it. Individual lives have always been at the mercy of accident, but now centuries can be blown away at a whim. Anybody who ignores that is cheating. Compared to that, nothing else in history mattered. Either the world embraces a working ethic, or the world as we know it is extinct. But Christianity roasted at Hiroshima and Auschwitz."

"I'm not going to argue," she said. "I know."

"You said you didn't know," said Harry.

"I don't know what you asked," she said. "But I know what I mean."

"I give up on that," said Harry. "But there's got to be a sensible answer. And meanwhile some people are mourning what Cadmus calls their lost innocence by debauchery, some are wandering with brains frozen like English peas, some are kneeling terrified in the churches and praying to something they don't believe . . . don't even *feel* any more. Millions going their own way, not believing it's a virtue to give or that the humble are blessed or that their neighbors are lovable, most of them not thinking they've done anything wrong but not able to understand why they're restless and dissatisfied. Marching toward the bomb in aboriginal, amoral bewilderment. Nobody to tell them what's right or what's wrong in the language they speak. All they're told is to stay in their own little corners and try to forget about the booger bear."

"What do you want, another man to come stomping down the mountain with a stone tablet?" Cadmus said. "There's been catasturphies before. Always will be. There's always some dummies you can't straighten. But these millions of people roaming around without a bell sheep, Harry, that's what a artist is for. A artist ought to fill in the holes for everbody. Show 'em how to get from what's gone to what's coming without cracking up. Tell 'em how to be alone, how to be proud of theirselfs, how to be alive and not rob theirselfs of the only thang they've got. A artist can't be much of a artist if he thanks being alive is something stupid and shameful."

"What would you suggest?" said Harry. He grinned at Blossom, who had accidentally dumped the contents of a salt shaker into her tequila sour and was looking at it as if wondering how to drink around the gray mound in the bottom of the glass.

"Dig down inside your own self deep enough till you find something," Cadmus said. "Be a window to your spirit and don't be scared of what's in there, because if you go down far enough it can't be bad, I wouldn't thank, but can only be life, and then throw out what's useless and face up to what's real and be joyous about it because there ain't no use being otherwise. That's how you start. Tahred me mightily to say it, though. But I ain't a artist. I'm just a guy that gets along."

Blossom tasted her drink. "Wooo," she said.

"Where does God fit in?" said Harry.

"You got a pretty small idea of God if you thank God's gotta fit in. All you know about God, son, is that you don't know nothing about God," Cadmus said. "I wisht people'd quit using that word. God ain't got no name. If God got a name then you might as well call it Ole Sam and thank about Ole Sam setting up yonder on a platinum throne and puzzling hisself about what's ever gonna become of this world. That's like a little kid thanking about his daddy and wondering why his daddy ain't done right by him. Makes me sick to my heart that we ain't grown up."

"Brother Chunk sure would be put out with you," said Walter.

"Nobody believes Brother Chunk any more," Harry said. "He rules people because they're scared, not because they think he's right."

"Well," said Walter. He looked at Harry. "I'd just as soon I hadn't brought that up."

Jason lit another cigarette. One was burning in the ash tray and he had one already in his fingers. "Smokem," he said. He assumed his Edward G. Robinson voice. "See here you guys. What I like is smoking, see? I like to puff on cigarettes, see? Reason I squint like this is because I got smoke in my eyes, see?"

"Let's dance," Pippa said to Ben.

Her body had weight, had a quality of being that went solidly into his arms and that made him more aware that he was holding a woman than that they were dancing. The band had reluctantly abandoned its Latin beats in deference to those who could not manage them, and now was playing "The Nearness of You." Doris and

Seton whirled past, making an exhibition of even that solemn tempo. The clean smell of Pippa's hair was against Ben's nose. He kissed her hair.

"Why wouldn't you tell Harry what you think?" he said.

"Because I don't need to."

"Tell me," he said.

"If you ever really know me, then you'll know. You don't know me now."

"How could I know you better?" he said.

"By holding me," she said. "By holding me so tightly I can't get away."

The lights went down and a spotlight hit the stage. The master of ceremonies came out, held up his thin arms for silence, rattled off several quick jokes which were met by scattered laughter, and then did a tap dance. Sweating, he bowed and Cadmus applauded loudly. "Guy who works that hard ought to get clapped for," Cadmus said. The master of ceremonies introduced the next act: the Ballet Alegria: three Mexican girls in straw hats, frilly blouses that covered their shoulders and breasts, and frilly skirts that clung to their hips below their navels, and two Mexican men in straw hats, tight pants, and vests. After the members of Ballet Alegria had finished hopping around, the master of ceremonies presented a woman he called, "Josefine, the romantic." Josefine sang and undulated in her sheath dress and tried to get a good look at the ringside table where the big blond man was doing the clapping, but the spotlight was in her eyes. Then a man played the guitar and sang. Anita Montiel, who was introduced as "sensational," danced in a scant costume and also tried to peer through the spotlight at the front table; she knelt, writhing and clawing at her hair and squinting at Cadmus. The next act was to be Lucy Gonzáles, Beautiful Dancer. But Blossom, who had been whispering as Cadmus bent his head close to her, suddenly stood up. "Why sure, honey pot," Cadmus said, getting up with her. The two of them walked across the dance floor to the stage.

Blossom stepped up onto the platform and someone in the audience whistled. She smiled and tried to curtsy, but her skirt was too tight. She settled for dipping her silver hair, bowing from the waist, and giving the audience a view that brought a lot of whistles. Cadmus looked down at the startled master of ceremonies and said something. The master of ceremonies shook his head. The members of the band began laughing. Cadmus repeated. The master of ceremonies shook his head and looked pleadingly toward the front bar where the manager usually stayed. The manager and a heavily built waiter with sloping shoulders and black slanting eyebrows came down an aisle. Blossom bowed again. The manager stuck out an arm, stopped the waiter, and looked at Blossom. The crowd whistled and clapped. The manager grinned. Cadmus said something to the manager, who shrugged. The master of ceremonies looked out at the audience as if to say the situation was beyond his grasp. Cadmus got down from the stage and returned to the table.

"Blossom wants to sang," he said.

"Can she sing?" asked Doris.

"I guess we'll find out pretty quick," Cadmus said.

The master of ceremonies finally got the crowd quiet.

—introducing mees blossom, the internationally known singer who comes to us from weecheeta fallas, tayhass, where she has sung recently—the master of ceremonies glanced helplessly at Blossom—at the dew drop een.

The crowd whooped and yelled as Blossom went to the microphone with short steps. She smiled beautifully. The sequins in her hair shot darts of light. Clutching the microphone, she opened her mouth and sang:

"Ratchit."

The band was playing "As Time Goes By," but the music squawked and died as the musicians realized Blossom was not singing in key or tempo and was not using the correct words.

"Ratchit ratchit ratchit . . . ratchit ratchit ratchit . . ." Blossom sang.

The Americans in the crowd shouted with laughter. The manager clapped a hand to his forehead and sat down on the apron of the stage. The husky waiter looked confused.

"Walter," said Cadmus, "you get these folks out of here. I'll meet you out at the Mirabeau."

"What's . . ." Walter said.

"Get humping, son. You don't want to get caught in no brawl in Mexico. What would the good voters thank?" said Cadmus.

The band had quit playing. The room was a riot of noise. Blossom bowed and smiled. An American corporal wobbled across the dance floor and grabbed at Blossom. Cadmus moved with amazing quickness, arrived at the stage simultaneously with the corporal, and pushed the corporal back. The corporal swung a long, wild looping punch that missed Cadmus by six inches; the force of it carried the corporal off his feet and flung him onto the floor. Three more soldiers rushed out of the crowd toward Cadmus. Harry came upon them from the side, hit one of them very crisply above the ear with the blade of his hand, and the soldier fell.

"Go with Walter," Ben said to Pippa.

She shook her head. He took her by the shoulders, shoved her toward Seton, ran onto the dance floor, and was promptly hit on the jaw by someone he hadn't seen. Ben staggered sideways and tripped over the corporal, who was trying to get up. Rolling over, Ben got one hand on the corporal's forehead and bounced the back of his head off the dance floor. Ben looked up to see Harry hammer three rapid punches into the face of another soldier and then kick him on the left kneecap. The soldier sat down, bleeding from a cut beneath his right eye. Cadmus was wrestling with the other soldier and had bent the soldier over the apron of the stage and was clubbing the soldier on top of the head with his fist. By then six or eight more people had run onto the dance floor. Two of them were young Americans who were drunk and looked as if they enjoyed fighting, and the rest were young Mexicans who were also drunk and looked as if they enjoyed fighting. The husky waiter moved through the flailing fists with his chin tucked against his thick left shoulder and a grin on his face; he was clearly a man with much experience in the ring, and he hit anybody who got in front of him.

Cadmus jumped onto the stage and picked up the smiling Blossom. She put her arms around his neck and kissed him. The soldier Cadmus had been wrestling with clamped a hand around Cadmus's ankle. Harry came by, kicked the hand loose, and yelled for Cadmus to run. Carrying Blossom, Cadmus pushed through the crowd toward the front door. Awed by his size, people stood back for him. Someone tackled Ben and knocked him down; he rapped his elbow on the floor and the pain of it made him cold. A fist landed on Ben's neck, but it was a blow without power. Another fist went past Ben's face as he twisted around, and Ben saw the fist collide with the eyebrow of the man who had tackled him. The fist was Harry's.

Harry pulled Ben to his feet as the lights went out. Shoving through the blackness and the tangled bodies, hearing grunts and thumps and curses, they went up onto the stage and through the curtain that led to the wings. They stumbled down a short dark hall and came into a room which was lit with bare electric bulbs. Harry opened a door. They plunged into another room, and someone shrieked. Romantic Josefine and sensational Anita Montiel scrambled away from their dressing table mirrors and reached for gowns to cover themselves.

—pardon us, please. is there a way out? Ben said.

The two women, clutching gowns in front of them, stared.

—get out of here, sensational Anita Montiel said.

—we would like to very much, Ben said.

Romantic Josefine went to the window, released one hand from the gown momentarily, and raised the shade. Harry lifted the window. He and Ben climbed through into an alley.

—thank you, Ben said to romantic Josefine.

She slammed the window shut and pulled the shade.

"The police ought to be here by now," Harry said.

Their footsteps echoed as they ran down the alley past garbage cans and littered wine bottles. The alley smelled of urine. At the end of the alley, Harry peeked around the corner. He motioned to Ben. Walking casually, they came out of the alley onto a quiet street and strolled toward the west away from the New Shamrock. Behind them, rockets showered above the plaza. They heard yelling from the direction of the New Shamrock.

"First time I've ever seen any trouble in that bar," Harry said. "But it's fiesta."

"Blossom's an exciting singer," said Ben.

"Wonder where she learned that song?" Harry said, laughing. "That song would start a riot any place."

They went down two blocks of adobe buildings, past walled patios and iron grill fences where flowers grew, turned left for two more blocks, turned left again and returned to Avenida Guerrero. Near the hotel they caught a taxi. "Mirabeau," Ben said to the driver.

"Better straighten your tie," said Harry. "And brush off your elbows. You hurt?"

"Not a mark."

"Me neither. We were lucky," Harry said, looking at a bruised knuckle on his left hand. "Except in an hour I'm gonna feel like I've got two sprained wrists."

"I'd forgot you were such a good fighter. Where'd you pick up that trick of kicking people?"

"I got four things out of the Army," Harry said, grinning. "A scarred back, a scarred leg, the GI Bill, and the willingness to kick folks. They've all come in handy. First time Doris got a look at my back she felt so sorry for me she asked me to marry her."

The Mirabeau was a large building among trees far back from the street. A gravel road ran up to it. On the side of the building opposite the road was a courtyard, three walls of which were made up of small rooms where the girls of the Mirabeau worked and lived. The courtyard was a quiet place where lanterns hung from the trees. The dance hall and bar of the main building formed the fourth wall of the courtyard. Inside the dance hall and bar it was the color of twilight. A juke box stood against the back wall near the dance floor. The juke box was the size of a refrigerator and shone with red, yellow, purple, and green lights; inside its window records revolved on a turntable. The music was blurred and scratchy, but it was loud enough to be heard all over the room.

Girls walked singly, or in pairs, or sometimes in groups of three or four, around the dance floor, between the tables, past the bar, and around the dance floor again, waiting for a signal to join a customer at his table or to go with him into one of the rooms off the courtyard. Most of the girls were short and dumpy with heavy hips and breasts, thin calves and ankles, round faces, black hair, and moist, peanut-colored skin. But there were other types: some thin and hard, some tiny and perfect as dolls, and some who were quite pretty. And above them all stood one woman who was perhaps six-feet-three in her high heels. She wore a pair of red silk briefs that were split up the sides but could barely contain her buttocks. Her long legs were bare and perfectly formed. Her pink blouse was sleeveless, and its top two buttons were undone. Her black hair was drawn into a long, knotted ponytail. When Ben and Harry entered she was dancing with Jason and laughing down at him, a wide-mouthed laugh that lifted her Indian cheekbones.

"There's Yolanda," Ben said. "She's still the queen."

Cadmus sat at the head of the table. He had not been injured in the fight except for a scratch on his left cheek. "And Blossom done that while I was carrying her," he said. Ben slid into a chair beside Pippa.

"You're right," she said. "They do parade."

"Who?" he said.

"The . . . girls," she said. She looked at him carefully. "Oh, Ben, when I saw you run out on that dance floor I was so afraid you were going to be hurt."

"Same thing occurred to me," he said.

"I mean it," she said. "I was so afraid for you that it frightened me for me. I don't know if I like that. Will you kiss me?"

"Right here?"

"No," she said, turning her mouth toward him, "right here."

As he kissed her, Ben saw Seton looking at him. Seton scowled and took Doris to dance. After the kiss Ben sat with his arm on the back of Pippa's chair, touching her shoulder. Her left hand was on his thigh beneath the table. Sheridan danced with Chub and then danced with several of the girls from the Mirabeau. Walter danced with Chub. Blossom sat weaving and smiling, and Cadmus told a story about his no-good brother Oscar Lawrence. Yolanda brought Jason back to the table. Jason tumbled into his chair, grinning and sweating. The white powdery-looking patch on top of his head intrigued Yolanda, who kept digging at it with her knuckles.

"She says I got no banana," said Jason.

"He won't go to me room," Yolanda said. Her laugh boomed around the table and made the other voices seem small. Her wide lips drew back from her teeth. "He got no banana."

"I do too," Jason said solemnly.

"Come on, Yolanda, let's you and me dance," said Cadmus. "We'll give 'em something to look at."

"Everybody wants to dance," she said. "But nobody wants to make love. How will I make any money?"

"I'll let 'em sell me a bottle of that colored water for you," said Cadmus. "Come on."

They sat in the Mirabeau until nearly three A.M. The girls of the Mirabeau never ceased parading except for summons to business which didn't seem to take very long at a time. Seton and Doris danced until Seton came back to the table, gray and exhausted, and then Doris dragged Harry to the dance floor. Jason had realized he was desperately in love with Yolanda but that it was true he had no banana and he was destined to suffer. He would lay his head against Yolanda's wide shoulder and she would scrub her knuckles through the white patch in his hair. Cadmus kept giving Yolanda money to keep her there. "I know she ought to stay with you for love, son, but this is hard reality," Cadmus said. Whenever Jason lit more than one cigarette, Yolanda would scold him and put out the extra one. "She cares," said Jason. "She cares bout me."

Walter had begun to loosen up. He had put away a large number of Carta Blancas, and his round face gleamed. The cultivated blank of his poker playing expression had vanished. His small eyes crinkled. He laughed and kissed his wife and sang fraternity songs. "If Brother Chunk could see me now," he said. "Where's old Brother Chunk? Where's he, I say?"

"Getting dressed up to go to heaven," said Cadmus.

"All dressed up to go to heaven," Walter sang.

Seton went off to search for the men's room, picking his way through the whores, avoiding their glances and their invitations. Sheridan came around the table and slid into Seton's chair. He looked past Pippa at Ben.

"Still won't give me a line on that proxy fight?" Sheridan said.

"There's nothing I can tell you. We don't know who's going to win it," Ben said.

"Of course you know," said Sheridan. "Or you have a good idea. By now you know the ones you've got sealed up, and the ones the opposition has."

"As a matter of fact, we don't know that," Ben said.

"It's actually that close?"

"Why are you so interested in it?"

"I told you. I like to fiddle with the market. But everbody's interested in this one. Could be a giant new corporation in the making."

"We have enough giants," Ben said.

"I'd give a lot to know who's going to win it," said Sheridan.

"So would I," Ben said.

Sheridan laughed.

"You must have a damned good indication or you wouldn't have come off to Mexico this weekend," Sheridan said. "You have to be confident you've won, or certain you've lost. Otherwise you'd be back there hustling."

"You don't know anything about it."

"But I know a lot about you. I've heard about you."

"I'm not going to give you any information," Ben said.

Sheridan turned to Pippa.

"Has he told you?" Sheridan said.

"We haven't discussed it," said Pippa.

"It doesn't concern her," Ben said.

"I'm just trying to figure why else you would have come to Mexico if the proxy fight wasn't already decided. I know this fight is a big thing in your career."

"It's not my career that matters."

"Sure it is," said Sheridan. "This is your job. A good lawyer never likes to lose a case. Especially if he wants to get ahead."

"Sheridan, I said I'm not going to give you any information about this, and I'm not. Let's drop it."

Sheridan shrugged.

"Suit yourself," he said. He took Pippa's hand. "Come on. Let's dance."

"No," she said, and jerked her hand away.

"Just one dance."

"No dances," she said.

"What's the matter? Are you in love?"

"You're very close to making me mad," Ben said.

Sheridan stood up.

"I never saw two people so edgy," Sheridan said. "What the hell."

He walked back around the table and went to dance with Chub.

"Ben, you're trembling," Pippa said.

"It nearly got me," said Ben. "All the sudden he nearly turned me on. It happened so quickly."

"Even your voice started shaking," she said.

"I thought I'd pushed it back, but my anger is still close to the surface. It scared me," said Ben. "If he'd said one more word I'd have tried to kill him with a chair. I don't want to be like that."

"It's not difficult to get mad at Bill Sheridan," she said.

"But it wasn't just Sheridan I was mad at. I was mad at being goaded."

"Poor Ben," she said. "You're a mass of open nerve ends."

"Cut it out. Don't say poor Ben. Screw that kind of talk."

"All right," she said.

"I'm sorry. Don't act offended. I'm just trying to . . . there's been so much . . . well, forget it. That doesn't do any good."

"All right."

"Look, I've poured my guts all over . . . I'm sick of . . . Damn, I'm getting inarticulate."

"You've stopped shaking."

"The shaking doesn't last long," he said.

"It does inside."

"How do you know?" he said.

"I feel it. Why don't we dance?"

"You don't want to dance."

"Not with Sheridan. I want to dance with you."

"Evidently you don't like Sheridan very much."

"There," she said. "They're finally playing a record we can dance to. I didn't want to polka."

At her elbow he walked to the dance floor and they turned to face each other and moved among the shuffling figures.

"This evening on the phone," she said. "I heard most of it. Are you going back to Dallas?"

"I don't know yet," he said.

By three, Seton had begun to complain that he wanted to return to the hotel. Cadmus announced he was tired of the Mirabeau and would transfer himself to another bar. He sent a waiter to phone three cabs. Yolanda tried once more to persuade Jason to go to her room.

"But I got no banana," he said, as if he now believed it. He was almost crying. "Got no banana and I can't remember where I left it."

Yolanda followed them to the door, dusted Jason's head with her knuckles and pinched his ear. Jason said she was a very affectionate woman. The cabs were waiting on the gravel road in the light of the doorway. Cadmus told the three cab drivers they all wanted to go to Tony's. Cadmus, Blossom, Ben, and Pippa climbed into the first cab. Harry, Doris, Jason, and Walter got into the second. Walter and Jason were singing a fraternity song. Sheridan said he and Chub would drop off Seton at the hotel and then would follow them to Tony's. Yolanda stood in the driveway and watched the three cabs pull out. As the cabs got to the main street and started to turn, Ben looked back and saw her still standing there.

In Tony's they sat under fish net at a table in the pink light of the bar, and Walter decided he wanted to be elected to the

United States House of Representatives. Everybody agreed that it was a good idea.

"Course I'm not ready to run for it right now," Walter said. "Few more years. Good record down in Austin. Stay clean. No scandals. Always on the side of the right."

"The political right, you mean," said Harry. "As opposed to the political left."

"No, I mean the right-doers," Walter said. "As opposed to the evil-doers."

"Where do you plan to get your campaign funds then?" said Harry.

"S'problem," Walter said.

"Maybe Brother Chunk will take up a collection," said Harry.

"Say," Walter said. Then he thought it over. "No, I don't think Brother Chunk is going to like me."

"You're not backing prohibition?" said Ben.

"I don't know. I don't know what to do," Walter said. "Sheridan's supposed to help me out. Where *is* Sheridan?"

"Tucking Seton away," said Ben.

"You sure they got the name of this place?" Walter said.

"I told the cab driver," said Cadmus.

"Some of these guys aren't too smart. He could have misunderstood," Walter said.

"Want to go look for 'em?" said Cadmus.

"It'd be silly, I guess," Walter said. "The minute I got out the door they'd turn up. Then they'd have to go look for me."

"They'll be along," said Cadmus.

Jason fell out of his chair.

"Tricky," Jason said. "Thought the damn thing was going one way and it went the other way."

A waiter helped him up.

"Go see if I can find my banana," said Jason, stumbling off into the darkness toward the rear of the room.

"Will he last the night?" Pippa said.

"Jason? Why he's just getting warmed up," said Ben.

"His wife's going to be mad at him," Pippa said.

"That's a fact," said Cadmus.

A pair of large dark glasses poked around a bamboo screen near the door, and white teeth shone. Alonso Guzman stepped out from behind the screen and came to the table, walking jauntily in his green suit with the double rows of military buttons and the tight pants. He bowed to each of them and asked if he might sit down. Ben nodded, and the young Mexican sat down and crossed his legs and looked for a moment at his pointed Italian shoes.

—i am happy to see you again. i have been looking for you, Alonso Guzman said.

—did you write your column? Ben said.

—oh yes. it went very well. there were certain unanswered questions, but i avoided them. there are questions that have no right to be asked. most newspapermen are so insensitive as to ask them regardless. but not me.

—will you have a drink? Ben said.

—yes. thank you.

Ben called the waiter, and Alonso Guzman ordered a beer. His eyes lingered for a moment on Blossom before he looked back at Ben.

—as an example of the questions i mean, why is not mr. anderson in austin? is not the legislature in session?

—how did you know he is in the legislature?

—i learned it at the hotel. someone heard him talking in the bar to mr. sheridan.

—the texas legislature meets every other year. this is not a year for meeting.

—how can they accomplish their business if they only meet every two years?

—they can't.

The young Mexican picked up his beer, gestured to the table, and drank.

—a drink. that is the first thing you texans think of. i spent one weekend at the university of texas and have never quite recovered. when i arrived in the city with three other students from the university of mexico we were met by a delegation of student politicians and they took us immediately to a beer garden with checkered tablecloths. we drank very much. the music was very loud. next door there was a bowling alley with negro pin boys and the pins kept falling with much noise. i recall that someone climbed a tree. it might have been me.

—that does happen, Ben said.

—how i envy the gay lives you lead. free from economic repression. your primary national flaw is that you want too much to be liked. many people from other nations cannot understand generosity or wanting to be liked. they are suspicious of you. but they can understand your exploitation and they hate it. me, i understand that you are both good and bad but you are better than you are evil. i want to move to the united states and work for a big newspaper. i would like to live in austin.

—that big weekend must have got you, Ben said.

—it was with much pleasure. there was a football game with the university of the texas christians. maybe a hundred thousand people came to the stadium i think.

—maybe half that number, Ben said.

—maybe. but there were many people. the girls had flowers. there was a great pageant of marching orchestras and girls who turned flips. we wore paper sunshades on our heads. one of my friends fell down unconscious from the heat and the drink. he remembers texas with bitterness, but i think that may be because he hardly remembers it at all.

—there is much there to dislike, Ben said.

—and much to like, as anywhere else.

"Anythang more he wants to know about me?" said Cadmus.

Ben translated the question.

—ah, very much. but it will come out in time. i do not like to intrude myself. yet i do not like to seem either pompous or calculating. how does one manage that?

—it's a question i've never given much thought to, Ben said.

—how typically texas. you simply go right on as yourself and rely on your natural self without worry of protocol or decorum. i would like to be that way, but i have been raised to observe the formalities. i have been raised to use the impersonal forms of the pronoun. i must remark, if you will forgive me, that the one with the blonde hair is a most striking woman.

—there is nothing to be forgiven for. but do not allow the big gentleman to hear you say that.

—he would take offense?

—one cannot say for sure.

—he would take offense because i am a mexican.

—he might take offense because she is his woman, Ben said.

—but racism is never far from your minds.

—nor from yours, evidently.

—very true. that is a pity. now i must drink my beer and go home to sleep. i do not have the gigantic energy of the texans. the weekend i was in austin my anglo student friends never slept. here we realize the value of sleep and we realize that what is frantic cannot be relaxation, but certainly it is true that we do not get much done either.

—i thought no one slept during fiesta, Ben said.

—fiestas are for the primitive. more and more of us are becoming too sophisticated for fiestas.

—but people remain the same. you must accomplish the purpose of the fiesta somehow.

—but surely i am not that bound to fear of the dark mystery. i can enjoy spiritual orgasm in other ways, Alonso Guzman said.

He arose and bowed again to each person at the table.

—thank you for the beer. i will see you in the morning. let me remind you if there is business with the police you should call me at once. here is my card.

—i thank you, Ben said.

The young Mexican turned and swaggered toward the door through the pink light.

"A difficult time," said Ben.

"What do you mean?" Pippa said.

"The *angst* has got us all. Him as much as any of us," said Ben.

"How come you didn't translate all that stuff?" Walter Anderson said.

"It wasn't worth it," said Ben.

"I caught some of it," Doris said. "But my vocabulary wouldn't stretch around the entire conversation."

"That's because we need another drank," said Cadmus. "Hey hombre."

When Jason came back he had a red curtain tied around his neck like a cape. A waiter trailed him as if undecided whether to yank the cape away or ask him respectfully to return it.

"Ho!" Jason said. "So we sing as we are riding so!"

"So what?" said Walter.

"I'll think of it," Jason said, swirling his cape.

—he must give that back. it came off the window, the waiter said.

"Foe," said Jason. "He's Red Shadow's foe."

—we'll pay for it, Ben said.

—but the window is uncovered, the waiter said.

Ben gave the waiter five dollars.

—does it matter if people see in? Ben said.

—not to me, the waiter said.

"What're you doing?" said Jason. "Dealing with my foe? We got to draw up sides here. I hate sneaky deals behind the back. I hate 'em. Don't you hate 'em, Walter?"

"Sure do, Red Shadow," Walter said, laughing.

"Hate sneaky deals and sneaky people," said Jason. He tried to pull his cape around his shoulders but it was not quite large enough. He put his left elbow on the table and propped his chin on the back of his wrist. "Hate 'em. They're scums of the very earth. Can't sleep nights for hating 'em. I think I'll get drunk."

"You think you'll get drunk?" Doris said. "You've been drunk for two days."

"Haven't," said Jason. "Besides that dirty hot air blowing in my face in the cab sobered up. I want to get drunk and hate sneaky people. Me and Walter will hate 'em together. Waiter! Bring tequila for the Red Shadow!"

—the red shadow wants tequila please, Ben said.

—he is the red shadow? the waiter said.

—so he says, Ben said.

The waiter laughed.

"Dealing with my foe again," said Jason. "Making jokes behind my back. Sneaky deals, Walter."

"All the sudden I don't feel too good," Walter said.

Jason downed the shot glass of tequila, wiped his mouth on his forearm, and gestured to the waiter.

"Walter, you do look a little green," said Doris.

"I'm not used to drinking this much," Walter said. "It's almost four o'clock. I wish Chub and Bill would get here."

"I'm ready to go to bed," said Doris. "Will you take me to the hotel, Harry?"

"Grudgingly," Harry said.

"I'll go by myself then."

"I'll take you," said Harry.

"You can stay up if you want to," Doris said.

"I'll take you," said Walter. "I need to lie down."

Pippa squeezed Ben's knee under the table and looked at him. He nodded. Four of them got up. Ben took money out of his pocket, but Cadmus brushed it away. "My party," Cadmus said.

"You guys gonna hang around a while?" said Walter.

"Yeah. We'll wait and see if they show up," Cadmus said.

"We can walk back to the hotel," said Ben. "We might pass 'em on the way."

"You sure it's okay for me to stay?" Harry said.

"Honey, it's fiesta," said Doris. "People are supposed to do as they please."

Harry considered that.

"I guess I'll go with you," he said.

"Strike with a blow," said the Red Shadow.

Blossom's chin had begun to sink toward the table, and Cadmus sent her back to the hotel with the others. "Pore thang wore herself plumb out with all that sanging," he said. She gurgled and let Walter support her as they went through the door. Pippa and Ben went out last. They ducked around the bamboo screen and were gone.

"They look good together," said Cadmus. "Handsome-looking couple, ole Ben and Pippa."

"Riffs," the Red Shadow said.

"Who's that?"

"Riding, riding."

Cadmus reached into the inside pocket of his white sport coat and produced the photograph of Jason falling off the burro. He looked at the photograph and then at the Red Shadow who was scowling fiercely at the waiter. Cadmus grinned and licked the edges of his crooked teeth.

"*Hombre, pronto tequilas,*" said Cadmus.

A breeze came up from somewhere to blow dust through the streets of Boys Town. Scraps of cellophane from cigarette packages skittered along between the low stucco and adobe buildings, past the entrances to the bars and the cribs where whores leaned against wooden doorframes and waited, their bodies partly blocking views of rooms with pastel walls and of crucifixes hanging among taped-up nude photographs from *Playboy Magazine*. Even at this hour many people wandered the streets of Boys Town. From the bars came loud music and the stomping of feet doing the polka. Peddlers roamed with beads, scarves, unusual sexual gadgets. In one doorway stood two fat ladies yelling about the wonderful exhibition they would put on for ten dollars; they had stopped a group of young soldiers from across the border. In the dark alleys there were scurrying noises. The sky above Boys Town was black and clear.

A dog had been run over in the street in front of Lile's Club. The dog was whimpering when they passed it on the way in, but it was almost finished and Guthrie took them inside to a table at the back of the room. Their guide, a young policeman with a mustache and a tiny pistol that looked as if it squirted water, glanced at the dog without emotion as he held open the door for Guthrie, his wife, and Waddy and Beth Morris. Senator Rose had returned in a taxi to their hotel on the Texas side of the river.

"Really, Sam, there are some *nice* places in Mexico, even on the border," said Beth Morris.

"I think this is great," Waddy said.

"It's dreadful," said Jane Guthrie.

"At least it's better than that place Waddy wanted to go to, for God's sake," Beth Morris said. "Thank heaven Albert was with us."

Albert, the policeman, grinned and smoothed his mustache with the tips of his forefingers. He had turned his chair around and sat with his elbows on the backrest and his back to the wall.

"I have an idea the police aren't popular in this district," said Waddy.

Albert grinned again.

"Why was it you didn't want us to go to that bar, Albert?" Beth asked.

"Pachucos," said Albert. "Very *bod.*"

"Albert's scared of the Pachucos," Waddy said. "Those guys would carve him a smile where a smile doesn't belong."

Albert grinned and nodded.

Other than Guthrie's party there were eight or ten Mexican men in Lile's Club, and fifteen girls who hadn't yet quit work for the night. A few of the girls sat on steel frame chairs around the walls. The others were at tables with the men, or at the bar. The driver of the limousine Guthrie had hired sat at the bar so that he could keep watch on his car through the window. Guthrie leaned back in his chair, crossed his legs, and rubbed his stomach.

"Sam *likes* this place, for God's sake," said Beth.

"I like it," Waddy said.

"Certainly you'd like it, darling," said Beth. "It has whores."

"It does?" Waddy said. "Where?"

"I notice the men are watching you, Beth. They like blondes," said Guthrie.

"Well," Beth said. "Well, maybe we *should* stay here for a while."

Guthrie studied the interior of Lile's Club and the faces. The walls were a different color than he remembered, and the bar had been moved, and he recognized no one. The girls were too young, of course; hardly any of them had been born when he used to come here. The bartender was old enough, but he was a stranger. Guthrie had never known who owned Lile's Club. The only ones who might possibly have hung on from the old days were some of the maids. And that was doubtful. This was not the sort of atmosphere for loyalty or longevity.

"You act as if you've been here before," said Jane.

"When I was in the Air Force," Guthrie said.

"You didn't tell me," said Jane.

"It was before I knew you."

"Links with the past, huh, Sam?" Waddy said. "Can't go back to it unless you know what you're looking for."

"God, that was brilliant," said Beth.

"I think," Waddy said, "I might divorce you."

She laughed. "Oh darling *don't* let's fight again," she said.

"One thing people don't consider about having money," said Waddy, looking at Sam with pale eyes through his glasses, "is that having money makes it so hard to get a divorce. A guy who pumps gas at one of our stations can tell his wife okay, you can have the television set and the record player and the furniture, and I'll take my clothes and the car. And their community property is settled. If you or I wanted a divorce, Sam, we'd have to be in court for months and it would cost millions."

"You're leaving out the matter of heart, darling," Beth said.

"Yeah, I'm leaving that out," said Waddy.

Albert grinned and smoothed his mustache, as if he had never heard such conversation.

"*Do* get some of those girls over here," Beth said. "I'd like to talk to one. One thing I haven't done in my life is talk to a whore."

"Haw!" said Waddy.

"Now what does *that* mean, for God's sake?" Beth said.

Watching her husband, Jane Guthrie saw his dark face suddenly lift and his eyes widen. He reached for a cigarette, his fingers scrabbling on the table inches from the package. Turning, Jane saw who he was looking at: a young Mexican girl who had just come in, a girl with a plump face and black hair and several gold teeth. The girl went to the bar and sat on a stool. She looked curiously at the table of tourists and then shrugged as if giving up any thought of doing business with them. Guthrie's face had relaxed again, but he tore the package as he tried to get a cigarette out.

"Sam," said Jane.

He lit the cigarette.

"Sam," she said.

"Huh?"

"What's wrong?"

"Nothing. I'm tired. It's been a long day."

"We should call and check on Jake," she said.

"Damn it, quit pestering me about Jake. We'll call when we get to the hotel," he said.

Guthrie beckoned to the plump girl with the gold teeth. She looked at the bartender, looked at Albert, and then came to the table. She walked as if her feet hurt. She looked sullenly at Beth and Jane and sat down beside Guthrie. She tapped her fingernails on the table in time to the juke box music.

"What's your name?" Guthrie said.

The girl looked at Jane before she answered.

"Juanita," she said.

"Have you been here long?" said Guthrie.

"A month," she said.

"Is business good?" said Guthrie.

The girl looked at Jane, who was watching her husband.

"Yes," the girl said.

"How old are you?" said Guthrie.

"Safanteen," the girl said. She kept tapping her fingernails on the table.

"Where do you come from?" said Guthrie.

"Sonora. Leetle town," the girl said. "I get out."

"Is *this* what you want to do, for God's sake?" said Beth.

"I wark. I safe my mawny," the girl said. "Thane I go to Mexico Ceetee or Monteerey and get mawry."

"A lot of girls have that idea. Not many make it," said Guthrie.

"I try," the girl said.

"Here. For you," said Guthrie.

"What for?" the girl said, looking at the twenty-dollar bill he had given her.

"Just for you," said Guthrie.

"I dawn wawn it," she said.

"Take it," said Guthrie.

"What I hoff to do?" she said.

"Nothing," said Guthrie.

"You crazee. You no geeve mawny for nawthing. I dawn wawn it."

"You touched his heart," Waddy said.

The girl looked at Guthrie. She stuck the bill inside her sweater and tucked it into her brassiere. She pulled her sweater down so that Guthrie could see what she was doing; her flesh bunched and wrinkled around the stained brassiere. Then she laughed at Guthrie. She stood up, walked toward the bar, and stopped. She looked at Guthrie and blew him a kiss.

"Stoopeed," she said.

Albert began to rise, and the girl went out the door.

"I hope she uses that money to buy a brassiere that's big enough," said Beth.

"I don't think they make them that big," Waddy said.

"Why did you do that?" said Jane.

"I wanted to," Guthrie said.

"She didn't appreciate it very much," said Beth.

"No," Guthrie said, "she didn't."

"What did you expect?" said Waddy. "She's only a whore."

At Waddy's request, Albert brought three more girls to the table. The conversation was a failure. None of the girls could speak English except for a few words they would not say in the presence of the two women. Waddy suggested an exhibition. Albert translated. The girls refused. They did not do that sort of thing, they said. Waddy laughed. The girls were offended. One of them said something which Albert didn't translate. The three girls got up and went to a table and sat with two Mexican men. They talked to the men, who kept glancing back at the table and frowning.

"You've made them mad," said Beth. "It was a fairly awful suggestion."

"Merely an idea," Waddy said. "They were ugly."

"I wouldn't have watched," said Beth.

"Who cares?" Waddy said. "Sam, call the car. This isn't much fun."

"Albert, get the car," said Guthrie.

Everybody looked at them as they went to the bar. Guthrie paid the check. The men at the tables stared at the tall blonde woman. The car waited with the doors open in the shadow of the building. The dog had crawled almost to the edge of the sidewalk, but now it lay without moving. Light outlined the olive shades in the windows of two of Lile's rooms, and blotches of light lay on the driveway from a string of bulbs that hung between the club and the wing of rooms. Waddy, Beth, and Jane sat in the back seat. Guthrie pulled down the jump seat for himself. Albert got in beside the driver, banged the door shut, and the black car roared down the street raising dust.

"What I'm looking forward to is the bullfight," Waddy said. "They're supposed to have a movie star fight one of the bulls. It ought to be funny."

"Are we going to stay for the bullfight?" said Jane.

"Sure," Waddy said. "We couldn't miss that."

The black car left the adobes of Boys Town and went down a street of houses that were dark behind flowered walls. The nearer plaza on Avenida Guerrero was still bright with lights from the whitewashed palms. People wandered through the tents and along the sidewalks and around the bars. There were sounds like pistol shots, and much yelling and singing as the driver stopped before turning onto Avenida Guerrero. From one of the bars came two men: one very tall in a white sport coat and canary slacks, and the other, chin-high to the tall man, wore what appeared to be a red cape. The two staggered down the sidewalk toward Avenida Guerrero and paused to let the black car turn in front of them.

"I know that big guy," Waddy said. "His father owns Frontier Oil Company. Name's Wilkins."

"Who's the fool in the cape?" said Beth.

"Don't know," Waddy said. "Maybe he's here to fight the bools."

"In his condition he couldn't fight a tomcat," said Beth.

The tall blond man and the shorter man in the cape clutched each other at the corner as if the black car had almost hit them. Waddy laughed.

"Wave at him if you know him," Beth said.

"The hell with it," said Waddy.

"Sam, dear, you wave at him," Beth said, putting her hand on Guthrie's knee.

"Yes, dear, you wave," Jane said.

The car turned onto Avenida Guerrero and started toward the International Bridge with its horn blasting people out of the way.

"Too late," said Guthrie. "I didn't know him, anyway."

"Sam's not in the mood for waving," Waddy said. "Plenty to think about without waving at drunks, isn't there, Sam?"

"Enough to keep me occupied," said Guthrie.

"Sometimes I wish I'd been a matador," Waddy said, "with nothing to worry about except life and death and bulls. Bools."

Moonlight swam on the tile roofs, and the small courtyard with the doorless toilet was black in shadow. A warm breeze brought up odors from the alley and from across the rooftops: smells of laundry and manure and wine and dust. From somewhere among the dark passageways below, a cat yowled. Dogs barked. It was quiet again. Behind him Ben Carpenter heard hands patting the sheets and pillows, and then a tiny tinkling. "I've found it," Pippa said. "It was all tangled up." He turned away from the window and looked at her white body on the white of the bed. At this side of the hotel, opposite the plaza, there were no fiesta noises. Because of the breeze he had turned off the squeaking ceiling fan. Except for the occasional drip of the shower the room was silent now that she had quit crying.

"I knew it was here someplace," she said. She sat with her knees drawn up. Her elbows raised beside her black hair and pointed at him as she snapped the gold chain around her neck. "I didn't want to lose this. I bought it in Rome."

"I thought you were asleep," he said.

"I couldn't sleep," she said. "Not now."

"I wouldn't have got up if I'd known you were awake."

"You held me. All the time I was crying. I couldn't help crying."

"To tell you the truth," he said, "you scared me. I was afraid to let go. I couldn't be sure whether you loved me for what happened or hated me. You called me some terrible names, but you were acting like you wanted to swallow me."

"Come here," she said. "Come away from the window."

He stepped out of the lime patch of light on the linoleum floor and went over and lay on the bed. She put her knees down and lay on her side, facing him, supporting her head with her left hand, and put the fingers of her right hand on his stomach.

"I feel like I've got four flat tires," he said.

"So do I," she said. "But I feel grand. I could die now. Let me die now. While it's like this."

"That's crazy talk."

"No. You don't know. I could die. I love you."

She leaned over and kissed him.

"I have part of you now for as long as I live," she said. "No matter what happens. I'm overflowing."

Her head dropped back. Her long black hair spread out on the pillow and came down onto her shoulders. The gold locket lay between her breasts. Ben reached down to the floor until his fingers touched a package of cigarettes and his lighter. After he got two cigarettes lit, he gave her one.

"These are strong," she said.

"They're Delicados. After you smoke these a while they make all other cigarettes seem like breathing mountain air."

"They bite."

"I don't see how this could have happened to me," he said. "It shouldn't have happened this easily. Could I have loved Jean the way I thought I did and then suddenly forget her and love you?"

"Be careful what you're saying," she said.

"I thought that's what you wanted me to say."

"I don't know what I want," she said. "Be careful with me."

"You are absolutely the damnedest person I have ever known," he said. "A Catholic mystic who says she loves me and to prove it she tries to break my back, goes into a crying fit, and warns me not to love her. Maybe that's the attraction. You're never dull or predictable."

"This is dangerous," she said. "It's dangerous for both of us."

"I forever surrender trying to make any sense out of you."

"Just lie here with me while we have each other. Be sweet the way you were."

"Was it different than you thought it would be?"

"I didn't know what to expect."

"You yelled," he said. "It was almost like a yell of outrage. Like you didn't want it at all. Like you were fighting it and it crashed through and got you. I hate to say this, but you reminded me of a mortally wounded animal. Gut shot and really mad about it. A fierce hysterical anger, or even deeper than that, and you called me those terrible names, and then it overcame you and you called me those terrible names with love and started crying like you knew the happiness . . . and terror . . . of the whole world."

"You must have thought I was ugly."

"Not ugly. Beautiful. But it scared me, all right. I figured it would bring the house detective, too. I guess they don't have one. Will it be like that every time? If it is, I'm going to wear a football uniform when I go to bed with you."

"It wasn't a small thing to me," she said.

"I believe that," he said, grinning.

"Pretty soon it'll be time for early Mass," she said. "Will you go with me?"

"I'll go as far as the church door."

"But you won't go inside?"

"There's nothing for me inside."

She got up and walked around the bed, found the ash tray, and put out their cigarettes. The locket brushed against his chest as she climbed over him to get back to her place in the bed. She pushed the black hair out of her face. The whites of her eyes flicked light as she looked at him.

"Even if it's not always true," she said, "tell me you love me."

"I love you."

She kissed him. Her lips were dry and her flesh was feverish.

"There is such a thing, isn't there?" he said. "Or does it matter what you call it as long as it eases the loneliness."

She kissed him again, and he felt her tears on his face. They lay and waited for daylight.

"Tourists," said Cadmus Wilkins as the black limousine turned onto Avenida Guerrero and sped away through the double rows of parked cars toward the International Bridge. "You got to watch them tourists. They got no sympathy. No sympathy at all."

"Bite sword," the Red Shadow said, stumbling against the big man and holding on so that he wouldn't fall off the curb.

Cadmus looked both ways along Avenida Guerrero. The plaza was littered with bodies. They lay in every position: some face down on the concrete, some with heads and arms dangling off the benches, some with hands folded on their chests. They lay among bottles and papers and broken balloons. It was like the aftermath of a battle. A few of the lights in the palms had been burst by rocks or shots. The music had stopped. In the east there was a touch of gray. The air was warm and damp.

"What we need is some native fruits," said Cadmus. "We've come plumb off without any provisions, Red Shadow. Let's step into one of these here bars and get us provisions and then we'll wander the streets and give 'em the message."

"Saaang as we ridin soooo," Jason sang. "Bite sword. Hey bite sword everbody."

"You're kind of on edge about something, Red Shadow."

"Foes."

"Little native fruit will fix that up."

They went into a bar. The room was lit by the glow of the juke box and by two neon tubes above the mirror. Feet scuffed on the floor behind them and glasses clanked on the tables, but they could make out no one in the darkness. When they went in the voices stopped, then began to hiss, and finally someone laughed. The Red Shadow stared into the darkness. Mexican voices said things that neither Jason nor Cadmus understood.

"Bargain with these people," said Jason.

Two barmen watched Cadmus. He stepped up to the cash register, cleared his throat, and said, "We want some native fruit."

—i don't speak english, señor, one of the barmen said.

Several people laughed.

"I'll have to talk Meskin to this gentleman," said Cadmus.

"Can you?" said Jason.

"Certainly," Cadmus said. He cleared his throat again.

—do i want of wine? Cadmus said.

—that is quite possible, señor, the first barman said.

More people laughed.

—red or white? the other barman said.

Cadmus understood that.

—red. presents itself, Cadmus said.

—what? the other barman said.

—presents itself the wine, Cadmus said.

—you would like to see it? the first barman said.

—displays itself, Cadmus said.

—he wants the wine to do a dance, someone yelled. They all laughed.

"This ain't going too good," said Cadmus.

—the yankees think that's all we can do, someone said.

Chairs scraped against the wooden floor.

—throw them out, someone said.

—the one with the cape. make him cry.

—tourists.

—imperialists.

More chairs scraped against the floor, and now Cadmus could see people standing up in the darkness.

"This ain't going a bit good," Cadmus said.

"What're they mad at?" said Jason.

"Us."

"What for?"

"Because we're rich," Cadmus said.

"Who's rich? I'm not rich," said Jason.

"Down here you are."

"No, you're the one who's rich. We'll all gang up on you. Hey men we'll hang that rich Yankee."

"This ain't playing," Cadmus said.

"Oh," said Jason. The shadows moved closer. "I guess not."

—the wine please, Cadmus said.

One of the barmen put a bottle of red wine on the bar. Cadmus gave him fifty pesos. The man made no effort to make change or to ring up the sale. Cadmus picked up the wine bottle.

—are they going to walk out? someone said.

—we should have some pleasure with the anglos.

Cadmus found himself looking down at a dark stocky man in farmer's clothes. Around that man stood half a dozen others. They were muttering and urging each other forward.

"Look here," said Cadmus. "Magic."

Cadmus put down the wine bottle and picked up a bottle of beer from the bar. While the Mexicans watched he slipped the wet label off the bottle and stuck it on a flat side of his wallet. Holding the wallet in the palm of his hand, Cadmus suddenly threw it hard against the low ceiling. The wallet fell back, and he caught it. The beer label stayed pasted to the ceiling. The men looked up at it. Cadmus picked up the wine bottle, grabbed Jason's arm, and they walked quickly out the door.

On Avenida Guerrero Cadmus headed immediately toward two patrolling policemen and began to walk along behind them. Faces appeared in the door of the bar Cadmus and Jason had left, but none came outside.

"We'd do best to get a little distance from here," said Cadmus. "Those guys in the bar don't like the police more than they don't like us."

"Thought this was a *frinly* country," Jason said.

"It depends," said Cadmus, "on where you happen to go. Come on, Red Shadow. Ain't you happy I'm a wizard?"

They went down toward the hotel, turned beside the plaza, and hunted for an empty bench. Cadmus discovered one that had been pushed back against the trunk of a palm a few feet from the sidewalk. He brushed off two wine bottles. They sat down. Cadmus produced his pocket knife and laboriously dug the cork out of the bottle he had bought. He passed the bottle to Jason for the first swallow. Jason drank, spat out pieces of cork, nodded, and gave the bottle back to Cadmus.

"Good," said Jason.

Cadmus swallowed from the bottle. He sputtered and nudged Jason in the ribs, almost shoving the Red Shadow off the bench.

"Great God! Look! A giant bat!" Cadmus said.

A winged figure had stepped out from behind the palm tree. The figure was short and appeared to have one large ear. Two huge black wings hung down from either side. The figure stood silently in front of them.

"Hi bat," said Jason.

"Good morning," the bat said.

"Damn nice bat," said Jason.

"I'm gonna go to New Mexico and chase goats with Waldo," Cadmus said.

"How bout a drink of wine, bat?" said Jason.

"Thank you very much," the bat said. "I have my own cup."

"Very accommodating bat," said Jason.

The bat moved out of the shadow of the palm tree and into the light from the one covered lamp that still shone from the leaves.

"Aw," Jason said. "That ain't a bat."

"I thank I'm kind of glad," said Cadmus.

He was an old man with a floppy black beret and with two burlap bags that were slung from his shoulders by a rope that went behind his neck. He reached beneath his shirt, took out a tin cup, removed a spoon from the tin cup, put the spoon into his pocket, and held the cup out. Jason filled the cup with wine.

"Thank you very much," the old man said.

"You give us a start," said Cadmus.

"I am sorry," said the old man.

"What you got in them bags?" Cadmus said.

"Things," said the old man. He shrugged. "During fiesta I can find many things of use. Food, bottles, magazines, cigarettes. Even shoes and pants and shirts. During a fiesta, people forget about tomorrow, you see. They forget they might need these things. Observe."

Out of his left bag, the old man hauled a pair of leather high-heeled shoes.

"Very expensive," he said. "The poor girl might have saved for months to buy them. But during fiesta they become insignificant, she escapes from them, and I pick them up."

"You talk better English than Cadmus," said Jason.

"For many years I worked as valet to a wealthy man in San Antonio. Then I got old."

"Have some more wine," Jason said.

"Thank you very much."

"I sure am glad you ain't a bat," said Cadmus.

"So am I," the old man said.

"You could've been a bat. Crazy things happen in a fiesta," said Cadmus.

"It is a revolt, like making love. We explode to keep from exploding," the old man said. "All the same I am glad I am not a bat."

"More wine," said Jason.

"Thank you very much."

"I believe I'll vomit some blood," said Jason.

"Are you ill?" the old man said.

"No," said Jason.

"I can vomit more blood than you can," Cadmus said.

"I can vomit more blood than anybody," said Jason.

"Do it," Cadmus said.

"It might make me sick," said Jason.

The old man turned up his cup.

"More wine," Jason said.

"No thank you," said the old man. He polished the cup on his sleeve and returned it inside his shirt. "I must finish my work before the dawn. Thank you very much."

The old man moved into the shadow of the palm. They heard him walking through the grass and bottles, and then he was gone.

"You know what I thank?" Cadmus said.

"What's," said Jason.

"I thank he really is a bat."

At the hotel desk, Guthrie had two messages. One was the number of a long-distance call from Corpus Christi, and the other was a note that said: *"Phone me the moment you get in. Very important."* The note was signed with the initials of Senator Rose. Waddy, Beth, and Jane went up on the elevator while Guthrie was looking at the messages. By the time Guthrie reached his floor, Waddy and Beth had gone off to bed. The door to Guthrie's suite was open. Jane stood by one of the windows. She looked at the papers in his hand as he came in.

"News of Jacob?" she said.

"Probably," said Guthrie.

He phoned the Senator's room. Senator Rose answered as if he had not been asleep. He said he would come to Guthrie's suite. Guthrie hung up the phone and poured himself a drink. Jane kept watching him. "What is it?" she said.

"Damn it, I don't know yet."

"Quit using that tone of voice to me, Sam. That's how you spoke to me in that bar. I don't like it."

"All right," Guthrie said, frowning.

Senator Rose came in through the open door. He wore Japanese pajamas, a robe and slippers, and his white hair was neatly brushed. He accepted a drink from Guthrie, glanced at Jane as if he regretted having to be here, and then sat down on the couch. The Senator crossed his legs, and Guthrie looked at his thin white ankles.

"A call came just as I got back to the hotel," said Senator Rose. "I thought I'd better take it because there might be something I could do. I hope that wasn't too presumptuous."

Guthrie shrugged. Jane looked at the Senator and bit her lower lip.

"Regardless, I took the call," Senator Rose said. "It was from the hospital. Sometime tonight, or last night rather, Captain Iles got out of bed and managed to get himself partly dressed and left the hospital. No one saw him leave. They can't imagine how he did it unless he climbed out the window somewhere. But a man in his condition . . ."

"They couldn't hold Jake if he decided to leave," said Guthrie. He smiled. "I guess old Jake wanted to go home. We'll find him."

"That's not all the story, Sam," Senator Rose said. "They did find him."

"Oh," said Guthrie.

"They found him on North Beach in Corpus Christi," Senator Rose said. "He was lying at the edge of the water. He was dead."

"Oh," said Guthrie.

Jane gasped and began crying.

"What do you suppose he was trying to do?" the Senator said.

Guthrie shook his head. He sat down on a chair at the writing table and put his face in his hands. "Jake," he said finally. "Jake, no." After a moment he looked up. He went to the coffee table, poured two inches of scotch into his glass, and drank it. "Well," he said.

"I'll start packing," said Jane.

"What's the use?" Guthrie said. "Jake's dead, isn't he? I'll phone the hospital and the funeral home and have the arrangements made. I'll phone Marge."

"I'm going back this morning whether you go back or not," said his wife.

"For what? To sit in that trailer and bawl with Marge? Don't fool yourself. You and Marge really aren't friends. You really don't care about each other."

"She's a human being," Jane said.

"Then why haven't you been having her to your parties? Why haven't you invited her up to pal around with you at the country club? You and Marge don't have anything in common. We'll handle the expenses and say we're sorry. I *am* sorry. But there's nothing else we can do. I didn't kill him."

"Marge is human and she's in trouble," said Jane.

"We're being nice to her. We're helping her," Guthrie said. "But you and I are different than she is. Admit it. We don't reach her and she doesn't reach us. She wouldn't come around bawling if I cracked my head and died. She'd probably laugh herself sick. No, we're staying here right through the end of this trip."

"Sam, won't you let anybody have dignity?" said his wife.

"Not at my expense," Guthrie said. He looked at Senator Rose. "What do you think, Senator? Am I right?"

Senator Rose spread his hands and said nothing. Jane went into the bedroom and shut the door. The Senator stood up. "Good night, Sam," he said. "Let me know if I can do anything."

"Thanks," said Guthrie.

In the bedroom Guthrie undressed, put on his pajama shirt, and sat on the bed. Jane came out of the bathroom in her nightgown, looked at him, and walked toward the living room.

"Where are you going?" Guthrie said.

"I'm going to sleep in there on the couch," she said.

"What the hell for?"

"You said we were different than Marge. Maybe so. But I'm different than you, too, Sam. Damn right I am. We'll never be the same again. And I just don't feel like sleeping with you tonight. I may not ever feel like it again."

She snapped off the bedroom light and left him sitting in the yellow cone from the table lamp. Guthrie sat for a moment and looked at the door reflected in the dark window. He could hear the commode gurgling. Then he walked into the living room. Jane lay on the couch on her back with her eyes open. He bent over her small dark body. She smelled of cold cream.

"Baby," he said.

"Go away, Sam."

"At least, you sleep in the bed," he said. "I'll sleep out here."

"Don't bother being gallant. I'm comfortable."

"You may as well use the bed. I have to make some phone calls, and I'd rather make 'em in here where I can take notes."

"Why didn't you put it on a practical basis in the first place?" she said. "That's what we both understand, isn't it?"

She got up from the couch, pushed his hand away, and went into the bedroom.

"Good night," he said.

"A friend of yours is dead, Sam," she said. "Why don't you cry?"

"I can't," said Guthrie.

She closed the door.

Guthrie placed calls to the hospital and to the funeral home. He couldn't find Marge. She was evidently between the funeral home and the trailer. He left word for her, and he called his house and told Roger to take Marge and the children up to Agua Verda. Guthrie said he would be there Sunday night. The plane could drop off Guthrie and Jane, and fly Waddy, Beth, and the Senator on to Dallas. Guthrie had ordered the funeral for early Monday morning. He could be back in Dallas by noon. His mind skipped past the funeral. He began to think of the things he would have to do in Dallas once A. C. Johnson gave in, the ends that would need tidying up, the conferences with his executives and attorneys and with the executives and attorneys of Ramco. He smiled at that. He would enjoy very much seeing young Carpenter's face. Then there would be conferences with Waddy and with Waddy's executives and attorneys. The arrangements would be involved and shrewd. Guthrie would need to concentrate. He would need to think out all that was happening.

Suddenly he stood up. He walked to a window and looked down at the empty street. Across the block and three floors below, a Mexican boy came around the corner with an armload of newspapers. The boy went along the sidewalk in the slowly dawning light, stopping to look into store windows and to shift his bundle of newspapers from one arm to the other. Guthrie watched until the boy was out of sight, and then the street was empty again.

The church was built of mud brick and painted white. They had walked several blocks from the hotel, asking directions until they fell in with a group of Mexicans who were also going to Mass. Some of the old women walked briskly and clutched their prayer books. But most of the people walked with an effort, dragging themselves toward the church, their heads aching and dazed with wine. It was Pippa who first saw the steeple and cross of the church rising above the neighboring shops and houses against the gray sky. Their heels clicked on the concrete sidewalk. The early morning had an odd smell of dust and wet grass. Then they came to the white church on the corner. The shadow of the church spread across the street. The Mexicans pushed open the iron gate of the fence that protected the grass in front of the church. The bells began ringing, and Ben looked up at the steeple. A few of the Mexicans also looked up. The cross on top of the steeple was large and looked like brass.

Holding his hand, Pippa took him down the wide walkway and up the church steps. She had covered her head with a scarf. She still wore the white cocktail dress and white high-heeled shoes, and her long black hair hung down from beneath the scarf.

"You look nervous," Ben said.

"Won't you come in?" she said.

"I'll wait out here."

"It won't take long," she said. "Please wait."

"Sure I'll wait. I wouldn't walk all the way down here and then not wait."

The wooden doors were open. She smiled quickly at him and then looked inside and turned away from him. He watched her dip her fingers into the holy water and cross herself. She knelt on a low bench at the rear of the church with her back to him, and she bowed her head. Through a stained-glass window sunlight came gold on the altar. Dust moved in the sunlight. The benches were filling up, and people jostled Ben in the doorway. Ben looked once more at Pippa's back with the black hair hanging down against the white dress, and at the soles of her shoes, and then he walked down the steps and went to the corner and leaned against the black iron fence and smoked a cigarette. Jean, he said to himself, goodbye Jean.

After a while people began coming out of the church. It was light now and had already begun to get hot. The smell of wet grass had burned away. The shops along the street had shutters or iron grills bolted over their doors and windows. The sidewalks were scattered with paper, bottles, and scraps of food. There were a lot of dogs on the street. Pippa came out of the church. She looked for him anxiously until she saw him and then she ran toward him. He met her at the gate. She put her arms around him. The Mexicans looked at them as they went past. Pippa raised her face, and there were tears on her cheeks and in her dark eyes.

"Oh Ben," she said, "I love you too much. God help me, I love you too much."

He smiled and kissed her cheeks and tasted salt, and they walked back to the hotel. She kept looking at him and squeezing his arm as if afraid he might go away. They went through the dim cool lobby of the Gran Hotel Reforma. The desk clerk slept with his head on the counter. Through the doorway of the bar they saw Cadmus and Jason sitting at a table. Cadmus was talking, the bartender was listening, and Jason, in his red cape, was knocking beer bottles together and singing. Ben and Pippa went up on the elevator to the third floor. He took her to the door of her room. "I love you," she said.

"You're a funny one," he said.

"When will I see you?"

"Let's sleep three or four hours. I'll call you."

"Do you love me?" she said.

"Yes."

"Say it," she said. "Tell me again."

"I love you."

She wiped her eyes with the scarf and looked steadily at him.

"Don't go," she said.

"I'm just going to my room to shower and sleep for a bit. You do the same. We need it. I'll see you in a few hours."

He kissed her on the eyes and then turned and walked down the quiet hall. When he got to the corner, he heard her key in the lock.

Ben sat on his lumpy bed, too tired to take off his clothes. The shouts of children came up from below in the courtyard with the doorless toilet. He looked at the ceiling fan, sighed, and forced himself to get up and turn it on. The blades began squeaking but they didn't seem to disturb the thick hot air in the room. Ben undid the top three buttons of his shirt. He looked at the bed. He was about to go to it and fall down when the phone rang.

He started to let the phone ring because he thought it was Cadmus who had seen him come in and would insist on having him come down to the bar. The phone continued to ring. Ben answered it. This was once when he would refuse Cadmus. He was dazed as he listened to the voice on the telephone; it had been so long since he had arrived at the birthday party, and they had done so much. He wanted to sleep. Then through the heaviness of his senses he began to realize that it wasn't Cadmus he was saying no to.

"You can't say no," the voice said. "You've got to come. I need you. I don't know who else to talk to."

"Walter?"

"Yeah, sure, Walter. Listen, are you drunk or what? Please, I need to talk to you."

The voice didn't sound like Walter's. It was a strained voice, rasping and broken.

"What room are you in?" Ben said.

"Two-oh-eight, my playing weight," the voice said. The voice made a peculiar noise that was something like a laugh. "Please come."

Ben put down the telephone, walked into the bathroom, blinked at himself in the mirror, and then washed his face in the tepid water from the cold tap. He tried to keep from thinking about what he would find in Walter's room, but somehow he already knew. Ben was cursing as he walked down the stairs to the second floor.

"Door's not locked," the voice said after Ben knocked.

As Ben pushed open the door he saw Walter sitting on the bed. Walter wore a pair of white cotton shorts. He was starting to get fat but his body still had a look of power, as if he could make two or three yards regardless what they did to him. His flesh was pink from the shower. A wet towel hung on the iron frame of the bed. He looked up at Ben with red eyes. There was a tray on the table beside the bed with a pot of coffee and two cups. Walter squeezed a can of tomato juice between his hands.

"Coffee hot?" Ben said.

Walter nodded.

Ben stepped around a pair of Chub's shoes, went to the table, and poured a cup of black coffee. On the floor beside the table lay the white shirt Walter had worn the night before. There was blood on the shirt.

"Well?" said Ben.

"Christ, I don't know what to do," Walter said in the rough cracked voice Ben had heard over the telephone. "I've been thinking about it and I don't know what to do. I hate to get you into this, Ben, but I've got to talk to somebody. To *some*body. I don't know who else to talk to."

"Where were they?" said Ben.

The red eyes glared angrily at him and then softened again.

"When I came back to the hotel Chub wasn't here," he said. "I called Sheridan's room and nobody answered. I figured they'd got lost or something, you know? So I took off my clothes and lay down. And then it hit me. Clear as it could be. I don't know where the idea came from. I'd never thought anything like that. But all the sudden I *knew*."

Walter drank from the can of tomato juice. A red dribble edged down from the corner of his mouth, and he wiped it off.

"I called Seton's room," Walter said hoarsely. "Seton was asleep. He said yeah they'd come back to the hotel with him. I was like a maniac, Ben. I went down to the desk and got a key to Sheridan's room. His room's just down the hall from mine. I went up and let myself into his room. And there they were."

Walter winced at the memory. His hands trembled as he looked at the can of tomato juice.

"I beat him up pretty bad. Wasn't really much of a fight. Poor son of a bitch just woke up, you understand, and must have had a hell of a headache. And here he was being hauled naked out of the bed before he could even remember where he was and getting hit in the teeth. I knocked him down a couple of times and would have kicked in his skull except I was in my stocking feet. I'd taken my shoes off to be quiet. He finally realized who I was and what it was all about, and he tried to fight. But I was mad and he didn't have a chance. Ever time I swung I hit him solid. He's sort of flabby, got a little paunch and little fat tits and a white flabby ass. I finally quit beating on him and just let him lie there."

"How much did you hurt him?" said Ben.

"I don't know. I don't care about that bastard. I want you to find Chub. I love her, Ben. I hadn't thought much about it one way or the other for years. But I've been thinking about it this morning. I want her back."

"*Find* her?" Ben said. "Where'd she go?"

"She couldn't have gone far," Walter said with an effort at a grin. "She didn't have on any clothes when she ran out the door."

"I'll try," said Ben.

"I want her back. I've given her a bad time. I want to make it up to her."

Ben phoned the desk and asked the number of Blossom's room. He nodded. "I'll be back in a minute," he said.

"Why would Chub do it?" said Walter.

"What about your pal, Sheridan?" Ben said.

"I should have known that son of a bitch was no good," said Walter. "After the way he treated Pippa this winter."

Ben stopped at the door and turned around.

"What about Pippa?" Ben said.

"I don't guess you heard about it," said Walter.

"What about Pippa?" Ben said.

The red eyes turned away.

"Not many people in Austin even knew it," said Walter. "But Pippa worked for Sheridan in his office for a while. I got her the job. He knocked her up and then wouldn't have anything to do with her. She went to Houston and had it fixed. She got real sick. It was a dirty shame."

Walking blindly, trying to put Walter's voice out of his mind, Ben found Blossom's room. He rapped on the door. "It's Ben," he said. "I want to talk to Chub."

Blossom peeked around the edge of the door, showing a naked shoulder. She smiled. Her hair looked like trampled snow. Chub stood in a corner of the room. She looked frightened. She was pulling Blossom's dressing gown around her.

"Chub," Ben said. "Let's go home."

"Did Walter send you?" she said.

"He wants you back. Damned if I know why, but he does. Come on."

Blossom patted Chub sweetly on the shoulder as Chub went out. Together, Chub and Ben walked down the hall. Chub seemed like a child in her fear and her bare feet with Blossom's gown dragging the floor. The gown made a swishing noise.

"How could you be so stupid?" Ben said.

"We'd been drinking. We went to sleep," she said.

"I don't mean that."

"Ben, what did he say? What did he say about me?"

"He loves you."

"Thank God."

"You sound like it matters."

"Of course it matters."

"If it matters, then why did you do what you did?"

Chub paused beside the door and looked up at Ben. Her fingers held the gown tightly around her.

"Ben," she said, "I think I've wanted him to catch me. I've wanted to get it all over with and take my punishment. I'll be good to him. You'll see."

"What about Jason?"

"Not now," she said. "Not now, please."

Cadmus and the Red Shadow were sitting in the bar when William Sheridan came into the lobby carrying a suitcase. Sheridan's face looked purplish and swollen, and he dabbed at his mouth with a handkerchief that had red blotches on it. His black hair with its handsome streaks of gray glistened with water. He seemed to have difficulty walking. His black glasses turned once toward the door of the bar, but there was no indication that he recognized the two men who were looking at him. A bruise neatly covered the dimple on his chin. He had brief conversation with the desk clerk, produced a handful of money, snatched up his suitcase, and limped out of the lobby into the white light of Sunday morning.

"Looks like the Good Ship Lollipop has lost a passenger," said Cadmus.

Jason put down the two beer bottles that he had been clinking together. He squinted toward the front window as Sheridan went past, but the sunlight was too bright for him to focus.

"Wuz that ole Shurdin?" Jason said.

"Yep. Appears to be heading home."

"Ole Shurdin sure could play guitar," said Jason. "Me, I'm in th' rhythm section. I play bottles."

He clinked the bottles together. The bartender yawned, examined his dark glasses, and polished dust off the lenses. Cadmus and Jason each took two more of the green pills from Cadmus's supply. They ordered two more beers. Jason slumped forward until his chin was six inches above the tablecloth. Jason's cheeks and chin were dark with whiskers. Cadmus scratched his own blond, almost invisible beard, and permitted himself to yawn. The bartender yawned again. Cadmus yawned. Jason yawned.

"This ain't no good," Cadmus said. "Let's go hire a orchestra."

"I miss my little girls," said Jason.

"Cheer up, Red Shadow. You're the spiritual leader of your people. You can't get down."

"I miss my little girls. I'm scum of the very earth," Jason said. "Poor ole Willy. Poor little girls. Poor Red Shadow."

"What you need is a shave and some good music."

"I need my little girls. Mah darters."

"You're at cross purposes, aint you, Red Shadow?"

"He made us human."

"What?"

"He made us human," said Jason. "Can I help it?"

"Guess not."

"Bite my sword all you scummies."

"Sometimes I don't know quite what to say to you, Red Shadow."

"I'll go into their damn tents and chop 'em up."

Cadmus sprinkled salt into his beer glass. The bartender switched on a transistor radio, moved the dial back and forth, and then switched it off. The front half of the room was aflame with sun.

The bartender came around the bar, edged past the pillar that Jason hugged with one arm, and pulled shut the drapes.

"You know what?" said Jason. "I don't even *like* Chub Annerson."

"Aw, now, Red Shadow, have some charity."

Cadmus heard footsteps in the lobby and then Ben came into the bar. Ben sat down at the table. His face was thin and pale. He ordered a cup of coffee and a bottle of mineral water, and he sat quietly as if absorbed in some personal problem. Jason kept saying that he missed his little darters. Cadmus sipped his beer and watched Ben. Finally Ben raised his eyes and looked at Cadmus.

"Son, you don't look like you had enough rest," Cadmus said.

"How do you keep from getting run over?" said Ben.

"Me myself?"

"Everbody."

"You don't," Cadmus said. "Everthang I've learned I learned because I didn't know how to duck. Always got hit square. That's part of it. You don't want to keep from getting run over, or you'll miss a lot. And let me give you a little tip. It don't ever quit hurting and you don't ever get used to it, but you get bigger and go long with it. Takes guts to live, and a lot more guts to be happy."

Ben drank his mineral water.

"I believe," said Ben, "I'm tired enough that I can go to sleep and not think about a thing. Getting tired enough is a good purgative."

"Except you got to wake up sooner or later," Cadmus said. "Until you're dead. I figure on getting a lot of sleep after I'm dead."

When they heard the elevator door shut and the old machinery rattle and clank as it lifted Ben toward the third floor, Cadmus got up and helped Jason to his feet.

"Come on, Red Shadow," said Cadmus. "We gonna go get a barber out of bed and get shaved and hire a orchestra so we can all dance our way to the bullfights. I don't see why folks get downhearted. This here is a fiesta. We got to have gaiety and carryings-on of that nature."

When Sam Guthrie entered suite 508–10 of the Cactus Inn, the bellhop had just lifted the aluminum covers from the breakfast plates Waddy Morris had ordered. The plates had been laid out on a table by a window. The waiter took the aluminum covers back to his pushcart and returned to the table with two glasses of orange juice and two white linen napkins. Waddy, wearing a pair of blue shorts, stood beside the table and blew on a cup of coffee. He glanced at Guthrie, who yawned and shook his head.

"Too early for you?" said Waddy.

"I always get up early," Guthrie said.

"Me too," said Waddy. "Never have been able to sleep past six. There's too much to do." He nodded toward the bedroom door. "Beth is always up by at least noon, unless she's been out late the night before. That's how it is with those damned aristocrats. Hell, when I was twelve years old I used to throw *The Dallas Morning News*. Had my papers on the porches by five A.M. Neither rain nor sleet nor cold nor all that crap could screw up my appointed rounds. Sleep is a drug. It's a bad habit. Nobody needs to sleep more than four or five hours at a time."

"I didn't quite get that much," Guthrie said.

"You couldn't have. What time did we get back to the hotel? Three? Four?"

"I didn't notice."

"Have a Bloody Mary."

"Coffee's all I want."

The waiter poured Guthrie a cup of coffee and then wheeled his cart out of the room.

Guthrie sat down at the table, rubbed his eyes, and yawned again.

"Remember my skipper? Iles?" said Guthrie.

"Yeah. He got beaten up."

"He's dead," Guthrie said.

"Well," said Waddy. He sipped his coffee, put the cup down on the table, and looked at Guthrie. "Tough luck."

"He got out of the hospital last night somehow and went roaming around and died."

"Silly stunt. What did he do that for?"

"I don't know. We're gonna bury him tomorrow at Port Agness."

"We'll have all this business cleared up by then," Waddy said. He sat down and crossed his legs and peered at a scattering of tiny red bumps on his ankles. "Where the hell could I have got these chiggers? They drive me nutty. I scratch them and they get scabs and stay all summer. But I can't help scratching them."

Waddy looked at the scrambled eggs and ham on his plate as if wondering what he was supposed to do with them. He sprinkled salt and pepper on the eggs, buttered a slice of toast, dropped the toast on his plate, and shoved the plate away. He sat for a moment in quiet debate as he drank his coffee. Then he pulled the plate to him again, cut off one bite of egg and one bite of ham with his fork, chewed solemnly, and shoved away the plate. He picked up the glass coffeepot which was keeping warm above a candle and refilled his cup.

"Wonder how much sleep Acey Johnson got?" Waddy said, and grinned.

"About as much as Simmons."

"No, I don't think I scared Simmons. I think he's past that."

"Because of Carpenter."

"You keep bringing up that name," said Waddy. "Forget him. Why do you let him bother you?"

"He's a pain in the ass."

"He's only done his job," Waddy said. "Or has he done something else?"

"I don't like the way he acts toward me. He acts like he's my judge."

"Sam, somewhere in this life you must have run into people who didn't like you. I've run into a few who didn't like me," Waddy said. "I've heard some of the things that have been said about me. Some of the bad things. So the hell what? They don't matter to me. They can't hurt me. That's one reason why they talk about me. They watch for any mistake I make. If I pick up the wrong fork at dinner, they say I have unspeakable manners. If I buy a big new Cadillac, they say I'm ostentatious. If I buy a new Chevrolet, they say I'm phony or cheap. If I wear a five hundred dollar suit that was tailored in London, I'm nouveau riche. If I wear a forty dollar suit from a department store rack, I'm a hillbilly. If I give a lot of money to one of their charities, it's a tax dodge. If I don't, I'm tight. So who cares what anybody thinks? I don't need a thousand consciences talking to me about myself, or even one conscience other than my own. I run my life my way as far as I'm able, and the hell with those judges who condemn me every day. They can condemn me all they want, but they sure better go along with me."

"I try to be that way, but sometimes they get to me," said Guthrie.

Waddy yawned.

"You've got me doing it," Waddy said. He looked at the bright dirty window. "No use putting this off. I might as well call Acey Johnson and see if he wants me to be unpleasant."

Guthrie had been sitting with his eyes shut and his face soft, as though drained by weariness and opposing demands on his emotions. He opened his eyes and saw Waddy smiling across the table at him.

"How are you going to get Johnson?" said Guthrie.

"How much do you know about bringing in a gas field?"

"Not much."

"Acey has just finished defining a field of ten gas wells on a four-thousand acre lease in East Texas," Waddy said. "He's in deep. He had to put together seven leases, and there was a lot of work in it. He borrowed two and a half million dollars to finance drilling those ten wells. He had to put up the rights to that property and an office building he owns and a bunch of producing oil wells to get the money from the First National Bank. If anything goes wrong with that gas field, the bank will have to take him over. Acey will be in very bad shape."

"What could go wrong with the field? Isn't it proved?" said Guthrie.

"Sure, it's proved. The structures are sound, the wells are drilled, he has a reserve of about twenty-five billion cubic feet of gas. But he doesn't have a gas contract yet, because he doesn't have a pipeline. The closest pipeline to his field is owned by Mortex, and it's ten miles away. Mortex is operated by a holding company called the Woodrow Corporation. Who do you think runs the Woodrow Corporation?"

"I know that. You and your father."

"That's it," Waddy said. "Acey has understood that Mortex is going to run a lateral line over his field. We require about a billion cubic feet of reserve per mile, and he had plenty of reserve to make it worth our while to go ten miles. Besides, we're old friends. But the next closest pipeline is thirty-eight miles away. They won't come to him. He could try to sell them a piece of his field to make them come, but there's not much demand for gas right now. The supply's abundant. And Acey has a short-term loan. If Mortex decides not to run that lateral line to his field, poor Acey."

"But how could you justify not running the lateral line to him if it would pay off?"

"I really don't have to justify it," said Waddy. "Anyhow, I told you the gas supply is plentiful. Mortex doesn't need Acey Johnson. If he won't play with me on this proxy fight, I won't let him play with my pipeline."

Waddy smeared strawberry preserves onto a slice of toast and took a bite. A bit of strawberry clung to his lower lip as he talked.

"I'll give Acey a choice," Waddy said. "He can either join us, or sell me his Ramco stock. Or dig up two and a half million dollars to pay the bank and then be left sitting there with ten useless gas wells spotted around on three hundred and twenty acre plots of a useless four-thousand-acre lease."

Waddy licked the strawberry preserves off his lower lip.

"How important do you think his friendship, or obligation, or gratitude to Simmons will be when Acey is looking at ruin?" said Waddy. "Not important enough, Sam. Acey won't like it, but there's nothing he can do except play with us. I don't especially enjoy doing it to him. If we cold win without Acey, I wouldn't do it. We've played plenty of golf together, and gone skin-diving together, and gone hunting together in Alaska. But this is a different kind of game. I refuse to lose it."

Waddy twisted around in his chair to reach for the telephone. Then he looked back at Guthrie and his eyes were pale and cheerless as clear gumdrops.

"I don't like to lose anything ever, Sam," he said.

Waddy picked up the telephone.

"Operator," he said, "I'd like to place a call to Dallas, please."

It required four taxicabs to transport them to the bullring late that afternoon because one cab was occupied by what Cadmus called his orchestra. Cadmus and Jason had spent most of the morning being shaved and massaged before returning to the hotel for clean clothes. In the hotel bar they were joined about two P.M. by Harry, Doris, and Blossom, and then shortly afterward by Walter, Chub, and Pippa. Walter and Chub were holding hands, a fact which seemed to puzzle Jason. The massage and shave had sobered up Jason to the point that he could walk and talk, but as he stared at Walter and Chub and at their interlaced fingers and their passionate glances at each other, Jason began drinking tequila sours as if he hardly knew what they were. And by the time Ben came down, a little before three, Jason had put on his red cape again and was desperately drunk and was threatening that people would bite his sword.

Ben sat down beside Pippa and ordered a beer. He had tried to phone Simmons, had received no answer, and now, seeing Pippa, he was afraid he might start to shake again. Pippa had put on a yellow dress with bare shoulders and back. The dress had white figures on it, and she wore white costume jewelry. She put her hand on the sleeve of Ben's blue linen sport coat, and he didn't look at her. Seton was the last to enter. He had doused himself with cologne and hair tonic and shaving lotion. He sat down at the end of the table near Pippa, crossed his legs, and let his right shoe dangle as he swung his foot back and forth.

"I am starving to death," Seton said. "I've been lying in my room listening to a serenade from my stomach. Across the river the country is fat with chocolate candy and cold sweet milk, but you've dragged me to the wrong side of the bridge with your mad ideas. If I don't get some decent food by midnight, I'll die. It's come to that, Cadmus. Your foolish trip has caused my death. My blood is on your conscience."

"It rides easy," said Cadmus. "What would you say if I told you I'm having 'em whip up a great huge monster of a tuna-fish salad with boiled eggs and pickles in it?"

"I wouldn't believe you," Seton said.

"That's what they're doing," said Cadmus.

"It's poison. You're giving me poisoned Mexican tuna fish."

"I ain't. We had some tuna fish in the bus. I got Damon to fetch it this morning and turn it over to the chef. Very famous chef. Name's Pedro or José or something," Cadmus said. "In a minute they're gonna serve you a big huge monster tuna-fish salad and a chocolate cake and a gallon of cold milk. Now what do you think?"

"Is he lying to me?" Seton asked.

Pippa, who had been looking at Ben, turned toward her brother. "I don't think so," she said. "I heard him telling them about it earlier."

Seton's gray face lost some of its sharpness. "Cadmus, you're only half wicked," said Seton.

"Shake my hand, friend," Cadmus said.

Seton looked at the large extended palm, and Cadmus laughed. Cadmus withdrew the hand and placed it on Blossom's shoulder.

She wiggled up against him and smiled delightedly around the table.

"Much as I dislike the idea, somebody ought to call Sherdian and get him up," said Harry.

"Sheridan took off," Cadmus said. "He came down early this morning and said he had some urgent business with Brother Chunk and he went on home. Told me he sure did hate to leave the Good Ship Lollipop and its frolicsome crew, but he ain't a guy to put pleasure before business."

No one spoke. Looking at his bottle of Dos Xeches, Ben wondered how many of them knew, or could guess, the reason for Sheridan's departure. None could possibly know the real reason except Ben, Walter, and Chub, and perhaps Blossom if Chub had explained why she had come naked to Blossom's door or if Blossom had connected the events. Ben glanced at Blossom, whose smile never flickered; it was impossible to tell what went on behind that bright empty face. Ben thought he felt Pippa's fingers tighten on his sleeve. And still no one spoke. He began to feel uncomfortable for Walter and Chub. But yet if the secret had somehow got out, if it had been guessed so easily, then how many of them had known about Sheridan and Pippa? Maybe nobody had known it except Walter who was keeping it quiet for his friend, Sheridan. Surely if any of them had known, Ben would have heard about it. Gossip traveled so quickly among his friends, and the circles of their friends, and the circles beyond that, so quickly and widely that often Ben knew embarrassing and intimate things about people he had hardly met. How much did it matter, he wondered, whether they knew about Sheridan and Pippa, or Sheridan and Chub? Most of them knew about Chub and Jason, and it didn't seem to make any difference; they thought little the less of Chub and Jason for their sins and none less of Walter for his cuckoldry. There wasn't much more damage that could be done. They all knew such dreadful things about each other. But how much did it matter to Ben if they knew the truth about Pippa's illness, and how much did it matter that *he* knew? Why should it matter? He had been lied to before. Certainly he should not have expected anything other than a lie; he should have recognized her, perhaps, as merely a symptom of his own illness; but the fact was that he had expected more. A few hours ago he was telling her he loved her, and now he wouldn't look at her. Instead he watched his fingernails against the brown bottle, and was aware that Pippa was very alive and anxious beside him, and he felt the tensions of each person at the table, and waited for someone to speak.

"We don't need Sheridan," Walter said finally. "We can have a good time without him."

"My opinion exactly," said Harry. "Here comes the tuna fish."

Three waiters marched in line to Seton's chair. The first put down a bowl piled high with tuna-fish salad, the second put down a chocolate cake, and the third put down a frosted pitcher of milk and a glass. Seton looked at the tuna fish, the cake, and the milk, looked at Cadmus as if about to gush with joyous tears, and then looked at the waiters who were smiling proudly at him.

"Where," Seton said, "are the goddamn crackers?"

"Hey, Ben, look at this here thang and tell us what it says," said Cadmus. "It's the newspaper that Meskin fella works for. I picked out our names in his column but I can't make out exactly how grand he's wrote it."

Cadmus passed Ben the newspaper which had been folded open to Alonso Guzman's column, the title of which Ben translated loosely as Chit Chat with Alonso. There was a smudged photograph of the young Mexican wearing his dark glasses.

"Don't sound very literary to me," said Cadmus.

"He lists all of our names and Wilma Rudolph as having registered at the Gran Hotel Reforma for the fiesta," Ben said. "Then here's what he says: 'Mr. Wilkins is the fabulously rich West Texas oilman from the booming West Texas city of New Hope where we have it on the best sources oil is flowing in the streets.'"

"He ain't checked that with my partner," said Cadmus.

"'Mr. Wilkins brought his guests to Nuevo Laredo in a fabulous bus that even has a television set. He is personally accompanied by the most fabulously beautiful blonde lady that these young eyes have ever feasted upon. Could be it romance?'"

"Hell, it's always romance," said Cadmus. "I thought all Meskins knew that."

"'Our distinguished visitors, including one of Texas's leading politicians, Rep. Anderson, plan to attend the corrida on Sunday to see movie star Pepe Romano fight a bull. Mr. Carpenter, a Dallas businessman who speaks excellent Spanish, is accompanied by his fiancée Miss Seton. They are all the kind of wild gay lovable Texans that your faithful correspondent met when he spent a weekend in the capitol city of Texas, Austin, and was treated to many a round of parties.

"'Also visiting this weekend but staying on the Texas side are the wealthy Mr. and Mrs. Woodrow Morris Jr. and Mr. and Mrs. Sam Guthrie, with the distinguished Senator Bertram Rose from Washington, D.C. We have it on the very best sources that Mr. Morris, of Dallas, is about to put across an oil deal in Southern Mexico that may make him as rich as Mr. Wilkins.'"

"Guthrie?" Harry said. "Guthrie's here?"

"I'd heard he was," said Ben.

"Let's go find him," Harry said.

"You don't handle business matters by poking folks in the nose," Cadmus said. "And I'm talking with authority as a guy who Waddy Morris might someday be as rich as. Except sometimes, of course, it does a body good to poke a fellow in the nose. It ain't exactly dignified, but it's therapy. How's that tuna fish, Seton?"

"Passable," said Seton.

"For Seton that was falling down gratitude," Cadmus said. "Floods my fabulously wealthy ole heart to hear it. How bout you, Pippa? You look like something's bothering you. We can't have that. Gotta have everbody happy."

"Everybody can't wade through things as capriciously as you can," said Pippa.

"Aw, honey pot, capricious ain't the right word," Cadmus said. "Thangs I can do something about, I do. Thangs I can't, I wish I could. But anyhow I'm setting here on this earth and can't nothing get bad enough to make me want it any other way. If it does, then I won't set here no more."

"You don't feel things deeply," said Pippa.

"What you mean is I don't get up and announce it," Cadmus said. "Inside this here massive chest, underneath this here baby pink skin, is a soul big as all humanity. Gentle and loving and . . . what else is it, Blossom?"

"Damn good," said Blossom.

"That's what I was trying to think of. Blossom, she's got a hell of a vocabulary."

"You must be terribly insecure to brag about your goodness like that," said Pippa.

Cadmus licked the salt from the rim of his Marguirita and touched his tongue to his crooked upper teeth. The dark crescents beneath his eyes seemed deeper as he looked at Pippa.

"I shouldn't of brought it up," Cadmus said. "Sometimes I feel like nobody's listening when I try to splain something to 'em. Take your own self, Pippa. I thought you was alive, but you so wrapped up in your own problems, whatever they are, that you won't let the real stuff bust in on you. What you need is to be shook out. Go run in the wind. Diddle your toes in the wet sand. Stand up on a mountain and scream till you can't scream no more. I know a place on the edge of a plateau up by Taos, New Mexico, pretty close to where my brother Waldo, bless him, chases goats, where you can see a hundred miles across the desert. Across the Rio Grande gorge way out yonder, and watch the rain blowing in for hours, the black sky creeping across that desert toward you until you can eventually feel the cold your ownself and the leaves start flipping around, and you see the rain blow right up to you and over you and on into the Taos Mountains and down the Hondo Valley turning everthang black until you can't see the tops of the mountains no more and can't hear the Hondo River running down in the valley. That's a good place to holler and yell. Then the rain is gone and the sun is on the pines and the snow is shining on the peaks and you can hear the river splashing again, and you think: What was I hollering about? Here I am, ain't I? What is there for me to yell about?"

"But you don't know me," said Pippa.

"Who knows anybody?" Cadmus said. "Who really does? What I'm gonna do now is drank. Too much talking is bad for the liver."

After lunch they went out to walk in the plaza. There were not so many drunks now. They could hear birds singing in the palms. The young girls were in their Sunday dresses. Children raced among the colored tents and balloons. People sat on the concrete benches with their eyes shut and the sun on their faces. In the shade there was the sour smell of old cheese but in the sun the air was dry and hot. Music crackled and blared from the speakers. At four Cadmus hurried to the equestrian statue in the middle of the plaza. He grinned and pointed. There it was: his orchestra.

"Went down to the New Shamrock this morning and the fellow promised they'd be here," Cadmus said. "Ain't they beautiful?"

Waiting in front of the statue were two guitarists, a violinist, an accordion player, and a man with a trumpet. They wore black caballero costumes and white sombreros. There were white fringes on their tight black bell-bottomed pants and on their short vests. When they saw Cadmus, the violinist tapped his foot and the musicians began to play. Cadmus grabbed Blossom and they did a polka on the pavement in front of the statue. People stopped and watched them. Blossom's skirt was very tight but she tried to polka; her breasts jiggled and bounced and seemed about to throw themselves out into the sunlight. Cadmus stomped his feet on the concrete.

"This here is what they call some kind of a Mexican shoe dance," he said, sweating and struggling for breath. "I forget the word for it. Sure is hard on the leather."

"Let's go on to the bullfight before Doris decides *she* wants to dance," said Harry.

"We're going," Cadmus said. "But ain't my orchestra beautiful? Hey, Red Shadow, how you like my orchestra?"

"Look lika buncha Riffs t'me," said Jason.

Cadmus rushed off and rounded up four taxicabs. He shoved the orchestra into the first cab with orders to play loud. "Plaza of the toros," Cadmus told the drivers. When he was satisfied with his procession, Cadmus got into the second cab with Blossom, Pippa, and Ben.

"Ben," Pippa said softly, her eyes moist as she looked at him, "something's happened. Something I don't know about."

Ben couldn't hold her stare. He shifted his look away from her eyes to the white pearl combs that pinned her black hair, to the white earrings he could barely see, to the white necklace that she now wore rather than the gold locket. On the left side of her neck at the curve of her shoulder was a tiny red bruise that he had put there. She had made no attempt to cover it. He looked down at the crease of her breasts just above the yellow top of the dress, and then down at the dark fuzz of hair on her arms. She clasped her hands. Her nails were clean and unpolished. In the cramped cab her skirt had come up over her left knee, which glistened under nylon.

"Ben," she said. "Why did Sheridan leave?"

"I'll talk to you about it later," he said.

Cadmus squeezed himself into the front seat, exhibited his crooked teeth, and said, "*Vamos!*"

They rocked back as the taxis shot away from the plaza. Blossom giggled and adjusted the bindings of her bosom. She leaned against Ben. Her face was dotted with sweat.

"Damn good," she said.

The bullring was an oval of wood and clay-colored bricks. A breeze had arrived to flap the flags around the rim of the arena. Banners and posters hung on the walls outside. The cabs deposited Cadmus and his group at the curb amid a swirling mob of Mexicans, tourists, police, soldiers, and peddlers of every sort. Cadmus assembled his party and marched them through the mob with his musicians playing at the head of the column. They were pushed and cheered and shouted at and applauded. Someone handed Cadmus a bottle of wine; he drank deeply and handed it back. At one of the gates marked *SOMBRA* Cadmus passed over the tickets he had bought at the hotel. The party marched through the gate. In the shade of the walkway beneath the stands Cadmus halted a vendor and ordered beer for everybody. Walter, who had been in the rear, came up holding hands with Chub. They were both laughing as they pushed through the crowd. Walter gave Cadmus a piece of paper and then stood with his arm around Chub's waist, as if neither of them could bear for their bodies not to be touching.

"What's this?" said Cadmus.

"Extra ticket," Walter said. "You had one too many."

"Couldn't have," said Cadmus. "Counted 'em my own self and I don't make mistakes. We all know that."

Cadmus looked down at the heads of his party and began saying their names aloud: "Ben . . . Pippa . . . Harry . . . Doris . . . Seton . . . Jason . . . Jason . . . Jason? Where's Jason? Anybody seen Jason?"

"He was in the cab with us," Harry said.

"He ain't here now," said Cadmus. "He's lost out yonder in that mob. Damn. It's all he can do to stand up by hisself, too. You all go get your seats and I'll look for him."

But when Cadmus returned as the red gate opened in the arena and the three matadors stood with capes folded to begin their proud entry, Jason wasn't with him. The Red Shadow was still lost in the mob.

With each of the first three bulls the spectacle got worse and the crowd got noisier and more abusive. Some cushions were thrown after the second bull, and a fight broke out in the upper stands on the sunny side where people were hooting at the matadors and hissing the picadors and whistling and booing the judge. Several soldiers with steel helmets and rifles raced into the brawl and restored peace. Someone tumbled down the steps and got up with blood on his face and the soldiers took him away.

"This wind isn't helping any," Waddy Morris said. "Look at him pouring water on his cape."

"What difference does the wind make, for God's sake?" said Beth.

"The wind makes the cape move and distracts the bull's attention. The matador wants the bull to go at the right part of the cape," Waddy said. "Don't you know anything?"

"I know this is a miserable way to spend an afternoon. I thought bullfights were supposed to be fun. All they're doing down there is running around and stabbing the bulls with knives and things and everybody's unhappy," said Beth.

"This hasn't been a very good day. I've seen good ones," said Waddy. "After a good fight, the people throw hats and flowers and shoes and stuff down to the matador. I saw a woman throw a mink stole in Mexico City."

"I might have thrown a mink stole to that first boy. He's cute," Beth said. "I love those tight pants."

"They cheat," said Waddy.

There was a string of sharp popping explosions.

"They're shooting, for God's sake," Beth said.

"Firecrackers, my dear," said Senator Rose. "Someone threw firecrackers into the arena."

After having failed to get his sword into the bull on four tries, the matador finally made it the fifth but the sword went in too far to the side and the bull stood swaying and bellowing, a long rope of slobber hanging from its mouth, yellow streaks of manure on its rump. The bull was close to the red barrera. The matador and his assistants began to worry the bull with their capes, trying to make him move his head back and forth to work the sword in. Gray and white striped cushions sailed into the arena. The matador's manager leaned on the barrera with his face in his hands.

"We shouldn't have sat down so close. They're going to hit us with some of that garbage," Beth said.

"Senator, pass me the flask," said Guthrie.

"You look tired, Sam. Did you sleep at all last night?" Beth said.

"No," said Guthrie.

"That really is too bad about your boat person," Beth said.

"Yeah, it was tough," said Guthrie.

"But we're celebrating," Waddy said. "Sam can't be sad today."

Guthrie touched Beth's hand. He looked at her long fingers with the cherry-colored nails, and when he looked up he saw that she was watching him and that her mouth had turned slightly down. Deliberately she removed her hand.

"Jane was the smart one, not coming to this thing," said Beth.

Guthrie took the flask of scotch from Senator Rose and drank from it.

"This is interesting," Waddy said. "Even when these are no good, they're interesting."

The matador stepped up to the bull and killed it with a blow from a short heavy sword into the base of the skull. The bull went down onto its knees and rolled onto its side. The monkey men came running in with their team of draught horses, hooked the bull to the chains, and dragged it out. Bells jingled on the harness. The carcass of the bull left a trail through the dirt. The matador looked up at the stands, and boos and hisses came down at him. He went quickly to the barrera to get out of the barrage of cushions. Workmen came in to scrape the arena floor and smooth the dirt and clear away the cushions and paper cups and cigarette butts. A man with a can of lime repainted the circles in the center of the arena. From up high in the stands, around the cigarette and Pepsi-Cola signs, the people yelled and laughed and whistled.

"I'm ready to leave," Beth said. "How many of these damned bulls are they going to kill in one day, for God's sake?"

"Six," said Waddy. "Let's watch this fourth one. This is the one the movie star is supposed to help fight. He's some Mexican cowboy star."

"The matador you think is so cute is up again," said Waddy.

"One more bull," she said.

The cowboy star rode into the arena on a white horse. He wore a white silk suit with white boots and a white sombrero. His face was thick and dark and his teeth were very white as he smiled and waved his hat at the crowd. The people applauded and then got quiet to wait for the next bull. The movie star dismounted, let them lead his horse out of the arena, and went behind the barrera to shake hands with the matadors and banderilleros. The first matador took his large pink cape, walked into the arena, bowed to the president, and with his cap in his hand made a gesture that included all the audience. He tossed his cap away and went toward the gate from which the bull would enter. The matador was very young and thin in his pink and gold suit of tights, pink hose, and black ballerina slippers. He pressed his lips tightly together, shook out his cape, and knelt thirty feet in front of the gate. The crowd hushed.

"He thinks it's time for desperate measures," said Waddy. "That's sort of dangerous."

"I do hope he doesn't get killed," Beth said.

"So does he," said Waddy.

The gate opened. The bull burst into the arena with two red ribbons fluttering from its shoulders. That first wild angry charge flung dirt on the kneeling matador, who made a pass with his cape and then leaped to his feet. Someone yelled, "*Ole.*" Some others applauded. The matador ordered away the men who had come out to run the bull with their capes and see which way the bull would hook. The bull slammed its horns into the wooden barrera and turned, looking for its enemy. The matador accepted it, did a series of passes, and the crowd approved him. Then the bull's left horn tore the cape out of the matador's hands, and the crowd booed and whistled again. At the president's signal a trumpet player in a sport shirt stood up and blew the music for the picadors.

The two picadors rode in, looking ancient and evil in their armor and with their lances. They rode through a shower of cushions and paper cups. Their horses, blindfolded by newspapers tied with red rags, kept turning their heads on their thin necks to try to tell where the danger was. The bull whirled, lowered its black-tipped horns, and charged the nearest picador. The horns whammed into the padding of the horse, raised up the horse as the lance ripped a gash in the bull's neck muscle, and threw the picador over the barrera. He landed with a clank in the passage behind the wall. The crowd laughed and clapped. The second picador moved into position with his lance aimed, and the men with capes turned the bull. The bull, with its neck bleeding now, was less anxious to charge again. The bull looked back and forth from the men to the horse and the lance. Then the bull bellowed. The manure looked gold around the bull's iron gray rump. The bull charged. The lance smacked into the meat of the neck muscle. The picador leaned hard on the lance. The bull got its horns into the padding of the horse but lost its fierceness under the gouging of the lance. The lance ripped and twisted in the neck muscle, and the bull's shoulders shone with blood. The crowd set up a frenzied booing. The band began to play, and the picador left the arena, riding slowly out through the flying paper cups and screaming voices.

"They hurt that bull bad," Waddy said. "They want to make it safe for the movie star."

The matador came out again. He had a Band-Aid on the back of his left hand. He walked stiffly to the bull, shook his cape, called to the bull, and the bull refused to charge. The matador knelt. The bull stood bleeding. The crowd booed and whistled. The bull bellowed. The matador got up and went to the barrera and got two banderillas.

"He's going to place his own," said Waddy. "He might as well. A kid could do it now."

With the two sticks, decorated with red and orange and green paper and barbed with steel darts, poised above and to either side, the matador made a quick graceful run. He went in past the horns and jabbed the banderillas into the bull's bleeding shoulders. Then he did it a second time. The bull made an effort at a charge. The wooden sticks clacked as the bull moved, and one banderilla fell out. The matador looked up at the dark yelling crowd. Soldiers and police stood at the exits. A swirl of dust blew in the arena, and the flags crackled in the wind. The band played. The matador went to the barrera, drank a glass of water, spat the water into the rust dirt at his feet, and took his small red cape and sword.

"What are they yelling?" Beth said.

"All sorts of things," said Guthrie. "They're yelling butcher and murderer and coward and calling for justice. There's a few cuss words, too."

"I'm glad I don't have to play to this crowd," Senator Rose said.

"People get upset everywhere," said Waddy. "Our crowds at home have their dirty moods. Ever been to a basketball game between Texas and Texas A&M?"

"It seems different to me," Senator Rose said.

"You're a politician. You'd know how to handle them," said Waddy.

"I'm afraid this goes a little beyond politics," the Senator said.

"This is what politics is all about," said Waddy.

"I don't like it," Guthrie said. "Let's get out of here."

"Squeamish?" said Waddy.

Waddy grinned and rubbed a red lump on his chin. He looked happy. Beth sat frowning. Her dark glasses mirrored Guthrie's face. There were gray specks, like ashes, on her white hat.

"I feel like everthing's about to be torn up. We ought to get out," Guthrie said.

"We'll miss the best part," said Waddy. "The movie star's coming out now."

"It's just that we're not in control of things here. We don't know what might happen," said Guthrie. "In the temper this crowd's in, they could go crazy and set this place on fire. That'd be a ridiculous way for us to die."

"Why, Sam, you're scared," Waddy said.

"It's a wise man who knows when to be scared," said Senator Rose.

"Don't stuff me with those crappy platitudes," Waddy said.

"I want to go," said Beth.

"I *am* going," Senator Rose said.

"Okay. If everybody wants to go, we'll go," said Waddy. He stood up. "It's a mean world, Sam. Even I don't always get what I want. But nearly always."

"I'm not scared. Damn it, don't tell me I'm scared," Guthrie said. "You want to stay? All right, I'll stay with you."

"Of course you would, Sam. I know that. But we'll go," said Waddy.

They picked their way down the narrow aisle toward the exit. The voices of the crowd blasted around them. A bottle crashed at the exit. Soldiers with rifles ran up into the stands with their bayonets slapping their hips. Beth held Waddy's elbow as Guthrie led them out. In the great roar of the crowd they came to the exit. Guthrie looked down. The movie star, waving his white sombrero, walked toward the middle of the arena with a red cape in his other hand. The bull stood with its head lowered. The bull's front hoofs were wide apart and were planted in blood.

At first when Cadmus stood up the Mexicans behind him yelled for him to sit down. But after three bulls had been killed, most everyone was standing up and those in the rear who couldn't see over Cadmus had learned to see around him. The tiers were very sharply banked, which made an easy angle for cushion throwing. Whenever Cadmus stood up cushions and paper cups and assorted debris would fly around his blond head. He would search the stadium with his eyes and then sit down and look at the bullfight.

"That rascal Jason," Cadmus said. "Where could he have gone?"

"He'll turn up," said Walter. "He probably went back to the hotel."

"Hope so. That boy was awful drunk," Cadmus said.

Harry, his hair brushed forward and his face flushed, was drinking beer and throwing paper cups and cursing loudly and asking Ben for obscene words he could yell at the matadors. Chub Anderson sat with a tight grim smile, and Doris had given up any attempt to look as if she enjoyed the bullfights.

"If that big cow messes on himself once more I'll throw up," said Chub.

"This is disgusting. Why don't they stop it?" Doris said. "There's no art in this. It's torture."

"What's happening now?" said Seton. He had covered his eyes with his hands and occasionally he peeked through his fingers. "Oh God, listen to that cow. Listen to him moan."

"Sure does beller, don't he?" Cadmus said.

"What're they doing to him?" said Seton. "Are they still poking him with that long stick?"

"They've quit that now," Chub said. "Now they're getting ready to put those little sticks in him."

"Oh God," said Seton. He peeked out, and then closed his fingers over his eyes. "I thought he had a chance when he knocked that man over the fence. They should have let him go. Don't they ever let the cows go?"

"They claim they let one go now and then," Cadmus said. "But I've seen about ten thousand of these thangs and I never saw a bull turned loose yet. Soon's I do, I thank I'll quit going."

"Look at the cowardly bastard," said Harry. "He ran up and threw those banderillas in there like darts. No style at all. Poor damn bull is drowning in its own blood, and the guy hasn't got enough guts to get close. Tell me a word, Ben. A sentence."

"Yell to him in English. He'll understand you," Ben said.

"I want a good dirty Mexican sentence," said Harry.

"I've told you all the dirty Mexican words I know," Ben said.

"I'll say the Mexican words again. What's that one about his mother?" said Harry.

A cushion bounced off Walter's shoulder. He whirled and glared up at the crowd, but the angry walnut faces paid no attention to him. Shadow had deepened across the arena so that only the upper rows of the sunny side were in the afternoon light. The arena band, its members wearing sport shirts and dark glasses, began to play. Cadmus's orchestra was silent. The violinist kept looking at Cadmus as if he would like to join in the yelling but wasn't certain if he had permission.

Pippa had not spoken since the parade of entry. She sat between Ben and Seton. She was very white and seemed solemn. Her hands were folded in her lap. She looked down at the arena as if she didn't see the matador or the bull or hear the crowd. Several times Ben started to talk to her and then thought differently of it.

The bull bellowed.

"Looks like the movie star is about ready to go out there," Walter said.

"He'd better do something good," said Cadmus.

"It's a nasty crowd," Walter said.

"Make 'em the right speech and you could start a revolution," said Harry.

"It's kind of hard to be a bull," Cadmus said.

"The bull didn't know this is what he was growing up for," said Harry.

"Who the hell does?" Cadmus said.

Behind the barrera the movie star took off his white hat and wiped his forehead with a handkerchief. Pippa turned and looked at Ben. His paper cup had got soggy, and beer was dripping out the bottom. He crumpled the cup and dropped it between his feet. He sat with his legs turned toward her to keep his knees out of the back of the man on the row below him.

"I want to know," she said, and her voice was lost in the yelling of the crowd.

Ben bent his head close to her.

"I want to know what's happened between us," she said.

"I'll talk to you about it later."

". . . now," he heard her say through the noise.

"This is not the place," he said.

". . . is . . . the place," she said.

One of her pearl combs touched his ear.

"All right," he said. "Why did you lie to me?"

With her fingers she turned his chin so that he was looking into her dark eyes.

"Is that it?" she said. "That's why Sheridan left? Walter told you?"

"That's not why Sheridan left, but Walter told me. Why did you lie? Why didn't you include Sheridan in your five, or however many it was?"

"Maybe I should have said fifty," she said.

"It's not how many, or how unlucky you were with Sheridan," Ben said. "It's the lie. Why did you lie to me? I would have had sympathy for your trouble, would have loved you more because of it. But I didn't want you to lie to me."

"Hey, Ben, look there!" shouted Cadmus. "It's your pal from Dallas!"

Several rows below and to the right Ben saw Guthrie going down the aisle with a tall blonde woman, a gray-haired man, and a man he recognized as Waddy Morris, Jr. Ben got up. He glanced down at Pippa, who looked back at him, long black hair coiled on the curve of her left shoulder, moist eyes holding his, and then he ran for the exit. He had begun to tremble and he shoved people out of his way as he ran.

"Ben!" Pippa said. "I didn't want to!"

When he found that he had been abandoned in a crowd of strange faces and wine smells and shoving bodies, to get his knees rapped by purses and his feet stepped on and foul breath pushed into his face, with his friends nowhere in sight, gone off to leave him to his destiny alone and bewildered on foreign soil, the Red Shadow decided to take command of his fate and make the best of it. He wouldn't go down without a trace. He was, after all, the Red Shadow. A fighting man at heart. A ferocious leader. The scourge of the very desert. It was true that he wanted his little girls and his poor suffering wife Willy and would even have been glad to see his mother, but there was no use calling for them. To remain in the mob was to be crushed. It was a time for action. Gathering his cloak around his shoulders, the Red Shadow lurched forward. Angry foreign voices in unknown tongues assailed his ears. Beer and pepper sauce and old fish and sweat attacked his nose.

Elbows flailed at his ribs. But he pushed forward, staggering, stumbling, trying to sing his fierce song: "Sooo we saaang as we riidin . . ." Into the arms of the mob rode the Red Shadow, and got tangled in an octopus of clutching fingers, a thicket of torment, a flea market of rags and bottles and sharp instruments that bruised his flesh. It seemed that he was walking on other people's feet, never touching the earth, and that his head was tucked beneath the wrong arm, and that he had his hand in the wrong pocket, and that there was something soft and womanly mashed against his face. And before he quite understood how it was being managed, the Red Shadow was carried in the mob through the gate past a ticket taker who could only grab what pieces of paper were offered him and those the police and soldiers could assort and tear away from the crowd.

By the time he untangled himself the Red Shadow was in a weird place that smelled remarkably like a barn. There were pens built of heavy boards, and he heard snorting and bellowing and clacks and whumps of hoofs kicking wood. People in funny costumes swarmed around him, all of them talking nervously. A man in a white suit and white hat sat on a white horse and cursed a smaller man who looked distressed and seemed to be apologizing. The Red Shadow had come through all of it with a bottle of tequila and a dizzy head. He went over and sat down on a coil of rope. Two very large horses, the biggest horses he had ever seen, with big round feet and bodies that looked like boxcars, stood huge before him with bells that jangled when they moved. Several men in black suits, with manure on their shoes, stood around the horses and smoked cigarettes with dirty fingers. They looked at the Red Shadow and said something. He thought perhaps they would like a drink. He offered his bottle of tequila. They grinned and passed the bottle around, drinking, and slapped him on the back. They were his new friends. Possibly his courageous band. He felt good with them. They had another drink. One of them sat down beside him on the coil of rope. A policeman in khaki came up and spoke to the Red Shadow. His friends pointed to the man in the white suit. The policeman nodded and went away. The man in the white suit quit cursing, put a white smile on his dark face, and rode off on his white horse. One of the Red Shadow's new friends said something, and the others laughed. The Red Shadow laughed, too. They slapped him on the back. He gave them another drink.

"I miss mah little darters," said the Red Shadow.

They laughed and shook his hand and slapped him on the back.

"I miss mah wife. Poor Willy. I love poor Willy."

They laughed some more and drank again and clapped his knee.

"I'm a scum of the very earth," the Red Shadow said.

His new friends nodded wisely and smiled and grinned.

Then all his new friends got up suddenly and ran away, taking their big horses with the jangling bells. The Red Shadow felt very alone again. He sat on the coil of rope in the cattle smell and listened to the faraway music and shouting and to the much closer kicking of hoofs against wood. But his new friends returned in a few minutes with their big horses, and they laughed when they saw him. He gave them cigarettes and another drink. They were very good friends.

"He made us human," said the Red Shadow.

His new friends laughed. One of them had blood on his black shirt. Another of them took a large drink from the bottle of tequila and fell off the coil of rope when he tried to sit down. They all laughed. It was great to be among friends, and there were so damned few. The Red Shadow sang his song for them, and they laughed. They all had another drink.

Twice more his new friends got up suddenly and left him, and twice more they returned to laugh and drink and slap him on the back and agree that he was certainly a scum. The policeman stopped by and had a drink with them, and he also agreed the Red Shadow was a scum who missed his little darters more than anything in the world. A man in armor and a flat hat came past limping and cursing and refused to drink. The Red Shadow and his friends scowled at the man in armor, but they began laughing again when he was gone. There seemed to be less kicking on wood now, but the noises from faraway were louder.

The fourth time his friends got up to leave him, the Red Shadow became curious. Sticking his bottle of tequila down inside the coil of rope where it would be safe, he staggered along the musty tunnel looking for them. When he had gone what seemed too far, he stopped. They had vanished, or he had missed them. He smoked a cigarette. He wasn't sure which direction he had come. The wooden beams and yellowed planks twisted oddly, and ripples moved across the walls. Maybe his friends would be back at the coil of rope now if he could find it again. He stumbled down the tunnel, searching, and saw a door with a handle on it and with light coming from a crack in the door. He put his ear against the crack and heard yelling and music. It was some kind of a party.

The Red Shadow pushed on the handle, the door opened, and he stumbled into an open space. The sky was above him, but there were red walls and a lot of people sitting. He looked down at the tracks his feet made in the dirt. There was a tremendous amount of yelling. Was it for him? He waved his arms, fell to one knee, and got up again. His new friends weren't out here, but the man in the white suit was. He was standing just over there, by that big cow that seemed to have cut itself, and he had a red cape like the one that Red Shadow wore. The man in the white suit stared at the Red Shadow and quit smiling. What was that man going to do to that cow? The Red Shadow thought he might be going to bandage the cow with the cape, but then the Red Shadow saw a sword in the hands of the man in the white suit. He was hurting that cow! That's why these people were yelling. They wanted it stopped.

The man in the white suit didn't move as the Red Shadow staggered up to him. The cow made an awful groaning noise. One red eye looked at the Red Shadow. Blood streamed down the cow's hide, and there were flies crawling around.

"I'll save you, cow," said the Red Shadow. "You'n me are buddies."

The Red Shadow snatched the sword from the man in the white suit. The man in the white suit looked astonished and backed away. The Red Shadow looked at the sword. He wondered how you went about biting a sword. People seemed to be running toward him. The Red Shadow tried to break the sword over his knee. It hurt. He fell down in the dirt. His hands felt sticky; there was blood on them. He looked at the bent sword and up at the yelling people. There seemed to be fights everywhere and great crashing sounds. All that work had exhausted the Red Shadow. He wanted to sleep now. He shut his eyes as hands grabbed his shoulders and legs and tore his cape.

They met beneath the stands. The noise in the shaded passage had a hollow sound, like wind and rain hammering on the roof, and dust hung in the passage. Ben ran down the ramp from the arena, turned the corner into the passage, and there was Guthrie.

Guthrie stared at him, for a moment not comprehending. Then

Guthrie's heavy brown face twisted into anger and a sort of wild delight. Guthrie laughed. Waddy Morris peered through his glasses, puzzled, as his wife stood holding his arm.

"Carpenter! You followed me here!" Guthrie said. He turned toward Waddy. "Here he is. This is the one who tried to torpedo me." Guthrie looked back at Ben. "What do you want now? Why did you come here?"

"I didn't follow you," said Ben. "But I'm glad I found you."

"You must want to make some kind of deal," Guthrie said. "No deals, Carpenter. It's too late for that. You don't have anything to offer any more. You're out."

"We're still in it. You're going to have to count proxies," said Ben.

"Then you haven't talked to Simmons today," Guthrie said. He watched Ben's face and saw that he was right. "You don't know what's happened. You don't know your last try was a flop. Well, let me tell you about it, Carpenter. It would give me great pleasure to tell you about it."

"I don't want to listen to you. I've listened to you long enough," said Ben.

"You'll listen to this. We talked to Johnson awhile ago, and he's folded like a bag of wet spaghetti. That whining and blubbering you and Simmons did turned out to be nothing but shouting at the ocean. Johnson is our man. You don't have a chance. You never had a chance."

Noise pounded at the roof. Waddy Morris smiled when he heard Ben's name. Light from the ramp cut across the passage between Ben and Guthrie. Ben could feel himself shaking and he fought to control his voice. He saw Guthrie's face, big and grinning, and the rage rose in him and he grabbed the front of his own coat to keep his hands off Guthrie. From above came a sound like a storm.

"Why should you feel proud of it?" Ben said. "You didn't do it. He did it." Ben nodded toward Waddy Morris with a movement that was almost a lunge. "He did it all. Without him, we'd have cut you off. You couldn't have made it on your own."

"Cry about it. Why don't you cry about it? I want to hear you," said Guthrie.

"I'm through crying, Guthrie. It's your turn now. If I were you, I'd be scared. You're going down."

"No, I've got it now. I've got what I want," Guthrie said.

Ben heard music. He glanced at the ramp and saw Cadmus

coming down, and Blossom mincing down in her tight skirt and silver hair, and Cadmus's orchestra playing madly behind.

"For God's sake," said Beth Morris.

"We're gonna have a little dance," Cadmus said. "Play that foot-stomping piece, hombres."

They all collided in the passage at the bottom of the ramp, with Cadmus's orchestra of violin, accordion, two guitars, and a trumpet milling among them and playing a polka. Senator Rose clapped his hands. Blossom, smiling beautifully, weaved through the sombreros, went to the Senator, took both his wrists, and pulled him toward her. "But my dear," he said. Cadmus jumped up and down and stomped his feet. Beth Morris stepped back from them, and Waddy laughed.

Guthrie glared at the musicians, at Blossom and the Senator, at Cadmus, and then at Ben again.

"Clowns," said Guthrie. "That's all you're fit to associate with, Carpenter. A pack of fools and clowns. You never knew how to do anything except insult me and then run off and cry to Simmons. It was a joke to fight you."

"It's a bitter joke," Ben said. "Enjoy it while you can."

From above they heard something that sounded like timbers tearing, and a loud rattling, and the yelling voices soared into hysteria. Harry came running down the ramp, splashing beer on himself.

"It's Jason!" Harry shouted. "Jason's out there!"

The noise from above was like waves smashing against the stands, and Ben felt that it was beating on his sanity. Police ran past, pushed through Cadmus's orchestra, and ran up the ramp with clubs in their hands. Harry grabbed Cadmus's arm and pointed up the ramp. Then Harry saw Guthrie and he struggled through the gathering crowd in the passage to get beside Ben.

"Jason's down in the arena," Harry said. "I think he's started a riot. Let's get this over with."

"Go on and help Jason," said Ben. "I don't need you. This is something I have to handle by myself."

"You sure?" Harry said, looking at Guthrie.

"Go on," said Ben.

"Ben can take care of hisself," Cadmus said. "Come on, Harry."

Harry ran with Cadmus up the ramp, fighting through the heavier stream of people that had begun tumbling down.

"You're just a gang of schoolboys," Guthrie said. "You never had to grow up. You came hunting me with a handful of pebbles. What're you gonna do now, Carpenter? Nothing's like you wanted it to be at all, is it?"

"Maybe it isn't," said Ben. "But I'm going to get you, Guthrie. I can do that much."

"You're whipped. Can't you see that, or are you still too much of a kid? I'm gonna dump you and Simmons and the rest of you bastards so hard you'll never stand up again. You made me mad, and I'm gonna hurt you for it."

"You haven't beaten me," Ben said. "You've beaten yourself. You're gonna collapse under the weight of your own greed, and I'm gonna be there to help it happen. You're corrupt."

Guthrie stepped toward Ben with his fists raised and his stomach pulled in. The collar of his golf shirt was turned up around his neck, and his coat seemed to have suddenly got too small for his shoulders. Ben heard Chub Anderson screaming from somewhere up the ramp. Blossom clung to the Senator, who kept saying, "But my dear," as he was bumped by the people who swarmed around them. The passage was suffocating, and Guthrie was larger and closer. Ben had begun shaking violently, as if all the past months were assaulting him and driving him into a definite decisive act, a statement, a terrible visitation that would either loose him from his purgatory or would obliterate him.

"I've been waiting for you to call me corrupt again," Guthrie said.

"You think you're getting what you want, but none of it's gonna mean a damn thing to you," said Ben. "It's all empty without integrity. You can't put yourself beyond that. You don't have any respect for yourself, so you can't have any for anybody else. That talk of yours about developing the economy is a bunch of crap and you know it. All you're doing is trying to feed your own dead soul, and it won't work. You're an insecure, frustrated man, Guthrie, or you wouldn't have sold out. I nearly feel sorry for you."

"I didn't cheat anybody," Guthrie shouted.

"I don't know exactly what you did. But I know there'll be other days between you and me."

"There won't be any other days for you," said Guthrie.

"Aren't you going to punch him, Sam?" Waddy said.

"Oh, Waddy, for God's sake," said Beth.

"Listen, Sam, this won't settle anything," Senator Rose said. "We should get out of here."

"Ratchit," said Blossom.

"Corruption! That makes me laugh," Guthrie said. "If I'm corrupt, why aren't you?"

"Because I can still feel. I've still got myself," said Ben.

"Then you haven't got very damned much," Guthrie said.

"But it's all there is, and I still have it," said Ben.

"Don't try to act pure. You don't fool me," Guthrie said. "You're nothing but the son of a thief."

The noise from above became like thunder, and there was the sound of thousands of feet drumming on wood and concrete, and the rage broke inside Ben. The rage exploded from him and left him feeling clear and certain and strong, and he saw the black mole on Guthrie's cheek, and he smashed his fist into the mole with all the strength his rage gave him. He saw the cheek split open as Guthrie fell back against the wall of the passage. Ben slammed his left fist into Guthrie's chest, knowing that second blow had been wasted the instant it had begun but hoping Guthrie would at least be sore there. Guthrie grunted. Blood streaked across the cut cheek, and the sight of it made Ben feel more clean in his fury. But before he could swing again Guthrie was on him. Things seemed to be happening very slowly, but Ben realized it had been only a couple of seconds since he had hit Guthrie and that his reactions had not been fast enough and he had lost his advantage. Guthrie's big knuckles cracked against Ben's left eye, and Ben tasted blood from his nose although he didn't at first realize what it was.

Then Ben was going down, surprised that he had felt the fist not as pain but as a jarring shock like a blow on a helmet. Guthrie leaped on top of him growling and Ben's shoulders banged onto the dirt floor of the passage. For a second Ben could not breathe. The two men twisted in the dirt. Harry would have kicked Guthrie's kneecap, but it was too late for that now and the fists kept clubbing Ben as they writhed in the dirt. Ben reached for something, for a hold of some sort, for anything that would cause Guthrie pain, any scratching or clawing. Ben managed to turn sideways with a violent heave and threw his elbow into Guthrie's mouth and saw Guthrie's wild eyes staring at him. He knew that if one of them could murder the other at this moment it would be done. Ben struggled beneath Guthrie's weight and felt the thick ridges of muscle on Guthrie's back and then for an instant could not see because blood was stinging his eyes and then he jabbed his fingers into Guthrie's throat and heard Guthrie's moan combining with a great thundering and then Ben got kicked in the side of the head and felt Guthrie's weight suddenly torn away and feet trampling on him and dizzily he crawled out of the passage and pressed himself against the wall.

Cadmus lumbered down the ramp and swept Blossom aside. Immediately behind Cadmus came a flood of brown faces in a torrent of yelling and screaming. The mob flowed over Guthrie, knocked him back, tumbled him over, rolled him against a wooden pillar and pinned him there and then spilled out like a burst river along the corridor. In the mob, as if caught in a current, were several police and soldiers; clubs thrashed, fists whirled, feet pounded, sounds gushed from thousands of throats. Ben saw Waddy Morris and the blonde woman and the old man ducking behind a pillar, and he saw his own friends running in front of the mob or scattering through it, and out by the gate he saw a flash of a figure with black hair and a yellow dress with white patterns on it. He tried to scramble up but the swarming bodies thrust him back down against the wall. The flood washed against the sides of the passage ripping posters and splintering beer counters and trampling souvenirs, and in a tumbling swirling battering tide poured through and around the arena crushing everything in its way.

The bus that said *OLE BEN'S HAPPY TIME MINSTRELS* was parked in front of the Gran Hotel Reforma, and the hunchback stood at the rear of the bus with a flag tied to a stick to direct traffic. Damon, his black cap square and his boots polished, sat in the Reforma Bar and drank what he hoped his passengers would think was coffee. Lights had come on in the palms of the plaza. The whitewashed benches were empty. A great silence lay over the plaza, as if the final spasm had been spent and everyone had gone off to sleep.

There were very few peddlers on Avenida Guerrero and hardly any cars. The heavy traffic from the Plaza del Toros had cleared the city, and most of the tourists had gone back across the International Bridge, above the wide and muddy Rio Grande, into Texas. Over in the plaza men with burlap bags moved among the benches and palms, around the statue, through the few tent pegs that still stood, moving in and out of the shadows among the papers and wine bottles and debris of the fiesta.

While Harry was paying the cab driver, an old woman with one baby parrot in a cage came up to Ben, Doris, Walter, and Chub. The old woman looked up at them from a cracked and wrinkled brown face. With sausage fingers she held the shawl at her throat.

—are his wings clipped? Ben said.

—señor? the old woman said.

—can he fly? Ben said.

—he can fly some far but not so much, the old woman said.

Ben gave her a dollar and took the parrot from the cage. He held the bird around the body, as he would hold a pigeon. The parrot tried to bite him but quit and clacked its beak and clinked its eyes.

"You can't take that back," said Walter Anderson. "You'll give everbody parrot fever or whatever they call it."

"I know it," Ben said.

Ben tossed the baby parrot into the air. The bird went up and flapped its wings and came down almost to the sidewalk before it knew it could fly, and then it flapped along two feet above the sidewalk with a few of its feathers falling out and fluttering down. The parrot finally rose to the roof of a shop and landed on a drainpipe. It sat on the drainpipe and bristled itself and then flew across the street to the next roof and was gone in the darkness.

"The cats will get it," said Doris.

"Maybe not," Ben said.

The hunchback bowed and saluted them with his rag flag as they walked into the lobby of the hotel. "Must have been a swell fight," said Harry. "Sorry I was too busy to watch it. I'd liked to have seen all those Mexicans walking on Guthrie."

"You'll probably get to see that fight again," Ben said. "Tomorrow I'm going back and start filing anti-trust suits as fast as I can think them up. I owe Guthrie that much."

The desk clerk looked at Ben's face.

—señor, would you like me to call a doctor? the desk clerk said.

—it is nothing. i have never felt better," Ben said.

—here is a message for you. the young lady left it. she and the man with the funny walk.

—thank you. i had expected it, Ben said.

Ben took the letter up to his room and sat on his lumpy bed

beneath the squeaking ceiling fan. He listened to the dripping shower and to the shrieks of children playing below the window. Lifting the envelope to the gray light, Ben tore open the gummed flap and took out a piece of paper that had been torn raggedly from a spiral notebook. He looked at the writing scrawled in ink on the lined paper. He lay back for a moment on the bed, holding the paper to his chest, and then he sat up and began to read.

Dear Ben:

I had almost decided anyway to tell you this afternoon that I'm not going to see you again. So it really doesn't matter what Walter told you or what you think I am. You said once that people get what they deserve. This is what I deserve. I tempted myself and tempted myself until I eventually fell, but I know it's no good for either of us. Without temptation I couldn't have had a choice, and without a choice what I am wouldn't have any value. But you have made it so that I have a choice, and I choose to give you up.

I am grateful to you, but you are destructive to me and I would be destructive to you. I don't want to be faithful to you or to any man. I realized this morning how really tempting you are to me, but at the same time how inadequate and temporary what you offer me is. I love you, and I don't want to love you. I am not one of those who believes he can have both; for me it's impossible, for love entails giving and I am already given. What one thinks or convinces oneself of doesn't matter, it's what one knows that is important. And you have helped me to clear away the confusion about what I know.

You want a woman who will be pure for you and will be yours, and I would be neither, although you came close to making me think I wanted to try. What I love is forever, but I will think of you as long as I can.

Pippa

Ben read the letter twice and folded it and put it in the inside pocket of his blue linen sport coat which was smeared with dirt and blood and had been ripped at the shoulder. He looked down at the pillow and smiled and shook his head. "Pippa," he said. And then he started laughing. He couldn't stop laughing. He went to the window and looked down at the courtyard where the children were playing with a three-wheeled wagon in the shadow of the doorless toilet, and he looked across the crooked patterns of the slate rooftops, past the slanted windows and iron balconies and potted flowers to the oyster sky with slashes of red, and he laughed.

Cadmus and Blossom were sitting in the chief's office inside the stone police barracks when Alonso Guzman knocked on the door. The chief, an old man with a bushy gray mustache, had been staring at Blossom with black agate eyes from beneath his straw cowboy hat and had been scratching the bone handle of the revolver he wore in a holster at his belt. The knock relieved Cadmus. He had brought Blossom because he had thought her appearance might get him into places where his bribes might not, but then he had discovered the chief spoke no English. Cadmus had begun to regret that he had not brought Ben rather than merely getting Alonso Guzman's business card to present to the chief and then trust to fortune. Cadmus had been trying to explain his errand in sign language and awful Spanish but he had got nowhere except further into confusion; the chief kept looking at Blossom and ignoring Cadmus. If there was anyone in the police headquarters who spoke English the chief had, for his own reasons, preferred not to summon him.

Alonso Guzman entered the office, bowed to Blossom, shook hands with the chief, who did not rise but only lifted his fingers from the butt of his pistol, and then shook hands with Cadmus. The young Mexican still wore his green double-breasted suit with the double rows of military buttons and the narrow pants legs, and he let his eyes behind the grotesque dark glasses stay on Blossom for a few seconds before he spoke to the chief.

—what is their trouble, uncle? Alonso Guzman said.

—i don't know. this madman beats on my desk and waves his arms and draws funny pictures in the air and tells me things that make no sense. i think perhaps i should lock him away except our cells are very crowded from the riot, the chief said.

—do you speak any spanish at all? the young Mexican said to Cadmus.

—to speak spanish some, Cadmus said.

Alonso Guzman shrugged. He sat on the edge of the chief's desk and looked at Blossom. From outside the door they heard an argument, a scuffle, and a blow. Then the sound of someone being dragged along the hallway.

"I now to speak English," said Alonso Guzman.

"Great," Cadmus said. "Look here, Alonso, all I want is to get my pal out of jail. He didn't mean to cause any trouble. He was just drunk. Poor fella feels bad enough anyhow without spending time in your jail."

"Drunk?" said Alonso Guzman.

"Absolutely," Cadmus said.

—of what does he speak? the chief said.

—of drunkenness. that is all i can make out so far, Alonso Guzman said.

—of drunkenness i have heard plenty. i think i will throw him out. but i enjoy looking at his woman.

—he is a yankee.

—do you think i am an idiot? i can see that he is a yankee. a man that big and tall could be no mexican.

—i mean he must be here for a purpose. do you have any yankees in your jail who might be his friends?

The chief yawned.

—who knows? from the riot we hauled in hundreds. they are stacked up back there. it repels me to think of them. in a day or so we will begin to sort them, the chief said.

Alonso Guzman looked at Cadmus.

"*Amigo?*" said Alonso Guzman.

"Hell yes. You bet. Don't know when I've liked a guy as much as I like you," Cadmus said.

—that is it. he has a friend in the cells, Alonso Guzman said.

—half the town has friends in the cells, the chief said.

—but this is a rich texas oil man whose name i have put into my newspaper column, uncle. let us at least examine the cells, Alonso Guzman said.

—for one hundred dollars, the chief said.

—you embarrass me, Alonso Guzman said.

—no you embarrass me. You would neglect to take at least one hundred dollars from this man? that is so stupid that it embarrasses me very much. what do you young people learn in your schools? what is happening to this country? the chief said. He scowled at Alonso Guzman and with his tongue pushed mustache hairs out of his mouth.

Alonso Guzman looked down at the polished toes of his pointed Italian shoes, glanced at Blossom, who crossed her legs and smiled prettily at the chief, and then looked at Cadmus as if wondering how to explain.

"What's he saying about a hundred dollars?" said Cadmus.

Alonso Guzman spread his hands. The chief made a snorting noise, as though trying to clear his nose and throat. Someone rapped on the office door and the chief shouted to go away. After a moment of silence the knocking came again. The chief cursed and scratched the bone handle of his revolver and told Alonso Guzman to open the door.

A policeman wearing sergeant's chevrons on his short-sleeved khaki shirt and with black stripes on his olive pants began apologizing at once for bothering the chief.

—mother of god, everyone bothers me today. my office has become a nest for maniacs and young fools, the chief said.

—but i have the instigator of the riot. i knew you would want to see him, the sergeant said.

—why would i want to see him? put him in the cells for a month and then bring him to me, the chief said.

The sergeant saluted and stepped aside.

"Jason!" said Cadmus.

The Red Shadow tried to grin, but his face was scratched and smeared with the wet red dirt of the bull ring and the effect was grotesque; it was the face of a muddy, weathered gargoyle with twisted lips above an absurd red curtain that was knotted around its neck. The cape was ripped and tattered, and Jason's shirt was torn across the front as if someone had grabbed his pocket and yanked down. Behind him was Cadmus's orchestra, the musicians looking foolish and frightened, strings dangling from their guitars, their big white hats crushed and marred. The musicians all began talking when they saw Cadmus. The police sergeant turned to look at them and they shut up.

Cadmus went to Jason and looked at him carefully.

"Guess all you need is a bath," said Cadmus, as Blossom kissed Jason on the cheek and the chief looked angrily at them.

—i would like to shoot them. our country is going to hell. in the old days i could march them out and shoot them for making me this trouble, the chief said.

—this is the friend, Alonso Guzman said.

—everyone tells me things that would be obvious to a donkey, the chief said.

The chief stood up. Sitting, he had looked to be a large man. Standing, the peak of his hat didn't reach Cadmus's shoulder. He scowled at Cadmus, went to Jason and scowled at him, scowled at each of the musicians in turn, and finally looked at Blossom. He studied Blossom for a long while. No one spoke. The chief shrugged and sat down and looked at the wall.

—two hundred dollars for the bunch, the chief said.

"How much?" said Cadmus.

"Two hondred dollar," Alonso Guzman said.

Cadmus pulled out his money clip, counted off two hundred dollars, and laid the money on the chief's desk. The chief kept looking at the wall, as if he had dismissed the entire affair from his mind and now wanted only to be left alone. Cadmus folded up the twelve dollars that remained, inserted the money in the silver clip, and looked at Alonso Guzman. The young Mexican nodded. Cadmus took Blossom by the arm, and with his other hand took the sagging Red Shadow. The policemen at the desk in the hall watched silently as Cadmus left the building with the blonde girl and the madman in the tattered red cape and with the five musicians and Alonso Guzman trailing behind.

They walked down the street from the police barracks, past the quiet shops, along the gray sidewalks until they came to the plaza where lights now shone among the palms. The warm soft evening lay blue on the plaza; from the shadows of the concrete benches and the whitewashed palms an occasional brown face looked out, a hand moved, paper crackled, a bottle clinked, a dog growled, a cat froze. At the equestrian statue, where he had found them that afternoon, Cadmus stopped and turned to his musicians.

"One more tune," Cadmus said. "Play 'Guadalajara' for us. You ain't played that tune all day."

"Señor, we thank you for the . . ." said the orchestra leader, who clutched his broken guitar and his smashed hat against the black and white design of his vest.

"Never mind," Cadmus said. "Just play that one tune while we walk off."

The orchestra leader nodded, tapped his foot, and the music began. It was an oddly off-key discord of sounds from ruined instruments, but the voices of the four who were able to sing came up in a thin high blending. Cadmus listened for a moment, then waved to the musicians and to Alonso Guzman. He again took both Blossom and Jason by the arm and started across the plaza through the black shadows toward the Gran Hotel Reforma.

"Poor Willy," Jason said. "I miss poor Willy. I'm a scum of the very earth."

"Naw," said Cadmus. "You're just a man."

Afterword

I am tempted to use one of the worn clichés of the literary journalist and say, "Edwin Shrake's *But Not For Love* enjoyed neither the critical success nor the popular audience it deserves." But I won't. Even though it is true. When commentators on Texas literature point to the 1950s and 1960s, they always hold up Bill Brammer's *The Gay Place,* William Humphrey's *Home from the Hill,* and the early novels of Larry McMurtry as representative works about the time and the place. There is no question that those writers captured a slice of Texas life that is worth remembering, but not a one of them does a better job of opening a window into the Texas of the depletion allowance and the nascent electronics industry than Shrake does. And he does a great deal more: he shows us the temper of the times among the urban intellectuals and upwardly mobile businessmen who are still struggling to find a place in postwar Texas. While the novels of Humphrey and McMurtry have remained in print and while Brammer's one novel was chosen by the Texas Library Association as one of five books for discussion during the Sesquicentennial year, *But Not For Love* has been unavailable to most readers. Avon did five printings, but it has been out of print for some years now. It has not had the fervid critical advocacy given Bill Brammer's novel by Texans interested in politics and in Lyndon Johnson (who is parodied in *The Gay Place),* nor has it caught the public attention by being filmed, as have a number of McMurtry's novels about Texas and Humphrey's *Home from the Hill.* But I think Edwin Shrake's second novel—his first is a forgotten paperback called *Blood Reckoning*—may capture a segment of Texas urban life in the Cold War years better than any of its counterparts.

The Texas that existed before World War II underwent a painful transition during the Eisenhower-Kennedy-Johnson years. The old-time, colorful Texas cattle and oil millionaires were giving place to new kind of entrepreneurs—represented by men like Sam Guthrie and Waddy Morris, Jr. Though Waddy's father had made a fortune in oil, Junior's interests have shifted toward electronics and other post-war technologies. And Sam is one of those self-made transistor millionaires whose soul is being dried up by his success. But the changes from cattle and oil to transistors and business machines are not the only mutations taking place in the state. Morals are changing, and there is an upsurge in liberal political thinking that goes against the grain of the old Dixiecrat days of Allen Shivers and the conservative democracy of Lyndon Johnson and Sam Rayburn. And, what is most important, rural Texas is giving place to urban Texas. The Texas legislature may still be in the hands of the rural lawmakers, but the men and women from the cities are starting to make a serious political presence felt in Austin. Brother Chunk and his red-baiting, prohibitionist, Bible-thumping reactionaries are still to be feared, but their dominance is not as great as it once was in Texas. The most important specter confronting the characters in *But Not For Love* may be The Bomb and its role in Cold War politics.

The characters we are most in sympathy with in this novel are breaking out. Under threat of nuclear disaster and in the wake of an all-out war, they are shucking the Puritanism of their ancestors and drinking the nights away. They are flouting the sexual taboos of their parents and ending marriages without undue ceremony. They are experimenting with drugs—though this is seen only when Cadmus is passing out green pills in Mexico—and they are challenging the shibboleths of old Texas—the political truths and the religious verities that reflect the days when men like John Nance Garner and Coke Stevenson spoke for Texas. In many ways, the debauchery seen in *But Not For Love* replicates of the American Jazz Age of Fitzgerald and Hemingway and the British Twenties disillusionment of Aldous Huxley's *Antic Hay* and Michael Arlen's *The Green Hat.* It almost seems as if the Twenties have finally come to Texas. Forty years late.

The most striking thing about *But Not For Love* lies not in the excellence of its characters or in the elegance of its plot; it is its capturing of the Zeitgeist—the spirit of the times. Shrake's novel is not a strong analysis of character, for there is not a fully rounded character in the book. The people who inhabit the Texas that Bud Shrake creates here are types. Each one represents a slice of Texas life in the Cold War. Cadmus is the proto-hippie whose message is one of peace and love and brotherhood—but we don't exactly know how he came to it or where it will take him. Or even what exactly it is. Ben Carpenter is the earnest do-gooder out to right the wrongs of a world gone crooked, a world that overwhelmed his father and made him a thief. Waddy is the spoiled rich kid with a ruthless streak, almost a replica of the smirking villain in the theatrical dreadfuls at the turn of the century. Sam Guthrie is the man spoiled by greed, and his wife Jean is the woman who sees it and is sorely distressed. Jake Iles and his slatternly wife are very much foil characters—role players who point out the growing ruthlessness of Sam Guthrie. Chub Anderson (she with "the morals of a cocker spaniel") and Blossom are good-time girls who always fill in the background in novels of the dissolute life. Three characters who struggle to come to life—but ultimately fail—are Pippa Parry, Ben Carpenter, and Jason Hopps, the Red Shadow who relentlessly proclaims himself "the scum of the very earth." Jason, who loves his wife Willie and their daughters, can't contain himself as he drinks at the Oui Oui Club and pursues the illicit pleasures of Chub Anderson—and any woman with the breath of life still in her body. Jason, were he the focus of more authorial attention, could be the dissolute hero we see so often in Fitzgerald. But since Shrake has such a crowded stage and so many plots to juggle, Jason is always a few paragraphs short of fuller development. Pippa, who had an affair with the scummy Walter Sheridan that resulted in an abortion, is almost real and almost the right woman to help Ben Carpenter out of his near total dejection at the turn postwar life has taken. But she hovers near the edge of roundness without ever quite coming to life. And, finally, there is Ben Carpenter, the reformer, the justice-seeker, the failed husband and father: he is Shrake's closest approach to a valid, real-life character whom we can understand and put ourselves in the place of.

I am not sure I would have these characters better developed. It might be that what Shrake has chosen to do in *But Not For Love* is just right for the themes and plots of the novel. Fuller characterizations would slow down the hectic pace of the stories—and it is the hectic that rages in everyone's blood that drives the plot lines. We simply don't have space and time to spend on Cadmus Wilkins, the ironic Christ figure who pronounces at the end that the Red Shadow—Jason—is not the scum of the earth but "just a man." Nor can we follow to its logical conclusion the Guthrie-Waddy story or the Ben-Pippa plot or the possible reformation of "the Red Shadow." We have other business to attend to. We are about seeing the gross and scope of life in Dallas-Fort Worth, along the beaches of North Padre, and at the Cinco de Mayo festivities across the border from Laredo. And what we see is a time of turmoil, a time of uncertainty, in a place struggling to cast off the Old South/Old West mystiques and join the rest of the country in the move to urbanism and technological advancement. *But Not For Love* gives us regional fiction at its best.

Shrake is an outstanding stylist. He uses words economically and makes us see the people and the places and the larger world. When we visit Sam Guthrie's mansion on the beach or go out to sea or into the bar with Jake Iles we get a perfectly presented picture of life on the Texas Gulf Coast. Every word fits:

> In the muddy darkness he could see several men standing on the dock. Lights were on in some of the boats, and he could hear voices. The café was open. The jukebox was playing. A screen door slammed. The morning smelled like wet laundry (50).

Or this from the Fort Worth segment:

> It was a two-story white frame house with blue slatted shutters, and it stood among elms on a quiet narrow street with broken sidewalks. The street was on a bluff in a high part of the city. Looking down to the west between the trees and the dark

> houses Ben Carpenter could see the tumbled blackness of the woods below, and beyond, where the earth slowly rose again from the turgid river, lights spread like Christmas ornaments against the purple night. Sunset Ridge was slightly more than a block long; it swung on a crowded boulevard and curved to the west past a grassy park, then turned south along the edge of the bluff for two hundred yards before it dropped abruptly down and was lost in the parking lot of a church above an expressway (139).

Fort Worth residents will recognize the description of Sunset Terrace down to the last detail. Forty years later, the street is unchanged. The house where the party was held looks as described, the vacant space across the street still looks out on the Trinity River and toward the west side of Fort Worth. Shrake makes the street as real for the reader as a visit does to the actual observer. What Shrake does here and elsewhere in the novel is to make us see. Fitzgerald could do it. Faulkner could do it. Not everyone can. It may be a gift. If it is, Bud Shrake polished his as a sportswriter and sports columnist on papers in Dallas and Fort Worth and later at *Sports Illustrated.* Like Hemingway and many other writers who trained on newspapers, Shrake took the best features of journalism and incorporated them into his fiction. His work is spare, clear, rapidly paced. He does not expect the reader to parse his sentences and seek out his meanings. Everything is up front. Shrake has no interest in the obfuscation of the modernists; he wants the reader to see and feel and spend a few hours in a world he creates for us. And I think it is no small accomplishment.

James Ward Lee